Return to **SHANGRI-LA**

THOMAS G. CASEY

authorHOUSE

AuthorHouse™
1663 Liberty Drive
Bloomington, IN 47403
www.authorhouse.com
Phone: 1 (800) 839-8640

Published by AuthorHouse 11/21/2019

ISBN: 978-1-7283-3692-3 (sc)
ISBN: 978-1-7283-3690-9 (hc)
ISBN: 978-1-7283-3691-6 (e)

Print information available on the last page.

Cover art by: Jay Ashurst

This book is printed on acid-free paper.

To my childhood hero, James "Jimmy" Doolittle, and his famous Raiders. On April 18, 1942, he led seventy-nine young Army Air Corps airmen who flew in sixteen B-25B bombers off the deck of the US Navy's newest aircraft carrier, *USS Hornet*. Doolittle's mission was to bomb five major cities in Japan, including Tokyo. The mission was a total success, and it raised the hopes, morale, and spirit of our nation to fight back and win.

When the mission was completed, news of the surprise raid was reported worldwide. On April 19, the White House Oval Office was crowded with reporters surrounding President Roosevelt, who was sitting behind his desk. They kept shouting, "Mister President, where did our bombers come from?"

President Roosevelt sat relaxed in his armchair, placed his cigarette holder between his teeth, smiled, and said, "They came from Shangri-la."

The attack on the empire of Japan had a serious effect on the Japanese high command, especially Admiral Yamamoto, who planned the Pearl Harbor attack. To save face, Admiral Yamamoto decided to attack and capture Midway Island. He sent a task force that included four carriers, battleships, and troop carriers. Unknown to Yamamoto, the US Navy's intelligence team had broken Japan's military codes. Admiral Chester Nimitz, who was commanding Pacific Naval Command Headquarters at Pearl Harbor, ordered Admiral William "Bull" Halsey to take three carriers and intercept Yamamoto's task force. In a one-day battle, Halsey's dive bombers and torpedo planes sunk four carriers, destroyed more than three hundred planes, and defeated their pilots. More than three thousand sailors went down with their ships.

The war in the Pacific was turned around thanks to Jimmy Doolittle and his raiders. The Japanese would never see another victory in the Pacific.

CHAPTER 1

Sunday, December 7, 1941
1100 hours
Franklin Square
Long Island, New York

The small town of Franklin Square, Long Island, was being covered with a blanket of new snow, making driving from church to home somewhat difficult for Charles T. Reed. He had to drive cautiously as the slow windshield wipers were hardly removing the heavy, wet snow landing on the windshield. His wife, Agnes, and their twelve-year-old daughter, Teresa, sat in the rear seat, and their six-year-old son, Charles Junior (who was also known as Chip), sat next to him on the edge of the front seat. Chip would take his scarf and wipe the inside of the windshield to clear the haze created by their warm breath. He kept telling his dad he could hardly see the large, chrome swan ornament on the end of the long hood. Charles told his son to keep watching to his right for any parked cars or people who may be walking on the road.

The large, black, four-door, convertible Packard moved slowly while cold drafts seeped through window seals, causing discomfort for all the passengers. The engine's heater was not providing enough warmth, especially to the rear seat. To add to Charley Reed's nerves while trying to navigate in the snow, Teresa was constantly complaining about the cold, even as her mother covered her with a heavy wool blanket.

This was Charley Reed's first real experience driving this car in snow. He had purchased the car at an estate auction two months ago in late fall. It was the car of his dreams. It was a 1940 Packard series 180 Phaeton with dual spare tires mounted in the front fenders and dual spotlights. It was black with a white canvas convertible and red leather seats. He told everyone he had bought it because Packards were President Roosevelt's favorite cars.

Charley soon learned he had one major problem because of his short legs. He had difficulty reaching the three pedals to operate the car safely, so he had his younger brother, Jim, install wooden blocks on the pedals. He was always nervous while holding the large, ivory steering wheel. He began to realize the long-nosed Packard was big and heavy and not easy to turn or park, which could sometimes make the car intimidating.

The three-mile trip to their home took nearly an hour. However, they reached the house without getting stuck or running into anything in the blinding snow. Charley was breathing easier as he reached Lincoln Road, where his home was located. Sitting on top of a hill, it appeared almost hidden under the snow. He also knew he would be facing a problem to get his heavy car up the sloping driveway covered in new snow. Below the snow and ice were coal cinders from the house furnace he had shoveled on the driveway earlier.

When he finally reached the driveway, he had no problem moving up the slippery surface. When he reached the side door entrance, he stopped to let everyone out. Anxious to get out of the car, Chip ran into the house and up a staircase to the kitchen door, where he was met by his grandmother, Julia. She told Chip to go back and tell his father to drive immediately to his brother Jimmy's house. She said, "Tell your father Jim just called and seemed very upset about something."

Chip ran past his mother and sister and out the door. He saw the Packard's stoplights come on in the garage as he ran as fast as he could, but he kept slipping in the snow while yelling to his father. Chip finally got his father's attention as he started closing the wooden garage door. "Daddy, wait! Wait! Uncle Jimmy called and said for you to get to his house right away!" Chip yelled out.

His father understood, pushed the door open, got back into the car, and started backing down the driveway. Chip watched as the big, black convertible rushed past him, sliding back and forth on the icy driveway. He saw the car reach the bottom of the driveway and then head down Lincoln

Road. Charles was expecting something was wrong with his mother, who lived with the brother.

Chip ran back into the house and removed his coat and boots. He entered the living room where he saw his mother sobbing in the arms of her mother. Teresa was standing next to the large Emerson radio and listening to loud and noisy news reports. Chip kept crying out, "What's wrong, Mother? Why are you crying?"

With tears in her eyes, his grandmother reached out and put her arms around him. "Chip, our country is being attacked by the Japanese bombing Pearl Harbor."

She then ordered Chip to get his sister and go to the kitchen and wait. She would soon be in and make their Sunday breakfast. She also told them to leave their mother alone so she could call her son Jimmy to let him know Charles was on his way.

Chip had no idea where Pearl Harbor was, but he did remember his father talking about his younger brother, Uncle Jerry, who was in the Army Air Corps and stationed there.

"Is Uncle Jerry in trouble?" Chip asked.

But he received no response.

Over the next few days, life at 171 Lincoln Road was unbearable as Chip's father went crazy at home listening to the radio night and day. He would disappear almost every evening for hours and sometimes come home drunk.

One night he returned from his brother's house, where he learned his brother Jerry was killed during the attack at Wheeler Airfield. The family also learned that day, the United States was now at war with Germany.

Four months passed since the attack on Pearl Harbor. The Reed family was devastated when they received word that Jerry had died from his wounds after being shot by Jap fighters strafing the airfield. During these first months of war, the news of US losses to Japanese victories also included Guam, Bataan, Corregidor, and more recently, Wake Island and Malaya.

On the morning of April 19, the family heard after church that the United States had bombed Japan. When they got home, Julia was holding up the newspaper showing in big, bold print "Tokyo Bombed."

It was a day of celebration. Their neighbors came over for cheering and drinking in the living room, while Charley played with the radio to get more news on the attack on Japan. He also took every bottle of whiskey and beer in the house and shared it until the supply ran out. Then he got in his car and went for more but did not return until hours later.

Over the next few years, Chip would be exposed to his father's frequent flare-ups, cursing the Japanese while preaching his hate for them every night at the dinner table. He would talk about all the atrocities the Japanese military were carrying out not only to Americans but to civilians in the Philippines. He would read the newspaper each night and sit by the radio for hours while listening to news reports. He continued to lose his temper and rave about the need to get rid of the little, yellow Japanese bastards.

One day his father arrived home with a wooden model of a Japanese fighter plane, explaining it was built by a friend at work. On a Sunday morning after church, he gathered the family in the front yard and poured lighter fluid over the plane. Then he threw it in the air. It crashed and burned on the lawn. He ordered Chip to go stomp on the burning plane to put the fire out.

Chip obeyed.

"That's it, Son. Crush those little, yellow bastards, and make them pay for your uncle Jerry!" Charles screamed.

Chip's mother became upset at her husband and his demonstration. She commanded him to stop his outrageous display of anger and cursing. She told him he had to stop his uncontrolled swearing and temper while showing so much hate for the Japanese, especially in front of his children.

When Chip turned nine, his uncle Walter took him to see his first war movie. It was called *Thirty Seconds over Tokyo*. Chip had no problem remembering the day when this famous raid actually happened. It was all over the newspapers and on the radio that Japan was bombed by American bombers. After seeing the movie, he learned the true story about the first raid on Japan. He talked all the way home to his uncle about how his father was so excited about that particular day—April 19, 1942. He ran down the road while holding up the paper with the headlines displaying in bold print, "Tokyo Bombed!" He stopped in front of each house and yelled, "We got them yellow bastards!"

Chip went on to express his feelings to his uncle about the Japanese, referring to them as little, yellow bastards, and he also said that someday he would be old enough to go to Japan and kill them all.

This concerned the uncle, who later that day advised his sister, Agnes, about Chip's language and anti-Japanese remarks.

"Oh, Chip's just mimicking his father. Pay him no mind," she said.

Little did Chip or any family member know or understand just how deep his hatred for the Japanese would affect his life in the years to come, thanks to his father. These acts of hate were slowly programmed into his subconscious and would surface many times throughout his lifetime.

In high school during a history lesson on WWII, Chip stood up in class and expressed his feelings. He added that it was a shame that the United States only had two atomic bombs available to use on Japan. He went on to say a few more would have made them pay for the murders and destruction they had done at Pearl Harbor and in the Philippines. They murdered thousands of innocent people in China, the Philippines, and the Americans on Guam, Bataan, and Wake Island. He also vowed someday he would personally get even with the bastard Japanese for killing his uncle at Pearl Harbor. This outburst got him a two-day suspension and a letter from the school's principal that was sent to his father, who actually praised Chip rather than punish him.

CHAPTER 2

June 1944

In early June 1944, the Reed family moved from Long Island to Westfield, New Jersey, to be closer to Agnes's handicapped sister. Charles Reed, an engineer with the New York Telephone Company, continued to commute by train each day to New York City and to the Brooklyn Navy Yard, where his office was located. The Reeds were lucky to find a comfortable house in a quiet neighborhood close to downtown and the railroad station.

When the news about the atomic bomb released on Hiroshima was first broadcast, Charley Reed celebrated with his buddies in New York City for two days before he arrived home. When news of the second bomb was dropped six days later, he decided to have a neighborhood party at the house. During the party he burned a number of collected Japanese flags on the front porch, nearly burning the house down. At the end of the war, the Reed family enjoyed many reunions with family members returning from the services. Chip Reed also became quite political, expressing his thoughts openly on the use of the atomic bombs on Japan. He would argue with anyone who thought the bombs were too extreme a punishment on the Japanese people. He even argued with the monsignor of his church.

Chip enjoyed growing up in Westfield. It was where he would build his character, which was quite different than his father's. Physically, he was taller and larger in build, but he had his father's facial features—handsome Irish smile, piercing green eyes, and a full head of wavy hair. He inherited his mother's fairness, compassion, and desire to always be in control. He wanted to excel in everything, including sports and hobbies; however, his scholastic records were never up to par. He liked spending most of his free time with his buddies and little time at home with family.

In Chip's junior year, the country became deeply concerned when the United States became involved in a new war in Korea. General McArthur was in command of the Pacific theater and in charge of the new war. After two years of frustration facing a red Chinese army backed by Russia, he advised President Truman that the United States could not win this war unless he was able to attack Manchuria. He suggested possibly making use of atomic weapons to help stop the overpowering Chinese Army. This cost McArthur his post in Japan. He was relieved by Truman, and he soon retired.

Chip and best friend, Bob Davis, were completing their senior year, and as did many other young Americans, they decided to enlist after graduation. Chip wanted to get into the US Air Force, and Bob choose the US Navy. A few months after their graduation, they were both in training camps. Chip wanted to fly, but he did not have the college credits, so he elected to go into maintenance, where he hoped to become a flight engineer. Bob Davis joined the US Navy and became a specialist in communications and ended up on aircraft carrier duty.

After boot camp Chip arrived at Sheppard Air Force Base in Texas and went through a special course on B-25s. The course was set up to train mechanics to be flying sergeants on B-26s being used as fighter bombers in Korea. The only problem was that the US Air Force sent every B-26 to South Korea, leaving no planes left to train on. The North American B-25s were the only twin-engine bombers available. Chip was chosen as one of the most likely to succeed in the special course and go to Korea, but the war ended in a truce before he finished the course.

Chip was ordered to go to Dover Air Force Base in Delaware, where he flew on C-54s and C-124s as a flight engineer. He spent his free time taking flying lessons, and eventually obtained his private pilot license. At the end of his four-year enlistment, he wanted to continue flying to earn his commercial license, so he enrolled at Emory Riddle Flight School in Miami. In spring 1959, he was hired by National Airlines based in Miami and started training to be certified to fly their Boeing 727s and DC-10s.

In 1965, Chip married one of the most beautiful women he had ever met. She was a National Airlines stewardess. One morning on a flight from

Miami to New York, she came into the flight deck and asked the crew if they would like a cup of coffee. Chip turned in his seat to examine where the sweet voice came from. She was tall and beautiful, and she easily filled out her tailored uniform. The only thing stopping Chip from leaping from his seat and formally introducing himself was the huge console between him and Mary Ellen Williams.

The courtship was fast. On a scheduled December return flight from New York to Miami a day before Christmas, Chip and his crew were grounded because of a two-day northeaster that paralyzed New York City and surrounding areas. It was a perfect time to get to get know more about Mary Ellen on a more personal level. After two exciting nights enjoying handsome cab rides in the snow to famous restaurants and nightclubs, he ended up proposing to Mary Ellen in a crowded and noisy Holiday Inn bar. They were married three months later in Miami.

In 1970, Mary Ellen had to leave flying to give birth to Charles Reed III. They lived in a classic but small Spanish house in Coconut Grove. Chip was planning ahead for retirement and began to invest in real estate. He studied law and got his real estate license. He also became interested in the restoration of World War II airplanes as a hobby and became a partner in rebuilding a North American P-5l Mustang. His real dream was to someday own a famous bomber, a North American B-25 nicknamed the "Mitchell," the same plane Doolittle used for his famous raid on Tokyo.

When Mary Ellen retired from National Airlines, she started her own business, a small gift shop in Coconut Grove. She was also determined to have a few items to make life even more exciting. She wanted to own a sports car instead of an old compact car she used daily for working and taking Charlie junior to school. Chip owned his own pride and joy, a 1958 Mercedes 450 SL. He told Mary Ellen to keep her hands off his toy, and he used the excuse that it was too complicated for her to drive. She laughed and used it when she could while he was flying on trips.

One night after Chip returned from a trip, he pulled into the driveway and saw a red sports car sitting outside the garage. The car was a famous Japanese sports model most of the jet-setters toured around Miami in. It was a Soto Z 3000. When he entered his home, Mary Ellen greeted him with hugs and kisses. Before he could ask or speak a word, she pushed him back outside and stood next to the little red sports car.

"Chip, I couldn't say no. It belonged to my old roommate, Joanne. She is being transferred to LA and had to sell it, and so I bought it."

"Honey, are you crazy? This thing is a pile of junk built by those little yellow Jap bastards. How could you do this, honey? You know how I feel about those Jap murderers?"

"Chip, my lord, isn't it time to stop being ridiculous about the Japanese? Chip, half the electronics in our home were made in Japan, and what about some of the instruments in your DC-10 cockpit? You know there are many Japanese who work at National and some fly with me. Darling, it's just a car, and I love it. What's more, I want it, and besides, Joanne sold it to me way below wholesale. I took the money out of my—"

"I don't give a damn about the money. It's the principle. And besides, these damn things are not safe, and you plan on going to your shop and taking your son to and from school in this thing?"

"Chip, have you forgot what I am driving every day? You think that Pinto in the garage is any safer? There were reports on the fuel tanks blowing up in accidents. Please don't bother to say it. I know you offered to buy me a big Volvo station wagon, but I am not ready for that scene yet, darling."

Chip looked into her sparkling hazel eyes and shook his head. "All right, but don't let my old man know about this. He'd kill me if he knew we owned a Japanese car."

She put her arms around Chip and whispered in his ear, "I knew you would let me keep it, and that is why I made a reservation tonight so that you could have your favorite dinner. I'm taking you out to Tony Roma's for those famous barbeque ribs."

The love between Chip and Mary Ellen was admired by all who knew them. Chip would brag about his feelings for her, which he felt ran deeper than a love affair. He constantly would brag she was his best friend with a tower of knowledge and the best mother in the world.

Life was full of adventures for the three of them as they explored a wonderful lifestyle. Thanks to Chip's added income selling real estate properties, they purchased the finest in luxury items such as popular powerboats.

One day he bought a popular twenty-foot Sea Craft outboard fishing boat complete with a trailer and loaded it down with fishing and diving equipment. They would take long weekends and tow the boat down to the Florida Keys, stopping at their favorite island, Islamorada. Chip had a good friend who owned a marina and apartments there. Ellen and Chip Junior loved to snorkel and dive on shipwrecks, while Chip would stick mostly to fishing for his favorite challenge, red snapper.

Chip also bartered a deal on a twenty-eight-foot Bertram sport fishing yacht with twin engines and a fly bridge. It, too, was loaded with plenty of electronics and even radar. Mary Ellen became an instant skipper and could run the yacht better than Chip. The three made vacation trips to the Bahamas Islands, including Bimini, Cat Cay, and the Abaco islands, where they would cruise the out islands, fishing and visiting with the islands' natives and enjoying their cultures. At one time Chip wanted to invest in a very popular tourist hotel in Hope Town, but Mary Ellen opted to buy a larger home in Coconut Grove. She won that battle.

Just short of the day of their seventh anniversary, Chip was scheduled to take a red-eye flight from Miami to Los Angeles. After landing at LA, he was greeted by a National Airline staff member and asked to report to National's operations office in the terminal. When he arrived, the National regional director took him into a private room and told him his wife, Mary Ellen, and his son, Charles, had been killed in a head-on collision with a pickup truck earlier in Miami.

A chartered Lear Jet was waiting to take him back to Miami. For the first hour, Chip sat and gazed out the small cabin window at the blue sky and the peaceful clouds below. He thought about the hours of joy and happiness he had with Mary Ellen and his young son. Then he broke down with an outburst of emotion, crying and screaming so loud the people in the cockpit heard him. The young copilot came back and sat down across from Chip, squeezed his hand gently, and mumbled how sorry he was for his loss. Chip wiped his eyes with a napkin and then looked into the sad face of the young pilot and thanked him for his comforting words and concern.

"Sir, would you like to have my seat up front? This bird is not as heavy as your passenger planes, but she is a spirited tiger and fun to fly. Maybe it could help take your mind off things at least for a little while."

Chip nodded yes and worked his way to the cockpit. He looked at the pilot, who smiled and pointed to the copilot seat. Chip climbed into the right seat, turned, and thanked the pilot. He put his hands on the controls, knowing it was on autopilot. He did not expect to take control, but the pilot suggested by taking his hands off his control wheel and gave Chip the signal he was in command. Chip was thrilled to be able to fly this popular Lear business jet.

Six hours after takeoff, Chip was at the Dade County Sheriff's Office, where he met with the deputy who was investigating the accident. He told Chip the young man was under the influence and lost control of his pickup truck as he was heading north in the south bound lane on US 1. The young man was speeding when he ran head-on into Chip's wife's car. He told Chip the medical officer at the accident scene reported that his wife, his son, and the young man were all killed instantly.

Chip had to go to the Dade County coroner's office to identify his wife and son. A young lady attending the bodies warned Chip that his wife's facial features were severely damaged and swollen. She suggested he wait to see her after they'd had some time to make her presentable. He agreed, but he wanted to see his son, who was presentable. She took him to his son and let him examine his remains. Later Chip told his friends that Chip Junior looked as young and beautiful as he did earlier that morning when he left for the airport.

He also wanted to see Mary Ellen's car, but once again, they told him he would probably want to wait on that as well. The deputy who had investigated the crash advised him that the car was a heap of twisted metal and that they had had to cut his wife out from the wreck. The interior was not one he would want to look at. He also said they took the car to a compound where it remained covered in tarps to keep photographers from taking photos. The deputy tried to comfort Chip, telling him to give them some time to clean it up first if he insisted on seeing it.

Chip asked the deputy, "What about the asshole in the truck who killed my family?"

"The young man, age sixteen, was killed instantly as he had suffered a broken neck and was thrown from the cab. The truck was a 72 Toyota, which we learned was stolen two days before the accident. The lad did not have a valid driver's license. Sir, your small sport car did not have a chance against the impact of that truck. It looked like it ran over your car."

Chip thanked the deputy and began to leave. But then he stopped, turned, and addressed the deputy. "Someday, Officer, I am going to make those fucking Japanese bastards pay for murdering my wife and boy."

The deputy was somewhat confused and reminded Chip the young man was not Japanese, but a child of an immigrant family from Colombia, South America. He also had a history of arrests with the Miami Police Department.

Chip looked at the deputy and commented, "They were two Japanese-built vehicles, weren't they?"

CHAPTER 3

It would take Chip Reed many years to recover from the shock of losing his wife and son. During these years while still flying for National, he spent most of his free time with his two friends and partners in their real estate office. He also helped to rebuild a number of warbirds and completed rebuilding another F-51 Mustang.

Chip flew up to New Jersey to visit his ailing father and was happy he did as his father passed away a week later. His mother, Agnes, had passed a year before almost on the same date. When he returned from Westfield to Miami, his emotions were running high and began to question his ability to command a National airliner right now. He decided to resign from National Airlines, completed restoration on his P-51. He taught his best friend and partner in the plane how to fly it. Months later his partner was killed in the fighter taking off from a small airfield south of Atlanta.

After his friend's funeral, Chip was ordered by the family attorney to return to Westfield as soon as he could in order to settle the family estate and view his father's will.

Westfield, New Jersey
The Reed's Home
127 Harrison Ave.
July 4, 1:30 p.m.

Chip decided it was time to sell his parents' home, the one he was raised in and loved. He flew to Newark Airport in New Jersey and rented a car. He drove to Westfield where he was meeting with a real estate broker named

Bobbie Whalen. She was an old high school sweetheart who had become a successful broker, and she knew his parents and their home well.

When Chip arrived, Bobbie was standing on the porch with the buyers, who appeared to be a very young couple with two children. Phil Bennett, a dentist, was moving to Westfield to open a new office. His wife, Patty, was a grade-school teacher.

Bobbie made the introductions, and they entered the house, which looked exactly the same as it did when Chip had left. Every chair and table along with bookcases and even the gas cook stove and refrigerator were still in place. Chip began to feel regret as he strolled the many rooms with the buyers.

Phil Bennett asked Chip if he was going to sell all the furniture. Chip told him, his wife, and Bobbie that he had no idea. Bobbie interrupted and made a suggestion to Chip. She said the Bennett's mentioned they would be interested in buying it all if he agreed. Chip made an instant decision and agreed to sell everything with the house.

The Reeds House
Fourth of July

"Hey, Chip, you're out of ice. Any left in the freezer?"

"You bet. Come on in, Bob. You know where the ice is."

Bob Davies opened the screen door and walked into the large open kitchen. He looked clownish in bright yellow Bermuda shorts, a green- and red-striped polo shirt, and a faded New York Yankees baseball cap. Bob was in his late forties was somewhat overweight because of his lifestyle, and he became a very successful stockbroker in New York City.

"Hey, old man, what are you up to, Chipper? The gang is asking for you outside."

"Hell, Bob. I thought I made enough burgers, but you guys are soaking them up, so I'm fixing some new ones. Chip turned and faced Bob with a hand full of chopped beef. "Bob, put some shape into this one." Chip threw the ball of raw chopped beef and onions to his friend. Bob caught most of the uncooked beef, but it disintegrated through his fingers and dropped to the floor. He picked it up, patted it back together, and threw it back to Chip.

"We'll cook that one for Fred Hager, I never could stand that little bastard," Bob remarked, wiping his hands on his shorts.

Chip and Bob Davies were like brothers and teammates throughout their high school years. They played next to each other as guard and tackle on the football team from their freshman to senior years. They were known as the dirty duo of the Westfield High Blue Devils. The only time they were separated was when they chose to enlist in different services after graduation. Chip joined the US Air Force, and Davies joined the US Navy.

At forty-six Charles was in better physical shape than most his old friends and men his age. Standing close to six feet, he looked younger than his age and displayed little graying in his dark brown wavy hair. His most distinguishing features were his bright green eyes and a long, deep, diagonal scar on his right cheek. When he was a senior in high school, he lost control of his 1939 Plymouth and went through the windshield after hitting an oak tree on his way home from his final football game.

"Hell of a party. Just like the old days, Chip. I hate to think this is our last hurrah in this great old palace. Man, we had some good times here, my friend."

Chip looked at his friend's well rounded smiling face, one that did not change over the past thirty-plus years. Bobby still looked sixteen. His pale hazel eyes nearly closed when he smiled, and his milky white skin, which was cursed with freckles, remained childlike and pleasant to look upon. His reddish blond hair still sported a crew cut that always looked self-inflicted.

"Yes, we sure did, Bob. We smoked our first cigarettes in this kitchen, remember? I stole them from my old man. They were Pall Malls if I recall."

"Jesus, you're right, Chip. I got sick and lost my cookies right here in this old sink." Davies rested his hand on the chipped porcelain bowl.

"Hey, Chipper, remember the time you were trying to get into Marcia Weldon's draws? You had her pinned right here on this butcher block table when your mom or was it your sister who walked in and caught you? Man, Marcia was one ugly bitch. Why you thought the rest of her belonged in a beauty pageant I'll never know, but I have to admit that she had the second greatest pair of hummers in high school next to Nancy Steiner, my old squeeze."

Chip broke into laughter. "It was Eileen, my kid sister, who saved my virginity that summer afternoon. She never did say anything to Mom or Dad, but I paid for that favor for years to come. Hell, I not only lost Marcia that day. I was too scared to ever try that again until I was at least forty."

They broke out in laughter and began to recall other memorable moments taking place in the old house. They were interrupted by Carol Davies, who came in looking for the ice bowl. She not only broke up their reunion, but she also reminded them there was a party going on in the backyard. She shoved them out the door to join all the friends who gathered to say goodbye to their old friend and the old Reed house. Later they would get into three station wagons and drive out to Clark Township to view the annual Fourth of July fireworks.

It was well after midnight when Chip found himself standing on the large oak-planked front porch of the old Victorian house, waving farewell to his friends as they drove off. Just when he thought everyone was gone, Bob Davies wandered around from the side of the house, pulling his zipper up on his shorts. He walked up the steps and plopped down in one of the big wicker rocking chairs.

"What the hell are you still doing here? I thought I saw you and Carol leave."

"You saw Carol leave, buddy. I had to take a whiz and told her I would be along later with you. I hope you don't mind driving me home. I just wanted to chat since I may not see you again for a long time."

Chip walked over and sat down in a wicker chair next to his friend. It was difficult to see Bob's face in the darkness as the only light that reflected on the porch was from a streetlight a half block away. He knew his friend was feeling his booze. He drank beer all afternoon and then switched to gin and tonic.

"What's eating you, buddy? Too much booze, or are you having problems at home with Carol?"

"None of the above, Chip. I just hate to think you're leaving us again. You know, when we were kids and decided to split after graduation, you decided you wanted to fly, and I wanted to go to sea. It was tough, but we were young and were facing new challenges, remember? But now we are older. You came back home, and it was like old times. I was hoping you would stay this time, especially now that you're on your own. I can't believe you already sold this old house. My biggest fear, this time when you leave, you will be gone maybe forever."

"No, Bob, not forever, and it has been bothering me too. Maybe I should have hung on to it longer, but I have lots going on in Florida and my partners in Lauderdale are getting a little uptight that I don't spend more helping them. Let's be honest, Bob. I really don't belong here anymore. This house is getting a new young couple with two beautiful children. They will enjoy its creaking boards and drafty windows. You will love them as neighbors, he is a dentist, and she is a teacher. I might add, she is really quite attractive."

"Chip, your life here could be fantastic. Do you know how many young divorcées are living around here and all with mega bucks? Carol and I could fix you up with a new divorcée or widow every night of the week. Please don't take me wrong. I know how you're still feeling the wounds from the loss of your wife and son. You really had it all until some young asshole with too many beers took it all away. Chip that was years ago, and maybe it's time to let go and start a new life for yourself while you are still young. I heard you tell Hager tonight that you were still trying to sue that Japanese car builder. Is this true? What makes you think you can still beat them? If I recall, it was proven in court nobody could have survived that kind of crash no matter what kind of car it was."

Chip remained silent. He stood up and walked to the edge of the porch.

"You don't understand, Bob. It goes deeper than that. The Jap's who own the fucking Zoto car company has a debt to pay to me and this country."

Bob got up, walked to the wooden banister, and put his arm around one of the large wooden columns bracing the large overhead roof. He stared out across the wide front lawn and into the black shadows cast by the huge elm trees that lined the street.

"All those boxes of shit that your dad saved, all those scrapbooks about the war with Japan, those photos of the A bomb blasts I helped you box up yesterday— are you going to keep all that stuff? I remember your dad really hated the Japanese. Didn't he nearly kill a Japanese businessman in New York City one night?"

"He sure did. He, Mom, and some friends went to the opening night in Times Square for the movie *Tora! Tora! Tora!*. They were standing outside the theater after the show when he overheard this guy say something to the effect that the movie was bullshit. He said there were far more destruction and casualties at Pearl Harbor than those stated in the movie. He was laughing about it. Keep in mind that Dad lost his brother at Pearl Harbor that day. He noticed the guy was Asian and figured him for a Jap, so he walked over, grabbed the Jap's silk scarf around his neck, and pulled him closer. With a right hook my Dad rearranged his nose, broke his glasses, and took out four teeth."

"Your old man was lucky, Chip. I understand this guy was a CEO of a big Japanese import company, wasn't he? How come your dad was never charged or sued by the bastard?"

"I really don't know, but I was told my dad whispered something in the guy's ear while holding his head off the pavement and then let him go. He stood over him and warned him not to get up. Dad never heard a word from him or from any authorities."

"So what's next, Chip? Now you're almost a retired airline captain and making big bucks in real estate. Do you just fly back to Lauderdale and sell more real estate? Do you buy a big sport-fishing boat or an island in the Bahamas?"

"No, I fly to Orlando, rent a car, and drive west to a little town called Lakeland to visit an old buddy of mine who once worked for National Airlines. He and an old friend of his are doing restoration work on old war birds."

"Oh, I forgot. You still dabble in those old fighter planes. Do you still have the slick little Mustang, that P-51?"

"No, I had a partner in that Mustang, a good friend and a pilot at National Airlines. He went to Georgia to visit his parents and was taking off to come home and crashed just weeks ago. We don't know what happened as the investigation is still going on."

"Jesus, Chip, I am so sorry about your friend, but will you be buying another Mustang?"

"No, this time I'm looking at a World War II bomber to go kill Japs." Chip began to chuckle, thinking about what he just said. It was even more difficult for Bob to fully understand.

"Now don't tell me. It's one of those bombers that dropped the A bomb on Japan, right?" Bob said jokingly.

"No, Bobby, nothing that big. The two bombers used to drop atom bombs on Japan were B-29s. The first bomb was dropped by the plane called *Enola Gay*, and it's on display today at the Smithsonian air and space exhibit."

"Well, I shouldn't talk. I spend all my bucks on country clubs, tennis lessons, three colleges, four sports cars, and a plastic surgeon. I also have a super-secret apartment on the lower east side in the city. You should see some of my guests. Chip, you spend one weekend with me in this place, and I promise you will never return to the real world."

"Why don't you just come on down and join me in Florida? I will tour you around the state, do some fishing and girl-chasing if that's what you want to do, you old horny bastard."

"Yeah, might just do that someday, Chip."

"Come on. Better let me get you home. It's late, and I have a 0830 departure out of Newark." Chip walked over to his friend and embraced him in a bear hug. Neither wanted to display their emotions, but they both experienced the wetness of their tears flowing gently down between their cheeks.

CHAPTER 4

Delta Airlines
Flight 1509
Newark Airport
July 5
0921 hours

"Excuse me. I hate to be rude, but that looks like a very interesting book you are reading. Isn't that the story of General Jimmy Doolittle and that famous first raid he did on Tokyo?"

Chip smiled at the inquiring man sitting next to him.

"Ah, yes, it is," Reed commented as he folded the book to expose a photo of Colonel Doolittle's plane as it was lifting off the deck of the USS Hornet.

"If I recall, that was a suicide mission. I mean they all crashed, didn't they?"

"Well, three crash-landed off the China coast, two inland, and ten of the crews bailed out over China. One crew flew to Russia, and this was the only plane and crew who landed safely. The Russians put them in prison and refused to release them or the plane back to the United States."

"Hollywood made a movie about this mission didn't they?" the stranger asked.

"Yes, in 1944, the movie was based on a book written by Captain Ted Lawson called *Thirty Seconds over Tokyo*." Chip opened the book to where photos of all the crews were. "Here is Lawson and his crew. They were the seventh bomber to take off that morning."

The stranger continued, "You know, I never could understand why Doolittle would want to lead those poor guys on what he must have known was a one-way trip. They couldn't land those planes back on the carrier, right?"

"That's right. The plan was to fly on into China," Chip replied.

"Who came up with this wild plan? They lost all their planes. Crews were captured and killed, and they did very little damage, I understand," the stranger said.

Chip closed the book, turned in his seat, and faced the man.

"It started with President Roosevelt demanding his chiefs of staff plan an immediate retaliation strike on Japan for what they did at Pearl Harbor. Those few months after Pearl Harbor attack were devastating hearing about how the Japs were kicking everyone's ass all over the Pacific. We lost Guam, Bataan, Corregidor and Wake Island. All the war news coming out of the Pacific was about our losses, and our country's morale was at an all-time low. He knew we needed to make a move of some kind, and we needed a victory to get this country off its knees. Our biggest problem was that we had no way to reach the Japanese homeland. Our two four-engine long-range bombers, the B-17 and B-24, could not reach Japan from existing bases at that time. Roosevelt called Stalin and asked if we could bomb Japan from eastern Russia, but Stalin refused as he did not want to face a two-front war with Germany and Japan."

The stranger shook his head. "So someone came up with the idea to use an aircraft carrier to get even?"

"Well, it was by sheer accident. In early January, the chief of staff of the US Navy, Admiral King sent a young navy captain named Francis Lowe to do an inspection on the new aircraft carrier about to be commissioned, the USS Hornet. On his flight back to DC, he flew over a navy airfield and noted one of the runways was painted out to resemble the deck of an aircraft carrier. What really got his attention were two twin-engine Army Air Corps bombers doing touch-and-goes on the runway. This strange sight planted an idea in the young officer's mind. When he got back to DC, he questioned his superior, Captain Wo Duncan, if bombers could be flown off the deck of an aircraft carrier? Both captains went to Admiral King with the same question, and he suggested they talk to General Hap Arnold, chief of staff of the Air Corps. Hap Arnold called in the most experienced pilot he had on staff, Major Jimmy Doolittle, for his input. Doolittle accepted the challenge to work with the two navy captains on putting together a possible strike on Japan.

"The navy wasted no time and began making plans, going over logistics for a surprise raid using the new carrier, USS Hornet. They looked over all the twin-engine bombers the US Air Force was using and found only two that would qualify. They were the new B-26 and the North American-built B-25. Doolittle wasted no time learning which plane could be modified to fly off the deck of an aircraft carrier, and he chose the B-25.

"After testing the B-25 with only two pilots on board an empty plane, he got his answer. This was the plane. Now he had to figure out how many he could get on a carrier to make the mission work. He came up with the formula for placing sixteen bombers on the deck with a takeoff roll of around five hundred feet."

"These planes on the raid would have a full fuel load and bombs, right?" the gentleman asked.

"Yes, they were well over their limits, but thanks to strong headwinds and a fast carrier, they were able to get all of them into the air."

The stranger shook his head. "By the way, my name is Wayne, Wayne Stewart." He held out his hand.

"Charlie Reed here, and p leased to meet you, Wayne." They shook hands.

"Did you have a family member on this mission?" Wayne asked.

"No, I just became attached to these raiders when I was a kid after seeing that movie called *Thirty Seconds over Tokyo* and reading the book written by Ted Lawson. I read all I could about the mission and each of the members of the crews. They meet every year on their anniversary date on April 18 to celebrate their mission and pay tribute to their lost buddies. Not long ago I had the honor to attend their fortieth anniversary in St. Petersburg, Florida. I met and talked to General Doolittle and his wife Jo, and I met many of the crews, especially the crew of Ted Lawson's ship called the *Ruptured Duck*."

"How many actually survived the raid?" Wayne asked.

"Well, out of the eighty that took off, three were killed during bailouts and crash landings with no losses over Japan. The day after the raid, eight were captured by the Japanese Army and taken to Tokyo and tortured.

The rest all made it out safely with the help of friendly Chinese. One crew running low on fuel knew they could not make China and flew to Russia where they became guests of Joe Stalin. Most of the Raiders went on to other theaters, and many flew many more combat missions."

"What happened to the prisoners?" Wayne asked.

"That, my friend, was one of the most tragic stories of the war. They were punished and tortured beyond belief and then put in solitary confinement until the war ended. However, a short time before the war ended, a yellow Jap bastard named General Tumi Soto ordered the execution of four raiders, but before execution day one died of beriberi. The other three were forced to kneel down, tied to crosses, and then shot."

"What happened to the other four?" Wayne asked.

"They were discovered in a Chinese prison camp after Japan fell and the war ended. They had no knowledge about the war from April 1942 until August 1945. Nobody knew about their existence until nearly the end of the war and they were liberated."

"My God, what a story they must have told," Wayne remarked.

"One of the prisoners named Chase Neilson tells his story in a book titled *Four Came Home*. He was the only raider who went back to Tokyo to testify before the war trials commission. Another Doolittle raider named Jake DeShazer returned to Japan years later as a missionary. He taught Christianity, and one of his first students was the pilot who led the raid on Pearl Harbor."

"Sixty four were saved by the Chinese farmers and peasants who carried them across China to safety. The Raiders leaned later that those wonderful men and women and children were all murdered by the Japanese Army, over 250,000 were sacrificed."

A soft bell went off in the cabin followed by a woman's soft voice. "Ladies and gentlemen, the captain just turned on the seat belt sign. We will be starting our descent into Atlanta-Hartsfield Airport. Please return to your seats, and make sure your tray tables are secure and your seat backs are raised. Thank you."

"Well, Charlie, time flies when you're hearing war stories," Wayne said as he wrestled with his seat belt.

"You're right. Sorry I got carried away, friend. Here, take this book, and read it. I know you will enjoy it." Reed passed the book into Wayne's lap.

"I can't do that. You haven't finished it yet."

"Oh, this is my travel copy, Wayne. I have at least six copies of it at home, two with most of the Raiders' signatures in it. Please take it."

"Well, thanks, and I will read it. By the way, are you getting off here in Atlanta?" Wayne asked.

"No, changing here for Orlando. Is this your home?" Chip asked.

"No, just a brief visit, I live in Wilmington, Delaware. I'm down here to meet with possibly my next wife and then fly over to Birmingham to meet with a broker friend who is trying to sell me a new King Air."

"Oh, you're a pilot too?" Chip asked.

"Oh, yes, it was a matter of survival. I do a lot of travel, and these damn commercial birds don't get me where I want to go, so I'm looking at a big twin. My company owns a twin Beech, a Baron, but we have outgrown it. Do you fly, Charlie?"

"Oh, yes, most of my life. I retired from National Airlines awhile back. I started out with National in Miami right out of school. As a hobby, I got into rebuilding war birds and rebuilt a couple of P-51s and an AT-6."

"Whoa, man after my own heart. I would give anything to climb inside of a Mustang and bore holes in the sky," Wayne said excitingly

"Yeah, they are great machines, but now I am on my way to look at my dream machine." Chip took the Doolittle book out of Wayne's hand. He put his finger on the plane that was in the photo on the cover, the North American B-25.

"You're looking at a B-25 to buy?" Wayne asked.

"If it isn't in too bad of shape, it was found in an old hangar out in Kansas two years ago. Two of my friends bought it and took it to Lakeland. They realized it was too expensive to rebuild, so they sold it to some asshole in Texas. I was told recently that he was in financial trouble and now wants to sell it, so I'm hopefully going to bail his ass out and put her back in the blue."

"Jesus, that's great, Charles. Say, if you do get it and put it together, I would love to come down and catch a ride with you."

"You got it, Wayne. Here, let me give you my card. It has all my numbers on it. I live and have a real estate office in Ft. Lauderdale."

While Chip was going through his briefcase, Wayne Stewart reached into his vest and pulled out a card that read, "Wayne Stewart, President and CEO International Land and Sea Leasing, Inc. Wilmington, Delaware."

"Sounds like a major company, Wayne."

"Oh, we do nicely. We lease heavy equipment and railcars and own a few small freighters."

Chip took a closer look at Wayne and noticed he was quite distinguished and well dressed even in casual clothes. He was also wearing a Rolex watch.

"You don't look old enough to be that important," Chip said, smiling.

"Oh, don't let the hair rinse fool you. I just hit the speed limit of fifty-five, been married twice, and have six children. In a few minutes, I will be meeting my next wife possibly. My old man is still active in the company at seventy-seven and has all his brains."

The Boeing 727 groaned as the first stage of flaps were set and the sound of the engines spooled back. Wayne and Chip's attention went to the cabin window as the plane banked sharply. The entire window was filled with the city of Atlanta and its suburbs bristling in the sunlight.

"Did you know, Wayne, this 727 is one of the hardest planes to land according to every pilot I know who has flown them, including me."

"Ladies and gentleman, we are on our final approach to Atlanta-Hartsfield Airport. Please see that your seat belts are fastened, your seat backs are up, and your trays stored. We are estimating our arrival at gate B15 in fifteen minutes."

Delta Gate B27
1213 hours

"Well, you were right about the 727 landings, Chip. I thought we crashed," Wayne said, laughing as they departed the plane.

A woman standing in the gate area caught Wayne's eye. "There she is, as pretty as make them," Wayne said as he and Chip entered the gate area from the gantry. He was talking about a very attractive and well-tanned redhead dressed in a tight satin white dress and brown and white spectator shoes. In a few short steps, Wayne fell into her outreached arms, and they embraced. Her purse fell to the floor, and Chip reached down and picked it up.

"Betty, this is Charlie Reed. Charlie, this is Betty," Wayne said, still holding his lady around the waist.

"My pleasure," Chip said with a bashful look.

"Hello," Betty replied.

"Say, Charlie, what time is your flight to Orlando?"

"Ah, let me see." Chip started to reach inside his blazer for his ticket.

Betty turned to one of the Delta aides and asked about the next Orlando flight. The aide looked at his schedule and remarked.

"Two fifteen, gate C19."

"Well, is that it, Charlie? Is that your flight?" Wayne asked.

"Guess so. I was due in Orlando at about three thirty."

"Good. We have time for a drink. Is that all right?" Wayne said.

"Ah, sure, I have plenty of time, but don't you two—"

Chip was interrupted. "We two have plenty of time, right, honey? We don't meet with Linda until tomorrow in Birmingham."

"Oh, Wayne, there's a change in that plan. Linda has a charter tomorrow afternoon and wants us to come to her office early. She said she would fly us to go see this plane you want if we can't get an early flight out. She said this way you could get a chance to fly this King something or other that you are interested in."

"That will work for me," Wayne said as they entered the crowded bar.

"I take it this Linda person is an airplane broker?"

"One of the best in the country, she was with Piper for years down in Florida, married a real nice guy, and together began a great life. They flew charters and went into the bush pilot business. Her husband was killed on a charter in Wisconsin, I believe. Linda went on to fly as an instructor pilot. That's how I met her. She flew me around when I was still working on my commercial. She is also this lady's best friend, right, Betty?"

"You bet, although I don't take to the wild blue yonder too well, Mr. Reed. That's where Linda and I separate."

"What do you do, Betty? and please call me Chip. I hate the name Charlie."

"Okay, Chip, I am a buyer for Saks Fifth Avenue, women's accessories mostly."

"And Atlanta is your home?" Chip asked.

"Until this madman changes it, yes." Betty smiled, and Wayne kissed her cheek.

The trio sat for the next hour talking about their experiences and future plans. At one point Chip jokingly mentioned Wayne should become a partner in his B-25 if he became its owner. Wayne did not hesitate and told Chip to call him if he ever needed or wanted an investment partner. Chip agreed, and while they were separating, they made promises they would stay in touch.

CHAPTER 5

Linder Airport
Lakeland, Florida
1630 hours

After a few bad turns and a stop at a 7-Eleven to get directions, he finally found Linder Airport. He also located the hangar called the Wings of Warriors, where he was told the B-25 would be stored. He got out of his rental and walked to the hangar. He found a badly lettered sign hanging over the door of the small wooden office that read, "We love old-fart pilots and biplanes." Chip laughed, and then he heard the sound of a radial engine flying overhead. It was a brightly colored yellow Texan T-6. He watched as it climbed into the afternoon sun and did a slow roll. He felt a rush and knew this was going to be a great day. Behind this door might be his future.

Chip opened the door and entered the dark and musty office. His attention was immediately focused on a woman sitting behind a desk stacked with papers, stained coffee cups, and half-eaten donut. She had a phone attached to her ear and a cigarette hanging from her mouth. He estimated her age to be between fifty and one hundred. She was rather plump and loaded down in makeup with the most horrible shade of red hair he had ever seen. She looked up at him, rolled her eyes, and motioned with her free hand for him to take a seat. He looked around and saw an overstuffed couch burden with books, papers, and parts to airplanes. He smiled, shook his head to say no, and remained standing. He did all he could to keep from laughing when he noticed two small fans at each end of the desk pushing around the foul air and smoke from the lady's cigarette, while an outdated air conditioner labored in a broken window in an attempt to push cool air into the small office. Finally, the woman put the phone down and put out the cigarette in a large overburdened ashtray.

"Okay, handsome, what's your bag? Are you selling something? If so, forget it. We can't make the fuckin' payroll this week."

"Ah, I am looking for Bergy, Roy Bergy."

"Yeah, so what do you want with him?"

"Ah, he invited me to come and see him. It's about an airplane. We are old friends from National Airline days."

"Oh, you're the guy from Lauderdale, the one with the deep pockets. Rotten Guts have been talking about you."

"Rotten? Who is Rotten Guts?"

"Roy is, you cutie. We call him Rotten because he passes rotten wind and you do know what farts are, right?"

Chip admitted he did, and then he began laughing. The strange lady joined in after that comment.

"My name is Lavoris Shoar, and no cracks about asking if I was named after a mouthwash. My parents owned a drugstore, okay?"

"Hi, I'm Chip Reed." He reached over the desk, and their hands met.

"Rotten said you would be here today, so come and follow me. I will show you where to find him."

Lavoris stepped from behind the desk and walked over to a narrow metal door that read, "Here is where wings are born." She opened the door and stood back.

"He's somewhere in there Mr. Reed, but be careful. There are three guys who went in there four years ago, and we haven't seen them since."

"Thank you, and by the way, please call me Chip"

"Chip?, wow, you have a strange name too. Did your folks own an ax company or a casino?" She laughed and waddled back to the desk.

Chip entered the poorly lit hangar. His eyes were quick to see the huge fuselage of a Grumman TBF Avenger standing before him. It stood on its long, leggy landing gear and flat tires. Its dark blue paint was faded, and most of its plexi-glass was broken or missing over the large cockpit. As he walked under its long, folded wing, he noticed the hull of another famous WWII Navy fighter, the famous Vought Corsair with both wings and tail section missing. He walked deeper into the packed-up hangar, tripping over aircraft parts when he suddenly saw what he was looking for.

Standing a few yards ahead was the familiar big twin vertical rudders of a Mitchell B-25. He walked faster not taking his eyes of the rudders. He noticed the elevator control surfaces had been removed, and most of the olive drab paint on the fuselage was chipped and faded. As he walked closer, he noted the entire plane looked as if it were cannibalized and in far worse condition than he imagined. The port engine was missing, and the wing was being held up by a jack stand. The port landing gear was down, and the entire wheel assembly was missing. He ducked under the belly beneath the open bomb bay and was pleased to see the starboard engine in place minus the prop, which was nearby on a stand. The main gear was down and sitting on its wheel as was the nose gear and its wheel. All the inspection doors and access plates were open under both wings. Oil and grease were both all over the floor, which made getting his footing difficult as he headed for the forward crew hatch. The ladder was down, and he carefully stepped up into the cabin behind the pilot's seats. As his head entered the cabin, his nostrils widened at the familiar smell of hydraulic fluid, oil, musty canvas, and body odor most common in these old planes. It was the smell all vintage pilots liked. It was like stepping into a new car and smelling the new leather for the first time.

He continued to make his way to the cockpit, crouching between the pilot and copilot seats as he scanned the instrument panel and the controls. He was surprised to see that not too many instruments were missing. He moved into the pilot's seat and sat down on the metal chair. The side window was open, and he took a deep breath of fresh air. The windscreen was dirty, but the light from the open hangar doors ahead made it possible for him to look around the rest of the hangar. He saw at least two Texan T-6 trainers in various degrees of completion. He saw an old Beechcraft C-45 off the port wing that looked airworthy. Standing in the sunlight of the hangar's big doorway, he spotted two men who appeared to be having a conversation. Chip figured the large man with the protruding stomach was Roy. He recalled when Roy was as skinny as a matchstick. He would crawl inside one of the huge engines on the DC-10, turn around, and pose for photo shoots showing how large the intake was.

Chip worked his way to the crew hatch, stepped on the ladder, and left the plane. He headed straight for the two gentlemen.

"Hey, you, Rotten Roy," Chip cried out as he approached the two men.

"Jesus, as I live and breathe, Chip Reed finally got here," Roy cried out.

"You bet." Chip walked up to Roy, and they embraced.

"Damn, it's good to see you, Chip. It's been too many years."

"Yes, you're right, friend," Chip said, smiling.

"Chip, I want you to meet my partner, Tom Rossi."

"Hello Tom, pleased to meet you."

"Likewise, Roy talks about you all the time and said you were coming today."

Tom Rossi was a small and fragile man with tiny features. He looked to be younger than Roy but actually was ten years his senior. He flew with the Eighth Air Force on B-17s in 1942 to 1944. He was a well-decorated navigator with thirty-four missions to his credit.

Roy reached over and took Chip's elbow and began to walk him toward the hangar. "Well, we know why you're here, Chip, so let's go check out the bird."

"Roy, I already looked her over, and she is a basket case. I was hoping to see a little more airplane put together."

"Oh, it's not that bad. You should have seen it when it came in on the four flatbeds. Hell, Chip, at least we got the wings and tail back on her." The trio laughed as they walked toward the bomber.

Bergy moved over to an old folding chair beneath the nose of the plane and sat down. He motioned to Chip to pull up a Coca-Cola crate standing on end. Chip moved it close to Bergy and sat down. Tom excused himself and commented he had to call his wife to check on a doctor's appointment she had to make.

"Chip, I have to level with you. This project is more than I can handle. I don't have the youth or the resources it takes to complete a project as big as this. I told the owner a month ago I was going to bring in a B-25 specialist to take over the project. This guy is a specialist on rebuilding B-25s, and his shop is just a few miles from here. His name is Bud West. He has a restoration shop and museum over at Kissimmee Airport."

"Hell, Roy, I know Bud West, I've met him many times at air shows. Is he going to take it on?"

"Yes, I think so if we can get the money. I told you my client is having problems and has not put in any new capital up for two months now. Hell, I have nearly thirty big ones out of pocket right now on my credit."

"What's the latest on your client? Can I call him and make him an offer? Do you think he may be ready?"

"You bet. I kind of hinted I may have a buyer, and he seemed to act like he would be willing to talk. And there is no time like the present, young man. Let's go in, and I will have Morning Breath get him on the horn."

"Morning Breath? Oh, you mean Lavoris," Chip responded.

"Chip, did you know Lavoris is a mouthwash?" Roy asked with a smile.

"Yes, Roy, I know."

"Well, she could stop a herd of cows with one outburst. So don't get too close or even think about kissing her." Bergy began to laugh. Then he stood up, stretched his long arms, and pointed the way to the office. When they arrived, Roy ordered Lavoris to call Mr. Blackburn in Texas.

As ordered, she picked up the phone and dialed Mr. Blackburn at his Dallas office. He picked up the phone, and Lavoris immediately put his mind to rest.

"Mr. Blackburn, Lavoris here, so don't panic. I am not asking for funds, but I have a man here who wants to talk to you about buying that piece of junk of a bomber you stuck Roy with." Lavoris smiled and handed the phone to Chip.

"Mr. Blackburn, I think I fully understand your situation and how disappointed you must be, sir, but this situation is not Roy's fault. The condition of the plane's airframe was in far worse condition than anyone imagined. As you know, it spent nearly five years in the jungle of Costa Rica filled with mud and water. Yes, sir, and I realize that, sir. But I have had planes rebuilt, and my contactors always ran into more problems than were originally estimated. Mr. Blackburn, I am in position to offer you cash for the Mitchell right now and take care of all the outstanding debts, including all the bills Roy Bergy has attached to the plane to date. That is fine with me, Mr. Blackburn. I will meet with Mr. Bergy and give you a call within a few hours with my offer. Say around six o'clock? Fine, Mr. Blackburn and thank you for taking my call. I'm sure you will be pleased with my offer. Thank you. I will be back to you soon. Good-bye." Chip handed the receiver to Lavoris, and she put it down in the cradle.

"Well, what do you think, Chip?"

"I think he will take any deal and run. I am sure he knows I know what he paid for the plane, and I will give him a small bonus like a finder's fee to make him comfortable with the deal. I imagine and understand he really wanted this plane. It's a shame that he fell on hard times."

"Chip, he's a guy you would have liked to spend some time with too. He flew F-86 Sabers during Korea and has three Migs to his credit," Bergy said.

"Well, I don't trust the asshole. He never kept his word when I would call and ask for some money. Hell, we're living out of tuna cans, and that mother sucker owns five furniture stores in Texas," Lavoris said as she lit a cigarette.

"Well, I'd better go and check in at a motel somewhere. Why don't we all meet later for dinner?" Chip said as he headed for the door.

"Sounds good to me Roy remarked. How about it Tom can you get your lady to the doctor, and maybe join us?" Chip asked.

"Naw, you guys go ahead. I promised the little lady I would take her shopping tonight after the doctor tells her she wasn't dying."

"Hell, I'll join ya. I haven't had a good meal since you won that ham dinner at the church picnic, Roy."

"No offense, Lavoris, but tonight belongs to me and my old pal here. We got lots to talk about. All you ever want to talk about is sex."

There was dead silence for a few seconds as Chip held his breath. He was not sure about the chemistry between these three and how far they went with humor.

Shit, I wouldn't park my fat ass between you three for a seven-course meal at Denny's. I don't need your company, boys. I can run down to 7-Eleven and pick me up a sharecropper and have a hell of a night rolling in whatever he is harvesting right now." She stood up, placed her hands under her large breasts, lifted them up, and took a deep breath. She picked up her purse and went out the door, singing "I'll Walk Alone."

"Don't worry, Chip. This is all part of a show. Lavoris was in theater once, maybe twice. She's a real trip. In reality, she is a very smart and wealthy lady and doesn't need anything, but she won't share anything either. She could buy your B-25 and the next two that show up. I put up with her cause she can barter like nobody I know. She is our purchaser, bookkeeper, and bank when we need it," Bergy said, laughing. "Say, Chip, I would like to call Bud West. Maybe he is free tonight, and we can meet after you make your deal with Blackburn."

"By all means, the faster we get Bud West on the project, the better. I will feel like I am about to kiss my retirement good-bye." Speaking of that, are you sure about the thirty thousand he owes you and no more, right?

"Yeah, that's 'bout right, Chip."

"Roy, hand me Blackburn's phone number, and I'll call him from the motel."

CHAPTER 6

July 6
1023 hours
Lakeland Linder Airport

Chip, Roy, and Tom stood in the hot sun just outside the hangar as the B-25J taxied up the ramp. Its props were barely turning over as the bomber rolled toward them. The popping sounds of its exhaust discharging through the short stacks became louder as it came to a stop in front of the hangar. Its gleaming, shining silver skin glistened in the bright sun, and Chip could feel the hair on the back of his neck begin to rise in excitement. This classic Mitchell was a museum piece, he thought. It was perfect. It had all the proper markings of a B-25J that served all over Europe and Pacific. She had two extra .50-caliber machine guns mounted on each side of the fuselage. Her upper turret had twin .50-caliber guns facing aft, and in her tail turret had a pair of .30s called "stingers." When the bomber came to a stop directly in front of the three men, Chip could see the pilot and copilot going through their shutdown procedures. Rossi ran beneath the wings and installed two wood logs in front and back of the main gear. The engines were cut, and the props slowly came to rest. The small crew door behind the nose wheel dropped opened, and the ladder came down. Bud West was the first to deplane followed by his copilot, Sam Jones. The two men walked over to the waiting trio.

"Bud, this is Chip Reed, my friend from Lauderdale."

"Hello, Chip. Nice to meet you."

Chip shook his hand and studied him for a moment. Bud West was a tall, lean man and younger than Chip remembered. He stood like a cowboy in his tight, washed-out, and stained Levi's and a faded denim shirt with a colorful patch over the left pocket displaying the logo of his company, Bud West's Sunshine Warbird Museum. He wore a soiled baseball cap with another similar patch. His shirt pockets were bursting with small notebooks and pens.

"Nice to meet you, Bud. You may not remember me, but we actually met a few times at air shows in Titusville and in Tampa."

West studied Reed for a second, trying to remember.

"Ah, I am really bad on intros. I'm so sorry, my friend. Please meet my second-in-command, Sam Jones," Bud said as Sam and Chip shook hands.

"Listen, Bud. I am happy to hear you are possibly interested in this project behind us, and now that I own this bird, I would hope we can come to some agreement or contract to finish the project and get her into the air."

"Well, that may not be easy, Mr. Reed. I am used to having this kind of project at my site, and this one is nasty and won't be easy working on her over here. I warned Roy about that after he told me about its condition awhile back."

"I understand, Bud, but I just bought this bird for more than I want to admit. And hopefully, I can take her to the Doolittle Raiders Fiftieth Anniversary in Columbia South Carolina next year. You are the only one who can make that dream come true. Can we at least talk?"

West smiled and pointed toward the hangar. "We will have much to do, and I hope you have a big checkbook, my friend."

"It's Chip, okay?" Chip said, smiling.

Bud put his hands on Chip's shoulders. "I will have you at the Doolittle Reunion, sir. Count on it." Bud smiled turned and walked toward Chip's plane followed by Chip, Bergy, and Tom Rossi.

When they arrived at the plane, Bud stood with hands on his hips and looked the bomber over from wingtip to wingtip.

"Probably going to eventually need two new Wright 2600s for starters. We will do what we can to save these two engines. I can always get my hands on a pair of rebuilt dash 23s later on. I will have my engine guys come over here to see if there is enough life in these two ladies to get this bird airborne. I might add, Chip, if we need to replace the 2600s, they are getting hard to find as are some other critical parts like main gears and wheels. Not many scrapped 25s around to pick up parts from anymore.

We'll have to have those Hamilton props rebuilt and will need all new tires and find some plexiglass for those broken nose sections. I'll send a crew over and get her in minimum flying condition to get a FAA transport permit so I can fly her over to my hangar for finish work. How does that sound, Chip?"

Chip shook his head and turned to Roy, who was grinning from ear to ear.

"You're going to teach me how to fly this thing, right, Bud?" Reed asked.

"Hell yes. That's part of the deal. Are you rated twin-engines?"

"Yes, prop and jets including 727s and DC-10s. I have more than two hundred hours in F-51s, Cessna 72s and 82s, Grumman Tigers, and a few hours in Texan 6s."

"Chip, we will start your lessons in my bird so we have you ready in time for the christening. For your information I have a young man flying into Orlando later to come over and make a bid on this J model I flew in with. It's been named *Panchitto*. You will need flying lessons on how to fly this B-25. With the likes of guys like you and this young pup from Delaware, sounds like we may just have a full class. You both buy very expensive antique planes and then want to learn how to fly them," Bud said, smiling. "Now what color do you finally want your bird?"

"Bud, I want to duplicate this plane like the ones that were on the Doolittle Raid in 1942," Chip replied.

"Well, to begin with, you have a B model, and that is a good start. You want to paint her olive drab with the old stars like General Doolittle's bird?" Bud asked.

"Yes and no. I want to duplicate Ted Lawson's plane, you know, the fellow who wrote the book *Thirty Seconds over Tokyo*."

"The famous *Ruptured Duck*, right?" Bud commented.

"You got it, Bud. Lawson and Doolittle have been my heroes since I was a kid."

"You may want to clear that with the Doolittle Raiders Association and Mrs. Lawson, Chip. I think she still lives out in California somewhere."

"Oh, I intend to. I spoke to her just before Ted died."

Bud reached out to Reed and offered his hand. "Mr. Reed, we have a deal. I will have a crew here early next week and a contract sent over here to Roy tomorrow."

"Roy, you and Tom will be on my payroll now … if that's okay with Mr. Reed here."

"You bet it is, and thanks, Bud. Oh, by the way, what are we to do about Lavoris out there in the office?" Chip asked.

"Lavoris? What is a Lavoris?" Bud asked, smiling.

"Not to worry, Bud. I will handle that project," Chip said, laughing.

The four men returned to Bud's plane where his copilot stood waiting. Bud shook hands with everyone and climbed aboard his plane. A famous cartoon character was painted on the nose section, and the name "Panchito" was painted around the cartoon.

In a few minutes, the two engines were fired up, Rossi pulled the cocks, and the Mitchell began to roll down the taxiway. Chip felt like he was a kid again looking through a chain-link fence at Roosevelt Field near his home on Long Island. He saw many B-25s coming and going during the war years. Now he was standing in front of his own B-25 nearly fifty years later.

CHAPTER 7

October 15
0945 hours
Lakeland Linder Airport

Nearly ten weeks had gone by since Bud West took over the new project, and for the first time Chip could see the magic and teamwork in Bud's specialists. The old Wright 2600-13 engines had been rebuilt and remounted on the wings, and two reconditioned Hamilton Standard props were waiting to be installed. All the control cables and control surfaces had been completed. Fuel tanks had been replaced or fixed, and new fuel lines had been installed. Bergy located new tires and wheel bearings for all three landing gears, and the Ruptured Duck, which was what it was now affectionately called, stood on her own three legs with only a tail jack in place to support the rear while the engines were being installed. It was agreed that as soon as the plane was ready and issued its transport permit, it would be flown over to Bud's hangar and completed there, which would include installing all the required electronics, reconditioned guns, painting, and detailing. Chip had decided he wanted to be close to the project, so he bought a used thirty-four-foot motor home and parked it next to Bud's hangar office. He also bought a used Buick Regal. He was able to use the RV as his home and office when he was not tending to business in Lauderdale.

October 17
0835 hours

Chip and Roy were standing at a workbench, studying plans on the Duck's hydraulic system when Lavoris approached them.

"Hey, handsome, here is a message for you from some guy you met in Atlanta, but he isn't there. He is in Florida at the Gainesville Airport, getting fuel. He is at an FBO there and wants to talk to you, pronto."

"What's his name?" Chip asked.

"Didn't give one. He said you met on a plane in Atlanta."

"Oh, yes, now I remember. I met this fellow when I was coming down here. Ah, his name is ... ah, Wayne, Wayne Stewart."

"Whatever. He is waiting, sweetheart, and it sounds like he's on his way here because he wanted to know if there were any good FBOs at this field."

"Well, I'll be damned. Hey, Roy, this guy is loaded and wanted to be a partner in the Duck at one time."

"I hope you aren't going to do that, Chip. You're not going to let a partner get involved, are you?" Roy commented.

"No, I'm not. Well, not unless this bird runs me out of money," Chip responded. Then he walked off and headed for the office with Lavoris to call his new friend.

When Reed reached the office, he went right to the desk phone and dialed the number off the memo.

"Flight 1, Colin here."

"Hello, my name is Chip Reed, and I am returning a call from a Wayne Stewart. Is he there?"

"Stewart? Oh, yes, he is on the patio with two ladies. Hang on. I'll get him for you."

Chip could hear the man calling out to Wayne and what sounded like a door bang shut. *I wonder what this guy is up to*, Chip thought.

"Hey, old man, how are you?"

"Just fine, Wayne. What are you doing in Gainesville?"

"Oh, we are on a little pleasure trip and celebration. I got engaged last night to Miss Betty. Remember you met her at the Atlanta Airport?"

"Of course I do, and my best wishes to you and Betty."

"Thanks, Chip. I am lucky. She's a dream come true, but so is her friend Lucky Linda. She is the reason why it's taking so damn long to get down to Lakeland. Linda is ferrying a Piper Archer down to Palm Beach for a friend and wanted company, so we joined her at six this morning and took off from Macon. We had to dodge some weather, so here we are."

"That's great, and you are planning on coming here?"

'You bet, Chip. It's in the flight plan. When we told Linda about your B-25, she immediately checked on Lakeland's location and said she wanted to stop by and meet you and the plane. Naturally, Betty told her you were single and a hunk, whatever the hell that means."

"Well, I look forward seeing you, Wayne. What is your ETA here? Do you know yet?"

"Linda figures we can be down there in about an hour or so depending on headwinds, so I would look for us around noon. Is your hangar easy to find?"

"You bet. Just look for the one that looks condemned. We are at the north end of the field. Ground control will get you here."

"Look forward to seeing you, Chip, and I hope we can maybe have dinner if it's okay with the pilot. Did you have plans?"

"No, and that would be great. See you soon." Chip hung up the phone.

"Lavoris, we are getting some company in a couple of hours. Do you think you could clean up this place a little?"

"Sure, you got a stick of dynamite and a can of high test octane?"

1234 hours
Lakeland Linder Airport

Chip and Roy stood in the shade of the hangar and watched the sleek Piper Archer II as it taxied up the ramp. It pulled in front of the hangar and stopped. Chip could see Wayne Stewart in the right seat and what looked like a woman sporting a baseball cap in the left seat. She removed her headset and shut down the engine of the Archer. Roy walked out and placed a pair of chocks around the nose wheel. The cabin door opened, and Stewart stepped out on the wing, waving his hand wildly. Chip walked around the wing and greeted Wayne as he helped Betty climb out of the rear seat. They stepped off the wing and greeted Chip.

"Good to see you, Chip," Betty said as she opened her arms and gave Reed a hug.

Chip kissed her on the cheek. "Good to see you, and congratulations, young lady. You've got yourself a neat guy here," Chip said, laughing.

"Oh, here, Chip. Meet my best friend, Linda."

Chip turned and looked up as Linda climbed out of the plane, stood up, stretched, and then closed the cabin door.

"Hi, Chip. I'm Linda."

Chip stood motionless. Linda stood tall, trim, and very attractive. Her short, wavy auburn hair spun around her long, tanned face. She wore little or no makeup, and her dark brown olive-shaped eyes gave her the appearance of being of Latin blood. Her wide, thin lips opened into a wide warm smile that created two deep dimples in her glowing cheeks. She was dressed in tight, washed-out designer jeans and a simple short-sleeve white cotton blouse with a red silk scarf around her neck. On her feet she wore a pair of vintage boat shoes without laces. Chip extended his hand to help her step down from the wing and added both hands around her waist to ease her down. He stood for a second, looking into her eyes, making her nervous as she gently removed his hands from her hips.

"Hello, Linda. Nice of you to bring Wayne and Betty by."

"This was my idea, Chip. I wanted to see your bomber."

After introductions to Roy and Tom Rossi, Chip led his guests toward the Duck. He had a terrible time trying to make small talk with Linda and even more problems taking his eyes off her shapely figure or erasing the scent of her perfume from his nostrils.

"Well, here she is, boys and girls," Chip said as they approached the bomber.

"Wow, she looks like she's almost ready for the blue yonder, Chip," Wayne said as he continued walking around the plane.

"Oh, we're a long way off, Wayne. At least two months before she gets in the air. Lots of wiring and new plumbing to come. We hope to at least be running the engines up in the next three weeks and checking all the fuel lines and tanks."

"Why a bomber, Chip? What made you want to own a B-25?" Linda asked.

"That's a long story, Linda. Let's just say it was a boyhood dream come true," Chip said, laughing.

"He's a romantic, Linda. I told you that," Stewart said as he walked toward the rear of the plane. "He fell in love with a plane and the story of its most famous mission back in 1942 when sixteen of these babies flew off a carrier and bombed Tokyo. It was our retaliation strike on the Japs for their attack on Pearl Harbor."

Chip turned and addressed Linda. "Wayne is right. I am naming this plane after one of the planes that were made famous on that raid, and it was called the Ruptured Duck. Here is a drawing on what the nose art will look like." Reed reached in one of his shirt pockets and produced a small envelope. He opened it and pulled out what appeared to be a cartoon of a comical duck braced by crutches.

"That's cute, and the name must have some story behind it, right?"

"Well, yes. I have a movie I will lend you called *Thirty Seconds over Tokyo*. It was made back in 1944 with some great old actors like Van Johnson, Bob Mitchem, and a real classy guy named Spencer Tracy. Once you see the movie, you will understand my love affair with this twin-tailed beast."

"I will look forward to seeing it. Now can I crawl up in that cockpit and see the business end of your machine?"

Linda sat in the pilot seat and immediately put her feet on the rudder pedals and took hold of the control wheel. Her right hand roamed the pedestal, and her fingers ran over the engine and prop controls as her eyes scanned the entire instrument panel. Chip watched her as he sat with his arms crossed in the copilot seat.

"Simple, isn't it?" he asked.

"Quite. And everything is where a single pilot could handle this bird with no problem. It looks like you have her pretty well outfitted except for your radios and transponder. Are you putting in radar?"

"No, not on the Christmas list at this time, but it could be later on when we are closer to final commissioning."

"What are your plans when she's all painted and ready for war?"

"Oh, I'll show her at shows around the country, but my main goal right now is to be at the Doolittle Raiders Fiftieth Reunion at Columbia, South Carolina, on April 18, 1992. Then do some air shows and maybe take her on a tour of the Pacific and even to China, where she and the Raiders are their heroes."

"Have many hours logged in 25s?" Linda asked with a smile.

"You hit below the belt. None actually. My dual time is in 727s and DC-10Bs. I will be starting lessons in a few weeks with Bud West. He is the fellow who is putting this bird together and the most experienced B-25 pilot I know. He says he will have me ready in no time. He claims this bird will handle like a Mack truck at first but will turn into a Mustang once I get to know her."

"I would like to be here when it rolls out, Chip. Will you put me on the VIP list?"

"I will do better than that. You can break the bottle of beer on the nose."

"Beer is not on the menu, Chip. More like a hundred-year-old French champagne?"

"When I get this bill for this project, it will be a beer. Count on it."

They both laughed, and without realizing it, Chip placed his hand over hers as they rested on the mixture controls."

"Sorry about that," he said, looking embarrassed.

"Why not push them into full rich, you know, takeoff position? I'm beginning to like your style, Chip Reed."

After an hour of touring the Duck, Chip suggested that they head for his motor home next to the hangar and get some refreshments. Unfortunately, when Chip attacked the small refrigerator, there were only three cans of Miller Lite, a Diet Pepsi, and an open bottle of club soda. He offered to go to the store, but Betty found a box of tea bags and made a batch of ice tea.

Linda had removed her shoes and tucked her feet beneath her as she sat coiled in the corner of the large sofa. Without looking at Chip, she concentrated on looking out the large picture window above the sofa.

"So, Chip, you have your bomber, and you're going to take it on tours visiting air shows around the country. Then you plan is to head for the Pacific?"

"Yes, that's the plan if I can afford to do it. I may need to look for sponsorships as many do."

"That's nonsense, Chip. I told you that if you wanted a partner or investor in this project, I would be more than willing to help, providing I can get some second seat time," Stewart said as he rose from his chair and walked over to the counter and refilled his glass with more tea.

"Hell, I would love to travel with you, Chip. We could have a ball hitting all the big air shows, and in the next few months, I will have nothing but time to kill. I plan on stepping aside and letting my eldest son take the seat. All I will do is advising and getting my allowance checks each month."

"Hey, lover, how about me, you know, the girl you want to marry and hates flying?" Betty said in a serious tone. She suddenly rose from the sofa and stood next to Wayne.

"Honey, this is not a full-time thing we are talking about. It just means we will be going to a few air shows. You can fly commercial. Don't worry," Wayne said, putting his arm around Betty's waist.

"Betty, you have just got to get into flying, girl, and enjoying it. Hell, I would kill to be able to fly a show circuit like this. You meet the greatest people on earth, and most of these guys who own these warbirds have wives who travel with them. It's like a big country club. All you need is a few hours with me on some weekends, and I will get you over this phobia … or whatever it is you worry about."

"I'm sorry. I know it's childish. I just get all tied up inside. My God, do you know how many Tums I took flying down here today?"

First, there was dead silence, and then all four began to laugh.

"Honey, we will work on it. It will be okay." Wayne gave Betty a gentle kiss on the lips.

"Well, Chip, what do you say? Want a partner?" Stewart asked abruptly.

"Wayne, let me sleep on that one, okay? Don't take it personal. I just need to see where I stand when this bird is finished, but I will say this. If I have to have a partner, you will be the first ask." Chip smiled and raised his glass in a salute.

"Hey, boys and girls, I have a date in Palm Beach, and it's getting late."

Linda put her shoes back on and walked over to Chip. "If you're not too busy, why not fly over with us to Palm Beach. We have a condo over there for the night, and tomorrow you can take a shuttle back to Orlando.

Unfortunately, we have to fly back to Atlanta at noon on Delta, and they don't make stops at Lakeland."

"Hey, that's a hell of an idea, Chip. Why don't you come with us? We can raise hell tonight and talk more about your adventure," Steward said while moving from the nose of Reed's plane."

"I wish I could, but tomorrow we have a meeting with the boss, Bud West, to make decisions on electronics and look over the hydraulic system."

"We understand, Chip. However, I would like to see you again if that's all right. I occasionally get some deliveries down here, especially Tampa and Orlando."

"Anytime, Linda. I would like that. I plan on being here until we move to Kissimmee when we get the bird running. Here, let me give you all my numbers." Chip took a business card from the counter and wrote down more numbers.

"Here is my card ... and all my numbers, and I have call forwarding plus a beeper, so you can reach me if you want." Linda handed the card to Chip, and he could feel that little extra squeeze of her hand. He hoped that he read her right. Unlike him, he kissed her on the cheek and repeated his intentions that he would like to see her again.

"Hey, let's think this thing over, ladies," Stewart said. "Linda, you don't have to deliver that Archer until tomorrow morning, right? Betty, you don't have to be in New York for your marketing meeting for two more days, and I have nothing to do but convince this young man he needs me as a partner. So why don't we just find a nice comfortable motel around here, check in, go out, have a nice dinner, and get our Palm Beach business over with early tomorrow morning. Linda, you said yourself that you needed to get that second radio fixed before you signed off the plane. Maybe Chip can get that done here."

All eyes were trained on Wayne Stewart as if he had just taken the last potato chip.

"That's a great idea, sweetie. I did not like the idea of staying in some guy's condo anyway. Oh, sorry, Linda. I know he's your friend and all that."

Linda laughed and moved closer to Chip.

"It's your call, Mr. Chip. Do you want us around for dinner tonight?"

"Of course. I mean, I have no plans, and it's a good idea. I will go over to the office and have Lavoris locate a good motel, and if you want to see a real Florida sunset, I have the perfect spot for dinner. It's over near Disney World, but it—"

Linda interrupted, "It's the restaurant at the top of the Contemporary Hotel, I bet."

Stewart was stunned. "Are you some kind of psychic too?" he asked, laughing. "That is exactly what I had in mind but could not remember the name of the hotel."

Linda turned to Betty and Wayne. "You will love it, and the best part is that its casual and we can relax since we did not bring any banquet rags to wear."

She stopped for a second and took notice of a photograph that Chip had hung on the hangar wall. It was a group shot of a group of senior men dressed in blazers, and all of them had some kind of emblem on their pockets. In the center was Chip standing next to a rather short balding man.

"This isn't your graduation class at National Airlines, I hope," Linda said, laughing.

"No, that was back in 1982 in St. Petersburg. It was the Doolittle Raiders' fortieth reunion. The man I am shaking hands with is the famous general himself, Jimmy Doolittle, or better known as the Boss to that gang."

Betty put her finger gently on the glass, pointing to Chip. "You must tell me sometime about your affair with this group. Wayne told me they hold a special place in your heart."

"I will be happy to." Chip reached up and took a set of keys off a hook next to the photo.

"Wayne, here are the keys to my Buick outside. Why don't you run over, get your baggage out of the plane, and meet me at the office. I'll have Lavoris work on your motel arrangements and set dinner for let's say seven thirty? Is that okay?"

Everyone agreed and left the hangar. Chip also advised Linda that her plane would be moved into the hangar and that he would get someone working on her radios as soon as possible.

Roy appeared and told Chip that Bud West had called and was in Orlando picking up his new prospect and wants to maybe introduce him to everyone tonight.

"Fine, Roy. Call Bud back, and ask if he would like to join us at the Contemporary for a drink?"

CHAPTER 8

1930 hours
Contemporary Hotel
Disney World

Chip Reed's party stepped off the elevator and walked up to the guest station.

"Reed party ... ah, for a seven-thirty reservation." Chip addressed the attractive young hostess as she looked at the book on the pedestal.

"Oh yes, we have your table ready, Mr. Reed. We reserved a round table next to the large tinted window with a great view." She escorted the foursome to the table. "Is this satisfactory, sir?" she asked.

"Perfect. Thank you, young lady," Chip said politely.

"Wow, look at the start of a colorful sunset. You were right, Chip. You can see clear to Tampa from here," Wayne Steward said as he moved Betty to her seat.

"Here, Linda, sit here. We still have a few minutes before that big orange ball falls into that purple sea," Chip said as he moved her chair out, and she took her seat.

"Thank you, and it is beautiful here. I keep forgetting just how flat Florida is down here. You can see forever," Linda said, laughing.

"Yeah, the only thing us pilots have to be careful of down here is radio towers, birds, and student pilots," Chip added.

"Hi, folks, my name is Mike, and this is Cora. We will be taking care of your party tonight." The two young waiters stood smiling besides each other. "Can we get some cocktails for you before we tell you about our specials?"

Chip was about to respond when he noticed the table directly next to them where a group of six men and women were about to be seated. Chip stared at them for a spell and noted they looked Oriental and naturally figured they were all Japanese. Chip looked up at Mike and asked him to have the hostess return. In a few minutes, a different, more mature hostess named Joanne Taylor stood at Chip's side and asked if there was a problem. He did not hide his emotions or the volume of his request as he said to the hostess that he did not want to be seated next to a bunch of Japanese who probably don't even speak English.

Not only did the hostess show concern and a bit of shock, but Chip's friends were a bit embarrassed and surprised as well.

"Sir, these people are not Japanese. They are from South Korea. We have more than four hundred of them staying here at the hotel. They are on a Disney tour, I believe, but let me see what I can do." She smiled and began to walk away when Chip called her back.

"I apologize, Miss Taylor. I have a problem with Japs. I'm sorry."

One of the Korean gentlemen sitting directly behind Linda turned in his seat and addressed Chip in perfect English. "Sorry if we offended you, sir, but we are from Korea as the hostess explained. However, my wife, Suling, is from Japan, speaks English, and would be most happy to talk to you about any problems you may have with doing business in Japan if that is your problem. She is with our government's immigration department and knows many Japanese officials in Japan."

Chip smiled and thanked the young man for his interest and suggested he would like to buy their table a bottle or two of wine. The young man just smiled and said no. He turned around and in Korean explained whatever he thought was going on with this gentleman. There were no comments or stares from the party, just friendly smiles.

Chip was pleased but embarrassed, and surprised no questions came from Linda, Betty, or Wayne during their dinner. They ordered their wines and dinner and enjoyed the spectacular sunset taking place.

After dinner the foursome moved into the lounge to have their after-dinner drinks. A colorful trio all playing Spanish guitars were playing a popular Latin song called "Meditation." It was one of Linda's favorites, and she asked Chip to dance before they even sat down.

As the foursome entered the elevator, Linda commented to Chip, "This was a great idea, Chip, and a wonderful evening. You sure had a colorful and full life. Your stories were most enjoyable. We were sad to hear about the loss of your wife and son. I am so sorry for your loss. You must have loved them very much," Linda said, looking directly into his eyes.

After arriving in the lobby, Chip and Linda separated themselves, heading out to the car.

"Linda stopped walking and asked Chip a personal question. "How come you didn't pursue a career with some big airline? You sure have the talent and ratings. Just how many hours have you logged to date?"

It was evident Chip was not going to respond Linda's comment about the losses in his life. He told her he flew with National for years and had logged more than 2300 hours.

"Now Miss Amelia, evidently, you have a few hours boring holes in the sky, and I have to ask. Have you ever considered flying for a major airline?"

"Well, like you, I was very happily married once to a guy full of crazy adventures. He was a great pilot and taught me most of my good habits. We would work here and there, brainstorming in a very old 1946 Stinson. We would sign on with charter services, even ran a medical supply company for a while, and then began to work for a big famous Texan oilman whom I won't mention. He had a fleet of jets and props and took good care of us. We just did not like his politics, friends, and social parties. We opened our own bush services up in Wisconsin and flew crazy fisherman and hunters all over the northern woods and lakes. It was fun and profitable until one day Randy, my husband, took off with a gentleman and his two sons on a hunting expo. It was late in January, and we had plenty of winter hanging around. But we had a nice break in the weather, or at least we thought. Randy took off early one morning, and we lost contact with him after learning about unexpected gales possibly on his route. It took three weeks to find his plane, and it was reported that all the passengers were killed. The NSTB has yet put their finger on the problem, concluding it may have been just bad luck with the weather. I never bought their story. Randy was too good a pilot. It took years before I went along with their theory. That was five years ago, but it still seems like yesterday."

They reached the car and looked for Wayne and Betty, but they did not see them.

Chip decided not to respond to Linda as he could see her eyes were starting to getting wet. He pressed his cheek next to hers and pulled her body closer to him and then realized what he had done.

"I'm sorry, Linda," Chip mumbled. "I was just trying to comfort you."

Chip tried to lighten the conversation up, so he smiled and stepped back. "Do you want to know something? If you had been flying second seat with me at National, I don't think I could have ever kept my mind on what I was doing. I would be spending all my time just looking at you. Did you happen to notice all those heads turn when you walked in the room earlier?" Chip was desperately trying to change the mood and bring Linda back to his presence.

"Chip, those eyes were on Ms. Betty Boobs, not my figure. If I had her figure, I wouldn't be flying for Airco Charters and Sales in Birmingham. I would be modeling for Sak's."

"Nonsense. You have a great figure, and none of Betty's parts would improve anything you already own." Chip paused for a second.

"Did that dumb line I just made make any sense?" he said, laughing.

Linda laughed and pulled Chip closer to her. At the same time, he relaxed his arms, pulled her even closer, and brushed his lips across her warm cheek. He began to realize for the first time in a long time just how much he was enjoying this moment. Things were changing in him, and he knew somehow this beautiful woman was going to be good for him.

"Hey, you two, we were trying to get into the wrong Buick. Can we go home now?" Wayne said, laughing.

Roy Bergy's Hangar
October 18
0845 hours

The small cabin door closed on the Archer's cabin. Chip watched Linda put on her baseball cap and adjusted her headset. He could see her eyes following her hands as they ran through preflight procedures, setting up radios, selecting fuel tanks, setting throttle and mixture controls. She looked up at Chip standing ten yards in front of the prop. He gave her the all-clear thumbs-up signal. Linda turned the starter key and the starter motor began to whine followed by the prop beginning to rotate.

The six cylinders fired off, and Linda throttled up. The nose of the Archer dipped on the nose strut. She put on her dark glasses and released the brakes. Chip could see her lips moving as she advised ground control that she was ready to taxi to the active runway. She removed her glasses, winked, and blew Chip a slow and sexy kiss good-bye. Then she advanced the throttle and turned the Archer on its port main gear and headed down the ramp. Chip never noticed the farewell waves extended by Wayne and Betty.

"Hey, looks like you found a new fan club there, handsome."

Unnoticed, Lavoris had been standing behind Chip, holding a large envelope. The return address showed it was from Mr. Blackburn's lawyers in Dallas. It was the final papers on the Duck, the final bill of sale. Chip reached out, put his arms around Lavoris, and gave her a big hug, almost lifting her large frame off the ground. Then he planted a big kiss right on her lips. Lavoris stood in total shock as Reed walked away, whistling, not aware he was covered in lipstick from under his nose to his chin.

CHAPTER 9

October 20
0945 hours
Bud West's Warbird Museum Office
Kissimmee Airport

"Hi, I'm Chip Reed. Is Bud around?"

The woman behind the desk was about to pick up the phone when she responded, "Oh, hi, Chip, I'm Sara Hicks. We talked a few times."

"Hi, Sara. It's my pleasure. I have been meaning to get over here for weeks, but the Duck has ... I mean, my plane has been keeping me pretty busy."

"A duck? You plan to call your B-25 a duck?" she asked, looking curiously over her glasses.

"Well, its formal name when it gets all its war colors on, and I will have a cartoon of a silly-looking duck on the nose area. It is named after a famous B-25 used on the famous Doolittle Tokyo raid," Chip said, smiling.

"Oh, the Ruptured Duck, of course. Bud told us about that. I remember the movie *Thirty Seconds over Tokyo* like it was yesterday. As a matter of fact, I believe we have a copy of the movie in our library in the next room. Would you like to buy one?"

"Sara, I have at least six copies of the movie. I had a friend make me up a bunch of illegal tapes I give to friends, but don't tell MGM." Chip laughed.

"Bud and Dolly are still having breakfast, and I just talked to him a little while ago. Would you want to join them? It's not far from here."

"No, I'll wait. I had no appointment time with him. Just told him I would be over to start talking about my flying lessons. He's going to teach me to fly a B-25, and that's not easy stepping out of a DC-10B. The only thing the two planes have in common is they both have tricycle landing gears."

"Well, why don't you take a walk outside and visit the museum and maintenance shop. Out there somewhere is an old fart named Curley who is wearing a Sunshine Warbird hat, a red one. Just tell him I said to give you the three-dollar tour, okay?"

Chip winked and walked out the door toward the open hangar. He stood for a moment just to enjoy the sights of the many collectable aircraft that were tightly parked in the hangar. There was an old Ryan PT-19 trainer next to a bi-winged Waco and a US Army J-2 Grasshopper. Just behind them, there was a Texan-6, a Grumman TBF Avenger, and a B-25 without wings, and a P-40 Flying Tiger. On the floor were pieces of a B-17 all over the place. Scores of old bi-planes were hanging from the rafters. Standing outside the hangar was a B-17G with all the engines covered in canvas and surrounded by work stands. Next to her was a Consolidated B-24 fuselage, and its wings off and stacked in crates. Chip continued to walk through the hangar when he caught sight of the red-cap old guy talking to a small circle of tourists. He was standing next to the remains of a B-26 without wings and telling his audience that these remains would someday be flying again. "That's what we do here, folks. We take these crushed and bent bodies and make them better than new."

Chip continued on past Curley and walked into the rear shop where all the serious business was at hand. He counted at least six or seven men working around the large room, some welding, some installing rivets or cutting metal parts out of new sheets of aluminum. He noticed signs he was trespassing but waited to get the word from one of the workers for him to return to the hangar. He also noticed a few of the workers as part of the teams who came over to work on his plane.

Reed began to walk outside the hangar and head down to Reilly's B-25 when a Dodge pickup pulled up and stopped. Bud stepped out of the cab and from the passenger side very attractive women stepped out.

"Chip, this is the beautiful machine that keeps me going. This is Dolly, my favorite wife."

"It's a real pleasure to meet you, Mrs. West. I have been looking forward to this day. Bud, as you must know, does a lot of bragging about you."

Dolly had one of those smiles that would light up a beachhead at midnight. She was beyond attractive with short dark hair and wide brown eyes, a gleaming smile, and an hourglass figure. Reed would soon learn that her most outstanding asset was her warm personality and love for Bud and his devotion to his trade, making dreams come true for lovers of warbirds. Chip knew immediately that he found a new friend in Dolly, and time would prove this fact many times over in the months to come.

"Well, let's go inside and talk about getting you up in the blue, Chip, and by the way, we will be finishing up on those exhaust valves and replacements on those rocker arms. They all came in yesterday along with all those O rings we need for the pushrod housings and your two new batteries. I figure we should have those two fans turning by next week. I'm sending over a tow bar today and tomorrow we will pull the Duck out and test those brakes for any leaks and problems. If we can get good compressions, good magneto readings with no major fuel leaks, or blow a jug and the controls are not hooked up backwards, we can get our transport permit and get your bird over here so we can start getting serious work done."

Chip was pleased to hear this news and followed Bud and Dolly into the office where they were greeted by Sara, who handed Bud a handful of pink phone memos.

"Give Chip a tour of the place, Dolly, while I make a few calls."

"Oh, I have already been through the hangar, Bud. Thanks anyway."

Bud asked Dolly to get him some coffee and show him their showroom. "Sell him some clothes, WWII stuff, things he will like to have, like monogrammed shirts and hats. Got to look good, Chip. You will be getting in to show business soon flying the Duck around the country, and you want to look good."

"Don't listen to him, Chip. He thinks he's starting up the Eighth Air Force again, loves logos and patches. Come with me, Chip. We do have some neat jumpsuits and flight gear that you may want to start thinking about." Reed followed Dolly to a large room filled with every kind of World War II flight suits and uniforms ever designed. There was a Norden bombsight, .50-caliber machine guns, bombs, handguns, badges of valor of all types, and beautiful models of hundreds of aircraft. What Chip found most interesting was the instruction books that where available for many kinds of warbirds, and he found the one he was looking for. It was the handbook for the Mitchell B-25 and even a tape of an old training film on how to fly the B-25. Dolly put them in a bag and simply said it was her offering to the Duck.

Chip and Bud spent a few hours in Bud's B-25, sitting in the cockpit, going over procedures and basic instructions. Unfortunately, they could not get the plane in the blue this day as one of the mags had to be pulled and a leaking hydraulic pump had to be replaced, grounding the bird. Bud told Chip he would have him up before week's end and felt that he would have no problem handling the plane. "These birds fly themselves," he would repeat to Chip. "But you got to help them down, preferably in a controlled crash."

Chip responded with a smile. Then Bud noticed Chip seemed to be somewhere else for the moment. Chip sat motionless, staring out the windscreen with both hands resting on the control wheel. Bud studied him for a second, thinking that Bud was in a trance. Finally, Chip turned to Bud and smiled.

"You know, Bud, I should have been on that raid with the Doolittle guys. I have had dreams of flying with them, doing that wild takeoff that morning from the USS Hornet. I even sat down one day and drew up my own bomb run that I would have made on that mission and that would have been a lot different than it was for those guys took that day. I would have flown southwest across Japan, hedge-hopping, shooting up anything military, and reaching the China Sea. I would have saved fuel and could have made it to Chung King."

"Chip, nothing wrong with dreaming. However, I remember they had to take that route south out of Japan so the Japs would not know where they were heading. I have had my share of those dreams, only mine was doing low strafing runs and ground support for the guys landing on Tarawa and Guadalcanal. I would love to have one of these modified 25 babies with a cannon and six .50sflying over the hill tops and putting delayed bombs right on the Nips in their caves. However, I don't think I was cut out to take a 25 off the deck of a pitching carrier."

Chip laughed. "Yeah, we were both cheated out of that war, weren't we?"

"Well, Chip, I don't know. It's kind of nice being around today and playing with the toys of that war. We are lucky to have this chance to rebuild and fly these old warbirds. That's the way I have always looked at it, Chip. Now what do you say we get out of this icebox and get in and get some coffee and talk about our first flight? And by the way, we did not get a permit to let you park your RV next to the hangar."

CHAPTER 10

October 30
Bergy's Hangar
Lakeland Linder Airport
1040 hours

The tow bar and the new batteries arrived early. Chip immediately had the batteries installed and hooked the tow bar to the nose wheel. Roy got his old Ford pickup and attached the tow bar as Chip crawled up into the flight deck and took his place in the left seat. He opened the sliding window and then reached down and took the manual hydraulic pump handle in his hand and began to pump. It took a few minutes; however, he checked the hydraulic gauge, and he had the pressure he needed for the brakes. He checked the landing gear's handle position to make sure it was in the down position. Then he gently pushed on the top end on the rudder pedals to check the brakes. Satisfied that he was ready, he put his head out the window and shouted down to Roy. "Pressure up, brakes set, and gear locked down."

Roy waved and shouted back, "Chip, when I hit the horn once, that means release the brakes. When I hit the horn twice, start applying pressure on the brakes, but do it slowly. Don't want to jerk your bomber off."

Roy started the pickup and ordered the chocks to be removed from the main landing gears. He then signaled Chip to release the brakes with one blow of the horn, and he responded. They agreed that once they got the Duck out on the ramp, they would take it slow and test the brakes. Roy put his pick-up in first gear and let the clutch out slowly. The truck stalled the first time, but on the second try the Duck began to roll out into the

59

bright sunlight. Once she was clear of the hangar, Roy slowed down and stopped. The Duck came to rest and Roy ordered the chocks put back in place, then stepped out of the pick-up and walked back to talk to Chip hanging out the window.

"Okay, we'll start testing the main brakes, Chip. Remember when I blow the horn twice, start applying pressure on the pedals. Don't push hard. Take it easy. We want to make sure that all the brakes are working smooth."

For the next hour, Roy and Chip tested the Duck's brakes on the ramp. They were both surprised and pleased that the brakes were working perfect with no serious leaks or cylinder failures. However, they did agree that the Duck was in desperate need for painting. There were patches of bare metal showing all over the plane and patches of green drab paint here and there plus the areas that received new skin. They felt embarrassed for the Duck but proud to see her out in the sun for the first time in many months.

"The Duck has more patches than a parquet floor in Bud's office," Roy remarked and sent Chip into hysterics.

Later that day four of Bud's men showed up and began working on repairs to both engines, replacing gaskets, fuel pumps, rocker arms, and push rods, and completing the new pre-oiling system. Bud was hoping that he could get over and try to start the engines before sundown, but he could not make it. The Duck was pushed back into the hangar to have the cowling installed along with attaching the connecting rods for the cowl flaps for the next day run-ups.

November 1
0830 hours

Bud drove to Lakeland early and woke up Chip. They went to breakfast and were back at the hangar by 0930. The Duck had already been pulled from the hangar and was sitting in the sun, chocked up and ready for engine run-ups. Bergy had allocated a large hundred-pound fire extinguisher and had it sitting outside the number-one engine. The weather was cool, but the sky was cloudless as Bud and Chip walked out to the Duck from the hangar.

"She's got a hundred gallons in each of her wing tanks. Oil is topped off, and hydraulic fluid in the green," Bergy reported, standing next to the open crew hatch after he and Tom Rossi pulled the props on both engines through.

"After you, Chip, but I want you in the right seat for this one," Bud said. Chip nodded, unzipped his windbreaker, and began to climb up the ladder to the flight deck followed by Bud. Roy walked out about twenty yards in front where he could see both pilots clearly, and then he yelled for Tom Rossi to stand by the fire bottle next to number-one engine.

Bud and Chip took their seats and began their preflight checklist.

"Battery switches on," Bud called out, and Chip reached over and flipped the two switches.

"Battery power is up," Chip replied.

Bud reached up and checked the lock on the escape hatch above them. Then he reached down and put his hand on the landing gear switches to make sure they were in the down position. He took hold of the hydraulic pump handle and began to pump.

"Keep an eye on that hydraulic gage in front of you, Chip. When it's in the green, set the brakes."

"Rodger that."

"Okay, let's see if we can get these old windmills to turn."

Bud proceeded to set the throttles, prop, and mixture controls, and then he switched the fuel boost pump on to low boost and checked for pressure on the gauge. He looked out the window and called out to Roy.

"Clear?"

Roy responded, "Clear number one"

"Number one switched on," Bud yelled out his window to Roy.

Bud switched the magneto switch from off to bot. Then he placed his finger on the energize/engage switch and pushed it up. He watched the prop begin to turn as the starter whined. After ten blades went through, he moved the fuel boost pump switch to high. With his third finger, he tickled the primer switch, feeding fuel into the cylinders. Once the engine caught and began to come alive, he would hold the primer down until he set the throttle so the engine performed and sounded to his liking.

Chip watched as Bud moved his hands and fingers like a computerized robot, never taking his eyes off the spinning prop outside his window until all fourteen cylinders of the Wright Cyclone settled in harmony. Once there, Bud adjusted the engine to idle at 800 rpms.

"Okay, now we make sure everything inside our fan is working properly," Bud yelled out, pointing to the engine instruments. "Chip, you got to watch all your pressures, oil, fuel, hydraulic, and vacuum." Bud reached over and tuned off the fuel boost pump.

Chip tapped on the cylinder head temp gauge as it was still showing no signs of life.

"Not to worry, Chip. It will come up in a few. How about reaching down and opening up those cowl flaps? We missed that on preflight. Mybad."

"Rodger that," Bud responded.

The number-two engine did not respond as fast as number one. Bud was giving Chip the chance to start the engine himself. Chip was all thumbs trying to energize the starter, count blades, and hit the booster bump, ignition switch, and prime toggle. It took a few tries, but soon he was able to master the procedure. With both engines running smooth, Bud explained to Chip they would just taxi out along the ramp and turn the Duck into the wind and do some run-ups. Bud signaled Roy to have the chocks removed. Slowly, Bud advanced the engines while he set his feet lightly on the rudder pedals to test pressure on the brakes. As soon as he was clear, he applied the left brake and advanced number-two engine's power to begin his left turn. The Duck responded, and a pleased Bud continued to taxi to the end of the ramp where he maneuvered the Duck into the wind and began a series of run-up checks. The number-one engine seemed to be nearly perfect. At thirty inches of manifold pressure, all systems, including prop checks and mixture checks, were in limits and showed only a fifty-rpm drop on the magneto tests. The number two-engine was not giving Bud what he wanted. The prop tests were perfect, and the mag checks were well beyond the hundred-rpm drop limits. He ran the engine through its paces a number of times, but nothing improved. He told Chip it was nothing serious and could be corrected in short time, but he wanted to do another compression check and maybe change all the plugs before they ran her up again.

After securing the Duck, Bud went over the engine problems with his engine men, while Roy and Chip began to clean up the oil steaks on the nacelles and flaps. Two of Bud's engine men immediately began pulling off cowling on both engines, checking them out for fuel and oil leaks. Bud came over to Chip and told him the Duck should be ready to leave for Kissimmee the next day. All he had to do was to call and register with the FAA. Bud was qualified as an inspector for the FAA, so he could approve the flight.

"Hell, if we have to, we'll take her over on the one engine."

Chip looked at Bud with concern.

Seeing Chip's reaction, Bud smiled and added, "Just kidding. We'll get them both running, Chip. See you in the morning."

"Hey, Bud, I got some info on the numbers and where the Duck was built."

Bud reached out and patted Chip on the shoulder. "It was built at North American Inglewood plant, and according to her numbers, she was the next plane off the line after Doolittle's ship. Doolittle flew 02344 on the raid, and the Duck has 02345. Quite a coincidence."

Bud smiled. "I knew that." He turned and walked off toward his pickup, leaving Chip speechless.

CHAPTER 11

Lakeland Linder Airport
November 2
0735 hours

Chip's first disappointment of the day came when he learned that he would not be flying in the right seat this morning on the Duck's first flight. Bud had brought one of his full-time pilots with him, a man named Sam Jones, a young pilot Bud and good friend he trained himself. Bud explained to Chip his reasons, and he understood and settled for the jump seat behind the crew.

Preflight was swift, and in a few minutes Bud, Sam, and Chip were in the cockpit, where the preparations for preflight were completed. Both engines fired up without any trouble. Rossi and Bergy took constant visuals beneath the wings and nacelles for any major oil or fuel leaks. Bergy had put two hundred gallons in each of the wing tanks at Bud's request. As soon as Bud had the engines warmed up, he signaled Bergy, and the chocks were pulled. Sam got ground control on the radio and got cleared to taxi to runway 5. Bud stood up behind the pilots during taxi to study the instruments and the way Bud and Sam were working together. As the Duck moved down the taxiway, Bud did some checks of his own on the props and mixtures. When they reached the runway, he turned the Duck's nose into the wind and began the run-up checks. The number-two engine started acting up on the prop control. The rpm drop was not satisfactory, but after two more run-ups, the problem cleared up. It was decided nothing was serious enough to keep from flying the short forty-three miles. They asked the tower for takeoff clearance. The tower responded and gave Sam departure frequencies and Orlando's radar frequency to get the code for their transponder.

After the nose wheel was centered, Bud advanced the throttles to their maximum travel. The two Wrights responded as did all the instruments. With everything in the green, he released the brakes, and the Duck began its takeoff roll down the five-thousand-foot runway. Bud was still standing but was advised by a hand signal from Sam to get seated. The Duck shook and vibrated as the props dug in and the takeoff roll began. Chip thought his plane was going to vibrate apart at one point. Finally, he saw Bud pull his arms back, and the nose to the Duck was free from earth. The main gears soon followed. The Ducks vibrations and sounds began to change as it became airborne. Sam asked Bud if he wanted to keep the gear down for the short hop, but he said no. As the gear and flaps were retreated, the Duck began its slow climb to 3,500 feet after cleared by Orlando control. They would fly direct to Kissimmee. When they reached their altitude, Bud began doing more checks on the engines and settings. Sam stayed on the radios and advised Bud of a few course changes. The flight would only take about thirty minutes from takeoff to touchdown, but Bud wanted to do a few touch-and-goes as soon as they cleared for Kissimmee.

Chip was fascinated by the short flight and happy to see Bud smiling at the Duck's response to controls and basic handling. More trial flights were soon to come. Right now the plan was to get the Duck down safe in one piece. When they reached Kissimmee, they contacted Unicom and got clearance to land on runway 6. Again, Chip refused to sit. He stood during the entire landing so he could watch the checkouts and airspeeds and get the feel of the Duck with full flaps, gear down and flying ten knots above the stall rate.

CHAPTER 12

November 5
1400 hours

Roy Bergy drove over to Kissimmee and picked up Bud, and by early afternoon they were back in Bergy's office in Lakeland. Chip had called a brief meeting to see what his friend Roy, Tom Rossi, and Lavoris were planning on doing with their lives. Bud West offered Bergy and Rossi jobs and even offered to take over the business. Bergy elected to stay with his company as did Rossi. Lavoris said she could care less what happened. She was going on a diet and was going to find a new Jewish boyfriend and to move to Palm Beach.

Chip Reed opened his briefcase and took out his checkbook. He asked Lavoris if she had totaled his final bill, and she replied, "My adding machine would not run that high." She finally laughed and presented Chip the large stack of invoices and an itemized bill. Bergy told Reed he was in no rush for payment, but Chip insisted on settling up. He wrote a check and presented it to Roy.

"Jesus, Chip, this is ten thousand more than we just billed you, and I can't take this," Bergy said as he stood up.

"Sit down. If he wants to give us a bonus, leave him alone," Lavoris added, laughing.

"Hey, you guys found my plane and made my dream come true. I will always owe you. So Roy, are you going to try to finish up some of these relics out here?" Chip asked.

"Yeah, there are a few bucks out there yet. We won't starve, but I would like to come over and help out where I can on the Duck if Bud won't mind," Roy said.

"Not to worry, Roy, and I owe you some flying time too. Now I have to get hold of my friend in Delaware. It seems that I may have to get him involved after all as a partner if I'm going to put the Duck in real shape and do the air shows this spring." He closed his briefcase and started to stand up.

"Sit down. What do you mean you are going to have some outsider put money in your plan? Are you crazy?" Lavoris said in a serious voice.

"I have no choice. My finances are not that good, and I may have to sell out my partnership in my real estate company. I figure to finish this project and get the spare parts together, that will just about put me on the line. I need a sponsor for the fuel and upkeep for the first year at least."

Lavoris reached down and brought up a large carrying bag that was in the shape of a colorful fish. She reached in and pulled out a big red wallet and opened it to her checkbook.

"What's it going to take to be a partner flyboy?" she asked.

Chip looked at Roy and then back to Lavoris. "Is she serious?" Chip said, laughing.

"Of course I'm serious. What's it going to take? I have close to 450,000 in this account that says I can be a serious partner. Now who do I make the check out to? I can either buy your big-ass out and own the Duck … or help you with your dream. What is it, Chip? I am in a buying mood."

Tom Rossi went into hysterics. "You should see the looks on your faces, gentlemen. Don't you see this lady is dead serious? And if you don't do something, I am going to propose to her myself."

"You're already married. Besides, you're not Jewish."

"Lavoris, I can't believe this. You are willing to buy into this company and be a partner in the Duck? I might add it will be a minor partner, that is."

"You bet," she said in her gravel voice. "Roy, you don't need me to be your boss. You can just keep paying me minimum wage and treating me like shit, okay?"

"You bet, sweetheart, but I will do it with respect, I promise."

"Well, Lavoris, you have a deal. We will have to wait until I set up a legal corporation on the Duck before I can take you in as an investor or partner. Will you give me some time?"

"Honey, I would give you my Victoria Secret underwear right off my body if you asked."

"Oh, spare us that … if they look anything like your outerwear," Roy responded, laughing.

Later that day Chip drove his RV, and Roy followed him in the Buick back to Kissimmee Airport. Bud West found a place for Reed to park on the airport grounds near his hangar, which Chip preferred rather than renting or buying a condo. He drove Bergy back to Lakeland, where they joined Lavoris and Rossi at a local restaurant to celebrate and have a kind of farewell dinner for the Duck's departure. Lavoris drew the short straw and had to buy dinner.

CHAPTER 13

Bud West's Warbird Museum
Kissimmee Airport
0945 hours

Chip sat on the old leather sofa in the museum's office. He was going through his logbook and noting the hours that he had logged with Bud in his B-25, which was called *Killer Bee*. So far, he had nearly twenty-five hours in the right seat, and Bud was letting him do most of the landings and takeoffs. They had flown to Dallas and to Charleston and were making plans to fly up to New Jersey to meet a new prospect for buying the Killer Bee.

"Hey, do you have any time in that book for any fun?"

Chip looked up, and standing before him was Linda Webber in a light blue one-piece jumpsuit, red sneakers, and a white scarf around her neck. Chip was speechless for the moment.

"Linda, where did you come from?" he asked nervously.

"Vermont, originally," she answered sharply with a big smile.

Chip began to stand up, forgetting that bills, brochures, and his logbook were still resting on his lap, which then tumbled to the floor. He stooped down only to meet face-to-face with Linda as she crouched to help him. For a brief second, they just looked into each other's eyes.

"You look terrific, lady," Chip said.

"Well, I hope so. I spent three hours yesterday getting made up for this trip."

They both stood up, holding onto his papers.

"I could use a hug and a kiss," Linda said as she let all the papers fall to the floor. Chip followed suit and put his arms gently around her, pulling her close to him. They kissed, moved apart, and studied each other for a second.

"I can't believe you're here. What brings you here … besides coming to see me of course?"

"I have a PA-28 Piper out on the ramp I am taking down to Miami. I sold it to a gentleman from Bogotá, Columbia."

"You sold it to a gentleman from Bogotá, Columbia? You're not going, are you?" Chip asked.

"No, my contract says Miami. How he gets it to Columbia is his problem," Linda replied.

"How much time do you have?" Chip asked.

"How much time do you need?" Linda said in a whisper.

"I have to fly with Bud West to New Jersey later, but let me check with Bud and see if I can go AWOL." He turned to leave and then turned back and looked at Linda standing in the mist of all his papers.

"Oh, sorry about that, let me introduce you to Sara over there behind the desk. She'll keep you company until I find Bud out in the hangar".

Chip introduced Linda to Sara and ran out the door to find Bud.

A few minutes later, Chip came through the door followed by Bud.

"Well, look here. Linda is back again," Bud said excitedly.

"Hello. I have been looking forward to this. Chip talks about you all the time. He says you're a high-time pilot. Do you have any dual time?" Bud asked.

"Oh, a few. About five hundred in Lears, Gulfstreams, few in Gooney Birds, and a few in DC-4s. The rest in single-engine Wacos and Pipers."

Mouth open, Bud was speechless as he just stared at Linda while she deliberately used her blinking eyes to flirt with him.

"Wow. I don't suppose you would want to fly up to Newark with me this afternoon?" Bud asked, smiling.

"What about Chip? Can he come too?" She flirted back.

"Ah, he needs to study today. Tomorrow he has a flight test," Bud replied, laughing.

"You're both nuts if you think you're leaving me on the ground. By the way, are you serious? I mean, about her joining us to Newark?" Chip asked.

"Yup, need to get going PDQ. How about it, Linda? We go up in four hours, spend the night in historic Morristown, and come back tomorrow morning. We'll be back here to have lunch with my first lady, Dolly."

"Well, I think I could do—"

"Great, get your stuff together. I'll let you fly right seat once we get over the beach. We'll fly the coast all the way to Virginia Beach and then to Philly and Newark. I just checked, and the weather is clear." Bud clapped his hands, spun on his heels, and began to shout orders to Sara to get the fuel truck out to Killer Bee.

"Killer Bee? What the hell is that?" Linda asked.

Bud commented, "Wait until you see the new nose art on this new 25. I just got jealous, I guess. Bud has a dopey Duck being painted on his, so I decided on a big bumblebee, and the name is Killer Bee." Bud laughed, reached out, slapped Chip on the shoulder, and then departed the office.

"Are you sure about this, honey?" Chip asked in a serious tone.

"Honey, wow, I'd better not leave your side now. You're starting to talk romantic."

One hour later the trio was at six thousand feet, flying right over the beaches of St. Augustine. Chip was talking to Jacksonville Central, getting new information on radar vectoring and altitude approvals to Newark.

Bud was not shocked to see Chip unfasten his harness and climb out of his seat. He took off his headset and handed it to Linda as she proceeded to bring her long legs over the console and settle down in the right seat.

The bomber was at eight thousand and flying on autopilot. Before Bud could speak, Chip reached over and took the plane off autopilot and looked over at Linda.

"She's all yours, gal."

Linda put her hands on the control wheel and rested her feet on the rudder pedals. She looked over at Bud, who was checking instruments. He smiled at her and nodded his head, but he kept his hands and feet on the controls very lightly. He knew what she wanted to do.

"Do it, Linda. It's all yours," Bud commanded.

Linda gently rolled the Mitchell to the right and rolled back on course and then rolled again this time to the left with more aggression on the bank. She learned what she wanted to know. Now she settled back and started flying the compass.

"Just like a pussycat, a big, fat, noisy pussycat," she said over the intercom.

Bud and Chip both responded with a hearty laugh.

Newark International Airport
Newark, New Jersey
1735 hours

The flight to Newark was perfect. The weather was cool and clear along the entire route. At the Newark FBO, a limo was waiting for them to take them straight to Morristown in the Watchung Mountains. When they arrived at the palatial home of Harry and Edna O'Conner, they were taken into a den where Harry and Edna entertained them. Later they were taken out to dinner and returned to spend the night. Bud completed his contract business and agreement with Harry O'Conner, who was a retired New York Lawyer with a desire to own a B-25 like the one his dad flew in WWII. He was now was the proud owner of the B-25 called Killer Bee.

After breakfast the O'Conners took Bud, Chip, and Linda back to the FBO at Newark, where Harry had a chance to go over his new purchase, Killer Bee. Edna and Harry took plenty of pictures with Bud and Harry under the newly painted artwork.

At 1000 hours, Killer Bee was airborne and heading south through cool, clear skies. Bud West requested a flight plan that would take them along the eastern coastline back to Florida, and it was granted.

"Gee, Bud, that seemed like an easy sale. Now what happens to Killer Bee?" Linda asked.

"Well, Linda, this was one of those special deals. Harry and Edna have no desire to keep the plane in New Jersey. They want me to take care of it and take it to air shows where they will come and join me and fly with me when they can."

"Wow. I only wish I could find a client like that. How about it, Chip Reed? Would you let me babysit your new Duck when it's all done?" Linda said, laughing.

"Who knows? You may have to some day when you feel we can live as one."

"Whoa there, pale face. Did I just hear a proposal?" Linda said over the intercom.

"One never knows, do they?" Chip responded, reaching over and grasping Linda's hand.

Bud West's Warbird Museum
Kissimmee
November 10
1510 hours

Linda stood close to Chip next to her Piper SA 28 Piper. A chilling wind blew across the ramp while dark gray clouds began to appear and move slowly down from the north. Chip reached over to Linda and pulled the collar of her light windbreaker up around her neck and then moved his hands to caress her tanned cheeks. Her eyes were nearly closed, and Chip could see the first signs of sorrow in them as tears began to form.

"Hey, what's this? A big girl like you with tears in your eyes?"

"Sorry about that," she replied as she attempted to wipe them with her hand, but Reed stopped her and pressed his lips gently on each eyelid.

"You'd better get up there, lady. This front is moving fast, and I don't want to be looking for you in the everglades later. You have close to an hour to get to Miami, so up you go." He kissed her hard and tightened his arms around her slim body.

"You almost slipped last night, Chip. You almost told me you really liked me. What made you stop? I was looking forward to a more romantic evening last night, but you were the gentleman and apt to sleep alone in another bedroom. Then you gave a comment on the way home. I really felt like you seriously cared for me?"

"Linda, I really do care for you, and yes, I almost said the word. But well, I'm still scared. So you have to be patient with me. Can you do that?"

"I guess I will have to, Chip. Meanwhile, I can and will say how I feel. I am falling in love with you." She pulled away from Reed's arms, turned, and stepped up on the wing. She opened the cabin door of the plane and quickly stepped in and shut the door, not leaving Reed any time to talk to her or kiss her good-bye. He stood gazing at her through the cabin window.

Then he walked around the wing and stood watching her go through the rest of her preflight ritual. As soon as the engine was running, she looked over at Reed and smiled. Then she released the brakes and began to taxi through the parked planes toward the active runway. Suddenly, the wind picked up and the gray clouds began to block out the afternoon sun. Reed felt a chill go through him as he watched the Piper disappear down the taxiway. His first thoughts were to get to the office and get on the Unicom frequency and tell Linda he did love her, but as he turned around, he ran into Bud West, who had been standing behind him the whole time.

"Don't let that angel get away from you, Chip," Bud said in a commanding voice. "I almost lost Dolly by playing it too cool."

CHAPTER 14

Bud's West's Warbird Museum
Kissimmee
1830 hours

For the next two hours, Chip found himself in a cloud and could not concentrate on paying his bills or going over to the hangar to check on the electricians installing the Duck's new radios. He sat in his motor home and waited for the phone to ring. He had already checked twice with Miami flight services to check on weather conditions. There were no serious problems reported, but the front was just now arriving. Chip felt stupid about not asking Linda what FBO she was going to use at the Miami airport. He looked through the cool drizzle distorting the big window over the dinette table where he sat with a scotch in one hand the other on the phone. Suddenly, it rang, and his hand jumped off the receiver as if it was electrified. He fumbled the phone.

"Hello?" he said nervously.

"Hi, can you pick me up at Orlando later? That is, if you want company tonight?" Linda asked.

"Are you okay?" Chip asked.

"Yes, why do you ask?"

"Don't mind me. I was just nervous about your flight."

"I'm on flight 1097 American Eagle, arriving at 2135 hours."

"I'll be there," Reed answered. "Would you like to have a home-cooked meal when you arrive?"

"I'm easy, but you already know that, don't you?" The phone went dead.

For the next four days, Linda remained with Chip and flew on two training missions with Bud and Chip. Most of the training was on emergency procedures, engine shutdowns, flying on one engine, and landing on one engine. They went over emergency procedures in case of hydraulic loss. Linda managed to log almost nine hours flying the B-25.

One trip was an overnight on Grand Bahamas Island with Bud and Dolly. They spent the night at the Grand Bahamas Princess Hotel in Freeport, where they played in the casino and danced all night. It was on this trip that Reed admitted to Linda that he was in love with her and wanted to continue a relationship. She agreed and told him that she would even consider moving her business to Kissimmee if she could get out of her present contact. Chip agreed it would be great, but deep down inside he had mixed emotions. He did not want to make any commitments yet. He had a difficult time telling Linda he was not ready for a commitment and felt he still needed time. She agreed and explained she would stay in Birmingham until such time he asked her to move down.

November 15
Orlando International Airport
1230 hours

Linda walked away from the Delta ticket counter and headed toward Chip standing in a maze of tourists and smiling at her.

"What's with you and that silly grin?" Linda asked, laughing.

"I just can't get over just how classy you really are. Just look around you, honey. Look at these animals dressed in tank tops, men in T-shirts, shorts, and sneakers. You would think they were home in their family living rooms."

"Hush now. These people might hear you," Linda said, putting her finger on her lips.

"I don't give a damn, Linda. This nation has turned into a bunch of slobs." Chip's voice rose even higher. "Just look at all those damn Japs standing over there with their Mickey Mouse ears on their squinty-eyed little heads."

"Hey, all you Japs, why not go to Disney World in France? It's cheaper and closer, and they love the Japanese." His voice almost reached full pitch.

"Did you understand me, Nippons? They love your kind in France."

"Chip, there is a policeman heading this way. Come on, you fool. I don't want to spend the night in a local Mickey Mouse jailhouse." Linda grabbed Chip by the arm and towed him into the large crowd, hoping to get lost in them. Chip continued to mumble about the lousy Japs.

They reached the departure gate where it was wall-to-wall people waiting to board the Delta 1011. Reed gently pushed Linda against a large pillar and put his arms lightly around her.

"Going to miss you, babe. Sure you can't get down for Thanksgiving?"

"Sorry, Chip. That's family time, and I promised Mom and Dad I would be with them along with my sister's family. Why don't you fly up to Cleveland and join us?"

"I, too, promised Dolly and Bud that I would cook the turkey ... or turkeys as it may be. They invited almost all their staff for Thanksgiving dinner. Besides, we may be taking the Duck up that weekend for a flight test." Chip released his arms and reached inside his sports coat. He came out with a small blue felt case and opened it. It was a single pearl on a gold band. He took it from the case and slipped it on the middle finger of Linda's left hand.

"It's beautiful, Chip, but you missed the finger," she said, staring at the ring.

"The next one goes on the right finger. This one is just to remind you who your steady man is. I looked for my old school ring, but I couldn't find it, so this will have to do for now."

Linda put her arms around Chip's broad neck and whispered, "I love you, Charles the Third." Chip stared into her eyes and smiled and kissed her lips.

The terminal loudspeaker broke their embrace.

"Ladies and gentleman, we are about to start boarding flight 678 to Atlanta, continuing on to Dallas. Please have your boarding passes ready."

"Well, this is it, love. You'd better go now. Remember you have been parked in a fire zone now for at least thirty minutes and will be lucky to have a car when you go out," Linda said, laughing.

Chip took her in his arms again and pressed his lips hard on hers. "I love you, lady. Have a safe flight, and call me when you get home tonight?"

"You know I will. I love you too. Now get going." Linda's voice began to fade.

Chip released her, smiled, and walked away.

When he reached the terminal entrance, he was not surprised. His car was gone. After inquiring and swearing at one of the airport security officers standing nearby, he learned his car was on its way to the Orlando Police impound lot.

"Next time, buddy, I'll see that it goes to the salvage yard," the security officer yelled back.

Chip quickly responded by shooting the officer the bird as he stepped into a waiting yellow cab.

CHAPTER 15

Bud West's Warbird Museum
December 4
0930 hours

Thanksgiving came and went fast. Now all the attention and spirit of the season were on Christmas. Chip talked to Linda almost every other day. She even called the Bud and Dolly West on Thanksgiving Day and passed on her best wishes and told Chip there was a possibility that she would be doing a charter in the Bahamas during Christmas week. Chip brought her up to speed on the progress or lack thereof on the Duck. He also told her how much he was missing her and would plan for the Christmas week.

Plans to get the Duck into the air were delayed because of new problems with fuel leaks and booster pumps. Bud decided it was good time to go over the spring air show circuit with Chip and choose what shows he may want to attend, including the annual fly-in at Oshkosh, Fun and Sun in Lakeland, and Valiant Air Command Show in Titusville, Florida, for starters.

"Chip, there is a call for you on line two. It's your partner, Mel Wolf, in Lauderdale," Sara called out.

Chip picked up the phone in Bud's office. "Hi, Mel, what's up? Are you serious? I forgot all about that damn property. Tell me, buddy. Is It the building in Perrine near Homestead? Holly mother of mercy, I clean forgot about it. What's the deal? Holy shit, Mel. You bet. How soon can you close? No, don't bicker. It sounds good, so take the bid and just close on that mother. And thanks. That's a free trip for you and the family to

Disney World. No, Mel, not Disney in France," Chip said, laughing as he hung up the phone.

Bud sat silently and watched as Chip was looking at a calendar in front of him.

"Bud, you know what a fool I can be sometimes, right? Well, about ten years ago, I picked up an old piece of property from a bank in Homestead. It was seven acres and had a fortress like building on the grounds, about sixty thousand square feet if I recall. It once was an overhaul depot for farm equipment, especially tractors. I totally forgot about it. Mel just called me to tell me he has a boat builder that wants to buy the property for a mill and a half. I paid less than $150,000 for the damn thing."

"Well, now we can go from watercolors on the Duck to some real enamel paint," Bud said, laughing.

"More importantly, I can call Lavoris now and tell her to put her bucks behind Roy Bergy and his operation. This is a gift from the gods and just in time. Now you can go buy those two new engines and get them down here and let's go flying, but first, we party tonight. I have to call Linda with the news. This is going to be one hell of a Christmas," Reed cried out as ran over to Bud and hugged him around the neck.

Reed could not reach Linda and left word to call him later. In the meantime, he put together a small dinner party for that evening at the best restaurant in Kissimmee, and he included Roy, Bud, Dolly, Lavoris, and Sara.

Later at dinner Chip admitted he did not have the greatest taste for gifts and gave all the ladies gold earrings and the men gold cross pens and pencil sets, complements from the Duck.

Bud West's Warbird Office
December 19

Chip came into the museum office and was surprised to see Sara sitting fresh as a daisy behind her reception desk.

"My God, what hit me last night? I feel like I got run over by a sixteen-wheeler," Chip said softly with both hands pressing on his temples.

"You should feel bad or even dead by now. Do you realize we finished nine bottles of Kendall Jackson reds and whites and then switched to something called Sambucca? Do you remember dancing with the restaurant owner? By now he has you classified as a male model in pink sneakers if you know what I mean," Sara said, laughing. "Wait there. Better yet, sit down on the couch, and I will get you some black coffee."

Sara returned with a steaming mug of black coffee and a glazed donut. She handed Reed an envelope. "This came in yesterday, and I forgot to put it on Bud's desk. It's from Chino, California."

Reed studied the envelope and the return address. It was from Ellen Lawson, Ted Lawson's widow. He opened the envelope carefully and read the short note along with a memorial card in memory of Ted Lawson's funeral. He read both documents over and over, and then he returned the letter and card back to the envelope and rested his head on the sofa.

"Chip, are you okay?" Sara asked in concern.

"Yeah, I am just fine. I just got permission from Ellen Lawson, Ted Lawson's widow, that she would be honored to have her husband's nose art of the Ruptured Duck on the nose of my bomber."

"That's terrific, Chip. Now you can sleep nights. I knew you were worried about that. How long ago did you write to her?"

"Oh, a month ago, I guess. I had to find her first, and that led me to the Raiders' historian, Colonel C. V. Glines, in Dallas. He sent me Ellen's address along with those of the remaining Raiders. There are two Raiders living here in Florida, one over in Naples, a Colonel Jack Sims, and the Duck's copilot, Dean Davenport, in the Ft. Walton Beach area."

"Why don't you write back to Ms. Lawson and fly here out here for the formal christening of the Duck? Maybe you could get those other two Raiders here too."

"What a great idea, Sara," Chip said as he stood up and put his arms around her and kissed her on the cheek. "You're a prize. You know that, lady?"

"Of course," she said, smiling, and she kissed Chip back on his cheek. "Get out of here, Chip, and write those invitation letters."

CHAPTER 16

Reed's Motor Home
December 22
1450 hours

The phone only rang once when Reed picked it up. He knew it was Linda.

"Hi, flyboy, how are you feeling now that you're a millionaire?"

"That's a laugh because you don't own a B-25, lady."

"Well, not yet. But I might be interested in the Duck if you ever need a partner who can fly her better than you."

"Hey, dem's fighting words," Chip said, laughing and knowing Linda was holding back on what he felt would be bad news, and she was.

"Honey, I have some bad news. That charter I was to have to the Bahamas fell through, and the boss wants me to take a small rock group from Nashville to Reno tomorrow."

"I knew it was too good to be true, and I was half-expecting this call. Listen, I have an alternative idea. Get out of that charter any way you can, even if you have to quit. I want you to meet me in New York City tomorrow night. We will stay at the Continental Hotel located off Central Park South, a great old New York hotel. We will go to Macy's, walk up Fifth Avenue, dine at the famous Rainbow Room, and go ice-skating in Rockefeller Plaza."

"Are you serious? New York? Did you know they are fighting a blizzard right now?"

"Of course, that's what makes it so beautiful, honey. It's the city of lights and the spirit of the people with rosy noses and red cheeks snuggling before fireplaces, drinking fine French wines while a blizzard rages outside."

"You sound like a travel agent, Chip, and you sold me. I have to work on this. Let me call you later."

"You'd better be there because I plan to be there even without you."

There was complete silence on the line. Reed could hear Linda breathing deeply at first, and then words began to come out with concern.

"You would go there without me? Would you be looking for other company?" she said in a faint voice.

"No, I am not looking to share New York with anyone but you. Please work it out. I will talk to you later. I love you, Linda." He hung up before Linda could respond.

Rainbow Room
New York City
December 24
2039 hours

Chip Reed's reserved table at the famous Rainbow Room was located next to a huge window looking out over the city. He watched large snowflakes swirling in the winds as they descended to the streets more than forty floors down. A heavy snowfall paralyzed the city earlier, and now it was making its way out to sea. Chip was hypnotized by the colorful lights that blinked and glowed throughout the sparkling black jungle of buildings below.

"Hey, lover, you do know you could have easily told the pretty hostess I was your wife and I was just running late."

Chip almost knocked his chair over along with the bottle of champagne in a cooler and the two tall glasses as he tried to stand up. He managed to stabilize the table and chair and then stood in shock, staring at Linda in the semidarkness. Her dark black dress blended in with the dim background, but Chip easily located her glowing tan face and white flashing teeth with his excited lips. He took her in his arms and tightened them around her hourglass frame, pulling her so tight she dropped her small handbag.

"You look fantastic, Linda. When did you get in? I was really worried the weather would keep you from flying into the New York area ... if you were even coming at all. Did the hotel give you any problem? I told them you might be late because of the weather but to send up my room service and orders on time."

"Chip, please slow down. I'm here now, darling. That is all that matters."

They sat and discussed the problems she had leaving Atlanta. Chip explained he had problems getting reservations at the Continental because of the weather and people not checking out. However, he did manage to get their special table for tonight with a little persuasion for the manager.

"We lucked out tonight. The Glenn Miller Band is here, starring my favorite female vocalist, Sara Vaughn. Tomorrow night I have great seats for the famous Radio City Theater to see the Rockettes with their annual Christmas show. Tomorrow night, honey, we get to see West Side Story."

"Sounds wonderful, Chip. Did you leave any room for us?" Linda said, laughing.

"Honey, the fireplace and French wine is all set up in our room, looking over Central Park. We will head to the hotel and our suite right after dinner and the show, I promise."

A tall, thin man appeared in a tuxedo under a spotlight. "Ladies and gentleman, for your listening pleasure, the Glenn Miller Orchestra. The Glenn Miller Orchestra opened up with "Moonlight Serenade," and the entire room applauded. Chip wasted no time taking Linda's hand and leading her to the small dance floor. They danced to all their favorite Glenn Miller songs and then sat and enjoyed the classic song style of Sarah Vaughn.

It began to snow again just as Linda and Chip entered their suite. It was everything Chip said it would be—the large fireplace with burning logs, a cozy fur rug with huge stuffed pillows.

The colorful lights from the city crystallized the huge window facing Central Park, while two bottles of selected French wines were nested in a cooler. Chip managed to find some romantic music on a nearby radio to set the scene, which would last until daybreak.

LaGuardia Airport
Delta Ticket Counter
January 3
1030 hours

"Chip, I can't tell you how much I loved these few days with you and the wonders of this great city. It was a fairy tale for me, and I hope the same for you. Right now there is a glow in my heart I hope never burns out for us and our future."

"Linda, I don't know what more I can say to tell you how I feel about you. I feel things are really different for me. So why not begin our lives together right now? Please come with me to Florida and start our lives together. Don't you feel it's that time?"

"Chip, darling, I can't right now. You have to give me some time. I did not want to ruin our weekend here in New York, but I have something I have to tell you. I have been given a wonderful opportunity for myself with our new charter service starting in one month at Love Field in Dallas. Richard has decided to make me operations manager and VP of all sales and services. He just purchased six new Boeing 727s, and we will be flying scheduled flights starting in March from Texas to California, Arizona, Utah, Kansas, Washington, and much more. We have quite a fantastic board and plenty of pull in Washington to get our routes approved. There is so much more to talk about, so can we just leave things as they are for now? I promise I will be with you in Florida as soon as I can to work out our future together. I love you with all my heart. You know that. Just be patient with me at this time please." She kissed Chip lightly on the mouth as her eyes filled with tears. She broke her bond from his body and then turned and entered the boarding ramp behind the boarding passengers and never looked back.

CHAPTER 17

Bud West's Warbird Office
Kissimmee
December 27

"Hi, Sara, is Bud around?" he asked as he stood in the office doorway.

"Well, welcome back, Chip. How was your time with Linda and your trip to New York?" Sara asked, smiling.

"It was fine. Now where can I find Bud?"

"He is over with the new owner of Panchito, going over the upgrades. Are you all right, Chip? You look like hell. Do you think you may have caught a bug up in New York because your color is not good?"

Chip did not respond and headed out the door for the open hangar. As he walked, he could feel the January chill in the air, and he pulled his jacked tighter around his chest. As he approached the silver B-25J, he stopped and just glared at the plane as it stood stately in front of the hangar. The sun was shining off its brilliant aluminum skin, which had just been washed and polished. It looked like it did the day it rolled out of the North American factory in 1941. Every detail was in place from the side-mounted .50-caliber machine guns to the .30-caliber machine gun protruding out of the plexiglass nose. The famous Disney cartoon of a Mexican cowboy wearing his big hat and waving two six-guns had been professionally painted under the clear windows of the bombardier's compartment. Chip felt somewhat jealous of this beautiful plane. To him, it was a serious piece of art in shinning metal.

Bud West was standing at the forward crew ladder and noticed Chip studying the plane, and he called out to Chip, "Hey, lover boy, 'bout time you got your ass out of those clouds and got back to work. I will be with you in a second. The new owner is up on deck checking out the new electronics."

Larry Murphy stepped down from the plane and joined Bud and thanked him for the latest work he'd completed.

Chip joined the two men and began walking to the warbird office.

"Well, how did the New York romance work out, Chip?" Bud asked, laughing.

"Don't really know. The American Express bill hasn't arrived yet," Chip replied, smiling.

Bud marched Larry into the office to meet with Dolly to go over the latest statements and log entries. Bud signaled Chip to come into his private office.

Chip wasted no time explaining what took place in New York with Linda and reveal that she was off to take over a new adventure in Texas. Bud just sat with his feet up on the desk and absorbed Chip's new woes.

"Screw it," Bud yelled out as he rolled back his old chair and stood up like a preacher. "What the hell? She did not tell you to get lost, did she? No, she just said in her own words to wait a little bit. Well, that is the way I read it, Chipper, so let's stop drowning and get back to work. There is a lot to do, man. I have decided that we are going to an air show in early March, so forget the Doolittle thing for now, Chip. Titusville is what you need to be thinking about now, so let's get the Duck ready for Titusville. You need some stick time, and we have lots to get done." With that, Bud walked over to Chip, looked him straight in the eye, and said in a stern voice, "Did you hear me, grunt?"

CHAPTER 18

Bud's Warbird Office
Kissimmee

Bud called a meeting in his office to instruct Chip, Sam, and Bergy how he wanted to set up the training programs, and he instructed the crew to go out and board Killer Bee.

With the Duck laid up, Bud took Chip, Sam, and Bergy up almost every day for training on Killer Bee. Each flight was better than the last. There were very few problems with Chip's landings and takeoffs, and that pleased Bud to no end.

One day Bud did challenge Chip about his last physical. He told him he needed an update and soon, or there's no air show flying for him. Chip said he would take care of it right away and explained he had a good doctor friend in Lauderdale that was FAA-approved. He would go down and see him soon.

One week later Chip was heading down the Florida Turnpike and headed to see his partner in real estate, Mel Wolfe, who was also a MD. Chip called Mel to make an appointment made for him right away. He arrived about an hour earlier than expected and decided to check into a local Howard Johnson Motor Inn, which was close to Wolfe's office and a block away from his old watering hole, Chuck's Steak House on Seventeenth Street. When Chip arrived at the doctor's office the next morning, the reception took him immediately into Mel Wolf's office.

"Jesus, Chip, how long has it been, man?" Mel Wolf walked over to Chip and wrapped his arms around him. Mel commented, "Man, you look like shit. What have you been doing? Spending all those thousands I got for you? Or are you getting too much action from those local bimbos?"

Chip laughed and admitted he was tired and brought Mel up to speed on what he has been doing on getting his B-25 together in Kissimmee. He also told his friend about Linda and his hopes for a new life with her, but now he needed to get his certificate up to date so he could be legal and fly his plane at the coming air shows.

Mel Wolf wasted no time and took Chip into an examining room where he performed a barrage of tests. Then he scheduled him for lab work and x-rays. Chip spent the entire morning with the good doctor. Later that day they decided to have lunch together at Chuck's Steak House.

"Chip, it will be a few days before I get all the lab work back. How about you hanging out at my pad, or you can even stay on my new Bertram yacht. I just bought a 38 sport fisher. I'll even take off in the morning, and we could head out tomorrow to the stream and fish for dolphin. They are all over the place right now."

"Sorry about that, Mel, but I have to get my ass back to Kissimmee as soon as I can in the morning. We are getting ready for an air show in Titusville in early March, and I have lots of training to do. I need a few more hours and lots of touch-and-goes to satisfy my instructor.

Early the next morning Chip was soon back on the Turnpike and heading north. He was amazed by the heavy traffic, and most it was composed of the variety of Japanese automobiles that seemed to be dominating the highways now. Of course, this did not sit well with him. Every chance he got, he would challenge a Toyota, Nissan, or Mazda, deliberately cutting them off in the crossing lanes. It was like entertainment time for him.

Bud West's Warbird Museum office
Kissimmee
1230 hours

Reed walked into the office only to be met by Sara, who had an urgent message for him. At first, his heart skipped a beat, thinking it would be a call from Linda. He opened the message and saw it was a call from Dr. Wolf's office marked as urgent.

Chip went over to Sara's desk and called the number. "Hi, this is Chip Reed returning Dr. Wolf's call."

"Yes, Mr. Reed, Dr. Wolf wants you to contact Dr. Storey in Orlando as soon as you can. He is a good friend, and Dr. Wolf wants you to go over and get some more lab work."

"Ah, thank you. Did he say what it was all about?"

"No, but I believe it is just a blood test he neglected to do and did not want you to come all the way to Lauderdale again."

Reed hung up the phone and went out to the hangar to find Bud and advise him he was back and all was okay with the medical exam.

Later that night, Reed received a call from his old friend Wayne Stewart, who advised Chip he and his wife, Betty, were coming down in a few days. Betty wanted to take flying lessons down there rather than up in Delaware, and Wayne wanted to talk more about getting involved with Chip and his B-25.

CHAPTER 19

Reed's RV
Kissimmee Airport

was more like a room in a frat house. After checking in, they visited Chip at his RV.

"We signed up Betty across the way at some FBO that has a Cessna

Wayne and Betty had arrived at Kissimmee in a new King Air Wayne had bought at an FBO in Dover. They elected to rent a car and stay off the airport property and for good reason. They did not want to intrude on Chip's request to stay in his RV, which school, and she starts next Monday with ground school."

"That's wonderful, Betty. I understand from Sam Jones, JD, his wife, also works there and said it is a good school run by a friend of theirs."

"By the way, Wayne, Bud wants to do a cross country later today, maybe over to Sarasota or St. Petersburg, and you would be welcome to join us if you like. You may even get some stick time if Bud is okay with that."

"Wow, I get to fly in the Duck. What a treat that will be."

"No, we are going in Bud's Killer Bee. He is babysitting, or we also may use Panchito, the new B-25J. He is getting ready for delivery. Bud is training its new owner and me at the same time."

Later that day the four fliers met in front of Panchito. Bud began to hand out instructions on who would sit where and who would be at the controls. He told them where they were going and what to expect for weather.

"Okay, you have your assignments, so let's get on board," Bud ordered.

In fifteen minutes Panchito was climbing into the hazy blue sky with scattered clouds hanging out at 2,500 feet.

Bud was in the right seat with Larry in the left seat while Chip sat in the jump seat between them, watching all the instruments. Wayne settled in the nose for the best view. Bud got on the radio and contacted Orlando for radar following. Chip heard him tell the Orlando controller he wanted to get clearance directly into Sarasota. He received his headings, altitude, and code for the transponder, which he immediately responded to. It appeared they were going straight out on 270 degrees at 3,500 feet.

"Okay, Larry boy, it's all yours to Sarasota." Bud took his hands off the control wheel and relaxed. He looked over at Chip and told him he would be flying them back. Chip was thrilled he was going to find out what it would be like flying Panchito, which was a little more sophisticated in electronics than the Duck.

As Panchito flew past the southern tip of Tampa Bay, Bud could clearly see the islands that lay off Sarasota's mainland and Sarasota Airport to the southwest. His plan, which he had not told his companions about, was to land at Sarasota, visit an old friend who owned an FBO called Dolphin Aviation, borrow his car, and have lunch downtown at a famous hamburger restaurant called Patrick's. Then they would take off and head south to Naples and turn east across the state, following Alligator Alley to Miami Beach and then up the coast to Cape Kennedy and home to Kissimmee. This would be about a four- to five-hour flight.

As the crew got closer to Sarasota, Bud called Tampa center and canceled their radar following. He called Sarasota Tower and advised he was in the area and would be flying over the island of Anna Maria and Long Boat Key. They responded and approved his intention.

"Okay, Irishman, I will take the controls," Bud ordered.

Bud dropped the nose of Panchito and picked up speed without throttling back. He had his eye on a bridge that connected the islands of Long Boat and Anna Maria. He dropped to minimum altitude minus a little and headed right for the bridge. There were some boats running around the waterway in a bay just east of the drawbridge. Bud decided to buzz them, just clearing a few masts, waiting for the small bridge to open.

He climbed over the small bridge and continued to fly west over the Gulf of Mexico just feet above the waves, once again scaring the hell out of a couple of day sailors enjoying the gulf winds.

The cockpit was strangely quiet. The confused crewmembers were trying to figure out what Bud was up to.

Bud broke the silence and said, "I'm just waiting for some screaming coming from the Sarasota Tower, but so far, nothing, which means they are all asleep or there is very little traffic today," Bud said, laughing.

Bud called the tower and asked for a right-hand downwind approach to runway 34, and he was cleared. He flew close to the city of Sarasota to give everyone a good view of the sparkling buildings surrounded by the peaceful blue and green waters of the bay.

"This is my favorite city in Florida, gentlemen, and you're going to eat one of the finest hamburgers you ever tasted in about fifteen minutes."

Bud made the approach to runway 34 and called for flaps and main gear. Larry Murphy was pleased to do so and almost as pleased to finally land from the stunt flying Bud was putting his new plane through, but he enjoyed every minute of it.

Bud met taxied to the FBO called Dolphin Aviation. They Bud and crew were greeted by an old friend of Buds, Ron Cararra owner of Dolphin. Ron and Bud hugged and exchanged greetings. Ron walked around the B 25J, commenting that it was the finest Mitchell he had ever seen. Bud introduced his three companions and then asked to borrow Ron's Lincoln to go to lunch.

"Lincoln? That went with Mary Lou along with the house and the Donzi boat. You're going to have to settle for a Ford Explorer." Cararra said laughing.

"Wow, so you are in the market again, you old playboy?" Bud said, laughing.

"No, now I am married to my old receptionist, who did not lock her office door in time one day while testing her new desk when Mary Lou walked in."

Bud and the three crew headed downtown to have the famous hamburgers at Patrick's restaurant Bud bragged about. Two hours later they were back aboard Panchito heading south into the blue. This time with Chip was at the controls heading for Naples.

Chip and the crew did get a chance to find out how fast thunderstorms could form over the everglades and had to get IFR vectoring from Miami and Orlando centers. The next two hours was spent dodging lightning storms and hard rain. When they finally landed, Larry and Bud found plenty of water leaks around seals around cockpit windows and sealed them up.

CHAPTER 20

February 14
Bud West's Warbird Hangar
Kissimmee Airport

Bud just finished towing the Duck from the paint room in the hangar where it saw the sunlight for the first time in weeks. The detail man was there ready to mask off the stars on the fuselage and wings, and the artist was going over the area with Chip where he was painting the cartoon of Donald Duck and the crossed crutches. Chip wanted it to be authentic and be located exactly where Lawson's cartoon was located. Meanwhile, the electronics were being installed by a mechanic who was inside finishing up installing the new radio and intercom system.

Bud jumped off the small tug and told his young mechanic to disconnect the tow bar and chock the wheels.

"She looks beautiful, Chip, and will be the queen of the warbird lineup. I am concerned about the Killer Bee looking so drab sitting next to her. By the way, did you call Roy and tell him we need him to flay copilot with you? He will need some touch-ups too. It has been a while since he flew the B-25, so let's schedule him up for a few go-around's with you soon. We have three weeks left, and you and I have some serious practice to do for the show."

Bud and Chip spent hours at the RV going over the flight plan they needed to use for the show. Both planes would take part in a simulated bomb run near the active runway. Bud explained their explosives going off at intervals after each plane made its pass. The explosions were powerful but would go off well after the plane had gone a safe distance. Bud showed

Chip the entire blueprint of the flight course, the locations of the explosions, the staging area, etc. Chip was excited but admitted to Bud he was nervous.

"Not to worry, old man. Roy has done this with me for years. He will make sure you are on time and over the safe area, but tomorrow we fly over to Titusville and do a few practice patterns so you get used to it. If Roy is not available tomorrow, I will put Sam up with you, and I will go solo." Bud smiled, rolled up the plans, and said he would see him for dinner and the final send-off for Larry Murphy, who was leaving with Panchito for Delaware in the morning.

Reed's RV
February 15
0835 hours

Reed was woken by a banging on his RV door. He staggered up and walked to the door, stopping to look out the window. He noticed a black Buick sitting outside and what appeared to be Betty Stewart in the seat. When he reached and opened the door, Wayne was standing there, stone-faced.

"Chip, hate to disturb you, but Betty has to talk to you." Wayne called out to Betty, who exited the car and approached Chip and Wayne.

"Ah, I am going over to the office and see if Sara brought some donuts in this morning. I will check with you two later." Wayne spun on one foot and departed for the hangar office.

"May I come in, Chip? I need to talk to you."

"Of course, Betty, but you will have to excuse the place. We have been working on the plans for Titusville."

Chip stepped out of Betty's path and immediately began to clean up charts and papers that were scattered all over the small kitchen table and the sofa. He never stopped apologizing for the mess.

Betty sat down and opened her purse and took out a well-used envelope and a newspaper. She opened the newspaper, which had a photo and article in it. She laid it on the table and then opened the envelope and withdrew a two-page letter.

"Chip, I received this last night from my daughter in Wilmington. She forwarded it to me. It was mailed from Ft. Worth a week ago. It is a letter from Fran Williams, Linda's stepmother. She did not know where to find you, so she wrote to me."

Chip reached for the newspaper and saw it was some kind of local newspaper from a place called Dennison. The photo showed a tangled vehicle on its side in what appeared as a large ditch. At first, he could not figure out what the car was as it was upside down and covered with debris. Then he could see it was a white SUV with Texas plates. Beneath the photo was a short explanation.

Early Tuesday morning this vehicle was located six miles south of Dennison on Johnson Highway. A women's body had to be cut out by the fire department. She is listed in critical condition at a Ft. Worth Hospital. Her name was withheld at the time. No other vehicles seemed to be involved. There were reports of heavy fog and rain in the area that morning, which may have caused the accident.

Chip looked up at Betty and quietly said, "Is this Linda? Betty, is this Linda?"

"I'm afraid so, Chip. From what her mother said, she was returning late from some conference near Wichita Falls and evidently got on a wrong road in a storm and lost control of her car. According to the police report, she did not remember running off the road."

"I have to get out there. What hospital did you say she was in?"

"I didn't, Chip. And when I called her parents, they told me she doesn't want anyone to see her until she has all her surgery completed on her head and face. She got pretty cut up from the glass and the dashboard from what I learned. When she got to the hospital, it was touch and go for a while as she had massive internal bleeding plus broken ribs and a fractured leg. She was in a coma for two days because of her head injury, but now she is fine. They had to do some serious work on her forehead and face. That is all I know for now. I did call last night and got a hold of her brother. He wanted to make sure I told you that under no conditions should you try to come and see her. She wants to wait until she gets her scars taken care of. I will give you his number, but you have to promise not to try to reach Linda under any circumstances. You can send her flowers and notes, okay? She loves you, so do as she asks."

Betty picked up the letter and put it in her purse, but left the newspaper on the table. Chip thanked her and walked her out to the car. She left to pick up Wayne, and Chip went back in the RV, sat down, and studied the photo again. This time he could not help but notice the model and name of the manufacturer of the SUV on the rear door. It was a Honda.

"I am without a doubt plagued by those miserable yellow Japanese bastards. Now they almost took another love of my life, but this time I am not going to forget or forgive if anything happens to Linda." Chip threw the paper in the sink and went back to his bed. On his route he grabbed a bottle of VO from the bar and carried it to his bedroom.

CHAPTER 21

Bud West's office
February 15
0945 hours

"You look like shit, Chip. Where did you go last night?" Bud asked as he ran through a ton of papers on his desk. "Here are all the forms and instructions we need for Titusville, and you and I have to fill out these requests right now."

Chip threw the newspaper article on Bud's desk. He picked it up and studied it for a second and then remarked, "What the hell has this to do with Titusville?"

Chip became a bit bitter and responded, "Bud, that is Linda's car. She had a wreck in Texas a couple of weeks ago, and I just now found out."

Bud sat down and listened to Chip pour his heart out about Linda and the restrictions that were put on him to not contact her. Dolly walked in and was also included in the conversation about Linda and her accident.

"Oh, Chip, I feel so bad for you right now. But from what I learned just now, Linda is calling the shots, and I would do as she asked and wait until she is ready to see you. I can understand her reasons. She is concerned about her face, I am sure, and I pray they can make her whole again." Dolly began to cry and began to leave the office, but then she turned around and addressed Chip as if she was trying to change the subject.

"Chip, I am so pleased you have decided to take your plane to the Titusville show. It will be good for you, and it'll take your mind off things you can't control right now."

"Dolly is right, Chip. We need to really start to focus on getting ready for the show. You need some more practice with me for the formation flying and qualification certificate for the show inspectors. That reminds me. Where is your new medical card?"

"I'm waiting for it in the mail from Lauderdale," Chip answered quickly.

The rest of the day was spent going over all that was needed to take over to the show, and that included tables, chairs, brochures, cans of oil, toolboxes, spare spark plugs, and the fake fiberglass five-hundred-pound bombs that were used for the bombing runs. Late in the afternoon, Bud took Chip up again with Sam and ran through the practice runs they would be doing over the actual runways at Titusville. Chip walked into the office and was immediately met by Dolly, who congratulated him again on deciding to take his plane to the air show at Titusville.

"You are going to love this show, Chip. They are doing a complete air show starting with the bombing of Pearl Harbor and continuing on to the Korean conflict. We learned this morning that a friend of ours named Tom Rinda, who owns one of the most beautiful F-86 Saber jets in the country, is coming to duel with John Peterson's Mig 17. This will be the first time this act has been seen."

"Sounds great Dolly, I just hope I don't embarrass your old man. I never bombed anyone before," Chip said, laughing while Dolly joined in.

A sweet feminine voice suddenly filled the room along with a heavy scent of a expensive perfume.

"Hi, are you Dolly West?"

Chip and Dolly both turned around and faced a very well-dressed and attractive young woman standing in the office doorway. She was silhouetted against the backlight from strong sunshine outside, which outlined her torso though the pale yellow dress she wore. Chip had no choice but to notice her shapely legs and hourglass figure. He had a tough time raising his eyes to meet hers.

"I'm Dolly West. Can I help you?"

The woman removed the light yellow scarf that was wrapped around her short blonde hair and walked toward Dolly with her hand extended.

"Hello, I am Lee Waters. A close friend of my dad just purchased some kind of bomber airplane from your husband, Bud West, and told me I should stop by his hangar sometime and introduce myself to you."

"Oh, of course, you're the friend from Boca Grande. I remember the O'Conners talking about you."

"Yes, it is Boca during the winter season and then onto my retreat to Toms River in New Jersey for the summer."

"Excuse me, Ms. Waters. This is Chip Reed. He has a plane similar to the one the O'Conners just bought."

Chip reached out and shook the women's hand gently, never taking his eyes off hers. She had deep, haunting dark brown eyes, and her tanned skin, which was highlighted by the right shade of makeup, was flawless. With high cheekbones, her square face was framed by golden blonde hair. When she smiled, she barely opened her lips as two shallow dimples appeared deep in her cheeks. She was strikingly beautiful, and she knew it.

"Pleasure to meet you, Ms. Ah—"

She interrupted Chip, "Waters, Lee Waters. At least for the time being."

"Lee, do the O'Conners know you were coming by this week?" Dolly asked.

"Yes, they are coming down this weekend, and we hoped to get together for a little visit. I understand they are coming down for a couple of weeks and take part in some air show."

"That would be the Valiant Command Air Show in Titusville. We are in the process of getting their plane ready right now. Would you like to see it?" Dolly asked.

"Love to … if you don't mind."

"Not at all." Dolly turned to Chip and smiled.

"Chip, would you mind? You can show her the Killer Bee and the Duck at the same time." Dolly was wearing her famous Colgate smile, the one that said, "Gotcha."

Dolly reached out and shook Lee's hand and told her she was pleased to meet her and walked away, leaving Chip speechless with this wild creature called Lee.

"Ah, this way, Ms. Waters, and I would be careful in those spikes. There is a lot of stuff out here you won't want to walk in and stain those nice shoes," Chip mumbled as he opened the door.

Chip walked directly to the open hangar where Killer Bee stood, keeping his eyes forward and not on the lady in yellow.

"Well, this is it, the Killer Bee," Chip said as they approached the colorful painted bomber. He stopped directly in front of the plane and watched the motionless face of the woman beside him. She took off her sunglasses and scanned the plane from wingtip to wingtip.

"What goes on in that glassed-in thing?"

"That's where the bomb guy sits. You see that apparatus in there? That's the bomb-sighting machine the bomb guy looks into at the target. When the target is lined up in his sights, he drops the bombs, and at this point he is flying the plane."

"Oh, really? And what is the so-called pilot doing?"

"Oh, a number of things lady, he may be in the restroom or looking at his road map to find out how the hell to get home or calling his mother and asking her to send more cookies."

"Are you always a smart-ass, Mr. ah—"

"Reed, but you can call me Chip, and I do apologize for being one just now. I was not sure if you were putting me on, so I tested the waters, if you pardon my pun."

"I know nothing about airplanes, Mr. Reed, especially ones with big fans on the wings. I grew up in the jet age. My older brother, Phil, would know what you're talking about if he was alive. However, I am here and alive, and I want to see what my daddy's old friends are up to. That's all."

She smiled and put her sunglasses back on and began to walk toward the crew ladder suspended behind the nose wheel.

"Are you sure you want to climb up there, Ms. Waters? I mean, you have a very pretty dress on and ..." Reed did not finish his thoughtful statement.

She kicked off both high heels and began to climb up into the plane. All Reed could do was watch her soft, round, tanned calves turn into harden muscles as each leg moved up the ladder. When Chip entered the cockpit, she was already seated in the right seat and holding onto the control wheel. Chip made his way to the left seat and sat down, never taking his eyes off her.

"Ah, please don't push anything or flip any switches. There are crew working all over the plane, and we would not want to do anything dumb."

"Like what?" She asked

"Oh, like closing the bomb bay doors while someone was standing in the open bay. It would not make for a nice sight and would sure mess up his day."

One look from Waters was all it took. Reed felt the ice pick go right into his heart. He was having trouble with the lady and could not understand his own attitude. She meant no harm. She was just curious, but he thought she was out to pull his chain for some reason.

"You know, I really do apologize, Ms. Waters. I don't know what's wrong with me today. Just a little uptight, I guess. This is my first air show, and well, please accept my humble apologies for being such a jerk."

With that, she pushed herself up from the seat and pulled her tight skirt up to her thighs, and in one swift motion, she swung her leg over the console, alerting Chip that she even wore matching yellow panties. Once outside, she put her shoes on and began to walk toward the office. Chip followed behind like a wounded animal.

"That is my bomber over there, that green one. I named it the Ruptured Duck," Chip said, laughing, hoping to get some kind of positive response from the woman who suddenly increased her step.

"You know that name sounds fitting for something you might be affiliated with, Mr. Reed. Don't bother taking me to my car. I can find it on my own. It's the red thing with no wings on it called a Thunderbird. Try to have a nice day. I will most likely see you at the air show."

Her voice tapered off as she distanced herself. When she reached her car, she took the yellow scarf from her purse, placed it around her head, and never looked back.

Chip walked back to the museum office where Dolly was waiting for him.

"Jesus, that woman is one piece of work. Hard to believe that she is any kind of friend to such nice folks like the O'Conners," Reed remarked as he walked past Dolly.

"I thought she was extremely attractive, didn't you, Sara?" Dolly said, laughing.

"Hell, I thought she was some high-class call girl that he met once on State Street in Chicago one time," Sara remarked while not making eye contact with Chip but still laughing out loud.

Dolly suddenly commented, "He isn't right, Sharon. Something is wrong. I'm concerned about him. I don't know if it's Linda or maybe the pressure of going to the air show now that the time has arrived. Bud made a few observations lately on his flying techniques. Chip seems to be fumbling over things—not forgetting, just fumbling." She took her eyes from Sara and walked to the window and watched Reed walking across the ramp toward his plane. "I heard Bud say something to him last week about his physical and wondered if he got his results back. Bud is concerned about him not being legal at the controls. He doesn't eat well and appears to be getting thinner, don't you think, Sara?"

Sara did not respond, and she continued filling out the applications and information forms for the air show.

Pre-air show meeting
Bud West office
February 20

Chip just finished writing a long letter to Linda, bringing her up to speed on the upcoming air show and how excited and nervous he was. He had sent her flowers every day for the past week but had not heard any response and was getting depressed. He sealed the envelope and started out for the hangar office to have Sara mail the letter.

The cool February winds were not kind. The weather was mixed with partly cloudy skies broken at six thousand feet. The winds were from the northeast and gusting sometimes to twenty knots.

The two B-25s stood like huge praying mantises parked in line, ready for an attack plan. Two service crews were on the wing of the Duck, finishing fueling her wing tanks, while other crew members were stowing boxes of brochures, pennants, posters, tripods and folding chairs. It looked like a small circus in play as each plane was loaded with air show stuff.

Meanwhile in the hangar office, Bud, his copilot Sam, Chip, and Roy Bergy were bent over the aerial chart of the area, laying out their route and going over radio frequencies that would be used for the short flight to the Titusville Airport.

"Excuse me, gentlemen," Sara said as she appeared in the office.

"Chip, you have a young lady on the phone calling from a Dr. Storey's office."

Chip went to Sara's desk and picked up the phone. "This is Chip Reed. What can I do for you?"

"Sir, we have orders for you to come over to our universal lab here in Orlando and meet with Dr. Storey. He has to ask you some questions about your family and about history of any cancer in your family. He also needs to draw more blood samples."

"Bad timing, Miss … whatever your name is. I am in the middle of a national air show. I will call you next week." Chip hung up and then immediately called his friend Dr. Wolf.

"Mel, Chip here. What is going on with this Dr. Storey wanting more blood and asking about cancer in my family?"

"Chip, don't get your shorts wet. We saw something in your tests here, and we want to make sure you are okay. Storey is a cancer specialist and a good one who deals with cancer-related diseases, and we want to be sure you're not in trouble. Only more tests can make us certain. Please go get the lab work done, okay?"

"Mel, I need that certificate. Now you have to help me here, or I can't fly my bird in this show coming up. Please send me a certificate or letter right away. I will take care of Storey when the show is over. I am giving you over to Sara, and she will give you the mailing address. Don't let me down."

Chip handed the phone to Sara and told her to give the doctor the information and to not take no for an answer. He also told her not to mention the call to Bud under any conditions.

Bud placed a small ruler on the regional chart and said, "When we take off, we will climb to four thousand and head southeast over Lake Tohopekoligo for about ten miles on a course of 145 degrees. We will then head down here to Lake Cypress and turn northeast on a zero fifty-five heading. This will take us over Lake X, where they test Mercury motors for the boating industry. I will drop down to a hundred feet over the lake and shake up their boat-testing guys for the fun of it. I will come back up and take position on your port wing, Chip. We will continue on to Titusville, contact Patrick, approach on 118.4 for clearance, and they will switch us to Space Center Tower on 118.9 for landing instructions. Chip, when we get to five miles out, you take a slow roll out to starboard and drift back, giving me at least a mile out front. Roger that?"

"Bud, when we land, do we go to a special area?" Bergy asked.

"Just follow me. There will be a truck of some kind that will be meeting us and taking us to the flight line for the active show planes. Are there any other questions? Chip, are you okay with this?"

"Rodger, I have no problems. Bud, how many of your staff will be on board with me?"

"Probably four souls. Harry O'Conner and his friend want to ride with you, and I will send two more of our ground folks to ride in the rear. Say, what's with you and Harry's friend Lee? I heard she gave you the North Pole when she was here last week. Did you step on her spikes?" Bud said, laughing.

"Buddy boy, that is one woman who needs to be caged and housebroken. I don't look forward to having her on board. Roy, you see that she is put in the rear compartment when we board. This flight is only thirty minutes plus, but that would be like an eternity to me if she is up front with us where I could see her," Chip said in a serious tone.

"Whoa there, Chip. She can't be that bad. I saw her a few minutes ago in a one-piece flight suit, and she fills it out with no questionable spare parts. Tell you what, Chipper. I will trade you her for the toolboxes. How does that sit?" Bud said, laughing.

"Forget it, sir." Bergy replied. "I pick the baggage here as I am in charge of weight and balance, and we will keep the lightweight lady on this trip if you don't mind."

There was no more said. The foursome picked up their charts and notes and walked outside to their aircraft.

Reed was walking around the Duck, checking everything that had already been checked by the ground crew and Bergy. He just wanted to be sure it was ready for flight. His hands were beginning to perspire, and he could feel the dampness begin to collect between his shoulder blades. He zipped up the lightweight flight jacket and tried to ignore the beads of sweat that already gathering under the hairs on the back of his neck and temples.

"I hope you don't mind, Mr. Reed. I will be riding along with you on this short flight."

Lee Waters stood next to him in a light blue skin-tight flight suit. Over her right breast was a colorful patch of the Killer Bee logo. She had on a white baseball cap with a leaping billfish on it and the words Boca Grande, Florida, lettered over the fish. On her feet was a new pair of white boat shoes.

"Well, hello, Lee. I heard that you requested flying over with me, and I am not only surprised but honored," Chip said in a sarcastic tone.

"You are wrong, flyboy. I was asked to fly with you to get to know you better. It seems like the office staff felt you and I may have gotten off to a bad start and thought it good politics for us to enjoy each other's company."

"I have no problem with that, Miss Waters. However, you will have to fly over in the aft compartment as we have a full house up front.

"Bullshit. You have your copilot, Harry, and two other crew members on board, making five souls, and that leaves room for one more up front in the glass nose. That's where I will be sitting."

Reed smiled and pointed to the crew ladder extended behind the nose wheel. Walters took the signal and walked to the ladder. Once she was in the plane, she was directed by Chip to crawl forward and strap herself inside the green house ... or the "glass thing," as she called it.

With both engines idling and all engine instruments in the green, the Duck was ready for preflight run-up. Reed's feet pressed firmly on the rudder pedals, applying the brakes, and then he released the hand brake. He watched as Bud West taxied Killer Bee slowly down the ramp toward the taxi strip. He could hear Bud giving his intentions on departure to someone operating the Unicom radio service on the field. Reed followed Bud to the active runway and took position for the preflight run-up. With all systems go after the run-up, Chip took position again behind Killer Bee, which taxied out on the runway and began its takeoff roll. Bud taxied onto the runway and centered the nose wheel. He watched Killer Bee as it broke its bond with the earth and began to climb into the cloudy sky. Reed released the brakes and advanced the throttles. The Duck wasted no time gathering speed as her nose wheel lifted off the ground. The noisy rumble and vibrations soon ceased as the main gear left the runway and the Duck took flight.

"Gear up," Chip commanded Bergy as he pulled back the control wheel and felt the Duck begin to climb into the cool air. "Flaps up," was his next command. In a few short minutes, Reed and his crew were at their prescribed altitude of four thousand feet directly over Lake Tohopekoligno. Chip leveled the Duck and trimmed the flight controls as Bergy adjusted the props, mixtures, and throttle controls and switched off the fuel-boost pumps. Chip was pleased with the new engines and performance so far and advised Bud by radio that he was about a mile behind him, level and awaiting instructions. Bud reported back to stick to their plan and watch for the change in course coming up at Lake Cypress five miles ahead.

When *Killer Bee* reached Lake Cypress, it made a rolling bank to the left and picked up its new heading to take them straight to the Titusville Airport.

"Hey, Duck, stay at angels four, and contact Patrick. Approach on 118.4, and slow down a few knots. I'm going down on the deck. Don't follow, and keep me in sight. I will be pulling up after my run over the lake and will take up the same position with you. Roger that?"

Reed thumbed his mic button. "That's a roger, but don't get wet down there." Chip laughed as he watched Bud begin his decent with increased speed.

"Roy, what the hell do you think he is doing?"

"Beats me, unless he has a bone to pick with the Mercury folks. Who knows?"

The colorful B-25 in its wild tan and green paint job appeared to be making a landing on the small lake from Reed's view. Then he noticed a number of small boats making crazy patterns with their wakes on the murky colored water. Bud began fishtailing Killer Bee and dipping its wings.

"Jesus Christ, he must be crazy. Look at him. He can't be more than twenty feet off the water."

The Killer Bee suddenly began to climb at a high rate, and Chip was closing too fast, so he pulled back his throttles and rolled out to his right so he could give Bud plenty of room to level off again at four thousand feet. Once he was level, Chip pulled the Duck up into position off Bud's right wing. Bud began calling for clearance from Patrick AFB approach control for instructions, something that Chip had forgotten to do.

After a few holding circles south of the Titusville Airport, the two bombers were cleared to land on runway 36. Bud followed Killer Bee around the pattern and landed behind Bud with a perfect touchdown. A "follow me" truck was there to guide the two planes to the warbird flight line on the west side of the field.

Chip taxied and parked the Duck as if he had been doing it all his life, and Bergy praised him for his professional touch with his plane and moved out of his seat to evaluate the plane's conditions outside. While Chip was gathering his charts and notes and putting them in his flight bag, a voice from behind startled him.

"That was just great, Captain Sky King. Noisy, but great. I had a front-row seat up there. Thanks. What was that crazy man doing with the other plane over that lake? I thought he was going to crash for a minute. Was that all planned?"

"Yep, Bud West wanted to make sure the belly of Killer Bee was clean so he dipped in the lake and washed her off," Reed said, laughing.

"Cute, very cute and very childish … but cute," Lee remarked as she made her way toward the hatch. "Oh, better have someone with a good stomach clean up the mess I made up there. I was all right until you started to make those circles before you landed. Sorry about that."

Lee Waters left the plane and headed over to meet with Edna and Harry to tell them about her experience. Reed did not have to examine the damage forward as he got a good sniff of Lee's problem as he went down the crew ladder.

Sara pulled up in her car and ran over to Chip with two envelopes. "Chip, here is some mail for you. I only brought two of the letters that seemed important."

Chip took the envelopes and noticed that one was from Linda and the other was from Dr. Wolf's office. He stuffed Linda's letter into his flight suit pocket and opened the doctor's letter. It was what he was waiting for, his health certificate. He thanked Sara and headed for the crew ladder to put the certificate on his clipboard and hand to Bud for the pilots' briefing. A letter from his friend Doctor Mel Wolf was also attached, telling him to get over to Dr. Storey's lab as soon as the show was over. He could be in trouble with a rare form of leukemia.

CHAPTER 22

Valiant Air Command Air Show (TICO)
Space Coast Regional Airport
Titusville, Florida
February 22
1100 hours

After going over some minor problems with Roy Bergy on numerous oil leaks, Chip strolled over to join Bud West under the wing of Killer Bee. Bud was examining the number-one engine's exhaust system while one of his crew was removing the engine cowling. Harry O'Conner was busy cleaning off oil streaks on the number-two engine's nacelle, while his wife, Edna, and Dolly West were helping unload the show materials from the rear hatch. Lee was helping Sara set up the tripods with the information stats on Killer Bee. A card table displaying brochures for Bud's Warbird Museum and photo albums where set up for public viewing by Sam and his wife, JD, and the ground crew was given instructions on cleaning up the two planes for the show.

"Find any serious problems, Bud?" Chip asked.

"Naw, just a loose exhaust fastener. Someone forgot to safety wire a couple of nuts. How is your bird, Chip? Any problems?"

"If you consider a person's breakfast of eggs, onions, and sausage splattered all over my forward bombardiers position a major problem, I would say yes."

"No shit? One of my guys?" Bud asked.

"Nope, one of your customer's friends, the one in the pretty blue tight-fitting jumpsuit over there which somehow escaped any unsightly stains of the aftermath."

"That's a good thing, buddy. I would hate to see that outfit removed from its frame right now. I'm counting on that outfit to bring lots of attention to our display and get more interest in our museum. Men like to see women in sexy flight suits. They think these ladies fly these birds. Know what I mean?" Bud could not help but laugh at the serious expression on Chip's face as he studied the lady in blue.

"Loosen up, Chip. She is only a woman. Hell, I had to beat up on Dolly for months to get her to think about what guys like to see at these shows besides warbirds."

"Yeah, right, and Bonnie taught Clyde how to rob banks. That woman is an accident waiting to happen, and somehow, I feel I just may be that happening," Chip said as he studied Lee stretching on the tips of her toes in the bomb bay while someone inside was handing her down an Igloo cooler.

"Come on, pal. Get your clipboard and pen. We have to get over to the pilots' tent for the briefing. They have coffee and donuts there too." Bud turned to JD and asked where Sam was hiding. "I need him to join us pronto for the briefing."

JD responded and ran to the forward crew ladder and called up to Sam, who was changing the cylinder head temperature instrument.

"He'll be right behind, Bud," she yelled and disappeared up the ladder.

Chip returned to the Duck and picked up his briefcase and clipboard. He went over a few things with Roy and told him to join him as soon as he was caught up with the unloading.

Pilots' Briefing Tent
1200 hours

As Bud, Sam, Chip, and Roy walked toward the big white tent, Chip handed Bud his clipboard with his current flying certificate and the new medical certificate.

"Good show, Chip. I have to hand all this in when we arrive," Bud said, smiling.

The big steamy tent was filled with pilots from all over the country, many of them from Florida. They were all dressed in colorful flight suits with their ranks and names printed on them. Some had huge logo patches sewn on representing their warbird clubs or a squadron insignia from the past. There was no age limit here. There were men in their seventies and young guys in their twenties. A number of women were also dressed in jumpsuits of all colors. They flew as co-pilots and team members with their spouses or boyfriends. There were a number of women volunteers working at a table that had information about the Valiant Air Command. The organization was building a couple of their own warbirds for their museum located nearby. They were totally dependent on club membership dues, donations, and this annual air show to keep them in business. The entire show was operated by hundreds of club member volunteers.

The briefing was done with the expertise of a flight commander setting his squadron up for a major mission. Joe Gibson, known as the show boss, and his assistant, Jerry Strom, went over every detail of the air show, including times for all the participating aircraft to be ready to take off. They had a huge area map and would show where the holding area was for each plane to go to and circle until called by the show boss. Special radio frequencies were established, and emergency procedures were explained. There were many questions asked, but the control team gave definitive answers for each one.

The air show would open with the National Anthem and the US Army skydiving team carrying the stars and stripes in a spectacular show falling out of the sky over the show and landing on the runway. The announcement would follow on the story of the bombing of Pearl Harbor with a show of Japanese planes attacking the field and simulated bombs going off. The second part of this program would be about the famous Doolittle Tokyo Raid on Japan by two B-25s simulating the bombing attack. Thousands of spectators would be sitting and standing along the active show runway.

Meanwhile, a specialized team of pyro experts had set up all the explosives and sound effects needed during the show. Small exploding devices would be used to look like machine gun bullets hitting the ground, and large detonations would simulate bombs blowing up along the north side of the active runway. Show sponsors had catered tents lined up along the show runway where they would entertain their special guests and families. Hundreds of other vendors from all over the country set up their booths, selling everything from expensive prints and paintings signed by famous artists to famous warbird plane T-shirt art. There were toy vendors, hat vendors, and even flight simulators for those who would like to fly an F-16. Food vendors were also present with the typical favorite fast foods and treats.

After the briefing, Bud, Chip, and Sam returned to the flight line and met with ground crews to brief them on the times when the B-25s would be leaving for their part in the show. They were lucky as they would be participating in the early part of the air show and would be on the ground as part of the air shows static display for the rest of the day.

"Hey, is there any place nearby where we can get a good burger?" Lee Waters asked.

"Right over there, Lee, in that little house on the edge of the field with the Bud signs in the window. They have super burgers and salads," Dolly replied.

"Great. I'm starved. How about it, Captain Ahab? Care to buy a lady a burger and a beer?" Lee said as she took hold of Chip's arm.

Chip pulled his arm away from her grasp. "You should be hungry, lady. You left your breakfast all over my—" Chip did not finish his response.

Bud jumped in and saved the moment. "Hey, why don't we all go and eat. Dolly, go tell the O'Conners we are going to the Stick and Rudder restaurant, and they can meet us there."

Bud turned and put his arm around Lee's waist, and in his schoolboy manner, he joked, "Come on, bluebird. I'll buy you a burger and beer as long as Chip has some cash in his shoe. I'm leaned out."

Chip, Bud, and Lee began to walk toward the restaurant while Dolly rounded up JD and Sam. JD caught up with the team and explained the O'Conners were talking to some old friends and going to give them a tour of the plane.

When they finished with lunch, it was well noted that Lee and Chip had little to say to each other. The atmosphere around the table was pretty thick with tension that everyone felt. Dolly tried with all her charm to impress Chip and Lee on how big this show would get before the end of the day.

"We will have at least four P-51s, a Corsair, two Hellcats, a B-17G, and a B-24 Liberator. I heard that we may see a P-38 come in maybe tomorrow, and we have two Marine Corps Harriers, an F-18, a C-130, and—"

"It's okay, Dolly. I have been to this show a few times before," Chip said, smiling, knowing she was trying to break the ice. Suddenly, the ice really cracked.

"Hey, Captain Chips, I am sorry I threw up all over your plane, and I know I should have been more … well, thoughtful and cleaned up my mess, okay? I'm sorry." Lee managed to get her words out but never looked up or had eye contact with Chip, who was quick to respond.

"Sorry we didn't have throw-up bags on board for you," Chip responded.

"Now that's funny, Chip, and a good idea. I never thought about throw-up bags on board. Maybe we should get Delta Airlines to supply us with some for advertising purposes, you know, like a trade? Hey, JD, make a note of that. Call Delta and get hold of their PR folks," Bud said, laughing.

"Bud, you really need help. You know that?" Dolly remarked. Then she and JD began laughing, and it soon became contagious as everyone joined in. Bud stood up and called out for the waitress and a check.

"Hey, sweet thing, you got a jealous boyfriend who would fight for you?" Bud asked the young waitress as she handed the bill to Chip.

"Sure do, darling, and he's my husband, he's that big guy with the red beard sitting right behind you."

Dolly leaned over, took Bud by the arm, and whispered in his ear. "Someday, buddy boy, you're going to get popped in the kisser with that dumb line now. Let's get out of here.

1400 hours

Chip found himself for the second time that day sitting at the controls of his bomber next to Bergy in the right seat. They were waiting for the signal to start their engines. As he looked out at the row of T-6s parked across the ramp, a line of taxiing aircraft began to pass by. The first planes were painted dark green with large red balls painted on their wings and fuselage. They were T-34 trainers painted up to look like Japanese fighters.

An authentic Japanese torpedo bomber taxied past followed by a famous Japanese Zero fighter. Chip could feel the sweat build up in his hands as he tightened the grip on the control wheel. He wanted to say something to Bergy and talk about how deeply he resented the Japanese. He elected to keep his thoughts to himself. Two Grumman Wildcats taxied by, one painted in the original colors of light blue with a white underbelly. Painted on her vertical tail were the words "USS YORKTOWN." A TBF Avenger torpedo bomber followed. Then he saw a long line of colorfully painted T-6s that were fishtailing back and forth so the pilots could see ahead over their radial engines. It was quite a sight, and all these aircraft would be taking part in the Pearl Harbor sequence.

"You know something, Roy? I just may switch my seat with that kid up there in the top turret. What's his name?"

"I think he said his name was Eddie. He works for Bud. Why would you want to climb up into the hot turret for heaven's sake? It's going to be boiling in that turret?"

"Oh, I thought I would load up those two .50s and shoot a couple of those meatballs out of the sky today, especially that damn Zero."

Roy stared at Chip but said nothing. Chip appeared in some kind of trance. He had a strange look on his face as he stared out the windscreen. Roy also noted that his knuckles where pure white as he gripped the control wheel. Reed looked very angry, and this bothered Roy.

"Hey, skipper, Sam is giving hand signals from Killer Bee to start engines. I got my fireguard over here. Are you clear on your side?"

Chip looked out his open side window and signaled the volunteer standing by with a portable fire extinguisher. He raised his finger and rotated it to advise the man he was about to start the number-one engine. The man indicated that the area was clear to start.

Chip carefully taxied behind Bud in Killer Bee while going through the checklist with Bergy. Two of Bud's staff were also on board. One was a young student standing in the upper turret, and one of Bud's best engineers was sitting behind Roy on a jump seat. The B-25s taxied up to the end of the taxi strip as the T-34 trainers began taking off in pairs followed by the T-6s and then the Zero and the Betty bomber. The TBF was having some mechanical problems and moved off the taxi strip. The two Hellcats paired up and began their roll. Bud moved his Mitchell onto the far side of the runway, leaving Chip plenty of room to pull up on his starboard wing. Both aircraft began their run-up checks and reported to ground control that they were ready to take off.

Chip's headset came alive with Bud's voice on the plane-to-plane frequency, "Chip, don't forget to go on the show frequency 118.1 when you get off the ground, and remember to reach for a high rate of climb to three thousand in order to give me more time for distance, then follow me to the staging area. Roger that?"

Chip understood and reported back to Bud. Bergy had already keyed the number-two radio on the show frequency.

Bud was cleared first and began his roll. As soon as Killer Bee rotated, Chip got the call from the tower to take off. Chip moved the throttles forward and released the brakes. The Duck began its short roll down the seven-thousand-foot runway. Chip watched Bud as he leveled out fifty feet above the ground gaining airspeed, and then he put Killer Bee into a high-speed climbing left bank, pointing her nose into the blue. As soon as the Duck left the ground, Chip called for gear up, rolled the Duck into a shallow bank while climbing and going through his procedures. He raised the flaps and maintained climbing upward, keeping his eye on Bud a mile and a half ahead. As soon as he reached his given altitude, he leveled off. Roy went over the power settings, cowl flaps, and shut off the boost pumps while checking all instruments. This maneuver by both pilots gave them the spacing they needed between the two aircraft. Chip was now a mile behind Bud heading for their holding area about five miles northwest of the airport.

"Okay, Chip, I'm almost on my turning point. Just follow me. Maintain thirty-five hundred, and throttle back to 120 miles per hour while we circle out here. We will stay in a left-hand pattern until we get the call. Roger that?"

"Roger, Bud. Are we staying at thirty-five?"

"Roger that, and you may want to give me some more room. When we get the call, I will increase my speed and head for the field and enter a left-hand pattern. When I turn for on my downwind leg, I will descend to five hundred feet and maintain this altitude for my fist pass and increase my airspeed to two hundred miles per hour. You do the same, but stay at one thousand. Don't forget to open the bomb bay doors on the final leg for effect. Be ready for those ground blasts. The explosives will be about thirty yards off your starboard wing, so stay right over the runway, and whatever you do, don't drift over the blast area. After the run, keep your airspeed at two hundred, and follow me. I will make a right-hand turnout and climb back to a thousand feet and enter the downwind again for the second pass. We may get some action from Jap fighters on the second pass, so stay cool, and don't run into anyone."

Chip could hear Bud chuckling.

"This is going to be cool. Just like the real thing," Chip yelled to Roy, but he wasn't listening. He was making adjustments on the engine controls and tapping on one of the engine's temperature gauges.

"The cylinder head temperature gage is jumping up and down on the number-two, Chip. Must be a loose connection, but we'll be okay," Roy reported.

Chip heard the call from the show boss to bring in the Mitchells. He did as instructed and followed Killer Bee out of the staging area into the flight pattern entering his downwind leg at a thousand feet. Bud had dropped down to his five-hundred-foot level and began to increase speed. Chip followed him down to a thousand feet, leveled off, and began to increase his speed. As he watched Bud begin his turn for the base leg, he dropped the nose too soon and began to turn too early and inside Bud. Bergy saw the problem and took control of his wheel moving it back to the left and kicked left rudder, forcing Reed to recover from making the premature turn.

"You're too close, Chip. Stretch it out," Roy commanded.

Chip also kicked the left rudder and brought the Duck level and back on course, but he lost sight of Bud, who was on his final approach and speeding across the runway. Roy had Bud in sight and signaled Chip to turn on the base leg. Bud reacted and dropped the Duck another hundred feet while he tried to get an eye on Bud, but Roy was blocking his view. So he banked again too early to start his final approach and dropped another hundred feet. By the time he realized he was well to the right of the runway and too low, he kicked the left rudder, but it was too late. The Duck had flown nearly forty feet north of the runway at six hundred feet and doing nearly two hundred miles per hour. The first blast jolted the Duck, causing Chip to hit his head against the side window. The Duck leaped and fell off on its left wing, and Chip recovered just in time to get the impact of a second explosion. This time Chip pulled up hard and climbed nearly a thousand feet before he got the Duck back under control.

"Well, I guess we blew that one, Roy," Chip cried out.

"Chip, what the hell is going on back there?" Bud called over Chip's headset.

"Get on the show frequency. They're calling you, Chip. Are you okay?"

"We're okay. Everything is fine, Bud," Roy responded.

"Chip, I'm going in for the second pass. You go straight out to the staging area and hang out. Do not do a second pass. Roger that?"

"Roger, that," Chip reported back.

"Stay on the show frequency. They will clear you when to land on runway 18. Roger that?" Bud replied.

"Roger that. Duck out."

Chip was too frustrated to even talk to Roy or look at him. He saw Roy's hand tapping on the number-two engine's temperature gauge again, and then he reached for the landing checklist.

"Sorry, about that Roy. I got the air show jitters, I guess," Chip said over the intercom. There was no verbal response from Roy, only a thumbs-up signal and a weak smile.

1420 hours

After landing and returning to the review area, Chip was not looking forward to seeing Bud and the reception committee waiting for him.

Bud had landed and taxied to his place, and he was immediately met by a golf cart and taken out to the nearby taxi ramp where he met with two men in another cart dressed in Valliant Command uniforms.

"I'll get the gear pins in and start the boys working on that cylinder head problem, Chip. Yell if you need me out there," Roy said as he climbed out of his seat and made way to the crew exit hatch.

Two golf carts parked in front of the Duck and waited for Chip to come down the crew ladder. As soon as he did, he was summoned by Bud.

"Chip, this is Bob Simmons and Fred Brenner. They are members of the Valiant board of directors, and Bob here is the chairman of this year's show," Bud said as they all shook hands.

They asked Chip to jump in the back seat of the cart out of the sun.

"Mr. Reed, Bud here has told me that you are still pretty green with your Mitchell, and he takes the responsibility for your actions over the field during the show. However, the crowd loved it and thought it was all part of the show, but you and I know that it could have been a disaster, don't we? We had no way of stopping those detonations once they were energized by that team's computer, and man, we thought that second blast would take you out. You were way off course, nearly over ground zero and three hundred feet below your minimum altitude instructions."

"I have no excuse. I just lost it, gentlemen, and Bud here has no business taking any of the blame. I got excited and lost it. I am deeply sorry, and I understand your concern. But I did have the plane under control, and it won't happen the next time, I assure you."

"Well, Mr. Reed, I'm afraid there won't be a next time, not for you anyway. If Bud here has one of his regular qualified pilots fly your plane, that's fine, but I'm afraid we have to ground you. We are sorry, but that's the decision and ruling of our show committee and board of directors. It's for the safety of the show, sir. Unfortunately, in the past few years around the country, there have been a number of accidents and crashes, and so far, we have been accident-free. We hope you understand and have no ill feelings toward us and hope to see you back next year. All you need is a little more experience, and I'm sure this man can give you that, right, Bud?"

Simmons smiled and reached out and shook Chip's hand. Then he excused himself. Chip stepped off the cart, and the two officials shook hands with Bud and rode off.

"Sorry about this, Chip, but it is their playground. Hell, you take second seat, and I will fly the Duck for the next two days. Sam and Roy can take the Bee up. Not to worry, okay?"

Chip smiled and patted Bud on the shoulder. "Where are we staying by the way? I think I would like to go take a real hot shower and crawl into a double scotch and soda."

"Oh, sure, I understand, Chip. We are staying at the Ramada down the road near I-95. Why don't you take my pickup over there and haul ass? We have Dolly's car and Sara's van to bring us all over after the show. Don't eat anything till we get there. We always go out to this rowdy steak house up on A1A on our first night here." Bud reached in his Levi's and took out a set of keys. "Here's my keys chip, now get going. We'll see you later."

Chip was about to crawl into the cab of the pickup when a voice from behind caught his ear. It was Sara holding a letter in her hand. Chip saw that it was from Linda and stuffed into his flight jacket. As he started to get into the pickup truck, he heard another voice yelling his name. It was the lady in blue.

"Hey, you have room in there for a suitcase and an ironing board?"

Chip turned only to come face-to-face with Lee. She was holding a suitcase in one hand and a duffel bag in the other. "Where's the ironing board?" he asked with a smile.

"In the bag with the iron, trust me. Now can I get a lift? You're going to the hotel to drown your sorrows, aren't you?"

Chip curled his bottom lip over his teeth and pointed to the other door of the cab. He was bruised by her remark, and for a brief second, he wished that she were a man so he could relocate her pixie nose.

For the first minutes, there were no words in the dusty cab as Chip drove across a dirt road toward the back gate of the airport. When he reached the gate, he asked one of the volunteer guards which way the highway and the motels were.

"You feel pretty bad, I guess. I don't know what happened up there, Chip. You sure looked good to me from the ground, but I guess these air show people were not happy with your flying," Lee said as she deliberately looked away from him and stared out the side window.

"Oh, just ignore me, lady. I'm having a bad hair day. I should have stayed on the ground and let Sam take her up. Hell, I thought I was doing fine until the fireworks went off under me. All I did was screw up my approach, drift off course, and drop four hundred feet lower than instructed. Plus I may have messed my pants when that second explosion went off. How's that for fucking up, lady?"

"Please. Do you have to use that language? I heard Bud say that it was mostly his fault not giving you more time training for this day, and you made honest mistakes that anyone could make the first time flying in an air show with all that was going on. He also said you kept your cool and prevented what could have been a disaster."

"Bud is just being nice Lee. Nope, I blew it, and if I could, I would take the Duck out of the show today and take a nice long flight out to Ft. Worth, Texas."

"Texas? Are you from Texas?"

"No, and I don't know why I said that. Well, yes, I guess I do. But that's a long story, and it looks like we just found our motel."

Chip pulled up in front of the motel, got out, and went around to open Lee's door, but she had already exited and was heading for the two glass lobby doors with baggage in hand. When they both reached the counter, Lee turned and looked into Chip's eyes.

"I'll just bet she's a brunette and a schoolteacher, right?" Lee asked.

"Who is?"

"The woman in Texas, the one you're running to so she can lick your wounds.'

"Can I help you, folks?" the young woman behind the counter asked.

Chip unlocked the door and entered his room. He threw the room key on the dresser and placed his clothes bag on the bed. He opened the bag and removed a clean jumpsuit. Packed within was a half of a bottle of Johnny Walker Red Label. He opened the bottle and laid down across the king bed. Then he took a long swallow from the bottle. It burned all the way down and caused him to cough. He got up and grabbed a plastic cup from the dresser. He went into the bathroom and ran the cold water and filled the cup. After drinking the water, he stared into the mirror before him. He was thankful it was dark in the small room as he did not want to see the face of the troubled man staring back at him. Suddenly, there was a soft tapping on the metal door. Chip walked back into the room and opened the door.

"I have the ice and the olives but no gin," she said.

"Sorry. You have the wrong room. All I have is scotch."

"That will do fine." Lee pushed past Reed, put the ice bucket down, went over to the nightstand, picked up the bottle of scotch, and poured some into a plastic glass.

"Don't you want some ice?" Chip asked as he studied Lee, who was still molded in her blue jumpsuit. She was barefoot, and evidently, he had just brushed her golden hair and bathed in perfume.

"No, this is fine," she said and moved closer to Chip, who moved next to the bed.

She put the glass down on the nightstand, reached up, and pulled the zipper of her blue jumpsuit down to the waist. She unbuckled the belt and let it fall to the floor. Then she unzipped the rest of the suit. She never took her eyes off his confused face and staring eyes. He displayed no emotions. She reached up with her hand and rolled the suit off one shoulder, and the rest of the suit slid off, dropping to her feet. She was totally nude and had the body of a woman half her age. Chip could see she had little use for wearing a bathing suit as there was no white skin anywhere. Her skin was golden bronze, and it appeared to be shining as if she had rubbed oil all over it. She was everything that Reed had imagined when he first saw her at the museum standing in the doorway and sunlight backlighting her perfect curves.

"You do want me, don't you Chip? It's been written all over your face since yesterday."

Lee stepped out of the jumpsuit and walked slowly toward him. She stood inches away, letting her firm breasts tease his chest while her hands moved to the zipper of his flight suit and began to pull it down. Chip felt as if he were frozen as he couldn't move. He stood looking down into her flawless face, which was now cleaned of all the makeup she displayed earlier. Her hands slipped under his suit and rolled it off his shoulders and down around his arms, restricting them from any movement. Then she pressed herself hard against his chest and raised herself on her toes to meet his lips.

Chip never noticed the letter fall to the floor from his flight suit.

"We have at least three hours before the gang gets here and our new affair ends."

Those were the last words to be spoken by Lee for the next three hours.

Quietly, Lee slid off the bed, got dressed, and left the room without disturbing Chip. A few minutes later and half asleep, Chip heard talking and laughing going on in the hallway followed by doors banging shut.

"It sounds like the crews are here. The show must be over," he told himself as he rolled over and noticed he was alone. He sat up for a second and then fell back into the pillows. He closed his eyes and tried to picture her lying beside him. He took a pillow and covered his face and took a long, deep breath. She was still there. Her scent was in his nostrils, and her body was pressing his. He rolled over and buried his face deeper into the pillow and began to curse her for finding a weakness he was not aware of. Did he fall for her act for the wrong reasons? Was he feeling sorry for himself because of his stupidity at the air show, or was he trying to hurt Linda for her lack of understanding when it came to his needs? Whatever the reason, Lee took all that away with the pull of a zipper. He lay there pretending that it didn't happen, but now he could not get Lee out of his mind and wanted to have her again. He wondered if she felt the same. Or did she just get what she wanted for the moment? He suddenly became angry with himself and reached for the Johnny Walker, but it was all gone. Then he noticed the letter on the floor. He picked it up and could not get the courage to open it and put it back in his flight bag.

CHAPTER 23

The phone started ringing, and hoping it was Lee, Chip picked it up and heard Bud's excited voice.

"Hey, Chip, we are meeting in the lobby in ten minutes and heading up the road for some steaks. Are you ready?"

"Ah, no, Bud, I really don't feel like anything right now. You guys go ahead. I'm going to hang out and catch some sleep. It's been a tough day for me."

"Chip, what's done is done, and hanging around and punishing yourself is not the answer. The answer is to climb back into the seat and get back up in the blue tomorrow with me and try again, okay?"

"Right, Bud and we will talk about tomorrow later. Have a good time. I will see you for breakfast, okay?"

He hung up the phone and rolled back on the bed. He reached for the remote and turned on the TV. He picked up the phone and asked for Lee's room, but after ten rings he hung up. *She probably went out with the gang*, he thought.

After falling off in a deep sleep, he was wakened to the sounds of laughing in the hall outside his door. He looked at his watch and then noted the TV was still on but was muted. He must have done this before he fell asleep. On the screen was some news reporter who was broadcasting footage of the air show from opening day. He waited to see the part about the bombing of Tokyo, but that was not displayed. There was only the sequence of the Jap planes bombing Pearl Harbor. He was about to call Lee's room when the phone rang. It was Bud.

"Hey, get on your duds and meet us in the restaurant. We need to get over to the flight line and start getting the planes set up. Roy already left with Sam for Kissimmee to get some parts and a new temp gauge for the Duck."

"I will be there in fifteen minutes. By the way Bud, have you seen the O'Conners and Lee this morning?"

"No, but they'll be at breakfast, I'm sure." Bud replied.

Chip went into the bathroom and turned on the light. He went back to his overnight bag and retrieved his shaving kit. Once again, he noted the letter but ignored it. He forgot to bring his shaving cream and cursed the motel for the little soaps, one of which he used for shaving lather. After shaving and showering, Chip got dressed and headed down the dark hall to the front of the motel where the restaurant was located. He entered the large room that was filled with men and women all wearing flight suits and baseball hats with various pictures of war birds on them. It was noisy and smoky, and Chip had a tough time seeing anyone from Bud's crew. Then he saw them in a corner. Bud, Dolly, Sam, JD, and the O'Conners sitting at tables that had been pulled together. He didn't see Lee anywhere.

"Good morning, Chip," Dolly cried out and waved for him to come to their table.

"Good morning, folks," Chip announced as he headed for a seat next to Bud.

"Get enough sleep, Chip?" Bud asked as he leaned close to Chip to whisper in his ear. "Did you meet with Lee last night? She took off without saying good-bye even to the O'Conners!"

"Don't know what you're talking about, Bud. I haven't seen her since I gave her a lift yesterday," Chip responded.

"Whatever you say, Pal, but Harry and Edna are really upset, so if you know anything about her cutting out, please at least tell them, okay?"

"Sure will Bud. Chip stood up and looked straight into Buds eyes. Bud, I'm really not feeling too good. You won't have a problem if I head back to Kissimmee, would you? I mean, you have enough folks here to take care of everything. You have my permission to fly the Duck for the next two shows if you like. I don't mind. Right now all I want to do is head back to Kissimmee and put my feet up and call Linda. I got a letter from her and need to talk to her."

"Okay, Chip, but I would feel better if you hung around. I wanted to take you back up with me today and go through the program step by step. I'm convinced—everyone here is—that all you had was some jitters yesterday, and we can prove to the boys in the front office that you're perfectly capable of coming back on flying status for the show."

"Thanks, but I really would like to go to my RV."

"Wait a minute," Bud remarked and leaned over and whispered in Dolly's ear. She reached in her purse and gave Chip a set of keys.

"Here, Chip. Take my car. We have plenty of transportation around. If you change your mind, let us know. Will you promise?"

"Roger that and thanks, Dolly. Bud, please make my excuses to the gang." Chip looked at Dolly while holding up the keys, winked, and thanked her again.

Chip headed straight for the front desk and was greeted by a young girl with brilliant red hair and a face full of freckles.

"Yes, sir, can I help you?"

"Yes, are you holding any messages for Charles Reed."

"Ah, no, sir, I have nothing here," the young lady responded.

"You can check me out then. I will be right back," Chip replied.

"Do you want to keep this on your MasterCard, Mr. Reed?"

Chip told her yes and proceeded down the dark hallway to his room. About halfway down the corridor, a short man in a flight suit stepped out of a room and began to walk toward him. When he recognized Chip, he made a comment as he passed him by.

"Sorry you got your wings clipped, old man. I was looking forward to burning a few of your feathers off yesterday," the stranger remarked as he passed.

"I beg your pardon. Were you talking to me?" Chip stopped walking and turned to face the man and noticed he was wearing a light tan flight suit with many patches attached. At first, he could not make out his facial features because of the darkness of the hallway, but as the man turned around, his face was highlighted under an exit sign. He was a short Asian man with dark skin and slick black hair. Chip figured him to be at least in his late forties.

"What the hell are you talking about?" Chip asked as he stepped closer to the stranger.

"Sir, we were instructed to tangle with the B-25s after you and Bud made your second flyby, but you loused us up, man," he said, laughing, and then he continued. "I was tempted to go out after you in the staging area after you blew that pass you made and harass you a little, but the air boss called us back to play with the little Wildcats, who are much too slow for me. You could have been a real challenge, maybe not as good as ole Bud West, but it would have been fun."

"Just what were you flying?" Chip asked.

"I own a Mitsubishi Zeke, one of the only model 52s flying today and a veteran of the South Pacific. You would most likely think of my plane as the Zero. Many people do as it was its famous name. I just like to come to the shows and show just what a fascinating airplane it is and love a good dogfight with ... let's say, qualified pilots?" He laughed again and stretched out his hand to shake with Chip. "I am Colonel Ram Kaisha with the Japanese Air Force, and you are?"

"Your worst nightmare you little Japanese asshole!" Chip said. With a closed right fist, he threw a solid bunch into the stranger's abdomen. As the colonel's head begin to drop, his hands reached down to grip his stomach, and Chip threw a right cross that caught the Japanese man on his left cheek and sent him spinning to the floor. Chip stood directly over the man looking down on him. The man was in the fetal position, moaning while holding one hand in his groin and the other over his bloody mouth.

"You get up, you little yellow bastard, and I'll take your fucking head off," Chip yelled out. He could feel his own body trembling and began gasping for air and thought his heart was about to leave his chest. Suddenly, a nearby door opened, and two young women in flight suits appeared.

"Oh, my God, what is going on here?" one of the girls yelled out while the other dropped to the floor on her knees to help the injured pilot.

Chip stepped away and began walking backward toward his room. One of the women went yelling down the hall toward the lobby. The other was talking to the pilot and helping him sit up. He was still groggy, and some significant swelling was beginning to show below his left eye. He looked up at Chip while pointing at him.

"You are a very sick man, sir, and I will see that you never set foot at this air show again." With that, he pulled himself up, and with the help of the young women, he began walking back to his room, still bleeding from his lower lip. He passed by Chip, who stepped aside to let them pass.

"I don't know what this was all about, sir, but Colonel Kaisha is a special guest of the Valiant Air Command. Did you know that?" the young woman remarked as she helped Kaisha to his room.

Chip did not respond. He opened his door, gathered his belongings, and walked back out in the hall only to come face-to-face with the motel manager, a uniformed policeman, and a half dozen guests, most of them in flight suits.

"Sir, I'm Bob Hicks, the motel manager, and this policeman is Officer Morgan. Would you mind coming with us back to my office?" The young man stepped aside and gestured to Reed to take the lead. The onlookers spread out as Chip walked through them. Then he noticed a figure running toward him. It was Bud West.

"Jesus, Chip, what the hell did you do?" Bud asked while walking next to him.

"I punched out a Jap's lights," Chip said as he stared ahead.

"A Jap maybe, but my friend, he is a very successful and famous officer in the Japanese Air Force. He's also a big-time board member of the defense board and brokers with our government for testing and advising his government on what type of planes they need, making him tight with our aircraft industry leaders. He is also a crack pilot, flies everything in our arsenal, and is sponsored by his government to fly at air shows all over the world. How bad is he hurt?" Bud asked in a whisper as they were entering the lobby area.

"Thanks for all that crap, Bud, but he is still a yellow Nip."

"This way please, Mr. Reed."

The manager commented pointing toward a door next to the front desk as Chip followed him. There were no words spoken. Bud stood with a few other onlookers as Reed disappeared behind the door.

Bud went running back into the dining room and found Dolly, who was still having breakfast. He excused himself, leaned over, and told her he needed to talk to her outside. Dolly got up and excused herself.

"Dolly, try and get hold of our lawyer Charlie Wendt. I think we might need him. It looks like Chip may have some legal problems."

"What's wrong, Bud? Is Chip the reason for all that commotion down the hall a little while ago?" she asked.

"Yes, Chip decided to tangle with Colonel Ram Kashia. I don't know what happened, but evidently, Chip punched him out."

"Oh, my God, Is Ram all right?"

"Don't know, sweetheart, but get on the phone and find Charlie just in case. Has everyone left for the show?"

"Yes, except for Harry and Edna. They are still waiting for Lee to call. She did leave them a note at the front desk that she was going to Miami. The front desk told them she took a cab to Orlando. I will go back with them and to the show and the flight line. You gave my car to Chip. Is he still going back to Kissimmee?"

"Don't know yet. I will catch up to you at the plane. Be sure to get the crew working on Killer Bee and the Duck. We are taking them both up today." Bud turned and headed back to the lobby.

Chip sat motionless as Officer Morgan sat at the manager's desk and began to ask questions about the incident. There was a knock on the door, and Bob Hicks got up and opened the door. Colonel Kaisha stood holding a towel next to his face along with the same women who came to his aid.

"I have come to see, Mr. Reed. Is he here with you, sir?"

"Indeed. Come in," Hicks said and stepped back into the office. Kaisha and the woman walked in as Officer Morgan stood up. Hicks moved a chair over and suggested that Kaisha take the seat, but he refused.

"I come to advise you that I am bringing no charges against this man. I may have provoked him with some childish remarks I made about his performance yesterday during the air show." With that, Kaisha stood before Reed and took a shallow bow.

"I hope you accept my apology, Mr. Reed. It was not fair of me to make fun of your flying skills." Kaisha spun around and bowed his head to the rest of the stunned faces and walked out of the office.

"Well, looks like all's well that ends well. You are lucky, Mr. Reed. He seems like a nice fellow, and we are happy to see that there is no damage here." Hicks smiled and reached out his hand to Chip, who ignored him. Then he asked Morgan if he could go. Morgan nodded his head yes, and Chip left the office and walked out to the parking lot and found Dolly's Cherokee station wagon. He totally forgot to check out. When confronted by his receptionist about Reed not signing his credit card receipt, Hick took the receipt and tore it up.

CHAPTER 24

Orlando International Airport
Delta Airlines Ticket Counter
1305 hours

Chip drove back to his RV, changed clothes, and drove directly to Orlando International Airport. He left no word at the office about where he was going and was not concerned about Bud, Dolly, or even his plane. When he got to the airport, he parked Dolly's car in long-term parking and went right to the Delta counter.

"There you are. Mr. Reed, one-way ticket to Dallas/Ft. Worth with a change in Atlanta. Your gate is twenty-six, and your flight is on time and boarding in fifteen minutes. Thank you for flying Delta."

Bud picked up his ticket and walked toward the gate. He saw a row of pay phones on a wall and proceeded toward them. As usual, all the phones were being used by what he referred to as visiting animals wearing bright Disney character T-shirts and stupid hats with mouse ears.

He went to the gate and noticed more phones. He started to dial Linda's office and then stopped. He dialed her home number, and as expected, her voice gave gentle instructions on how to leave a message. He put the phone down and went to a nearby chair and sat. He put his head back and began to relive the last few interesting hours of his life, starting with the light blue flight suit slipping down around one of the most beautiful sculptures of human flesh he ever held. Then her scent came and he could smell the vapors of her body fill into his nostrils. He opened his eyes, expecting to see her standing before him. It was all in his head but almost too real. "Why did she leave without a word?" he kept asking himself. Then he would think of Linda and close his eyes again and try to remember her lying in front of the fireplace in New York City. The white silk robe kept sliding off her warm body every time he gathered her into his arms. He wanted so hard to keep Linda on his mind, but Lee was satisfying his physical needs now. He wanted her again, and this bothered him.

The flight to Atlanta on the 757 was smooth while Chip put his thoughts together on what he would say to Linda and the things he wanted to talk about. He knew that she was the right woman for him and knew that his love for her was real and no match for anything Lee could ever give him.

Chip felt he nearly walked halfway across Georgia at Hartsfield Atlanta Airport to get to his next gate and flight to Ft. Worth. When he got to the gate in terminal A he noted that his plane was late, so he went over to a nearby snack shop, bought a coffee, and sat down at one of the small tables. He finally located Linda's letter and opened it.

> My deares Charles,
>
> First, I want to thank you for all the wonderful flowers and letters. I miss you so much and can't wait to see you again. The doctors here have been wonderful, and Richard and the directors are being generous to me with finding me the best surgeons and hospitals to continue getting treatments. I will be going to the Mass General burn unit in Boston as soon as all the papers are final. They have two of the best plastic surgeons in the country I have been told, and they want to see my scars. I don't know when I will be going, but I will give you notice if I have time.
>
> I understand that you are ready for the first air show and the Duck is all painted up with your cartoon on the nose. I wrote to Sara last night and asked her to take pictures of the Duck with you under the cartoon at the show.
>
> It is time for my therapy now, so I will close and wait to hear from you. Good luck at the air show, and give my love to Bud and Dolly. And don't forget Sara.
>
> All my love,

Linda

Chip read the letter again before he folded it back into the envelope. He kept asking if he was doing the right thing by surprising Linda with a visit when he had promised to wait for her when she felt ready.

The loudspeaker broke the silence of the waiting area. "Ladies and gentleman, the flight from Dallas/Ft. Worth has arrived at the gate, and we will be boarding on time."

Chip sat and watched the faces of men and women walking off the plane. He even became entertained by the various shapes of people and their attire, which could easily qualify them for a strange fashion show. As he began to rise from his chair, he was suddenly aware of an attractive woman in a dark blue suit and a wide-rimmed matching hat. She also wore what appeared to be a silk scarf wrapped partially around her head and nearly covering her face. He studied her as she walked slowly through the maze of people debarking and waiting in line to board. When she finally was clear, he noted a tall man in a dark gray suit come up behind her. He put his arm around her. Then as she turned, they embraced, and he kissed her. They talked for a second and walked away from the area.

"No, it can't be." Chip kept repeating to himself and found he was stalking the couple and following them down the crowded terminal. Suddenly, they stopped and stepped into a newsstand. He ducked behind a large column.

He was able now to see her face up closer, and there was no doubt. It was his Linda. He stood paralyzed and careful that she made no eye contact with him. The man finished paying for a magazine and returned to her side, and they resumed walking toward the center of the terminal. Chip stayed close behind.

They walked the entire length of the terminal and stopped at gate 7. Again, Chip had to duck behind another support column. There they stood with their arms around each other and their cheeks touching, talking quietly. The man suddenly kissed her on the lips and then on her forehead. They separated a little, and she removed a handkerchief from her sleeve and wiped her eyes. They kissed again. She placed her head on his shoulder, and they held each other tightly. Her head turned in Chip's direction, but they did not make eye contact as her eyes were closed. Chip could clearly see that there was what appeared to be a bandage around part of her forehead, hidden partly by the scarf. They kissed again, and the man turned and walked away. He turned back, and they exchanged smiles.

Chip turned and headed to the closest Delta information booth he could find and waited in line for a chance to speak to a representative. He was trying to figure out what was going on with Linda. Who was the tall, well-dressed, distinguished man with her, and why would she not have told him there was another man in her life? He never thought to look and see what the schedule board read at gate 7.

The next flight was going to Boston.

"Yes, I don't have a ticket but would like a one-way to Orlando on the very next flight," Chip said to the Delta representative.

"Sir, that would be flight 1256 and leaving in forty minutes from terminal C, gate 27. We only have one first-class seat available."

Reeds Motor Home
0500 hours

Chip rolled his legs over the side of the sofa and sat up. His head was pounding, as the rain hitting the top of the motor home sounded like a steel band pounding in his ears. He sat for a second and studied the empty bottle of VO on the coffee table. He rose and walked to the refrigerator. He opened the door, pulled out an open container of orange juice, and took a large swig. It was sour, and before he could reach the sink, most of it got through to his stomach. He spent the next few minutes hugging the toilet.

The rain stopped within the hour, and Chip found himself at the wheel of Dolly's Cherokee and racing to Bud's office. His head was clear, and he began making new plans for the days ahead. He felt it was time maybe to leave the area and look for new ground to build a new life. He thought about Texas and maybe running into Linda. Then he changed his mind and began to think about Southern California, somewhere near Chino. He began to sell himself mentally on it. He told himself this was what he should do and made plans to maybe get back into real estate. He thought there were plenty of air shows he could go to and other B-25 specialists he could go to if the Duck needed repairs.

He got to the office only to find Sara and Roy. They were just leaving to head over to Titusville and surprised to see Chip.

"Where is everyone?" Chip asked.

"They all left for breakfast on the way to the show. Bud has been trying to find you. Last night he saw Dolly's car at your dark RV and decided just to let you be. He is hoping you will be at the show this morning. He has talked to the show officials, and they agreed to let you go up again today but not as the command pilot," Sara explained in a cheery voice.

CHAPTER 25

Valiant Air Command Air Show
Titusville Airport
0945 hours

"You know something, Chip? You have really turned into a basket case. What the hell are you talking about taking the Duck to California?" Bud placed both of his hands on Chip's shoulders and looked him straight in the eyes as they stood in the shade beneath the wing of Killer Bee.

"I'm sorry, Bud. I just feel I have to get out of here and start a new life. I feel boxed in now. It's hard to explain. It seems everything I really cared about and loved has left me. Do know what I mean? I think I may have even lost Linda now," Chip said, looking away from Bud while shaking his head.

"Chip, that's bullshit. You are letting that mistake you made yesterday control your brain. It was a simple mistake, and you learned from it. That's hardly a reason to pick up stakes and leave. There's something else going on, isn't there? Is it Linda, or does it something to do with Lee Waters? Now don't tell me that you didn't jump her bones. I know better. She mentioned to Dolly on the phone yesterday she may have crossed the line with you. What did she mean by that?"

"She talked to Dolly?" Chip asked.

"Yes, and I have no idea what she told her, and that is all I know. Lee is a big girl, and what happened between you guys is your business, so don't sweat it," Bud said.

"Has she … ah, has anyone else heard from her since yesterday?" Chip asked carefully.

"I think she got word to Harry and Edna. She went to Miami to visit a friend, and then she is going to Chicago for a few days to visit family. You know, she is going through a real tough divorce right now and having a tough time. Evidently, she learned her doctor husband was having an affair with his young assistant," Bud said as he reached over and put his hand on Chip's shoulder.

Chip nearly slipped and admitted what happened with him and Lee. He wanted to tell Bud about his trip to Atlanta and what he saw, but he decided not to. "Bud, is it possible I can just take Roy and my plane and go back to Kissimmee?"

"Chip, can't it wait until tomorrow? We need the Duck for the show, and I want to let Sam and Roy take Killer Bee. I will take the left seat and you the right on the Duck, and we'll do the show this afternoon, okay? Then you and Roy can haul ass after the show and fly back to Kissimmee. I need to hang around for a while with the officials and go over the program and how it all worked out."

"No problem, Bud. I'll fly with you and will make plans later to head back to Kissimmee."

"That's better, Chip. Now what about Linda? Does she know what you are up to, and is she part of your plan to run away too?"

Chip made no reply. He dropped his head, turned, and began to walk away.

"I'll advise the show director that the Duck will be in the show this afternoon, and you will be riding right seat."

Bud began to raise his voice as Chip continued to walk away. "I'll have us gassed up and ready to go. I hope you really think more about leaving. I mean that." Bud spun around and walked out to the flight line with his head down, kicking at stones or anything in his path.

Valiant Command Pilots' VIP Tent
March 10
1200 hours

Bud, Sam, Roy, and Bob Simmons (the air boss) were sitting near the entrance of the tent and talking when Chip Reed appeared. They exchanged greetings, and Bud stood up and addressed Chip.

"Chip, Bob here says that he and a few members of the board are willing to give you another shot today as long as I am with you. What do you say?"

"I appreciate the offer, Mr. Simmons, and really grateful. I am sorry about yesterday. As Bud may have told you, I just need more time with my plane and a lot more time to think about my abilities to concentrate on following instructions at air shows," Chip said and broke out into a smile.

"Well, yes, I understand. We just don't want any ill feelings toward our organization as we take great pride in our shows."

"I understand, sir, and I don't have any hard feelings toward anyone. I just want to practice and come back next year if that is okay with you."

"Of course, and you will be welcome, son. Well, I have to get back to work." Simmons stood up and reached out to shake Chip's hand. "Take care of yourself."

Simmons walked toward the back of the tent where a few pilots were chatting over coffee. One of the pilots was Ram Kaisha. Chip thought about going over to talk to him, but Bud's big hand caught him by the arm and told him, "Chip, I would let sleeping dogs lic." Bud's remark was well taken, and Chip turned to Roy and suggested they head to the plane and begin the preflight inspection.

1435 hours

Chip thumbed the radio button. "Space Center ground, this is Army Baker 25 ready to taxi to active runway zero-niner."

"Baker 25 proceed to runway zero-niner and hold."

"Roger, Ground. Zero nine and hold."

Bud moved the throttles slowly and began working the brakes to turn the Duck onto the taxi ramp. He looked at his open window and waved at Dolly standing by the nose of Killer Bee. Bud raised his hands and cupped them around his mouth, yelling to Dolly that he loved her. Sam in Killer Bee waved to Bud, letting him know he was ready to follow him to the active runway for run-ups.

The run-up checks were complete, and Bud and Chip were satisfied the Duck was ready to fly. Bud notified the tower he was ready for takeoff and received permission to precede to the active runway.

"Tower to Army 25, you are clear for takeoff. Climb to 2,500, and proceed to staging area."

The bomb run was perfect. Bud led the formation, and Sam and Killer Bee followed behind. The two bombers made a perfect run, dropping their fake bombs and making dramatic climbs at the end of the runway. The entire crowd cheered as the loudspeaker described the reenactment of the performance as a dedication to the famous Doolittle Tokyo Raid held on April 18, 1942.

CHAPTER 26

Valiant Air Command Air Show
1830 hours

Bud, Roy, and Chip were going over the post flight checks on the Duck, while Dolly, Sara, JD, and Sam were loading up chairs, tables, and boxes of brochures in the aft compartment of Killer Bee.

"We have plenty of fuel for the hop over to Kissimmee, Chip, and the oil levels are all within limits. She is ready to roll, guys," Roy reported to Chip and Bud.

Bud slapped Chip on the shoulder. "Okay, get going. We will be over there with Bee in an hour or so. Harry and Edna want to take a little tour this morning, so I thought I would let Harry sit in the left seat and fly up the coast along the beaches. Got to keep them happy, you know?" Bud said, laughing.

"By the way, Chip, you said you may do some sightseeing over the islands, so pay real attention to the no-fly zones over Merritt Island and Patrick Air Force Base. You may want to contact Patrick as soon as you clear Space Center tower and ask for clearance to do some sightseeing of the NASA complexes."

Chip and Roy got on board, took their seats at the controls, and began their preflight and start-up exercise. With battery power on, they started checking all switches, settings on mixture, throttles, and props. Roy began tuning the two radios and notified Titusville Ground they were getting ready to leave.

After starting the engines and getting ground clearance, Chip began to move the Duck forward when his headset suddenly came alive. It was a controller from the tower on ground frequency asking him to hold. There was another plane that needed to be released at mid runway.

Chip looked over at Roy as he reached for the throttles, pulled them back to idle, and applied the brakes. Taxing down the runway ahead of him was the red spinner and the black nose of the famous Japanese fighter called the Zero. The sleek fighter was painted pure white with a black cowl around the engine. There was a red stripe that ran diagonally from the canopy down past the wing root. On the vertical tail section was a painting of a red sun with striped rays fanning out across the rudder assembly. The big red ball on the fuselage and the paint scheme was common on this Japanese navy type aircraft. Chip could clearly see Ram Kaisha in the cockpit with his fur-lined helmet and goggles pulled tight around his head. He paid no mind to the waiting Mitchell as he entered the runway and took off.

"Army B-25, you are first for takeoff now. Please switch to tower departure 118.9. Have a good flight."

"Roger, ground, switching to tower frequency.

"Army B-25, you are cleared for takeoff."

"Army 25, we are rolling," Chip responded.

Reed released the brakes and advanced the throttles. The Duck began to roll and vibrate as it gained airspeed. Chip watched the Zero making a steep turn eastward into the cloudless sky. He received a call from the tower asking about his flight intentions.

"Space Center Tower, Army 25. I will be heading straight out, turning east over Mims, and heading to the Indian River. Then I'll head south toward Melbourne and west to Kissimmee, my final destination."

"Roger, Army 25. Contact Orlando Control as soon as you reach your cruising altitude. You may want to use Orlando radar following. There is a lot of traffic around this morning. Keep an eye out for a single white red-nosed Zero fighter who left before you. He is out there flying north of Merritt Island and has no reported flight plan."

"Roger, Space Center Tower. Thank you, we will keep an eye out for the single plane in the area of Merritt Island."

"Chip, I see him. He is at eleven o'clock at our altitude about two miles out," Roy reported.

"I got him, Roy. It has to be that fucking Jap," Chip responded. "Roy, I'm going up to four thousand and level off. Check with Space Center Tower, and ask them to approve a right turn to come around to a heading of 270. We will pass over Melbourne and head back toward Titusville, and maybe we best advise Patrick control and contact Orlando Center before we hit Melbourne."

Roy received clearance and instructions from Patrick and frequency changes to contact Orlando control center and request radar following.

"Chip, you know we are pretty light. I only put enough fuel on for the show, about 250 gallons in each tank," Bergy said as he pointed to the fuel gauges. "We can't go looking for bikinis for too long if we are heading for Kissimmee."

The seasonal weather displayed a typical Florida spring morning. Big cumulus clouds were scattered endlessly across Cape Kennedy and the Atlantic seaboard, bottoming out at three thousand feet and climbing to five thousand. Above the clouds the sky was pale blue and the brilliant sun sent blinding sunrays through the yellowed plastic windows above the two pilots.

This was the world Chip Reed always loved. He enjoyed the freedom to take his plane and play in the valleys between the castles separating the giant cotton-like clouds. He loved to climb above them and then push the nose over of his plane, throttle back, and float blindly down until he broke out the bottom. Then he'd throttle up and punch into another cloud and climb until he broke out on top. This was the thrill of flying that he missed after he sold his F-51 Mustang. These maneuvers would not be as entertaining in the Mitchell because of its size and weight, but that would not stop him from trying. But in this air space, he had other plans.

The Duck was level and cruising due west over the Indian River northwest of Cape Canaveral. Chip saw the huge NASA buildings and the famous launch pads. He was looking at all the NASA facilities to the north as he began to bank left to head south. Meanwhile, Roy was scanning south, waiting for Chip to start his turn to change course when the Duck suddenly shuttered and rocked and banked hard to port. Four hands and four feet fought each other at the controls to bring the Duck back to level before Chip could ask what happened.

Appearing directly out in front of the Duck was the Japanese Zero fighter climbing fast into the sun. It had flown under the Duck, speeding ahead while fishtailing back and forth as it climbed into the clouds. Chip and Roy were still on the controls as the Duck bounced in the wake of the fighter's slipstream.

"Jesus, Mary, and Joseph. What the hell is that idiot doing?" Roy cried out.

"I'd say he is trying to make a fucking statement. Where is he?" Chip cried out as he squinted into the sun.

"Chip, I don't see him, but don't change your flight level at this time. He may be back there and coming over the top this time," Roy reported as he turned and looked back out his window.

"I'm going up and get closer to the bottom of those clouds," Chip said as he switched to Patrick's tower.

"Patrick, this is Army B-25, November zero two sierra, and I need clearance to climb to five-five."

"Army Baker 25, you are clear to five-five. What are your intentions at this time? Patrick tower. Over."

"Ah, Patrick, I will be turning north on a new course—295."

"Roger, Army, but be aware that if you get close to leaving our control, you may want to contact Space Center."

"Roger, Patrick. Will do." Chip switched back to the Space Coast Tower frequency.

"Army two-five Space Center Tower, please keep an eye out for two T-6s and a Zero playing tag somewhere north of you."

"Roger, Space Center. We just had a near miss with that Jap Zero. He just buzzed us twice."

"Do you see him, Roy?" Chip asked.

"No, I don't see him on my side. Chip, why not report him and what he is doing to us to Space Center Tower. This asshole is dangerous."

Roy saw the flash first as the Zero flashed by from right to left. He was doing a four-point roll as he cruised by less than fifty yards ahead of the Duck's nose. Chip was frozen on the controls as he watched the Zero climb back into the clouds. He reached for the throttles and prop controls and pushed them forward while pulling back on the controls, picking out a large cloud formation, and heading for it.

Roy keyed in. "Is this smart, Chip? I mean we may not see where he may be coming from next in the clouds. He could be using the clouds to hide, thinking you are still below. This guy is dangerous and some kind of mental case," Roy yelled out.

"He's not a mental case, Roy. I busted him in the chops yesterday remember? He brought no charges, so I guess this is how he is showing me he is going to have the last word up here where he thinks he has me cornered."

"Chip, let's get the hell out of here, back over the mainland where at least we will have witnesses who may see what he is doing. I can't believe that we are not on someone's radar scope right now."

"We should be on Patrick's scopes, but nobody is calling us."

Chip dropped the nose of the Duck and made a rolling right bank as he throttled back.

"Roy, keep your eyes open. We will be coming out of this cloud any second and I will start heading for the deck. Maybe if I outrun him and stay on the deck, we can get to the mainland, and I doubt he will come back again."

"Chip, we have to cross the south end of Merritt Island, and you can't go below thousand feet."

"I know, Roy. Be alert now. We are about to come out of the clouds, so keep your eyes north, I will watch south." Chip took a long look ahead and was a few miles farther south than he'd figured, so he banked right to set up a course to take him back over the southern end of Merritt Island.

"Jesus, there he is, and here he comes again, heading dead on, coming straight at us. Holy mother of mercy."

Chip automatically reached for the throttles and brought them back to slow the Duck's airspeed to two hundred miles per hour. The black dot coming at him was growing larger and closing at the rate of more than four hundred miles an hour. Chip was not going to blink as he figured the Zero would pull out hard to his right and climb expecting Reed to dive to the right, but Chip made up his mind he would not take evasive action.

Kaisha did exactly what Chip expected. He did a high-speed turning bank to his right and climbed, passing very close to the Duck.

Kaisha planned to climb and roll over to his left and then bank and drop down to catch up alongside of the bomber. He made the left bank and rolled over and ended up flying off Chip's starboard wing when he suddenly heard something changed in the sound of the Nakajima Sakae 21's engine. Kaisha immediately rolled away from the Duck, and leveled off, but still remained close by to the Duck. He matched the speed of the Duck and throttled back so he could listen to his engine and check his instruments.

Roy was looking right at Kaisha and noted his head was down. He was paying no attention to Roy or the Mitchell off his wing. Suddenly, the Zero's speed fell off as Kaisha banked away and out of sight from Roy.

Kaisha had throttled up to listened to his engine more closely. He was watching the oil pressure and the cylinder head temperature, which were all normal, but he knew something was wrong as the engine began making pinging sounds followed by loud bangs. He tried to analyze what was going on based on his instruments. He looked ahead and saw the Mitchell was higher and about a mile ahead. He decided he would head for the Space Center Airport at Titusville, and he hoped whatever was going wrong with his plane wasn't serious. All he wanted now was to get closer to Titusville and land. He throttled up and began climbing, and in a few seconds, he was flying past the Mitchell on its starboard side.

Unknown to Kaisha, one of his exhaust valves had broken off and fallen into the cylinder. The piston in the cylinder crushed the valve into pieces, and the cylinder began to disintegrate. In a matter of seconds, the cylinder would explode, destroying the internal workings of the entire engine.

The noise in the engine began to increase, and for the first time, Kaisha became nervous and uncomfortable with the situation. He began thinking he may have to leave his plane while he checked instruments again and noted the oil pressure was stable and there were no signs smoke or fire, so he proceeded to fly alongside the Mitchell. He positioned himself off the Ducks right wingtip for a second, looked over at Roy, waved, and sped ahead. He had no idea Roy was on the radio reporting to Space Center Tower about the colonel buzzing them again.

Chip didn't know that Kaisha had a serious engine problem, so he pulled off his power, dropped back a good distance from the Zero, put his nose down, and increased power. He planned to bank, roll out right, increase speed, and come up on Kaisha's starboard wing to get a close look at him and shoot him a bird, but this was not going to happen.

Kaisha thought Chip Reed was maybe planning to come underneath him and accelerate past putting him in the Mitchell's slipstream, which could toss him around, possibly making him lose control. He had no idea his engine was about to blow up entirely as he went full throttle to pull ahead.

Chip laughed to himself as the Zero moved ahead at great speed, feeling he had spooked the colonel. Suddenly, Chip and Roy saw a white and gray trail of smoke appear from the fighter followed by darker black smoke. Reed thought it was a ploy by Kashia as he prepared for his next move. Chip increased the Duck's speed and began to close the gap between the two planes. He was trying to guess what Kaisha was up to when a yellow and red fireball suddenly enveloped the plane's engine and nose section. The Zero suddenly appeared to jump up and then climbed while spinning around. It looked like a flaming torch surrounded in black and white smoke.

Parts of the Zero started flying off right into the Ducks flight path. Chip took evasive action, banking hard left and diving down to get out of the stream of parts and pieces from the Zero. Chip realized his right wing would be going over and though the path of the Zero's black smoke when a large explosion shook the Duck violently, causing the right wing to flip up, rolling the Duck on its port side. Both Chip and Roy were doing all they could to get the bomber under control.

After a few maddening seconds, the Duck leveled off at two thousand feet heading due south. Chip and Roy both knew something hit the Duck up forward as a rush of cold air blew into the cockpit from the nose area. They both figured they may have damage on the glass nose section. Roy immediately knew the Duck was hurt as the plane's trim went crazy. Chip fought the controls to get the Duck settled down in level flight.

"My God, are we hurt?" Chip asked as sweat began to run down his forehead from his cap and burn his eyes.

"Don't know, Chip. There is a blast of air hitting my legs and something hit my right leg. I have a lot of pain below my knee and it must be bleeding because I feel something running down my leg." Roy looked down and saw a large jagged hole in the skin of the Duck below his right knee. He also started to see blood now appearing through his flight suit around his lower right leg.

"Oddly, it doesn't hurt much, but it may be serious. I am beginning to lose feeling in my right foot. His voice tailed off. "Shit, I got a piece of metal sticking out of my leg, Chip. He reached down and pulled a metal fragment out of his leg and held it in front of him. It was a piece of jagged aluminum about the size of a tablespoon covered in thick blood.

"Jesus, Roy, you have to make sure it did not sever an artery. Take your belt off now and tie it tight above the wound to stop the bleeding. I'm declaring an emergency right now and going to get you down as fast as I can."

Roy took Chip's advice and managed to get to his belt off through his flight suit and then struggled to get it around his leg below the knee. He finally got it on and tightened it as best he could. He reported to Chip it was working as he could see the blood appeared to stop running.

"Space Center Tower, Army 25, we have an emergency. We just had the Jap Zero blow up right in our flight path, and we got hit with parts of that plane. My copilot is hurt and bleeding but conscious and alert. We are not sure how much damage was done to my plane. We are about two miles from the end of Merritt Island at two thousand. Do you copy?"

"Roger, Army B-25. You are cleared to come straight in runway 18. We will have emergency EMTs waiting for you when you land. We have had reports coming in about a plane on fire and crashing into the sea in your area. Did you say it was the Zero?"

"Roger that Space Center. We did not follow it down, but it's at least three to four miles northeast behind me, over."

"Army B-25, there were reports that a chute was seen in the vicinity. Did you see anything?"

"Negative. No chute sighting. It was too far behind us. Wait a minute. Stand by, Tower."

Roy began yelling out to Chip as he leaned his head against his side window.

"Jesus, Chip, we are losing fuel fast." He looked at the fuel gauges and noted a steady drop in the starboard tank gauge. He leaned forward and looked again at the right engine and then back to the engine instruments, which indicated no problem.

"I can't see any wing damage, but I do see fuel escaping from behind the wing, so there must be some damage done to one of the tanks."

Chip's heart skipped a beat as he noticed Roy pointing at the fuel tank gauge. He saw it was dropping fast.

"Army 25, Space Center Tower are you reporting damage to your plane?"

"Roger, Space Center Tower. Evidently, we have a hole in the right wing and are losing fuel fast."

"Roger that, Army B-25. You are clear to land 27 straight in. You will have a slight crosswind from 155. We will have emergency crew standing by. Do you have the field in sight yet?"

"Roger, Space Center. I have the field in sight. I'm about to cross the Indian River now, and I'm dropping to fifteen hundred." Chip pushed the intercom button. "Roy, can you handle the flaps and gear? I will handle the controls."

Roy nodded yes and took out his landing checklist and began going through procedures. He had already switched on the fuel pump. When he reached for the flaps, he noted for the first time the hydraulic pressure gauge was reading most of the pressure was gone.

"Chip, we may have another problem. Something must have hit our hydraulics somewhere. We have lost half the pressure".

Chip looked at his airspeed. It was indicating 160 miles per hour, and he told Roy they were going in and ordered him to set flaps and drop gear.

They both heard and felt the landing gears releasing and breathed easier but only for a second. The right gear was showing a red warning light. Roy turned and looked back out his window, stretching his neck to look at the landing gear under the right engine's nacelle.

"Chip, it looks like a door is hanging open and banging under the wing. I can also see there are parts of the tire flipping around. The gear appears to be down but not sure if it's locked."

"Space Center Tower, we seem to have some damage to our right main gear. I would like to do a fly-by for visual to check on wheel position. We are also indicating we may have a hydraulic problem and may have loss of flaps."

"Stand by, Army. Can you make a flyover and do another pattern? Do you have enough fuel? For your information, Bud West just took off with Sam Jones in a P-51 Mustang and is on his way up to give you a look over. Can you see the silver Mustang taking off on runway 27?"

"Roger. I see the Mustang tower, stand by our fuel report." Chip looked over at Roy, who gave Chip a thumbs-up indicating they could go around again.

"Tower, my copilot says we can do it. I will stay level at two thousand. Tell Bud West I will extend this leg until he can catch up with us," Chip said.

"Chip, Sam, and I are coming up on your port wing, so keep your airspeed at 165, remain at two thousand feet, and stay on course. We are going to fly under you and take a good look at the damage. Whatever you do, don't puke an engine or change altitude or do something dumb like land on us, okay?" Bud said.

"Gotcha, Bud. Give me all good news, will ya, feller?"

The Mustang went back and forth just below the belly of the Mitchell. Bud was sitting in the rear seat behind Sam and taking a good look at the Duck's underside. There were numerous holes in the starboard wing, flap, and aileron. Fuel was still exiting from two locations. The landing gear doors as well as the bomb bay doors had been punctured, and the right outboard gear door was hanging on what appeared to be on a single hinge. The right main gear was down and appeared to be locked, but the bad news was the tire had been shredded by whatever had come though the landing gear door. Plus it appeared hydraulic hoses were flipping around. This was not good news for Chip and Roy.

Bud was trying to come to figure out what he would do in this case. He made up his mind to tell Chip the bad news. There were no options. He explained that he would have to attempt holding the Mitchell's right wing up for as long as he could when landing, carefully dropping the left wing and gear on the runway. He explained to Chip that he would need to bleed off his airspeed before dropping the right wing and gear on the runway. Only then could he drop the Duck's nose to make contact with the nose gear. The Mitchell had a lot of great points, but landing on a blown-out tire was not one of them.

Bud thumbed his microphone button. "Chip, the news is not good. I have no way of making this sound easy. Your right main wheel is shredded, but the nose and left gear are okay. Chip, there's no easy way to get this plane down on a blown tire. She may want to go out of control the minute that right gear hits the runway and maybe not. The bad news is you could end up tearing up a wing and engine ripping off and spinning you out of control. However, if you follow my instructions when the time comes to put the Duck down, I can tell you what to do. Our other option to think about is playing it safe and doing a controlled belly landing in foam or in a grassy pasture. I only hope you have enough fluids left to bring the gear back up if we decide to put her down on her belly."

"Space Center tower, Army two five, can you tell me what our options are now? Can you handle an emergency belly landing?" Bud asked.

"Roger, Bud. We heard you, and we are looking at our options. We want you and Chip Reed to keep in mind that we still have a show going on. We really don't think a possible controlled gear-up landing is going to work here at this field. That said, just to the north of the field, there are plenty of open fields, but I don't know if we could get emergency equipment to you. Plus with all the dry grass, a landing might ignite a grass fire, which we could not control, and again, it would be difficult getting equipment to the crash site. Bud, you have a couple of options but you may pay hell to get permission, I would guess. There is Patrick Air Force Base with one active runway and the space shuttle runway. I feel Patrick with only one active runway would not want any kind of trouble with a crippled bomber if it crashed. I have no idea who to talk to over at NASA to use their shuttle runway."

"Thanks, Space Center. I will talk it over with the Reed crew. Stand by."

"Bud, Roy, and I now understand the Space Center's problem, and we are looking at a possible answer."

"Chip, try to see if you can at least get the mains back up. We will stay with you, but you need to start heading due west away from the air show."

Chip took Bud's advice and added power and turned west away from the air show. He reached down, raised flaps, and retracted the gear. He got the green light on nose wheel and left main landing gear showing they were retracted and locked. The right gear may have not retracted fully.

For the very first time, Chip knew he was really in serious trouble. He knew he could lose his life, his good friend Roy and his plane if he lost control of his plane. Once again, he had to depend on getting the best advice available in order to survive. He radioed Bud West.

"Bud, Roy, and I have been going back and forth on options, and the best one we can come up with is getting back to Kissimmee. We would be closer to your hangar and your team of mechanics and engineers if we do survive. Do you think Kissimmee would consider working with Roy and I landing on a runway or open field? To make things more urgent, I'm looking at Roy's face, and I can tell he is in real pain and he is turning pale. He just told me he is confident he would do all the right things when the time came and asked me to get us back to Kissimmee. Please help me get us down any way you can."

"Chip, Sam and I have been talking maybe it will be best for you to land with gears up. We feel you will have a better chance for survival. Landing on a blown tire is not easy, and even with experienced pilots, it takes all their skills. I will contact Ben Houston, the airport manager at Kissimmee, and see if they are willing to help us. If he says yes, Sam and I are going to help you get to Kissimmee as long as you have enough fuel. Tell me what you fuel situation is now and do you think it's enough to get you there?"

Chip looked over at Roy who was reading the levels and calculating in his head to see if he could find the answer. Is there enough fuel to make Kissimmee?

"Bud, Roy just gave me a nod and said okay and told me we have maybe a hundred gallons plus."

Roy reached down and checked the flaps and the landing gear lights which were still showing right gear unlocked. He suggested that Bud and Sam take a close look at the right landing gear and report its position.

"Bud, right gear is showing red light. Can you get a look at it and let us know if it is all the way up?"

Sam moved his Mustang alongside the Ducks right wing. Bud took a good look at the landing gear and reported it was not all the way up.

"Bud, we are heading for Kissimmee where maybe I can hopefully put her down on one of the runways. If we do run out of gas there are plenty of lakes and swamps between here and there."

There was complete silence from Bud. Suddenly a voice from Space Center came on all headsets. "Chip Reed, all us at Space Center including staff and all the air show pilots and crews are sending you our best wishes and good luck for a safe landing."

Bud thanked the center and advised Chip he just received good news from Ben Houston. Kissimmee had approved bringing the B-25 to the field. He would call as soon as all the plans were decided about preparations and runway information.

"Okay, Chip, here we go. I need you to listen very closely so I can guide you to the airport and directions on routing."

"I understand, Bud, and I'm ready for your commands."

"Chip, keep at two thousand feet, and conserve all the fuel you can. We'll guide you around to the south out of Orlando's traffic control so we don't get involved with their traffic. I will advise them we have an emergency and our intentions are to land at Kissimmee."

Bud continued to instruct Chip to fly his plane and keep cool. "Chip, continue to stay at two thousand feet. I will advise Kissimmee of our plan and work out your approach. They don't have emergency foam equipment and will have to get it from Orlando if there's enough time. We pray when they hear the facts about the condition of your plane, they don't change their mind and we have to look for safe pastures."

"When the time comes, I will help you with the emergency procedures. You both will have to work together on this. For example, you will want to kill both engines just before you flare out and close both firewall values. Place your mixtures to shutoff followed by throttles, magnetos, and battery. Whatever you do, don't feather the props. You want them flat so they bend if they hit. If they are feathered, they will act like knives and dig into the runway or the field, possibly tearing engines and wings off.

"Here's another thing. You will be coming in on final with full flaps and flaring out at around a hundred plus miles per hour, nothing less. At this point, you have to keep your tail down and nose high, but don't stall. When you hit, be prepared for anything that can go wrong. You may go straight or could drop a wing and put you out of control. For now, just fly the plane. I will go over all this again as soon as we get within five miles out and start to line up on the runway they direct us to."

"Roger that, Bud. Roy and I are confident we can make it happen. Just hang in there with us, old buddy. Say, if I break the Duck's back, are you going to get me a new one?" Chip said in a nervous laugh.

"You're not breaking that bird's back ... or yours. Now just stay cool while I talk to all the nervous folks over at Kissimmee. We are going up a few more hundred feet to chat with them. You stay cool and stay on course 270."

CHAPTER 27

Kissimmee Airport
1340 hours

Donald Barker was controlling air traffic at the Kissimmee Airport and first learned of the incoming B-25 from Ben Houston. Houston warned Barker about the condition of the plane and that it may have to land gear up. He suggested they call Orlando and order foam trucks and hope they could get to the field in time. They both discussed the runway best to use for the landing.

Two trucks containing foam that were ordered by Kissimmee were on their way in minutes from the Orlando Airport Fire Department. Barker got a hold of the airport personnel and hangar staff to come to his office to explain the situation.

When the two foam trucks with police escort arrived, they were directed to the runway to be used and told to stand by to start foaming. When ordered, they would put down a path forty feet wide and more than three thousand feet long. It would be up to Chip Reed to put his plane down at the right spot to take advantage of the foam and its ability to control any fire that might occur. Another foam truck with a boom and hose gun was also dispatched from Orlando to spray the aircraft after it came to a halt.

Bud and Sam were flying off the port wing of the Duck and communicating constantly with Chip, asking how Roy was doing. Bud had also been working with Don Barker and received the latest report on field conditions to give to Chip.

"Chip, are you cool? I just got word from Don Barker at Kissimmee. He has the emergency trucks on the way and will be putting down a carpet of foam as soon as they get there. Chip, best install Kissimmee on one of your radios now. It is 124.45, and they will be giving you approach instructions. Do you copy?"

"Roger that. Runway 15, and going to frequency 124.45."

Chip looked out his side window at the brilliant yellow monoplane off his left wing. Sam and Bud had their cockpit covers slid open, and Chip could clearly see the sober expressions on their faces as they studied the crippled bomber. Sam raised his right hand and was pointing ahead as Bud's voice returned over Chip and Roy's headsets.

"There it is, Chip, at eleven o'clock. I've been talking to Orlando and Kissimmee, and everything will be in place in time. You need to slow down the best you can to give them all the time we can. They will have plenty of foam to save you both and the plane. Kissimmee wants you to line up on runway 15. You will have to keep your airspeed at 120 on approach and bleed off to one hundred and then eighty by the time you are ready to flare out. Crab it in if you have to slow down.

"Chip, you will need full flaps before you begin to flare out. Keep right on the centerline, and remember you and Roy will have to pull those shutoff valves together. Remember mixtures to shutoff, throttles up, and mags off as soon as you are ready to touch down. Keep the nose up, and let the tail skid first, but not too high. You just want to drag it a little, okay?"

"Sure, Bud, I typed all that down. No sweat."

Chip could see Bud was smiling and managed to get off a weak salute to his two friends now in the final stage of preparing to land.

"Bud, I will try to get this down in one piece. Besides, I have an old B-25 expert sitting up here next to me, and he will make sure we get down in one piece."

"Roger that, Chip. We are going ahead to take a closer look and will join up again with you on final." Sam and Bud gave another wave as the Mustang increased speed and pulled away from Chip and Roy.

"How are we doing, Roy?" Roy seemed somewhat in a daze but managed a smile.

"Well, Roy, if we were coming back from a raid on Berlin, I would say just peachy. It just pisses me off we were shot down today by a Jap Zero. That bothers me."

Roy responded, "What's worse, it was over Florida in peacetime," Roy said, laughing.

Chip switched his number-two radio to the Kissimmee Tower frequency. "Kissimmee Tower, this is Army B-25, November zero two sierra baker. We're about seven miles northeast starting a straight-in approach for runway 15 if approved."

"Baker 25, we are ready for you. Pattern is clear, and runway is being foamed. We have all our emergency equipment standing by. Winds are calm, eight to ten from 130. Good luck, gentlemen."

"Roy, half flaps," Chip commanded.

Chip felt the nose come up as the flaps extended and could also feel the drop in airspeed, so he increased his throttles, but after glancing at his airspeed at 165 miles per hour, he decided to raise the Duck's nose up again to slow her down. He began to close the distance to the runway, and it was coming fast.

Sam was matching Chip's airspeed flying as close as he could so that Bud could easily see Chip and be able to advise him of the plane's attitude and speed. He constantly told Chip to concentrate on the runway and airspeed.

Chip was doing all he could to concentrate on the seven-thousand-foot runway coming up at him. He was getting nervous now, and he checked his airspeed. It was 130 miles per hour. *Damn*, he thought. *Too fast, I have to slow down.* Once again, he reduced his throttles and raised the Duck's nose.

"Roy, call out the numbers for me." Roy did not respond. Chip could see out the corner of his eye that Roy's left arm was reaching down, meaning he was ready to shut off the all valves. He called out again for Roy to give him the airspeed so that he could concentrate on the approach without taking his eyes from the runway.

The next few seconds felt like everything was going into slow motion. Chip could hear Bud's strong voice over his headset. "Your nose is high. Drop the nose a little, and if you need to, try crabbing to slow yourself down. Go to full flaps now."

Two hands found the flap lever, but only one hand, specifically Roy's, got hold of the lever. Then the flaps began to drop. Chip could feel the slight lift and loss of speed as the flaps went to the full down position. The ground was coming up fast, and just as Chip began to pull the control wheel back, his headset exploded again.

Sam was at a point where he had to move away from the Mitchell and gave Bud the time and chance to relay last-minute instructions to Chip and Roy.

"Chip, you look to be a little too high and fast and very close to touchdown. Get ready to close mixtures and throttles before you hit."

Chip and Roy closed all the valves. Chip's right hand moved to the two mixture controls and ran them into the shutoff position while Roy handled the throttles. Chip reached for the two magneto switches and moved them to off.

A loud voice from Bud filled Chips headset. "You got it, Chip. Drop your tail, and hang on."

Those would be the last words Chip would hear. He pulled back slightly on the controls with both hands and yelled, "Roy, brace yourself." Roy suddenly remembered the overhead escape hatch, reached up, and unlocked it. Put his hands on his control wheel, ready to help Chip in case he might lose control and not drop the tail.

The tail skid hit first, spraying foam before it touched the macadam runway. The impact of the Duck's belly slamming onto the runway was terrifying to Chip. For a moment it seemed like it was going airborne when it bounced, then it hit the runway again and stayed level. However, this time they heard the horrible sounds of screeching metal, which was broadcasted throughout the Duck's hollow hull as it plowed down the runway through the white foam.

For the first time in the past hour and fifteen minutes, Chip lost total control of his aircraft. The impact of the Duck after hitting the runway tossed both pilots forward, causing head and shoulder injuries. The one thing they both forgot was to tighten their harness straps and seatbelts.

Chip hit his head on the shield over the instrument panel and blacked out for a moment. He recovered and took command of his plane the best he could, using his rudder pedals and trying to keep the Duck going straight.

The uncontrolled bomber sped down the foam-covered runway, rattling and shaking as the sound of screeching metal continued. The Duck slid and began twisting side to side while turning to the right and then to the left. Chip was thinking he would run out of foam when the Duck suddenly spun sideways and began to slow down. Then suddenly it was over, the noise stopped and the Duck came to rest. Suddenly, there was nothing but peace and calm, a blessing to Chip's ears. All he could feel was the severe pounding in his temples. He sat for a second, slid open his window, and looked over at Roy, who was leaning forward against the control wheel while blood was running down his cheek. He took hold of Roy's shoulder and shook it gently, but Roy did not respond. He called out again to Roy and tried to move him back against his backrest but was unable to get the leverage he needed, so he released his harness and seat belt. He stretched across Roy and pushed open the escape hatch. Then once again, he tried to wake Roy and noticed the large deep gash across his forehead.

Sam and Bud landed close by and parked the Mustang They got out and ran as fast as they could toward the Duck. They looked on in horror, watching the last throes of the Duck sliding toward them. Bud was praying it would not twist and turn herself all the way around, dipping a wing and skidding off the foamed runway. It was almost certain that if it did leave the runway foam, it would slam into a drainage ditch, which could tear the Duck apart and possibly cause it to burst into a ball of flames.

Bud and Sam stood for a second and watched as the crippled bomber plowed side to side though the foam and then went into a final turn and came to rest with both wings level. It was all over. The Duck sat motionless covered in foam, resting sideways on the runway. Bud took a deep breath, and along with Sam as they he continued running toward the plane.

The emergency responders, firemen, and medics were closing in on the Duck as Bud and Sam passed them on the run. The big green foam truck took position directly in front of the Duck to begin pouring foam on the cockpit and nose. Bud started screaming at the top of his lungs as he reached the crews, ordering them to stop.

"No, not yet not yet. No fire, no fire," Bud shouted as he motioned to one of the small fire trucks to pull up closer to the cockpit. In seconds Bud had climbed onto the truck and then onto the nose of the bomber.

He crawled, slipping and sliding up the nose, and he reached over the windscreen to get to the opened emergency hatch. Suddenly, it popped open, and he seen the hand and arm of Chip Reed coming out followed by his head. He was bleeding but grinning as he looked directly into Buds smiling face.

Bud's first words were, "You made it, buddy. You did good." He then reached down to help pull Chip out of the cockpit. After a short tug-of-war, he managed to pull Chip clear of the hatch. Chip immediately told Bud he knew Roy was hurt bad and not responding. Bud moved Chip down to waiting medics and leaned down through the hatch to examine Roy. He backed out of the cockpit and began yelling to get help as he could see Roy was unconscious with an open wound on the side of his head. Bud tried with all his strength to move Roy but he did not budge.

Two young rescue medics were climbing up a ladder under the cockpit and reached out to Bud and asked him to move away from the hatch to give way for two young rescue medics to have access to Roy. They helped Bud down the ladder. Once down, Bud and Chip stood watching the efforts of the rescue team removing Roy from the plane.

Bud looked at Chip and placed his hands on his soaking wet shoulders. "Hey, you made it, Chip. You were able to save your plane and walk away after a perfect crash landing."

Chip studied Bud's smiling face covered in sweat and with dirty foam stuck to his glasses, his hair, his shirt, his jeans, and his boots.

"Bud, you look like shit."

Chip looked at his plane and could see the medics in and outside the cockpit working on Roy. "Jesus, I hope I did not kill Roy," Chip said as he began to tear up.

"Chip, he hit his head and has a large cut, and that is why he's unconscious, I am sure. He will be just fine when they get him out."

It took nearly ten minutes for the rescue teams to get Roy out of the cockpit. He was unconscious, and it took two very young and strong paramedics to get him out of the plane onto a gurney standing by. His head and face were bloodied and the entire right side of his flight suit covered in blood from the knee down.

Bud overheard one of the paramedics say he could find no pulse. Meanwhile, because he was walking under his own power, Chip was escorted to another ambulance where a medic was taking his vitals while his partner was cleaning a long deep gash over his left eye and nose. Bud sat next to him, still telling him what a great job he did on the landing.

"She's in fine shape, Chip. The Duck will fly again, I promise you, and again, it's all because you did a great job saving her."

"How is Roy doing?" Chip asked.

"Fine and for now don't worry about him. They are taking him over to the hospital. That's where you are going too for a good checkup."

"Bullshit, I want to look over my plane first."

Chip and Bud walked around, inspecting the Duck's damage as ground crews were already at work cleaning off the foam with water with hoses. Bud's crews from his hangar were making plans as to how they would be lifting her up. A huge crane had already been dispatched from Orlando and was on its way.

Bud felt he could comfort Chip with his plans. "We'll pick her up, put the gear down, change that ugly tire, and tow her home. Don't worry. I see no serious damage to be concerned about. Now get your ass back in that ambulance, and go get checked." Bud walked Chip to the open ambulance and helped him get to the waiting medic, who then sat Chip down.

"Chip, Dolly is on her way to the hospital to meet you there. I will stay here and talk to the crew who are taking care of Roy. I will also wait around for that crane to arrive. You just do what they tell you now. I will see you later."

Chip refused to sit back on the gurney, and he asked them not to close the door as he wanted a last look at his plane. After a brief moment, he looked over his shoulder at the medic, shook his head, and passed out, falling into the medic's arms.

The medic turned to his partner and said, "Did I just hear him say he was sorry, old girl?"

Four hours later the Duck was standing on her three legs again. The tire had been changed, and a water truck came out and rinsed the entire aircraft down. There was extensive damage done to the belly and both bomb bay doors were destroyed along with the nose wheel and right main gear doors. A number of frames were badly buckled, and major skin damage was showing stress along the sides of the fuselage.

Bud and Sam saw that both props had stopped in positions that saved the engines, which was the good news; however, Dolly West received bad news when she reached the emergency room at the hospital in the ER they were stitching up Chip's head wounds. She was told by an ER doctor that Roy was dead on arrival. He had died from losing too much blood.

The hospital staff attending to Roy noted that the belt he had wrapped above the wound was not tight enough to stop the bleeding.

It would be much later that Chip would learn of Roy's fate. He had been put into a private room so that they could do more extensive tests on his neck, his nose, and his back, which he was complaining about. Dolly sat beside his bed and tearfully broke the news to him about Roy. A nurse appeared next to his bed, asked Dolly to leave, and gave him a shot, and the visions of his long day faded into a silent, dark world.

CHAPTER 28

Osceola Hospital
Kissimmee, Florida
March 11
0815 hours

Chip woke up to the scent of sweet flowers. The first thing his eyes could focus on was the large bank of lights over his head. He wanted to move his head but couldn't. His hand moved cautiously toward his head, and his fingers touched a metal and cloth frame that surrounded his neck. Then the voice came to him. It was faint at first but kept repeating in a whisper.

"Chip, it's me, Linda."

Chip rolled his eyes and found Linda's smiling face staring down on him. At first, she appeared out of focus, and he tried wiping his eyes. Finally, he was able to see the most beautiful woman he had ever set his eyes on, but she was not the same for some reason. Her hair was not right and covered too much of her face. Her flowing auburn hair was longer and her eyes were dark and sad, even though they were softened by the warm tone of her silky white skin. Her lips parted as she leaned forward while her hand gently stroked his forehead. Then she ran her fingertips through his uncombed hair. She closed her eyes and kissed him lightly on the lips.

"Chip, you do know who I am?"

Reed moved his lips, but nothing came out. He felt as if his mouth was full of cotton as it was so dry. He blinked his eyes and managed to whisper. "Of course I do. Where am I?"

"You are in a hospital, Chip. You were in a crash landing in your plane yesterday. Do you remember?"

He closed his eyes tight and suddenly remembered. His fingers curled into his palms and tighten into throbbing fists. Of course I remember," he said to himself while visions of the crash began to return in his mind.

"What is wrong with me, Linda?" he whispered. "What is this thing around my neck?"

"You're going to be just fine, Chip. You had a serious concussion and possibly damaged some neck muscles. They have you in a neck brace to keep from moving your head. They told me they will be doing CAT scans later to make sure you have no spinal damage in the neck. They had no idea that you had any serious neck problems until you woke up screaming in the middle of the night."

"Did you hear about Roy?" Chip asked.

"Yes, Dolly told me everything when she reached me late last night. I took the first flight I could out of Boston as soon as I convinced the doctors I could make the trip and be back as soon as I could. I landed in Orlando about an hour ago, and Sue came to pick me up and drove me here. She had to get back to Titusville to the air show, but she told me Bud and a fellow named Sam are flying over this morning from the air show to check on you."

"Linda, can you make this bed move and crank me up so I can see you better?"

Linda picked up the control box resting on the bed besides Chip. "Ah, I'd better not. There are too many buttons on this thing, and I'll go and get the nurse."

A few minutes went by. Then a young nurse appeared next to the bed with Linda.

"How are we doing? I'm Pam, your caretaker this morning," she said though a big smile. She reached over and took the control box in her hand, and the back of the bed began to rise slowly. She stopped the movement when she thought he was comfortable. Then she pushed the side bar down and moved a pillow behind Chip's head. Smiling, she turned to Linda and explained how the control box worked.

"If you need me, just hit this button. If he feels uncomfortable, push this one to lower his head, and if he gets fresh, well, do what you have to do to survive." She smiled as she leaned over to look into Chip's eyes.

"Now you behave yourself. I will bring you some breakfast in a few minutes. You are scheduled to go down to x-ray at ten o'clock." She stood up, smiled, patted Chip on his hand, and left the room.

"Well, you can't complain about the scenery and the service around here, old man," Linda said in a warm smile.

She reached over and took Chip's hand and held it tight. "You are going to be just fine, and I'm so sorry about Roy and your plane. But Dolly says that you did a magnificent job getting it down."

"Do you know if they moved it yet?"

"Yes, later in the day from what Dolly told me on the way here. It was somehow jacked up so they could lower the landing gear. Then they towed it on its own wheels to Bud's hangar at the museum. From what she said, it couldn't be in too bad of condition. I'm sure Bud will tell you everything when he arrives."

"Lavoris, oh, my God, Linda, you have to call Lavoris at Bergy's hangar in Lakeland. She has to know about Roy."

"Relax, darling. Dolly covered all those bases last night. Evidently, Roy only has one son who lives somewhere in Wisconsin. His wife, Helen, is taking it very bad and has a sister looking out for her. Now don't you worry about anything right now. Let's just worry about getting you well and out of here as soon as we can, okay?"

Linda tightened her hand around his, leaned over, and kissed him again. "We have a lot to make up and a lot to talk about, but not now. You need your rest, and I have to get back to Boston. I was scheduled for surgery today, but I convinced the doctors I would be back for tomorrow's appointment. Try to get some sleep."

Chip wanted to tell her about his plan to go to Dallas and also how when he arrived at Atlanta, he saw her with another man whom she embraced and kissed. He decided this was not the time and did not want her to think he was spying on her. "Linda, we haven't talked about your accident. I understand you just ran off the road. Is that true?"

"Yes, I totally lost control of the car. It was a horrible experience. The right front tire blew, and the next thing I knew I thought I was flying and rolling around. What made it worse was it was late at night and I was driving too fast and was not on the right road heading to Dallas. If it wasn't for my lights staying on, I would not have been noticed in the deep ditch."

"You were lucky, and you were alone, right?" Chip asked.

"Yes, I was coming back from a conference where I was trying to market our new charter services in Wichita Falls. Richard, my boss, drove up with me but decided to fly to Denver with a friend of his at the conference. It was his car I destroyed, a brand-new Toyota SUV."

Chip closed his eyes, and the only thought he had was the fact that another Japanese car almost took his new love away. He raised his hand and motioned to Linda to call the nurse. His neck was really hurting, and he wanted to get something for pain.

A different nurse appeared and gave Chip a shot in his arm. She looked at Linda and told her he would most likely go to sleep pretty fast for at least two hours.

Linda stood silently by his bed, staring at his tired face. She picked up her purse, reached over, and kissed him on the bandaged forehead. Then she pinned a small envelope on his pillow.

1525 hours

Pam came into the room to give Reed a cup of ice cream she had saved from lunch. She also gave him a shot for his neck pain and two Advil's for his headache. She left the room but not for long. She returned with a rather puzzled look on her face.

"Mr. Reed, there is a little gentleman at the nurse's station who wants to see you, but he wanted your approval first."

"He wants to see me. Who is he?"

"He did not say, but I'll go out and ask. He must have something to do with that air show your friends are in. He is wearing a jacket with all kinds of patches and wings on it. He's kinda cute too. He is Oriental looking with jet-black hair and dark almond-shaped eyes."

Chip sprang straight up and began to roll his legs out of the bed, but Pam threw a body block at him, grabbed him by the shoulders, and pushed him back.

"You can't get up, sir. You could pass out and hurt yourself."

"Pam, you go out and tell that little yellow bastard that he killed my best friend yesterday. You tell him to get his little yellow ass out of here if he knows what good for him. If I could get out of this bed, I would break his fucking neck."

"Mr. Reed, I can't tell him that. Now you just lay down and don't you move, or I will call my supervisor and put you in restraints. I will tell him you are not in any condition for any visitors today. Now you cool your jets, and I mean it."

Within minutes a short, middle-aged, balding man with thick glasses and pockets full of pens arrived. He had a name tag attached to his white coat and held a clipboard with a lot of papers.

"Mr. Reed, I am Dr. Carter. I have a few reports on your lab work. You know we took many blood samples for our lab when you arrived. It's a standard procedure. However, today the lab contacted me and brought to my attention you may have a blood disorder that needs immediate attention. Did you know that?"

"Yes, my doctor in Ft. Lauderdale recently told me I have a problem, but he is working on it. He also told me about a doctor I need to contact in Orlando, some kind of specialist, and I planned to see him soon."

"That's a good idea. You don't want to fool around with this kind of blood disease. Leukemia could lead to serious complications and even death if not treated."

Chip felt a sudden chill run though his body. Now he had a serious new problem to face and deal with. He wondered if it could keep him from flying if he needed some kind of special treatment.

"Thank you, Dr. Carter. I will take care of this as soon as I leave here. Now I understand why my doctor in Lauderdale wanted me to see a specialist in Orlando. Thank you for your concern."

1735 hours

Pam returned to bring Chip's dinner and explained she was going off her shift. He wanted to ask what the little Oriental man had to say to her, but he felt it best the whole incident be forgotten.

Reed's mind was not on the tray of food. He used his fork to toy with the meatloaf and mashed potatoes on the dish. He was hungry and ate the string beans, tasted the soup, ate a slice of bread, and finished off a cup of rice pudding. What he really wanted was a good shot of Scotch, and his wish was almost about to happen.

"Well, hello, Captain Marvel."

Chip turned and looked at the doorway. There she stood as breathtaking as she looked the first day he had seen her. Dressed in a Navy blue suit with blue stockings, spike heels, a matching blue handbag and a large white straw hat pulled down low over her forehead.

"This isn't exactly the Ramada Inn. What happened? Did you refuse to pay your bill?" she said as she posed, leaning against the doorframe.

"I wish I could say you're a sight for sore eyes. You don't happen to have any scotch in that bag, do you?" Chip said.

Lee walked slowly to Chip's bedside. She removed her hat and placed it along with her purse on the foot of his bed. She carefully wheeled the portable serving table away from him, and without saying a word, she leaned over and kissed him hard on the lips. Chip never closed his eyes. He just stared into her smooth, round face as it retreated behind strands of silky soft blonde hair. His nostrils widened as the scent of her welcome perfume put him at ease. When she pulled away, her mouth opened slightly, and her eyes became glassy. She slowly brushed away her hair, which nearly covered her face. Chip suddenly noticed tears were beginning to run down her dark tanned cheeks.

"I'm so sorry about your friend, Roy. He was such a nice man. But I am pleased to see that you are all right."

"What are you doing here?" Chip repeated.

Lee backed away, picked up her purse, and took out a small lace hankie. She wiped her eyes, turned, took hold of a nearby chair, and pulled it up next to Reed's bed.

"I'm here to apologize for one and to pay my respects. Is that all right?"

"Apologize for what? Running away?"

"Yes, you might say that. I could not stay around and do what I wanted to do or act like I wanted to act. My good friends Harry and Edna think I should be wildly in love with my husband, Dr. Strangelove. They adore him and hate me for not forgiving him for screwing his assistant, a little redheaded nurse. I knew if I stayed around, I would have been too obvious about my feelings for you when I am supposed to be grieving about my divorce. They would not have understood."

"What makes you think I would have let that happen? I did not show you any reason to continue to stay for any kind of a relationship."

"You didn't have a chance, remember? I got up and left you. Chip, you made love to me four times in those few hours. It was the kind of lovemaking that women only dream or read about. You did not screw me like I was some kind of a one-night stand. I bet you wished that I were still lying beside you when you woke up, didn't you? Just think. Had I stayed, we could have gone on making love, and you wouldn't have punched out that Japanese fellow. Was that a sign of frustration when you found me gone, or were you just mad that I didn't say good-bye?"

"You take too much for granted, lady, and you couldn't be further from the truth about my feelings or my reasons for punching out the Jap. I admit that I enjoyed our time together. But that ended when you walked out that morning, and it is not coming back, not now. How did you know about the Jap?"

"I have my sources, and judging from your attitude right now, Miss Texas must be back in the picture again. I was under the impression she was on the back burner when we met."

"Well, your impressions suck, and incidentally, you just missed her. She was here a few hours ago when I woke up."

"And she has gone already and flown back home. I already checked on your visitors and told the pretty little nurse out there I was you long-lost sister. From what I hear, Miss Texas is some kind of Amelia Earhart who flies all over the world in corporate jets and a VP of some small charter company."

"What she is and does is no business of yours, Lee. I hate to be rude, but I would like to get some sleep. Take care of yourself. Leave the scotch if you have any in your bag, and go and have a good life."

Lee stood up, smiled, and picked up her hat and purse. She leaned closer and took his hand and moved it against her breasts.

"She can never give you what I can, Chip. Get some sleep. I will be back when you are released and take you to my new Sarasota beach house, which has a great view on the Gulf of Mexico. I can and will help you recover from all your wounds, and I mean all of them."

She bent down low to reveal her breasts, took his hand, and moved it again against her breasts as she pressed her lips hard against his, forcing him to open his lips with her tongue. She stood up, put his hand back across his chest, and walked out without another word.

Reed closed his eyes, his mind totally awash. He even found a laugh working its way up in his chest. "My God, that is some kind of woman," he said to himself. Then he fell off to sleep, and the last thought that crept into his mind was the vision of Lee lying beside him and how much he enjoyed making love to her.

1945 hours

"Hey, Crash, how ya feeling?"

Reed did not have to look up. He knew by the sound of the voice that it was Bud West with Dolly, KC, and Sam.

"Hey, sport, you look pretty good gift-wrapped. What is that growing out of your neck?" KC said, laughing.

"That's his big ass. It came up around his neck when the Duck hit the deck," Bud said while patting Dolly on her backside.

"Bud, what a terrible thing to say," Dolly commented.

"Yeah, but it's the truth," Chip said, laughing.

The visitors were able to get enough chairs around the bedside. Bud presented Chip with some strange-looking flowers he took out of his flight jacket.

"What the hell is this?" Chip asked.

"Don't know. They were growing out of a tube on someone's dinner tray outside in the hallway."

"Seriously, Chip. How are you feeling?" Sam asked.

"With the exception of this damn brace, pretty good."

"Well, your reports look good. No serious damage anywhere. You had a good bang on the head, and to think I was leading you around and checking out the damage of the Duck. Man, you could have dropped dead right there, or so I was told by your doctor this morning."

"Speaking of the plane, how bad is it, Bud?"

"Well, the crew and I gave it a good once-over. I haven't been able to look into it in depth as I have been over at the show all day; however, from what I learned, there is no major structural damage, just a lot of sheet metal and possibly a new set of gear, wheels, and bomb bay doors. If all goes well, we could have you back in the air maybe in six months."

"Well, let's hope it is not that long, and I guess the trip to the Doolittle Reunion next month is out of the question, right?" Chip said sadly.

"Hell, I'll talk to the O'Conner's, and maybe they would like to go meet the Raiders. We will take Killer Bee and Panchito up there. How does that grab you?"

Chip smiled. "Do you think they will invite Lee to go?"

Dolly looked at Bud with a puzzled look.

"I don't think— Well, I don't know. I don't think anyone has heard from her since the other night."

"I heard from her. She was here a few hours ago."

"She did what?" Bud responded.

"She was here dressed like a lotus blossom on a mission from Bloomingdales."

"What about Linda? She was here too, wasn't she?" Dolly asked in a nervous voice.

"Oh, yes, but they didn't meet. Thank God. Linda left early, had to get back to Boston."

"Yes, she told me when I picked her up earlier that she had to get right back. She was scheduled for surgery and put her doctors off a day. What did you think of the scarring on her face? Did she show you? She was wearing that big wig to cover what she could," Dolly explained.

"You know, I thought something was different about Linda, and she did not even attempt to show me any scars. You say she was wearing a wig? That is what made her different. I knew something had changed."

"Chip, what the hell was Lee doing here?" Bud asked

"Came to see how I was and to invite me to get well at her new condo on the West Coast in Sarasota. I believe that's what she said."

There was dead silence as each of Chip's guests tried to search for the next words and who would use them.

"Well, that was nice of her. She did include Linda in that invitation, I would guess," Dolly asked, but Chip did not get a chance to respond. Bud did it for him.

"Hey, we are treading where angels seem to take baths or something like that. That's none of our beeswax, and hey, I just noticed the big hand on my Mickey Mouse watch. We have to get our butts back to the Valiant museum for the big auction tonight. It starts in an hour, and we haven't eaten yet." Bud stood up and leaned over and patted Chip on the shoulder. Then he headed for the door followed by the rest of the team. Dolly came back and kissed Chip on the cheek and whispered that everything was going to be all right, and then she joined the others as they left the room. A few seconds went by before Bud appeared again in the doorway.

"Hey, flyboy, there is going to be an investigation, and you may be in the doghouse big time when they see you are not up to date with your complete physical, and that could cost you your license, but I will get that straightened out, not to worry. Second, you dirty old man, you did get a piece of that jump suit the other night, didn't you?"

Chip laughed. "I gave the FAA my certificate at the pilots' briefing, don't you remember? It was on my clipboard with a copy of my license. Furthermore, my friend, you will never know about the jump suit. So, don't send Dolly around to find out."

Bud smiled. "I will go back and check on your paper work and all the FAA forms when I get back to the show."

Chip lay quietly, thinking about the news on his health problems. He also thought about the loss of his wife and child and now possibly Linda. He thought about his friend and how a Japanese crazy pilot took his life. Now his thoughts went to thinking about his plane and its future, and he began to get ideas to somehow punish the Japanese for taking away his wife and child and Roy. He recalled hitting the Jap colonel who had caused his plane to crash and kill one of his best friends. As he closed his eyes, he saw a vision of flying his plane into the factory in Japan where the Zoto sports car was built. He suddenly sprang up in bed and realized he may have found a way to do it when the time came. His main problem would be able to live long enough with this new threat on his life to plan a trip to Japan. He thought immediately about the Doolittle mission and how they were able to reach Japan and escape to China. What if he could reverse that mission route and fly from China to Japan, find the factory, and destroy it?

Chip's thoughts were interrupted by a nurse who brought him his lunch. She smiled and commented on how bright he looked, and they exchanged smiles. When she left, he immediately went back to planning how to get the Duck to China.

Wayne and Betty Stewart arrived as Chip was having a snack and apologized for not coming sooner. Wayne reminded Chip that he and Betty had to attend a wedding at the naval academy in Annapolis. They had to fly up to Maryland the weekend before the air show as their daughter was a bridesmaid at the wedding of her closest college friend.

"Betty and I went over to the hangar and saw the Duck, and to be truthful, Chip, it was not as bad as I expected," Wayne said as he pulled up a chair for Betty next to the bed.

"Hey, guys, thank you for coming, and Wayne, that is a good report coming from you since you knows planes. I have been lying here, thinking about the Duck's future and mine when we get her back in the blue," Chip said, smiling.

"From what we heard from Bud, you should be out of here in a day or two. We also want to extend our deepest sympathy about Roy not making it after the crash."

Chip lowered his head for a minute and thanked Betty for the kind words. Then he shifted gears to give Wayne something to think about. "Wayne, we spoke about a partnership at one time, and I want to run this by you while it's still fresh in my head. I have not talked to Bud and Dolly about this idea yet.

"I have been thinking that we missed the Doolittle reunion for this coming year for sure, but I may go up with Bud and Killer Bee to the next reunion if the Duck is not ready," Chip continued. "How would you like to come with me on a Doolittle Tokyo Raider tour? We fly the Duck to Hawaii and then to some island hopping on Pacific Islands, tour China and end up in Tokyo. We ship the Duck home and do air shows. What do you think?"

"Well, first, I would say yes for sure, but what is the purpose? That is a long way to go for a vacation, and I just can't imagine what it would take to have parts and pieces we would need to get to Japan eventually."

"That is where you come in with your partnership, my friend. We will need a bunch of bucks to pull this off. Think of it. It would be a kind of flying exhibit to show the people of the Philippines, the Solomon's, and China as a reminder of the little bomber that served from their countries in WWII. I bet the Chinese would do back flips to have a B-25 with the Doolittle numbers on her tail landing in Chung King, Chu-Chow, and

Beijing before heading for Japan. I might be able to even get a Raider to join us for the China leg. We would continue on to Tokyo from China, reversing the route the Doolittle guys took on the raid in 1942."

"I suppose we would have to ship the Duck to the South Pacific to even begin a tour, right?" Wayne asked.

"Wrong, Wayne. We get extra fuel tanks like Doolittle did and fly right from the States to Hawaii, Midway, and Wake, and then to the Solomon's island, hopping up the chain to China. The whole idea is to follow the Doolittle mission and use that historic mission as our base for publicity. We may get lucky because of the trip and get a lot of publicity. Hopefully, some writer from some magazine would go for the story and maybe trigger a sponsor or two."

"I take it there are no women allowed on this venture. Is that right?" Betty asked, laughing.

"Of course, Betty, not as passenger, but you can join us at the romantic places as we move along. You would meet us in Hawaii and then in the Philippines and China and come home with us from Tokyo. I figure it would take us six to eight weeks." Bud smiled and winked at Wayne. "Do we have a deal partner?"

CHAPTER 29

Bud West's Warbird Museum
April 1
0920 hours

Chip stepped out Bud's red pickup truck. He stood for a few seconds as he pulled the zipper up on his windbreaker. A cool breeze was blowing over the ramp under graying skies. Directly in front of him was his pride and joy, the Ruptured Duck. It was the first time he had set eyes on the drab-colored bomber since he'd been pulled out of it nearly a month ago.

"Not as bad as you expected?" Bud asked as he arrived and surprised Chip.

"Worse, Bud. Maybe it's because it looks so helpless up on those jacks."

"Come on. I will give you the nickel tour," Bud said as he took Chip by the arm.

When they got back to Bud's office, Sara was waiting for Chip to give him a few messages and a bunch of mail. She said that a doctor in Orlando and his doctor friend in Lauderdale were calling constantly. And Linda called quite a few times asking where you were.

"Thanks, Sara," Chip took the handful of notes and mail and followed Bud to his office and closed the door.

"Well, you want to be alone and call Linda? I'll go get us some coffee," Bud said.

"No, and you'd better sit down so that I can explain a few things. The day I got out of the hospital, I lied to Lee and told her I was getting out two days later. I took a cab to my RV, picked up some clothes and cash, and took the same cab to Orlando Airport. I flew to Boston and found the hospital where Linda was being treated. When I walked into her room, there was this tall gent bending over her, holding her hand, and kissing her on the lips. Before I could retreat, Linda spotted me and asked me to come in.

"She introduced me to the gentleman as her boss, Richard Mears. He had been with her a few days, going over her health and the business moves he was making. She reached out for me with her arms, and of course, I fell into them. Her boss looked on.

"'Chip, Richard came to tell me I was no longer going to be in marketing. He is giving me a VP position with the company as the company's chief pilot and planning officer. He has just bought another small regional airline in California, and I will be moving to offices in San Francisco or LA. They are still working of the logistics about where it will be best for me to operate from. I will have my own team. Isn't this wonderful?'

"I politely asked Mr. Mears to give Linda and me some privacy. He did leave the room, but he was not very pleased. I asked Linda about what we had talked about just days before in my hospital room, about her coming to join me and building our lives together. All she could say was she was sorry, but she could not say no to this new challenge where she could have access to fly her own plane. He even bought a Gulfstream for her to travel in when needed.

"Of course, I played the total ass and wished her well. I even shook her hand and then turned and walked out of the room. She tried to call me back, but I kept going. When I got near the elevators, Mr. Mears was sitting in a waiting area on his phone. I just waved to him and got on the elevator. I flew back to Orlando and called Lee to come get me."

Bud pushed himself back from his desk and put his boots up on the desk. He folded his arms across his chest and slowly shook his head with a sad face. "So you lost Linda, you think. Then run to Lee's bed and hope all ends well, right?"

"No, that is not right, Bud. Yes, I did lose Linda for sure to her career. I am also sure from the looks of her boss, maybe to him too. He just looks like he has been waiting to possess her, the slick bastard. Lee, on the other hand, well, she is no doubt one of the most exciting and sexiest women I have ever met, but she wants me on a leash."

Sara knocked on the door and brought in two coffee mugs steaming with hot coffee. Then not saying a word, she departed.

"Bud, Wayne and Betty came by when I was in the hospital, and I understand he has been hanging out with you a lot while Betty is still working on her private license. Has Wayne said anything to you about a partnership in the Duck?"

"No, but he has been paying for lots of airtime with me in Killer Bee and with Sam when I am not available. Do you think he wants to buy the Duck?" Bud asked.

"No, just a partnership, and here is why. I have decided that when the Duck is ready, we will fit her out with extra inflatable fuel tanks like Doolittle did for his planes. You know big bladder tanks in the bomb bay. Wayne and I will fly west and take the best route we can to LA or San Francisco and fly then to the Hawaiian Islands for a starter. From there, we will begin to island-hop through the Philippines and the Solomon's. My main goal is to fly to China, land at Chu Chow, where the Raiders were supposed to land to refuel, and then fly on up to Chung King and then on to Hong Kong before I cross the China Sea and head for Tokyo. There is where we will end the tour, and we will make plans to ship the Duck back to the States. Or who knows? We may even donate her to the Chinese in Beijing for an exhibit."

"Jesus, Chip. Have you any idea the type of support you will need to make that kind of tour as you call it? You have two half-tired Wrights on her wings right now, and think about all the parts and pieces you may need like tires and generators and other stuff. You would have to have a support plane just to follow you around!"

Bud was not pleased with the idea and would not be easy to sell, but there was Dolly. Chip knew she was a romantic and loved adventure, and that might be the ticket to Bud's heart.

Chip explained to Bud he would be his coordinator for his support and have things where they belonged if needed, and he had enough contacts in the Pacific where he could make life easier for the crew. Then Chip told Bud about Wayne going to put a million-plus dollars up in the museum's account to cover costs on anything that would be needed. However, this did take the chill off the plans. Plus Bud would now be under a paid contract for his service.

After an hour of more of discussion, studying the world map in Bud's office, they began to put pins and strings on the map showing the best routes for Chip and Wayne to take. This would give Bud time to see what facilities were available on route to ship needed parts to. The three of them again put on their jackets and went out to the hangar to review what the Duck needed.

CHAPTER 30

After an hour of looking over the damage and work in progress, Chip agreed that it could have been a lot worse. Bud was trying to make Chip comfortable, explaining there was some structural damage, but he added that he felt the Duck would be flying again in six to eight months. He motioned for Chip to follow him over to the office as it was getting colder, and a light rain began to fall.

Chip took a seat on the couch in the office and removed a letter from inside his jacket. He opened the envelope and removed a letter and a photograph. He held the photograph up and called out to Dolly standing at the counter. "Hey, want to see what a real pilot looks like?" he said, laughing.

Dolly walked over and took hold of the picture. "My God, is that Linda?" she said, frowning.

"You bet, and is she a thing of beauty or what?" Chip said, smiling.

"She is gorgeous. Where was this taken? That looks like an F-16 behind her."

"It is. She told me months ago she just joined the US Air Force so that she could fly one."

"Oh, really? You are kidding, right?"

"Yeah, just kidding. This photo was taken at an air show down in Texas last year. She flew a charter there with some folks who said their son flew that plane. He is a captain in the Air Force. She borrowed his jumpsuit for the picture."

"I hate to ask, but when are we going to see Linda? She never did say how long she would be in Boston with this latest surgery," Sara said.

"Well, it's a long story, Dolly. She will have a tough schedule when she gets back to Dallas. It looks like they bought a regional airline and are starting another small charter operation out of LA or San Francisco, and her brother Phillip, who is a commercial pilot and a trial lawyer, became a new partner in the company. Her boss has also promoted her to VP, and he is sending her to California to run a new office."

"Wow, now she has family involved in her company, so that is good for her too."

"Yes, I guess so, but he was also part of my nightmare that I lost Linda. What I am about to tell you is a bit embarrassing and only for your ears," Chip said in almost a whisper.

"That day I left the air show with your jeep, I went to the RV, changed, and then went to the airport. I bought a ticket to Ft. Worth/Dallas with a stop in Atlanta. While I was at the gate to leave, the plane had just arrived from Dallas and was unloading its passengers. I noticed a woman who looked like Linda with a man, but I could not see her face too clearly as she had a scarf and hat almost covering it. She was with a tall, good-looking young man. I followed them to another gate, and there she put her arms around him and kissed him. I was able to confirm it was Linda, but she never saw me. She was hiding her scars with that hat and scarf. I learned from Linda recently that the young man turned out to be her brother escorting her to Boston. I was ready to give her up until she arrived at the hospital, called me and explained about her brother."

"Dolly, do you think Larry would like to sell his bird?" Chip asked.

"You are not getting any ideas on adding another bird, are you?" she asked.

"No, I was yanking your chain. I will wait for the Duck to be ready, thank you." He laughed as he returned the photo into the envelope and back into his jacket.

Bud stuck his head through the office door and addressed Chip. "Hey, Chip, you have a visitor outside."

"Who might that be?" Chip asked.

"Guess? It is sitting in a candy-apple red 450 SL with the top down. It has green eyes and very long nails."

"That bitch is here? Oh, my God, I'm sorry. I did not mean ..." Dolly covered her mouth as her eyes widened in embarrassment.

"Dolly, it's not your mother," Bud said, laughing. "It's the bluebird lady."

"Hey, Chip, why not go for a ride with her and throw up all over the front seat."

Chip stood up and looked out the window. Bud was right. There she was in a red Mercedes, talking to Sara.

"What the hell does she want?" Dolly remarked.

"His body silly, what else honey. She is here to collect our patient and make him well again."

"Bud, you forget this man is spoken for, and she needs to be told that."

"Dolly, not to worry, I can handle Lee." Chip said and excused himself.

As Chip approached the Mercedes, Sara spotted him and bid her farewell to the occupant and walked toward him, smiling. As she passed, she whispered, "Careful, Chipper. She has her fangs out."

Chip moved up to the open car and looked down on Lee. She kept her eyes straight ahead, ignoring Reed's presence. He said nothing and just looked down upon what appeared a coiled viper ready to strike. Sara was right. Lee was dressed in a skin-tight yellow jumpsuit in a pattern that resembled a diamondback rattler. The low-cut top left nothing for the imagination, and the cool air was playing havoc with her tanned skin as goose bumps were appearing all over her smooth arms and shoulders. The brief shower left droplets all over the car, and Reed noted that the interior was dry. She probably just put the top down for the effect, and it was working.

"You're going to freeze those things off if you don't cover them up," Chip said in a lighthearted tone.

"What the hell do you care? You don't answer any of my calls."

"Maybe I don't want to. Ever think of that?"

"You really are scared aren't you flyboy. You are too scared to find out what is eating at you down deep, afraid you might learn something about yourself, now is that not the truth?" She took her hand and swept her long blonde hair from around her face and looked straight up into Reed's eyes.

For a moment, Chip could not concentrate on anything but her raw beauty, even when she tried to appear hardened. "Lee, let's go get some coffee so we can talk. Wait here, and for God's sake, put a sweater or a jacket on if you have one. And put that top up. It's not exactly July out here today." Chip spun around and walked back toward the office. Lee reached behind the seat and pulled up a light sweater, never taking her eyes off Chip as we walked away.

"Chip, you should be modeling in those Levi's. Not many men can fill out a pair of those canvas bags as good as you," Lee said loud enough for him to hear.

When Chip arrived in the office, the look on Dolly's face gave warning that Chip needed to handle this with tack and all the innocence he could create. Sara carefully slipped out from behind the desk and said she was going to powder her nose.

"Dolly, I am going to have a cup of coffee with Lee and have a long talk with her. Tell Bud I will be back in an hour or so. Please get that mother Teresa look off your pretty kisser, I will be okay Dolly, I know what I am doing?

Orlando
Interstate 4

"What did Bud say when you told him you were going to Sarasota?" Lee asked.

"You don't want to know, and I don't believe I am doing this," Reed said as he sat tense, watching vehicles rushing backward past his window. "Hey, Mario, can you lean it out? What's the hurry? Did you know that little red cars get more tickets than any other color?"

"Relax, Chip, or would you feel better driving?"

"No, I hate little red sports cars, especially built by foreigners."

"Ouch. I thought this one would impress you. That's why I bought it."

Chip looked over at Lee, who would not return his stare. "Jesus, you are something else, and even if you did, I wouldn't believe you anyway," he said, still staring at her.

Lee reached over with her right hand and placed it on Chip's thigh and then slowly moved down to his crotch, but not for long, he grabbed her hand and placed it on the wooden shift knob on the console.

"Just drive, Lee. Just so there is no misunderstanding, we are spending the night at your condo, but we are coming back tomorrow morning. That's the deal, remember?"

"You bet, and I'll tell you what. If you are that uncomfortable, Chip, you can have the keys to the car when we arrive, and you can leave anytime you want. I have another car, and well, we can work out something to get it back. Is that satisfactory with you?"

Reed did not respond. He noted they just passed US 27. He figured there was at least another hour and a half before this ride from hell would end in Sarasota. His thoughts suddenly went back to his luggage sitting in the rear seat. Lee was watching him in the motor home when he packed, and had to be blind not to note he packed enough clothes to last a long stay somewhere. As he packed he was questioning his real reasons for doing it, and why did he climb into that little red trap to begin with.

Bud West's Warbird Office
April 2

Bill Scott, one of the museum's retired volunteers who once gave tours of the museum, came running into Bud's office. "Where is Bud, Dolly?"

"Out in the hangar, I'd guess. Why, Bill?"

"A sleek Gulfstream executive jet just parked on the ramp, and one of its contents is a very shapely lady heading this way. I think she's the one who visits Mr. Reed once in a while. You know the pilot and the one from Alabama? She is heading this way."

The office door opened and Linda appeared. Dolly stood uncomfortably silent behind her desk as Linda smiled and immediately began to explain her unannounced surprise visit.

"Hello, ladies. I am so sorry for the surprise visit," Linda said, smiling. "I decided enough is enough. Chip and I needed some time together, so I took a short leave and hope I did right. Do you think he will mind?

Dolly looked at Sara and smiled. "I think he will be thrilled, Linda." Dolly smiled and reached out and hugged Linda.

"Dolly, I have to get my gear off the plane and let my crew go. They need the plane back in Dallas. Where is Chip, is he out in the hangar?"

Dolly turned and stared into Sara's long, blank face. She was clearly looking for an answer. She turned and faced Linda, knowing she may not fool her with a lie but could not bring herself to tell her the truth.

"Linda, honey, don't take this wrong, but I don't think this is a good time. Chip is not here and I don't know when he will be back. He has been acting a little down lately and has a lot on his mind. To tell you the truth Linda, I don't think he is gotten over the accident and Roy's death yet. I don't know what to tell you. I wish you had called earlier when he was here."

Linda appeared to be looking right through Dolly. She could see from the look on her face that she was uncomfortable about something and trying hard not to say what was really on her mind; however, Linda chose not to challenge her. She suddenly felt strangely out of place. "I'm really sorry, and you are right, Dolly. I should have called." She put her arms around Dolly, kissed her on the cheek, and thanked her.

"Tell him I was here, will you?" she said softly into Dolly's ear and then released her arms and stepped back. Her eyes began to swell as she forced a weak smile. Then she turned and headed for the door.

"Linda, for what it's worth, I know he loves you very much," Dolly said softly, but Linda never responded. She opened the door and walked out on the ramp, leaving Dolly and Sara nearly in tears.

"You should have told her, Dolly. It's not fair to—"

"It's not my call, Sara. It's not my call."

A gust of cool air and the sensation of cold raindrops touched Linda's face, mixing with the falling tears as she walked slowly toward the awkward-looking bomber suspended on huge jacks beneath its wings. The three landing gears were fully extended, their tires barely touching the hardstand. A number of workers were standing inside the bomb bay, and nearby, a young man dressed in stained white coveralls was pouring gas into the tank of a portable generator. Linda walked up to the nose of the bomber and stood below the colorful cartoon painted on the nose, a Donald Duck character with crossed crutches surrounding its head. Beneath in bold red letters was written "RUPTURED DUCK." She stood, staring at the cartoon when a voice came from behind.

"It sure looks like a ruptured duck, don't it, lady? Hi, my name is Steve, Steve Doster. I'm working on this plane, and I am sort of in training while finishing school." He offered his hand but then realized it was full of grease and put it back into his coveralls.

Linda turned and looked into the youthful face of the lad as he began to start the auxiliary ground generator. Then he stopped and walked closer to Linda and looked up at the cartoon.

"It looks pretty beat up now, but it will be like new in a few months. That's what we do around here, you know? This baby made a belly landing here just a while back, and two guys got out. But one of them died, an old guy. The other guy, the owner, Mr. Reed, got banged up, but he's fine now."

"Did you see the crash, Steve?"

"Oh no, I was in school in Orlando. Mr. West is letting me work on it for experience. You know, just doing odd jobs for the crew. They let me watch how they put the new skin on. Sorry. I mean the aluminum sheets on her ribs. My dream is to get a ride in her when she is all finished. I've been trying to talk to Mr. Reed if that was possible, but I keep missing him. He was here earlier with Mr. West, but he left before I could talk to him. Mr. West told me it may be a few days before he gets back. Man, I wouldn't come back for a year if I was in his shoes."

Linda turned and faced the youth with a confused and puzzled look on her face.

"Why? What do you mean?" she asked.

"Well, I was bringing that generator out from the hangar when this new red Mercedes 450 SL drove up, and behind the wheel there was a drop-dead beautiful blonde lady in a drop-dead pardon the expression outfit. She asked if I knew where she could find Mr. Reed, and I told her he was with Bud West in the office. Just then, Miss Sara came from the office, stopped to talk to her, and returned to the office. A few seconds later, Mr. Reed came out of the office, walked over to the car, and appeared to have a little cool chat with her. I guess he made her put the top up, and I don't blame him. She was not modest about showing her assets if you know what I mean. If she was my girl, I wouldn't let her out in that outfit. Mr. Reed got in, and off they flew. I guess when you own a classic bomber like this one you can afford beautiful blondes and red convertibles."

Suddenly, the young man realized he had talked too much. He apologized and then reached up and slapped the cool metal of the plane below the cartoon. "Yes, sir, one of these days I will be riding in this beauty." He turned and smiled at Linda. "Nice talking with you. I need to get back to work, and you might better get out of this drizzle. From the looks of that sky, we are about to get really soaked."

He was right. By the time Linda reached the cabin door of the Gulfstream, she was soaking wet. She opened the cabin door and stepped in. She gave out orders to the pilot and changed into dry clothes before she took her seat in the cockpit. The backup pilot moved to the cabin and sat down.

"Decided not to stay?" the young pilot besides her asked as he began flipping switches on the console and the overhead panel.

Linda did not respond. She placed her headset on her head and picked up her preflight checklist. The rain began to beat hard now on the jet's thin airframe and obscured her vision to see outside the windshield. She wanted to imagine herself standing in front of the Duck next to Chip the first day she met him and how he told her the story of his dreams. She thought she was part of that dream. Now it was just that—a dream that may have come to an end and one that may have to be forgotten.

She turned to her copilot. "Teddy, let's light them up and get moving. I will handle ground and taxi clearance. Once we are in the air, I will call Orlando Central, check on weather in route, and give them a flight plan."

CHAPTER 31

Reed's Motor home
April 9

Chip read the four-page letter twice and for the second time tried to call Linda in Dallas, but he was given excuses by a young receptionist telling him Linda was in meetings and could not be disturbed. He stepped up to the stove and took the small coffeepot and drained its remains into the badly stained cup. He then walked over to the nearby door and left the RV. He walked over to a nearby folding chair, sat down, and looked across the unusually quiet airport grounds.

Off in the distance, he noticed a Piper Tomahawk flying on the downward leg to the runway. He figured it was probably some new student shooting touch-and-goes, and his thoughts immediately flew back to the days when he was taking his first private lessons in a two-place Cessna tail-dragger at St. Petersburg Albert Whitten Airport. He thought about his instructor, Ed Mears, a 250-pound, six-foot-plus Texan who took up two-thirds of the small cockpit. He laughed when he thought about the day when Ed made him fly straight into a boiling thunderhead over Tampa Bay. Chip thought Mears was nuts, but he did what he was told. As expected, after entering the black cloud, the little plane was tossed around like a leaf. Big Ed took control of the plane just as it fell out of the cloud only fifty feet above Tampa Bay. Mears looked at him and yelled over the noisy engine as the plane strained to gain altitude, "Don't ever fly into one of those fucking things."

Reed found himself laughing out loud at the memory, but it lasted only for the moment. His laugh converted to deep sobbing followed by tears. With his face buried deep in his hands, he cried Linda's name over and over and said, "I'm so sorry. I'm so sorry."

1410 hours

Bud West knocked on the screen door of the motor home and called out for Reed. There was no response. He opened the door and walked into the living room area. There were clothes thrown about on the sofa and chairs. In the small kitchen, dirty dishes, empty boxes of TV dinners, and empty bottles of beer were lined up in the sink. There was a heavy scent of stale beer in the air as he worked his way back through the narrow passage to the master bedroom at the rear of the motor home. He found Chip fully dressed and lying on his back on the bed. As Bud approached, he saw that Chip's eyes were open, and this scared him. He thought he was dead.

"What's up, Bud?"

"Jesus, Chip, you scared the hell out of me. Are you all right?"

"Sure, just lying here, thinking about where I put my .45 Colt."

"Hey, you are kidding, right? That is not funny, my man."

"Not to worry. I haven't got the balls to blow my brains out. That takes nerve," Chip said as he rolled out of the bed and sat up, looking at the bewildered face of Bud West.

"Hey, just got the word, Chip. We've got Killer Bee to take to the Doolittle reunion at Ft. Walton Beach. The O'Conner's can't make it, but they are tickled to let me take their plane to meet the Doolittle Raiders. How about that? We are going, and we can take the crew of our choice. Larry wants to join us with Panchito."

"That's great, Bud, just great. I have all the papers and schedules of the reunion somewhere out on the kitchen table in that mess. There are forms to fill out if we want to go to some of the dinners plus the name of the hotel and who you need to contact about bringing the plane to the local airport."

"Well, I'm looking forward to getting up there and meeting all those guys. You met some of them, haven't you Chip?"

"No, not really, and that's why I want to get there, Bud."

"I don't suppose you can convince Linda to meet us there?" Bud asked.

Chip reached over the bed and opened the blinds to the small window, and stared out. "Not on your life, pal, not on your life. I blew her away like the fool that I am."

"Well, how about Lee? Are you thinking maybe?"

Chip interrupted Bud, "That's also out of the question. Did I tell you about the afternoon I shared with her over in Sarasota after I woke up from a nap?" Chip asked, still staring out the window.

"Ah, no, I don't think so, but you're about to tell me, right Chip?"

"Yeah, I took a nap, and when I got up, Lee was not to be found in the condo. So I got dressed and wandered down to the pool bar, and there she was putting the charm on a young blond stud I recalled her talking to the day we arrived. I think he is the tennis pro there. Anyway, there she was, her hand placed on his brown thigh, thinking nobody could see her action below the table. I saw it and knew the act. That's when I went back to the condo, packed, and told Lee to take me home, but she said to just cool it and she would be back in the condo soon. I found her keys and took her car and came home."

"I think you should give Dolly a bad time letting you take off with Lee, and furthermore, I think you need to get on the horn and beg Linda to come back. But first, you've got to answer me one question about Lee. What was she really like in—"

Chip gave Bud no time to finish his question. "She was everything you would or could imagine in bed. Plus she used the ole Kraft blue cheese trick."

Bud looked at Chip with total desperation on his stone face. That was the look Chip was looking for, the look that always made him laugh. He put his hand on Bud's shoulder and smiled. "Let's find those papers and get started on our trip to Ft. Walton Beach."

"Are you going to tell me about the blue cheese trick?" Bud asked.

"Naw, that is not your kind of thing, Bud. You're too religious." Reed laughed and walked toward the door of the RV, knowing Bud was going nuts trying to figure what he meant by the blue cheese trick.

CHAPTER 32

Bud West's Warbird Museum
Kissimmee Airport
April 13

The next few weeks went fast for Chip Reed and Bud West. The work on the Duck seemed to slow to a crawl, and then there were engine problems on Killer Bee that required a new engine. Finally, the Bee was ready to roll and just in time to make the Doolittle reunion. Bud, Chip, Dolly, and two of Bud's good friends named Bill and Irma Schultz climbed aboard Killer Bee and took off for Ft. Walton Beach. It took only two hours to arrive at the FBO in Destin, just outside Ft. Walton Beach.

Bud and Chip went into the open bomb bay and removed chocks and safety pins, while Dolly placed two aluminum trays below the engines to catch any spills that may leak out. They did this to protect the hardstand, and they wanted to make sure they made themselves welcome guests. After a brief postflight check, they secured the hatches and walked over to a nearby car where a young volunteer was waiting for them to take them to the headquarters hotel for the reunion.

The next few days were filled with hours of activities surrounding the famous Doolittle Raiders. There were twenty-nine of them along with their wives and families present for their annual reunion of their famous raid on Japan. The Doolittle Raiders were present to help raise funds for a local chamber of commerce project. There was plenty of time at the public events for Chip to meet with each Raider, his childhood heroes. His only disappointment was that he would not meet Ted Lawson, who had written the book *Thirty Seconds over Tokyo* and who had flown the famous B-25B, the

Ruptured Duck. This was the plane he named his aircraft after. However, he met with the other members of Lawson's crew—Dean Davenport (copilot), Hank Potter (bombardier), Dave Thatcher (gunner), and Charles McClure (navigator). He enjoyed showing photos of his plane, but he felt uncomfortable explaining his unfortunate crash landing and the death of his best friend.

Chip had the opportunity to sit down with Dave Thatcher, the gunner/engineer on the crew of the Ruptured Duck. He was a tall, rather lanky figure with a smile that lit up any room. They found a small seating area away from the crowds. At first, he was somewhat uneasy asking Thatcher about his experience, especially about the crash that nearly killed them all and the total loss of the plane. Thatcher removed his blazer and sat in one of the armchairs.

"Dave, what I saw in the movie and read all about those final minutes, it appeared strange that Ted Lawson would put his gear down to land on a sandy beach full of rocks and driftwood."

"As you know, I was in the rear of the plane and had no idea what Lawson and Davenport were doing in those last moments. I learned later on from Davenport that he was arguing with Lawson about the putting the gear down, knowing that could cause them to flip in soft sand or in the water, but before anything could be changed, both engines quit at the same time."

"My God, for an experienced pilot, that was not a smart move by Lawson, was it?" Chip asked.

"Well, the strange truth is that Lawson did not want to lose his plane and actually thought he could land on the beach and take off again."

"I hate to ask, but I am sure it was on the mind of the entire crew. You were out of gas. How could he even think he could get fuel and take off again in those conditions?"

Thatcher smiled. "I guess we will never really know, will we?" He reached out to shake Chip's hand. "I really have to get back to the party. We are on a tight schedule as you can imagine. It was really nice talking with you, and I hope you and your Duck get back in the blue soon. Congratulations for saving her after your crash, and here's one piece of advice. If you ever have to land in the sea, do it with your gear up. Maybe someday I will be able to meet you and you're Duck at some air show."

Dave Thatcher stood up and put his blue blazer back on, smiled, and walked off, leaving Chip a very proud man who had been able to meet and chat with a survivor of the original Ruptured Duck.

Chip went on to meet more of the Raiders and was introduced to the Raiders' historian, Colonel C. V. Glines. After spending an hour with him, he bought two books that Glines had written, got them autographed, and went about gathering more autographs from the Raiders, including meeting and being introduced to the General James H. Doolittle himself.

After making the rounds, he told Bud and Dolly he was going to try to get a few Raiders over to see Killer Bee and get some pictures, but Bud put a damper on that idea as they needed to get up and out of local weather coming in.

Unfortunately, Larry Murphy and Panchito ran into heavy weather over Tennessee on his way home and had to divert to Columbia, South Carolina, before he could proceed to Georgetown, Delaware, where he kept his plane.

April 20

The return flight to Kissimmee was comfortable and ahead of schedule. There was plenty of blue sky with few clouds and a healthy tailwind. Killer Bee flew like the champ she was, and Chip was able to be in command at the controls for the entire flight. During the flight he experienced some strange tingling in his hands and his fingertips. At first, he thought it was due to the resting of his elbows on the armrests and changed his position. It would leave and come back, sometimes in one hand but more so in both. He examined his hands a number of times and made sure that he did not alert Bud as to his actions. Then he thought about his head injury. Maybe this was some kind of nerve thing from the accident, so he dismissed the problem and kept the sensation to himself.

When Chip got to his motor home, he immediately went to his answering machine, but the call he was hoping for was not there. However, there were three calls from Gina at his doctor's office. He took a bottle of J&B, a glass, and a few ice cubes and went outside. He sat in his lawn chair and scanned the late afternoon skies for traffic, but there was none. He poured a double and put his head back and closed his eyes. Suddenly, the tingles came back into his hands, and he dropped the glass. He thought his fingers went numb, and they did. He grasped both hands and began to massage them. He knew something was going on and decided to call his doctor friend in Ft. Lauderdale the next morning and tell him about the tingles.

April 21

Chip finally broke down and made the call to Ft. Lauderdale and spoke to his doctor friend.

"Chip, I don't like beating around the bush, and I know you don't. I have the preliminary results back from the lab, and you are possibly in the early stages of leukemia, we think. We are going to have to run more tests on you, my friend. So what is your schedule for the next few days?"

"Richard, you just told me I have leukemia? Is that not a death sentence?"

"No not necessarily, but you will probably need some special treatments. I won't know what they are until we get more tests done. I will talk to my good friend who is a cancer specialist. I gave him your information a while back and they have contacted you before but you would not return calls. He is right there in Orlando, Chip. Here is his number again, so promise me you will call him today."

Chip promised he would call, and hung up the phone. He wondered if he should have mentioned the tingling feelings in his hands and asked if it was related.

Chip began being concerned that his life may be shorter than he planned. He began to have flashbacks on his life, mostly about Linda and the Japanese who were responsible for taking away his wife and son and also more recently, his good friend Roy Bergy, who died because of a dogfight with a Japanese colonel and his Jap Zero fighter.

How can I get even with these yellow bastards? He asked himself. *Somehow I have to make plans now. It could be maybe my time might be getting short. I need a plan to destroy that Zoto factory and its owners in Tokyo. If the Doolittle Raiders can find Tokyo, so can I. I don't need a carrier to get me there either. I have the right plane that can do it. I just have to come up with a well-planned reason to explain to the governments of the United States, China, and Japan why I need to show my plane in China and Japan on a history tour of the Doolittle Raid.*

CHAPTER 33

Warbird Museum
April 26
0930 hours

"Good morning, Sara, and I hope you have some coffee brewing."

"It is in Bud's office, Chip. You have a message from some guy in Waco, Texas. He said something about a big rubber tank you and Bud were looking for. What the hell is that all about?" Sara asked.

"Oh, we are trying to do a Doolittle thing with the Duck. We were looking for a three-hundred-gallon bladder tank, a collapsible type to install in the Duck's bomb bay. It will hold the extra fuel we need for crossing the Pacific. Did you tell Bud he called?"

"No, but here is his number, and remember he is two hours behind us in time, I think." Sara laughed.

Chip ran out to the hangar and located Bud and told him about the Texas call.

"Did he give a price or what kind of shape it is in?" Bud asked.

"I did not talk to him yet, figured we would do that this morning. Sara has his number in Waco."

Bud called the Waco number. "Yes, we understand. When was the last time it was used? I see, and have you ever had it pressure checked since? Okay, here is what we can do. We will pay the $1,200.00 plus the freight, but it has to be leak-proof, or it goes right back. Do we understand each other? Good. I will give you my secretary, Sara, and she will give you the shipping information. We will send you a cashier's check today ... overnight. We need that tank pronto."

"What? Oh, name is Bud West. I own the Warbird Museum in Kissimmee, Florida. Yes, that's me, and I'm happy to know you are familiar with my work, sir. By the way, what is your name? Charlie Bush? Well, that's easy enough to remember. Thank you, Charlie Bush, and let's hope your old bladder is in good shape." Bud hung up the phone, looked at Chip, and laughed.

"Well, you have a new extra tank … if it fits, don't leak, and isn't rotten. It was used in a C-47 for years down in New Mexico for a freight company," Bud commented as he walked back out of the office Mr. Bush sounded like a nice guy. Then he stopped and looked back at Chip.

"Hey, we got lots to do today. We want to get the bird in the air this weekend and shake all the rivets, plus we need to service both engines with oil, set mags, install the new props, and get Wayne out here to start flying with us."

"Bud, I am going to DC next week to visit the Chinese embassy and the Pentagon to get all the info I can on China and copy the charts and maps I will need. Mostly I want to talk to the Chinese authorities about entering their air space and see what we need for documents and clearances there. I would also like to visit the Japanese embassy and talk to them about the same problems with flying through their air space as I will be flying from China eastward to their homeland when the time comes."

"Chip, I still think you are crazy, you know that? And I hope Wayne owns more than the Bank of England. This is not going to be cheap, and looking at the hours you will be putting into the Duck, I would guess you will have two more engine changes before you reach China. Keep in mind my friend, these Wrights you are using are not from the factory. They are rebuilts. Your list of extra parts you need will put your weight right up there, so let's be smart and ship ahead when we can."

Chip said nothing but watched Bud walk slowly off to the hangar. He knew Bud was concerned, but he also knew he would fly to meet him where ever he was in trouble.

CHAPTER 34

Warbird Museum
May 3
0745 hours

Chip slowly climbed up the crew ladder to the Duck and took his place in the left seat. Sam followed close behind and climbed over the console and took the right seat.

"Well, Chip, we are getting ready for the Ducks first flight. Are you nervous?" Sam asked quietly.

"Not really. Where is Bud?" Chip asked.

"Oh, he is doing a last-minute preflight check outside making sure all the tires are round and all the inspection plates are closed," Sam said, laughing.

"Shit, I was supposed to be doing that. Damn. Guess I'm still not up to par yet, and when Bud climbs up here, he will remind me," Chip mumbled.

He was right. When Bud appeared, he stood between Chip and Sam the ordered Chip out of his seat. "I will take the first flight today, Chip. There are things I need to know and you have no fucking experience yet to know about them. It is still my plane until I sign it off to you, okay?"

Chip said nothing as he and worked his way back behind the console where Bud was waiting to change places. It was tight, and they held onto each other passing eachother. Bud got to the seat and handed Sam the check prestart checklist while Chip settled into the jump seat.

After five minutes going over the checklist, Bud was ready and began to start the engines one by one as Sam watched the gauges and set the throttles and mixtures. In less than ten minutes, the nose wheel of the Duck broke the bonds with the earth and the Duck began its minimum climb rate into the early cool blue sky.

For the next hour, Bud put the Duck through some tough paces, making tight banks, feathering both engine, setting up stall speeds while making hard turns, and putting strains on the control surface cables. The only problem they had was when one of the engines cylinder's temperature gauges failed and a loud whistling sound came in from the new plexiglass replacements in the nose section. Satisfied with the test fight, Bud called the tower and asked for landing instructions.

Not a word was spoken by the crew as they stepped off the ladder.

Bud turned to Sam and told him to take her to the hangar and put on the new props. She is as ready as she can be.

Chip was pleased to hear those words, but Bud did not direct any orders to him. Bud walked off toward the office, kicking puddles in his path. "What is with him, Sam? He has not spoken a word to me, and I own this fucking bird."

Sam laughed. "Chip, that's Bud. He is just not happy with you leaving and taking this bird around the world. I guess he feels like it is still his baby and belongs at stateside air shows not touring the Pacific Islands and China."

Sam walked off to the hangar and began yelling for staff to bring the tug and tow bar to move the Duck into the hangar.

Chip went to the office to address Bud on his attitude. Bud was sitting behind his desk with his feet up, reading the local newspaper.

"Hey, when are you going to tell me how the flight went? You never said a word during the tests and ignored me when we landed. What is your problem?" Chip asked.

Bud folded the newspaper and tossed it on the desk. "I have no problems. The Duck has no problems. It's you. You, sir, have a problem. This idea of yours about taking that plane on a tour of the Pacific is nuts. What's the point? No one in the Solomon's or the Marshall Islands wants to see the Duck. China could probably care less, and Japan does not need to be reminded about WWII. I doubt that you will be welcome. All you will be doing is wearing out a great plane, and it will be worthless by the time you reach Japan, if you even make it there."

Chip had no comment. He just stood and studied Bud, and for the first time, he saw a side to this man he never noticed. He showed sincere concern, and he was not supportive of Chip's plan. Chip also knew he could not explain what was really on his mind, namely his plan of destroying the automobile factory, the Duck, and himself.

"Bud, you just gave me an idea. What if I decided not to do the Hawaii thing, pass up on the Solomon's and Marshall Islands, and just ship the Duck directly to Singapore or Hong Kong and save all that time and possible maintenance failures in route?" It would certainly be cheaper, and the time would be spent where I wanted to spend time, specifically China and the cities that were most important to show off the Duck, such as Chou Chow and Chung King, where the Raiders had traveled. "Bud, I have to go to DC to get the clearance from the Chinese and Japanese embassies. They may just kill the entire plan, but I have to try."

Bud smiled and then stood up. He walked over to Chip and put his hand on his shoulder. "Now you are making more sense. I can only hope they both blow you out of the water, but go find out. You best get a hold of Wayne and get him in here and get started on the best way to ship the Duck to wherever you decide to go."

CHAPTER 35

May 15
Washington, DC

Chip and Wayne flew to Washington, DC, to keep their appointments with the Chinese embassy and meetings with the State Department. They were awaiting word from the Japanese embassy and hoped that by the time they were in DC, an appointment would be set up. Chip finally did get the call from a Major Yasui Ping at the Japanese embassy. He said he could get the appointment and to call him when they arrived in DC.

The meetings with Chinese officials went extremely well with total cooperation from General Wo Jung, the military attaché to the United States, who not only liked the idea of having a B-25 touring his country but also agreed to furnish Chip and Wayne all the important documents and visas he would need to be able to clear customs for the plane and the crew. He also recommended using the port at Hong Kong where they would have all the proper lifting equipment to handle the plane.

"I am sure you are aware that the Chinese people look upon your military like the Flying Tigers and the Doolittle fliers as heroes for fighting the Japanese for invading our country," General Woo Jung commented. Then he went to his bookshelf behind his desk and pulled a copy of *The Tokyo Raid* book and showed Chip and Wayne all the Raiders' signatures he had collected.

"I was always impressed with your President Roosevelt and the comment he made to the press when asked where the bombers came from and how he maintained the secrecy of that mission. He simply told them they came from Shangri-La. We also praised him for the total support he provided to our people with food and medical help after the war."

"General Wo Jung, you might say my mission is to return to China and show my plane to your people. I would love to show it to the new generation and explain where the Raiders mission and so they could see a real B-25 like the one used and how it looked back then. Most citizens at the crash sights only saw the wreckage of the planes." Chip reached in his briefcase and pulled out a photo of the Ruptured Duck.

"You might even say, Mr. Reed, you are returning to share the memories of Shangri-la after fifty years later with the remaining Doolittle Raiders. I honor your reasons and plans. Please have someone keep me informed on your travels."

The meetings with Japanese officials revealed that they would have to get clearance from their military leaders and the Ministry of Defense in Japan. The Japanese ambassador, Zha Liyou, could not authorize their request, but he would see that their request was forwarded right away to the official powers in Japan.

While waiting for their flight at Reagan National Airport, Wayne was on his phone with his oldest son, Robert, giving him the orders to find the best shipping company qualified to carry a B-25. They would have to carry the plane intact without dismantling the wings and engines. It was a tall order, but Wayne knew it could be done with the right company. None of his own ships were designed to carry a bomber on an open deck. The biggest problem was deciding what port they would use on the West Coast with a direct route to Hong Kong.

By the time Chip and Wayne landed at Orlando International, the problem was solved by Wayne's son. He found a Japanese shipping company that would be able to handle the B-25 without disassembling the wings, but it did require that they secure many special permits and find a insurance company for coverage.

Robert advised his father that the company had two ships that would leave San Francisco and Seattle twice a month. The estimate for the freight and insurance was nearing a quarter million dollars, given the expenses getting the plane to the closest airport and transporting it to the shipping dock at the port and best way to make the transfer.

Bud West was anxious to hear what Chip and Wayne learned and met them at his office as soon as they arrived. Dolly had set up some finger foods, and Bud had a few beers on ice just in case they were hungry and needed some refreshments.

Chip wasted no time bringing Bud up to speed. "It went well, Bud. We have what we need from the Chinese, and we found a shipping line that can take the Duck in one piece without dismantling, thanks to Wayne's son Robert. What we don't have is the blessings from the Japanese government, but they are working on it. The Chinese general at the Chinese embassy came up with a great line. He said after fifty years, we are finally returning to Shangri-la."

Bud laughed and also commented that it would make good headlines and that the Doolittle Raiders should be advised of the plan. He then went over a few items that still needed attention on the Duck before it flew again. The installation of the bladder fuel tank was a nightmare and continued to leak when under pressure. Most of the problems were rooted in making the connections and feeding tank lines into main tanks through a transfer valve he'd designed.

The next morning when Chip arrived at the office, Sara was waiting for him with a handful of pink slips with phone numbers. Chip went through them fast, looking for calls from a Texas area code, but there were none.

"Chip, this Dr. Webber at the oncology center has called a number of times. He needs you to come to his office for lab work. What is going on, Chip? Do you have a problem we don't know about?"

"Not to worry, Sara. It's just some blood work, no problem, and I will call the doc and set up an appointment. Please don't say anything to Dolly or Bud about this as you know how they get worried over me."

"Chip, Dolly got most of the calls and talked to this Dr. Webber, so you may want to talk to her."

Chip was on his way to Dolly's office when Wayne came flying into the office. "Chip, just got a call from Robert, and he said that if we can make a commitment today, we can get on the freighter called *Silver Moon*. It is leaving out of San Francisco on June 20, almost a month away. We need to find an airport with access to the waterway around San Francisco Bay. The agent also said if we confirm today, we can get complementary cabins all the way to Hong Kong."

"Wayne, I have an idea. Let's get hold of the Commanding Officer at Alameda Air Station and explain our plans. Think about this, a B-25 retuning to Alameda where Doolittle loaded his planes on the Hornet in March of 1942. I think they would jump through hoops. Let's hope we can use the same wharf, so all we need is a barge to get us to the freighter, right?"

"Hell of an idea, Chip. I will have Sara call Alameda and get someone with authority so we can tell our story too and hope they agree. It would be a great event and another new addition to the Raiders' story."

"Damn, Chip. This does not give you guys much time to get your act together," Bud commented.

Wayne looked at Chip and Bud and asked, "how long did they feel it would take to get the Duck ready for San Francisco?"

"Bud, how about it, can we have the Duck ready in time to get her to San Francisco? Wayne, can you find out how long it will take to sail the Duck to China?" Chip asked.

"Don't know, but I will find out. However, at least we are getting her to China in spring hopefully before monsoon season," Wayne commented.

"To answer your question Chip, I think it takes about ten days. These new freighters are fast, and it may be only a week. I will find out the schedule of Silver Moon and get back as soon as I can." Wayne left the office and headed home to advise Betty.

Chip went to his RV and began to gather his papers on the Duck and locate his passport. He then went to the hangar and located Bud, who was inside the number-two wheel well, working on a leaking hydraulic fitting.

Bud came down off the ladder and began to wipe off his hands. He gave Chip a sort of cold look, which Chip was getting use to now. Chip knew Bud was still negative on the idea and did not want to see Chip and the Duck going on this adventure. Chip felt part of it was because he was not invited.

"Bud, Wayne's son has got us lined up for a freighter out of San Francisco to take the Duck intact, and they even offered a couple of staterooms if we decided to go with the plane. That is the good news. The bad news is that the ship has moved up the departing date two days, now scheduled to leave on the eighteenth giving us less than a month to get the Duck ready to go. We need to be on the docks at least by the sixteenth. Our plan now, if the US Navy cooperates, is to land at the NAS at Alamedas wharf. We will have to make plans for a barge and lifting equipment to meet us dockside at Alameda. From there we will head for the freighter and have the Chinese shipping company arrange to have the Duck put on deck. So my next question is this: Can you have the Duck ready in time?"

"I can have it ready, but one thing I thought about was removing that leaking bladder tank out of the bomb bay. Now that you're shipping the Duck, I did not see any need for the extra fuel tank, but I just had second thoughts. Who knows where you will be flying to? And you may need the extra three hundred gallons. Just don't use it unless you have to, okay? And remember it leaks seriously only at the inlet filler access."

"Listen, Chip. I was not at all excited about your plan in the beginning when there were more complications and outrageous expenses you and Wayne were going to face, but you were too excited to think about. Sending the Duck right over to China without all the island-hopping will make a big difference, and now I am supporting you.

"By the way, Dolly told me you had been over to see some specialist doctor the other day. What is going on with you? You did get the medical info you need for the embassies and customs, I hope. You need shots, lots of shots, and I asked Dolly to set up an appointment with you and Wayne tomorrow to get them, so make sure you and Wayne have your med records. You will need."

"There is nothing for you to worry about. I will need to get some kind of treatments when I get back from China. It has something to do with my blood. That's it. I will call Wayne and check with Dolly where to go tomorrow for the shots." Chip laughed and hugged Bud and thanked him for being so supportive.

Later that afternoon Wayne got a call from the Japanese embassy in Washington, advising him that their flight into Japan had been approved. They would need to fill out the proper paperwork and get the official documents they needed before they could leave the airport in China. The Japanese defense administer would advise them on how to enter Japanese airspace and said they would be escorted by a flight of F-15s at some point over the China Sea.

Wayne left Orlando that night for Washington to meet with Japanese officials at the embassy. He had all the Duck's papers along with Chip's ID and health records with him to get them cleared. They said there was no need for Mr. Reed to come as long as all his documents and shot records were presented.

CHAPTER 36

Bud West's Warbird Office
Kissimmee Airport
May 24
0945 hours

Chip received a call from Commander Edward Sherman, the commanding officer at Alameda Air Station. He told Chip he had received an approval from the US Navy Department at the Pentagon for his request to land the B-25 at Alameda. He needed an address to send all the forms with the radio base frequencies and active runway for Chip to use. He also wanted at least a twenty-four-hour notice of his ETA.

Chip was delighted and thanked the Commander. He gave him an estimated time on what he thought would be the day of his arrival, but he said he would send final plans as soon as he could.

Bud's entire workforce was working on the Duck as Wayne, Chip, and Betty were loading the aft compartment with luggage and emergency canned foods they might need, much of which was not found in China. His crew had already completed installing spare parts, generators, starter motors, carburetors, hoses, clamps, and many tools. They tried to think of everything Chip and Wayne might need.

Bud had suggested the flight schedule. They would leave at 0900 from Kissimmee the next day and fly directly to Hobby Field in Houston and then on to Denver. Their last leg would be over the Rockies to Alameda. He figured with no maintenance problems, they should easily make Alameda in three days. He also had made arrangements with the Chinese shipping company to include two Wright 2600 engines Bud had bought.

Chip would take the left seat, and Wayne would take the right seat for the takeoff to Texas. At Houston, they would rest, re-fuel and Bud would take right seat to Denver and left seat to Alameda. Bud was making sure all the systems were working perfectly before the Duck was loaded on the freighter.

Bud chose Chip to land at Hobby Field outside of Houston for a good reason. He knew Linda had offices in the Dallas-Ft. Worth area and felt Chip would be more comfortable not being close to her office so he would not be tempted to pay her a visit. He also felt Chip did not need to deal with any emotional problems that could affect his flying abilities.

The crew agreed on the flight plan, so Bud contacted Orlando Flight service and filed the flight plan.

May 26
0815 hours

The morning air was still as the sun rose into the clear skies in central Florida.

There was plenty of activity at Bud's hangar as the Duck was rolled out in front of a crowd of employees. A fuel truck was standing by to top off all wing tanks while mechanics were inspecting the engines for oil levels and any visual leaks.

Bud, Chip, and Wayne came out of Bud's office dressed in specially designed jumpsuits with logo patches that included a cartoon of the famous Ruptured Duck. Another patch was Bud's war bird logo. They were followed by Dolly, Betty, and Sara. They received a warm welcome by the staff and mechanics all clapping and wishing them a safe flight.

They all took part, walking around the Duck as part of their preflight inspection. Then one by one, they each went up the crew ladder into the plane and took their assigned seats.

The takeoff was perfect as the Duck rose into the sun and banked left to start their first leg to Panama City, Florida. Then would turn westward and fly along the Gulf Coast and to Houston. This first leg was perfect with no mechanical problems, and the weather was clear all the way. It was also a chance to test the auxiliary bladder tank. At Hobby Field, they taxied to an FBO and got a rental car and spent the night at the Ramada Inn near the Johnson Space Center.

At daybreak they were off the ground and flying directly over Dallas on their way to Denver about four hours ahead of schedule. So far, the weather was perfect with spring skies and little winds aloft at nine thousand feet. They would spend some time when they landed at Denver. Bud and Chip had friends there who were restoring B-25s, and Bud was really looking to scrounge parts where he could.

The flight over the Rockies was rough, even at ten thousand feet; however, it was clear, and the view was spectacular. As they approached San Francisco, they called approach control and radar guidance to Alameda Air Station.

The view of San Francisco was like a postcard with large ships moving around and one about to go under the Golden Gate Bridge. It appeared there was some kind of sailboat race going on in the Bay with lots of white sails moving fast and close together.

"Hey, guys, look at two o'clock. There it is the *USS Hornet* parked at Alameda docks. Wow, this was the same sight the Doolittle guys all saw when they arrived. Wow, what a sight." Chip was so excited he nearly lost control of the Duck, but his copilot was on top of things. Bud called out to Chip while laughing, "Chip, I got the plane." He leveled the Duck, dialed in Alameda's control frequency, and called for landing instructions.

The navy officials at Alameda Air Station were more than pleased to have the Duck landing on their runway. Commander Sherman, base CO, was there with a crew to meet them in a jeep and escort them to the wharf where a huge cherry picker was waiting to hook up to the Duck and swing her over to a waiting barge. When the Duck was told to hold and shut down, the crew went through procedures and then exited the plane and met with Commander Sherman and his aides. They shook hands and introduced themselves and thanked him for all he had done, making preparations to move the Duck to the barge. The captain walked them to a waiting car and explained he was taking them to the officers' club to relax and have snacks. He also told them that his well-trained crew would see their plane would be carefully prepared for lifting and that he would have them back in time to watch.

After some enjoyable time with the captain's staff and guests, including a navy veteran named Joey Cook, who served on the Hornet and told them some great stories about the Doolittle airmen and the day of their emergency launch, they were taken for a quick tour of the Hornet and its museum.

When they reached the barge, they saw that the navy crews were still busy securing the Duck and using tarps to cover the engines. Two giant tugs were securing the barge and getting ready to tow it out to the bay and to the docks where the freighter was located.

About an hour went by after the Duck was secured on the barge and the crew watched as the tugboats maneuvered the barge to tow it into the bay. Chip looked at Wayne and Bud and asked Commander Sherman how they could get to the pier where the freighter was located. He told them his staff car would take them over to San Francisco to the docks. They all shook hands and got into the staff car and departed.

When the threesome arrived at the pier where the freighter was tied up, they were greeted by the captain of the Silver Moon, Captain Chen Hsiang. He welcomed them aboard, and Chip turned over all the necessary documents.

They roamed around the ship for the next two hours waiting for the tug and the barge with the Duck on board to arrive. The ship's crew was all excited about having this big twin-engine bomber placed on the foredeck of the huge bow area. Once the Duck was placed down on the deck, the crew immediately began to tie her down under the watchful eye of Bud, who made sure the ropes and chains where all in the right place not to damage the Duck's landing gear, etc. He located the two engine covers in the Ducks rear compartment and helped putting them around the engines. It took two hours to get all the lines in place and inspect everything. Bud gave the ship's crew a thumbs-up on their work.

Wayne was really impressed with the big ship and the tour with Captain Chen. He told the captain he had a small fleet of freighters which served mostly the north Atlantic from Boston, but he had nothing of this size with the comforts the Silver Moon provided, especially the staterooms they offered to anyone who wanted to sail to Hong Kong.

The trio got into a taxi and drove to the San Francisco International Airport. Once they arrived, they sat in a lounge and downed beers and scotch and made their final good-byes to Bud in the crowded cocktail lounge. Bud was booked on an American flight back to Orlando. Wayne and Chip were leaving later that evening on a Delta 747 to Hawaii, and held up getting tickets to Hong Kong at Betty's request.

"Hey, Chip, I did forget to tell you, Betty is on her way to Honolulu from Orlando but changing in Dallas. She will beat us there and will meet us at the airport. She has a special hotel she wants us to stay at and would like to take the tour of the Memorial at the USS *Missouri*. Are you okay with that? It means booking our tickets to Hong Kong, for a couple of days so we can visit Pearl Harbor and Honolulu."

Chip had to laugh, and he picked up his glass and toasted Betty. "Here's to the smart one," he said. "That is a hell of an idea. I would love to spend some time in Honolulu. There is a retired pilot friend of mine who has a condo there and has an in with the US Navy. He has told me if I ever get to Honolulu, he can get me on the admiral's VIP gig and do the tour of Pearl Harbor by water. I will call him when we get in."

"Well, I had better get over to Delta and check on our flight." Wayne said as he got up and headed over to the Delta information counter.

In a few minutes, Wayne returned, laughing. "You are not going to believe this one, Chip. If we stay for three days in Honolulu, we can catch a redeye to Hong Kong and not cost a dime for the upgrade to first class. But we have to leave at four in the morning. Are you okay with that?"

Chip agreed it was a deal, then raised his glass in a another toast. "Here is to those beautiful beaches of Hawaii and those grass skirts, which are probably plastic now." Wayne picked up his glass and clicked Chip's. "Let's go have some fun."

Honolulu International Airport
April 18
Delta Gate 9

Betty was there at the gate, waiting in a colorful Hawaiian wrap complete with flowers in her hair.

"My God, girl, you look like Esther Williams on an MGM pool set," Wayne said and laughed as he dropped his small bag and took her into his arms.

"Well, guys, we have a limo waiting at baggage, and we are off to have brunch on the beach at the famous Outrigger Hotel. Tomorrow after you sober up, we are heading to Ford Island to visit the Pacific Aviation Museum and the USS Missouri. I have all the info and tickets we need and the only bad news is some kind of holiday and traffic and the tours will be in full swing." Betty put her arms around Chip and Wayne and began the long walk to baggage.

Chip excused himself from Betty's tour and spent the next morning working with the Chinese shipping company, which had an office in Honolulu, to get up dates on the Silver Moon and where and when it would be unloading the Duck in Hong Kong. He learned the ship would be going to a pier at Pillar Point, where the Duck would be unloaded and then moved by barge to the Lap Kok Airport (Hong Kong International Airport). There is a fire station at the north end of the field located on a seawall where they could lift the Duck to a hardstand and be towed to a nearby FBO where it would be uncovered and checked out. The freight company, Ku-Man Pacific Ltd, would make all the arrangements for the barge and delivery to the FBO. They were expecting the Silver Moon to arrive in Hong Kong in six to seven days at the docks at Pillar Point.

Chip located Wayne and Betty and told them that they should stay a few days longer. He wanted to leave as soon as he could to set up a hotel and be at the dock at Pillar Point when the Silver Moon arrived. He was not challenged by Betty and Wayne, who surely wanted a second honeymoon, and agreed that he should go ahead. Wayne would arrive a few days later. This would give Chip the time he needed to explore how he could purchase legally some kind of explosives like fireworks.

Warbird Museum
Kissimmee, Florida
April 18

Sara looked up and was nearly knocked off her seat when she saw the stunning, well-tanned face of Lee Williams dressed in a bright yellow sundress.

"Hi, Sara, how are you and the West gang doing? I noticed that the Duck was not in the hangar. Are Bud and Chip flying today?"

"Ah, good to see you too, Lee, and no, Bud and Chip are not flying the Duck locally today. If all went well, the Duck is sitting on a freighter in San Francisco heading for China, and Bud is arriving from San Francisco later today." Lee was speechless for a second and moved over to one of the stuffed chairs and sat down.

"Is this some kind of a joke? I know I may not be popular around here, but telling me stupid tales just to play with me is not funny."

"It is not a joke Lee, Chip, Wayne and the Duck are heading to China."

"Chip is sending his plane to China after all that it has been through?" Lee asked.

"Ah, this is all part of a plan Chips plan and something he decided to do. He always wanted to take the Duck and do a tour in China and end up in Japan eventually."

"Where is Chip now? Is he on the ship?"

"No, he and Wayne are still in San Francisco. Bud will be coming back here. Chip and Wayne are going to China with a couple days layover in Hawaii according to the message I got yesterday from Betty, who flew out to meet them in Honolulu."

"Do you know where they are staying in Hawaii?"

"No, they did not say. But I will be hearing again today from Chip, and I will find out."

Lee stood up, reached in her purse, and presented Sara with a business card with her numbers on it. "Please have Chip call me when he can, or at least you can call and let me know where he is."

Sara just smiled as Lee walked out the door. Then she ran into Bud's office and found Dolly working at her desk.

"You won't believe who just stopped by," Sara said, laughing.

Dolly looked up and set down the pen she was using. "I have a sick feeling it was Miss fancy hot pants Lee, right?"

Lap Kot International Airport
Hong Kong
April 22

Chip was able to rent a car and get directions to Pillar Point, where the Silver Moon would be arriving, where he could meet the shipping company representative. It took almost an hour to challenge the traffic from the airport to the docks at Pillar Point, and when he arrived, only small barges were tied up at the docks. He was able to talk to an English-speaking dockworker who gave him directions to find the freight line office nearby where he could find an official he could talk to about the Silver Moon arrival.

Bill Knight, an Englishman, was the shipping company representative at the small office in a warehouse. Chip was pleased to find someone who not only spoke English but was a sincere gentleman who was fully aware of the cargo coming in on the Silver Moon.

"You know the Moon would not under normal conditions pull into these shallow waters around the Point docks Mr. Reed, but because of your plane's requirements, it was the shortest distance to barge her over to the airport across the least amount of time on the open water."

Chip thanked him as he pushed on to get a date they expected the Silver Moon to arrive. Bill Knight went to a desk and picked up a pile of papers and began to run through them. He looked up at Chip and said, "She should be here in two days. Where are you staying? And if you give me your phone numbers I will call you."

"I have no idea where I am staying right now, but my partner, who is coming in later this week, recommended the Hong Kong Ritz Carlton."

"Well, your friend has good taste. The Ritz is first-class and in the center of everything. Here, I will get you a number to call and the street you need to find, which in itself may take you more than an hour to reach from here." Bill Knight picked up the phone book, and in a few seconds, he had written down the address and phone numbers to call.

"When your plane arrives, you will be met by customs and some people from the local embassy plus lots of press. Beijing has ordered a lot of press coverage on the arrival because of the nature of your famous WWII plane. I hope you have all your papers in order. If not, you may lose your plane until it is legal. These custom folks don't mess around."

"Thank you, Bill. I have all the documents. as does the captain on the Moon. We sent copies of all our plans to Beijing weeks ago. Please call me when you get new information on the arrival." Chip shook Bill's hand, thanked him, and headed out the office to his car.

He was in luck when he got to the reservations counter at the Ritz. There were cancelations, so he booked two rooms for the week with options to extend if he had to. He was told he had received a call from the shipping company's local representative who told him there had been a lady person calling and looking for him. Chip figured that it was either Betty or Sara and that he would make the call back but was told there was no number given for the return call.

Chip put in a call to Sara and Dolly in Florida, but because of the time of the call, there was no answer, just the machine at the office. He immediately called Bud West on his private line. He had to wake Bud up, but Bud did not care. He wanted to know everything. Chip told him the Duck was due in two days and about the complications of getting her off the ship and to a local FBO at the airport. Bud was pleased about the report, and he also advised Chip that Lee stopped by and was looking for him and that Sara had told her that you and the Duck were heading for China.

Chip spent most of the next morning going over the maps of China, the phone contacts he needed to make, and what airports he would be asking the Chinese permission to land at. First on his list would be finding Chuchow, where the Doolittle Raiders originally were supposed to land for fuel after the raid before they flew on to Chung King. Chip felt he would fly from Chuchow to Chung King and head for Shanghai and from Shanghai he would cross the China Sea to Japan. He had to set his flight plan and have it approved by the Chinese Defense Headquarters. He also needed an updated book on airports in China and frequencies he needed. He had been advised that the Chinese and Japanese air defense forces would be escorting him time to time and that he would be given the military frequencies to use for instructions.

Chip was heading down to the main lobby to look for a restaurant for lunch when the phone rang. "Yes, this is Chip Reed, who is calling? Yes, I know who she is, but please tell the party that I have checked out of the hotel. If she insists on asking you questions, please just tell her you have no more information." Chip thanked the hotel operator and hung up.

The small café was more like a coffeehouse with a limited menu. However, Chip was not that hungry and ordered scrambled eggs and coffee. The café was pretty crowded with what appeared as either English or Americans who appeared to be businessmen, not tourists. He was about to pour his second cup of coffee when a familiar voice came from behind. He turned his head and rose out of his chair only to be face to face with Lee Williams. She was smiling and glowing with excitement, and in one move she had her arms surrounding Chip's shoulders. Her bright red lips separated and found his mouth. It was a long and hard kiss that Chip did little to resist. For the moment he was enjoying the scent of her perfume and the warmth of her body next to him.

The next two hours were filled with emotion and passion as they made love in ways he never dreamed of. "My God, you are going to kill me," Chip cried out as he fell back in a spread eagle on his back, looking up at the ceiling. Lee rolled over and joined him, relaxing her long, tan body next to his and putting her lips to his ear and telling him that he would never escape her now.

The rest of the evening was spent roaming the streets of Hong Kong, stopping in small lounges, and having drinks, and if there was music, they would dance for hours. When they returned to the hotel, there were three messages for him, two from Wayne and one from Bill Knight at the dock office.

When they reached the room, Chip took Lee in his arms and began to explain his plans, which could not include her. After his long explanation, Lee pulled him in close and whispered in his ear, "Not to worry lover. I had no intention of staying any longer than today. I have plans to be in Honolulu for a few days and will be flying out this afternoon."

Chip was somewhat disappointed but also relieved as he knew it would be too much of a distraction right now with the Duck arriving and Wayne on his way.

"Lee, you are a beautiful woman, and believe me, I enjoyed every moment with you. Maybe when this tour is over, we can resume our relationship."

Lee kissed him gently on the lips, went over, and picked up all her belongings scattered all over the room. She did not hesitate at the door when she was ready to leave. She looked at him and told him not to get up and left the room.

Chip finally caught up with his calls—at least those to Bill Knight. Wayne was not answering any calls, so it was thought he was on his way.

Bill Knight called to let Chip know that the Silver Moon was going to dock around 1400 hours and the customs agent and a Chinese newspaper man were already hanging around the docks.

Before he left the room, he got another call. It was from Betty. She was totally upset and advised Chip that Wayne may have had a slight stroke and was in a local hospital. The doctors did not advise him to continue on to China. In tears Betty kept apologizing with every other word. She told Chip that as soon as he was released, she was taking Wayne back to Boston to make sure he had the best doctors look at him.

"Betty, what you are doing is the right thing. You tell Wayne to get well and get back home and not to worry about the trip. I will call Bud later today and see if he is still interested in making the tour, so please stop worrying about me and the tour. Just get him home and let me know how he is doing, okay?. You might tell him that the Duck will arrive today and that I will send you a report later after I get the Duck off the ship."

CHAPTER 37

Docks at Pillar Point
Hong Kong
1700 hours

The Silver Moon was snug up against the long dock. Chip, the customs agent, Bill Knight, Wen-Ling Wo, and a gentleman from the Chinese government arrived. A number of newsmen with photographers were marching behind Chip, heading for the ramp where the Silver Moon was preparing to get the Duck ready to be lifted to the barge. Chip could see his plane was right where he last saw it, sitting on the foredeck, still covered with canvas over the engines and cockpit and nose. As the ship's ramp was lowered to the dock and secured, he could see Captain Ho and his first officer, Jack Chen, coming down the ramp both and waving to Chip.

"It was a good crossing, Mr. Reed. We had no problems with your plane at any time."

"I am pleased for that, Captain, and here is our welcome committee— the custom officer, whose name I do not know, Bill Knight from your company, and a gentleman sent by the Chinese government, a Mr. Wen Ling Wu. I believe I got that right. There are also members of the press who want to take pictures of the plane being moved to the barge later."

"No problem. My crew is already preparing for the lift, and I see that we have the crane here and moving toward my ship."

It took about an hour to get the plane untied and another hour to set the lifting rings. There was plenty of confusion about who was in charge of the lift. Chip got a ladder and climbed on top of the wing and rode on the Duck all the way to the ground. He then removed the cockpit cover and the nose cover as crews removed the two engine covers. Soon Chip was doing a walk-around inspection as Captain Ho was dealing with the customs agent, Bill Knight, and all the paperwork. All was in order, and Captain Ho came over to tell Chip all was okay and the plane was now released to his custody. He explained he had to get aboard the Silver Moon immediately as the tide was going out and he was in shallow water to begin with.

Two tugboats arrived, and in less than a half hour, the Silver Moon was moved from the long dock and turned around heading into the channel. Meanwhile, Bill Knight was instructing a crew on another tug to tow a barge up and have it secured. His crew would be lifting it again and setting it down on the barge for its trip to a dock at the Hong Kong International Airport. Once again, the Duck was secured to the deck of another barge. Chip talked to one of the tug crews and got permission to travel with the plane to the airport to be sure the lifting was done with no complications. Bill Knight told Chip he would drive over and meet him at the dock and make arrangements at the nearby FBO to get the Duck over to one of their hangars so a complete inspection could be done.

Hong Kong International Airport
Flight 1FBO

Chip was delighted to have met an American who was the general manager of the FBO, Eric Strong. He was a large and muscular man with brilliant red hair shaved to the skull and a smile a runway long. He took charge immediately, getting the Duck towed into one of the huge hangars. He met with Chip for an hour and went over the plane, and he was able to supply much-needed experienced mechanics to start doing inspections on the engines, flight controls, electrical systems, etc. During their time together, Chip was able to explain his idea on his tour of China and why he was doing it. He had brought six copies of the book *The Tokyo Raid* the Raiders' most read and endorsed book, and a video tape of the movie *Thirty Seconds over Tokyo*. He felt these items would come in handy with people who could help him.

"I am aware of the book and the movie, Chip, and really honored to have your bird here at my hangar. I think what you are doing with touring the plane in the places the Raiders had visited after the raid is a fantastic idea, and I hope the Chinese will appreciate it. I know for a fact that the Doolittle Raiders and the Flying Tigers are their superheroes. Well, some of them are." Eric laughed and put his large arm around Chip's shoulders as they walked toward the Duck.

"I do have a problem, Eric. My second-in-command and partner in this adventure is in Hawaii at a hospital in Honolulu. He may have had a stroke according to his wife who called me earlier, and now I have to send home for a copilot who is the guy who built this plane and taught me how to fly it."

"Mr. Reed, your problem may be solved. We have a company here flying C-54s, DC-3s, and C-46 Commandos. All freight, no passengers. At least they are not supposed to take passengers, but they do all the time. They fly to cities all over China and Taiwan. Their chief pilot is a good friend named Jack Anderson, and he is also American and has plenty of good pilots flying for him with multi-engine experience. Maybe we can shake the tree with my buddy and get you a copilot who could help you. They all know China like the back of their hand. The company is Aero Asia and is based next door. Come. We will walk over and meet Jack Anderson and see what he can do for you."

"Hey, what have I got to lose? It would maybe take weeks to get my friend over here, and having a copilot with experience flying in China would be a plus, especially if he speaks Chinese to the control towers." Chip and Eric both laughed as they walked through the puddles on the ramp from a morning shower toward the Aero Asia hangar, where Chip could see the familiar shapes of DC-3s and a C-54 parked on the ramp.

As soon as Chip entered the office of Aero Asia, he was reminded of Bud West's office. It was full of airplane parts, hanging models, calendars with WWII warplanes on them, and even a full size Bendix prop against a wall. He was introduced to a young man who he learned was half Chinese and half Canadian. He was small and in excellent physical condition, Chip figured he did a lot of working out.

"Hi, my name is Charlie Chea, and I am the world's greatest pilot." He shot out his small muscular arm and opened his hand to shake Chip's.

He had Chip's immediate approval. He liked this little man and felt he had just found his new pilot. Charlie had a great personality and was not shy about his talent.

"I see you something to do with the Mitchell B-25 over at Eric's hangar. That's my favorite of all World War II bombers and most famous in China. I would very much like to have a tour of your plane if you don't mind, sir."

"Charlie, this is Chip Reed, the owner that plane. Mr. Reed is planning on doing a tour on parts of China where the Doolittle Tokyo Raiders were to land and also visit the towns they were escorted through back in 1942."

"I know the story well, Mr. Reed. I once lived in the town near where they were to land and get fuel, but they ran into bad weather and had no idea where they were, so they all crashed all over the countryside."

"Well, Charlie, I am impressed, and maybe Eric here will share a book I just gave him on the Doolittle Raid. But chances are you have it or read it, right?" Chip asked, smiling.

"Oh, you bet, Mr. Reed. I have all the books on the Doolittle Raid at home and many photos of where they stayed. I even went to the hospital where they cut off the leg of one of the Raiders. Can I go over and look at your plane now?"

"Charlie, you have a lot of high time in twins, and Mr. Reed is looking for a copilot for this adventure. Do you think Jack Anderson will let you go for a few weeks?"

"Wow you bet he will, but I will ask him right now while he is putting in the radio in Bonnie the Bitch, our C-46. I will go out and talk to him fast. Maybe you will come with me, Mr. Reed, and meet with Mr. Anderson and explain that you need me?"

"Sure, but first, we need to talk about getting you paid and if you are qualified to fly the Mitchell. It is not as easy as the C-47. It is more like driving a semi. If your boss approves, we will go over to my plane and do some preflight and check you out on systems. When I think you are ready, we will do a wheels-up around the area so you can get used to handling and procedures."

An hour later with permission to take leave of absence for two weeks, Charlie found himself putting on the safety belts and adjusting his seat. He was sitting to the right of Chip going through the cockpit preflight.

He reached over and handed Charlie the checklist and told him to start calling the items out.

Chip had not completely drained the main tanks before shipping, but he was concerned about the new fuel that had been pumped in the wing tanks. Earlier, he had a crew come out and pull the props through to make sure nothing was build up in the bottom cylinders. He thought maybe he should have changed the spark plugs, but he did not want to waste the time now. He was anxious to get the Duck into the air for a test flight.

After completing the run-up procedures and much to Chip's surprise, no spark plugs were causing any serious magneto drops. All systems were go. Now came the fun of taxiing to the active runway. He could easily see he was going to be behind many flights trying to fly out of Hong Kong. When it came his time, Charlie did all the radio work with ground and tower control. The Duck was now called US Army Bomber!

The take ff was standard procedure, and the call for gear retraction and flap positions were textbook. The Duck flew into the afternoon clear sky with ease and grace. She was the center of a lot of attraction from the start when moving around for her takeoff. Air crews and passengers alike were in awe watching this strange olive twin-engine plane with old American WWII white stars in blue background markings on her wings and fuselage taxiing around the field.

Chip was impressed with Charlie and his communications with the tower and control center. He was given permission to fly out of the traffic patterns and fly over the outer islands and around but not over the city of Hong Kong. For the next two hours, Charlie and Chip took turns making banks and turns and setting up a variety of airspeeds to get Charlie used to what the Duck could do and how she would handle on the controls. Again, Chip was really impressed with Charlie's natural touch for a plane he had never flown before. When they landed and got back to the hangar and went through the shutdown procedures, Chip was convinced he had a good man in the right seat. Now he could plan his adventure.

Back at the offices of Aero Asia, Charlie and Jack Anderson brought out all the area maps and began to go over the routes they would recommend to get Chip to the sites he wanted to visit and to put their plane down on a flight plan that would be sent for approval by the Chinese Defense

Department. Of course, they avoided all military bases and chose the fields they could use for refueling or emergencies.

That night, Chip left messages on Bud West's answering machine letting him know the Duck was doing just fine and that he had a new copilot who was half Chinese and who could help him with getting around China's airspace. Plus he was really good on the controls. He also asked Bud to let Wayne know how things were going and to bring him up to speed.

There was also a message for Chip from Sara, who said this doctor in Orlando insisted that he get a shot to help boost his red blood cells. There was a clinic near the American embassy in Hong Kong run by American doctors, and they would have a standing order for the prescription shot; however, it was serious, he needed to get the shot. Sara repeated this three times. She also told him if he was feeling weaker than usual to tell the doctor at the clinic.

Chip had an early breakfast, and then he went to the front desk to get information on the location of the American embassy. It took nearly an hour through traffic, but he finally reached the embassy and had no problem locating the clinic nearby.

"Yes, Mr. Reed, we did receive a prescription from a Dr. Webber in Florida, and if you follow me, I will have you taken care of."

The nurse had a name tag that read "Nellie" on it, and Chip figured she was left over from WWII. She appeared to be an American nurse or Red Cross aide who stayed in China for some reason. She looked older than the famous wall.

"Here we are. Miss Su Ling will take care of you."

Nellie left the small sterile room and Miss Su Ling. She was a very attractive young woman, and started preparing a small vial with a needle in it. She asked Chip what arm he would like the shot in, he told her the left arm and rolled up his sleeve. Without a word spoken, the nurse gave him the small shot, which he hardly felt, and then took a small round bandage and covered the puncture.

"Now if you will follow me to the lab, we also have orders to draw blood today."

"I don't suppose you can tell me what the hell that shot was for, can you? Ma'am, there will be no blood drawn today."

Su Ling just smiled, and in superb English she tried to explain that it was nothing more than a booster shot to help the red cells. She said it was called procure or something like that. However, the doctor wanted the blood work done.

"Miss Su Ling, I'm not going to have blood drawn today, so let's get me out of here, okay?"

She then took him back to the front desk, and he was handed an invoice for $145.00. He wanted to comment on the cost but just handed Nellie his American Express card, which she said she could not use. The Visa card worked.

Bud West's Office
Warbird Museum
Kissimmee, Florida
1000 hours

"Hello, yes, this is Dolly West. Can I help you?" The woman's voice on the other end of the phone was one Dolly had not heard in months.

"Dolly it's Linda, you know that old flame of Chip's?"

"Linda, my God, what a pleasant surprise. How are you, girl?"

"I'm just fine, how are you, Bud and Sara?"

"Oh, we're all the same, still busting our fanny's building planes and having fun with nonpaying customers." Dolly laughed, and Linda joined her.

"Well, Dolly, I have to ask. How is Chip, and how is the Duck doing these days? Is he doing any air shows?"

"Chip is in Hong Kong with the Duck. He arrived there last week. You remember Wayne, his partner? He had a mild stroke while playing honeymoon with Betty in Honolulu. He was supposed to join Chip in Hong Kong, and then they were going to tour China and Japan. Chip had to find another pilot, and according to his reports, he has a Chinese pilot named Charlie who seems to be working out fine. According to a call to Bud yesterday, they are leaving Hong Kong and heading to a few places Chip wanted to visit, including Chung King and Singapore."

"My goodness, is this that idea that Chip had years ago about following the path of the Doolittle Raiders? He used to joke about that, saying he should have been on the original raid ... or wished he had."

"Bud and I have not figured the reasons for this whole trip. Bud tried to talk Chip out of it, but with Wayne's big pocketbook, they decided it would be fun and a great adventure, so off they went."

"When you hear from Chip again, please let me know where he can be reached. I would love to talk to him about a wonderful job position he could have in my new company as an operations manager. This is perfect for Chip, and he can still play with the Duck. We have plenty of hangar space here in Ft. Worth."

"Linda, I will be most happy to pass on that information to Bud. I am sure Chip would love to hear from you. We will call you with the information as soon as we have it. What number can we reach you at?"

Linda gave Dolly all her information, and they said their good-byes. Dolly called Bud at home and gave him the news. Bud explained to Dolly that Lee had shown up in Hong Kong but that he had no idea what she and Chip were planning. Bud laughed. "It seems like Chip is back in the den with two tigers now."

CHAPTER 38

Aero Asia Company
Hong Kong
Jack Anderson's Office
1100 hours

Chip and Charlie where given the approval of their flight plan as far as travel to Chung King, but they would have to reschedule a new plan to reach Singapore or Beijing if it was in their plan. Chip had no plans for Beijing but needed to reach Singapore to make his flight across the China Sea to Japan and realized he may have problems with Chinese and Japan defense authorities.

Chip was also wondering what he could carry on board for explosive that would increase his impact on crashing into the Zoto factory. He knew that buying any kind of bombs was out. He also figured he could fill up all tanks with fuel at some FBO at Tokyo International Airport and locate the Zoto factory only thirty miles north east of Tokyo.

What he had to do was crash into the factory at the right time to minimize the loss of civilians working there, maybe at lunchtime. He did research and learned the plant was pretty much run by automated robots building the current models of the Zoto sports cars. This would mean there were fewer employees, but he learned they did not leave the factory for lunch as the factories had their own cafeterias. The innocent civilians were a concern but not enough to change his mind. He had waited all these years and soon the Zoto factory and hopefully all the owners would be destroyed. This would be their punishment for killing his wife, his son, and his uncle plus all the innocent Chinese they murdered after they helped the Doolittle Raiders escape.

Chip was thinking hard on what and how he could get explosives. Suddenly, he realized who would deal with gunpowder and explosives, and a light bulb lit up and exploded in his head. "Fireworks, that's it, the answer," Chip said to himself. "I can carry up to maybe two tons of fireworks in the bomb bay; however, why would I want them, and how would I tell the Chinese authorities? I could say I was taking them to Japan, but for what reason?" He explained to the Japanese embassy in DC he might decide to maybe leave the Duck in Japan to donate it to the government. They could sell it to a buyer or put in a museum. He figured this may soften the regulations on taking the Duck to Japan to begin with. However, for what reason would he be carrying frireworks?

Aero Asia
Jack Anderson's Office

Chip had scheduled another test flight before he and Charlie left for the first leg of the trip. He met with Charlie at the office, and they walked out on the ramp where the Duck was being fueled and being readied for flight. He also got a call from Bill Knight at the shipping company, two big engines just arrived on the sister ship to Silver Moon from San Francisco. Chip totally forgot that Bud had sent them just in case. He immediately went back to the office and talked to Jack Anderson to see if he would store the two Wright 2600 engines for him until he made arrangements with the shipping company to deliver them to Aero Asia. Jack Anderson agreed and told Chip it was a shame he had no use for the Wrights if they were for sale. They were too many horses for the planes in his service.

Chip caught up with Charlie and continued walking toward the Duck. He looked at Charlie and said, "Charlie, you're a guy who seems to know the movers and shakers around here. Do you have a friends or contacts I could use to buy wholesale fireworks to take with us?"

"Fireworks, you want to carry a load of fireworks in the plane around China's airspace? Mr. Reed, you would be grounded for sure and locked up if the authorities knew this."

"Well, what if we just loaded up the plane at the last stop before I fly out to Japan?"

Charlie laughed. "Japan has plenty of fireworks you can buy over there, Mr. Reed."

"Yes, but not wholesale, and I need a lot of them. It is for a celebration with friends I want to meet me when I reach Tokyo to end my adventure. I would just find some folks over there who can properly shoot them off at my expense and help me celebrate my tour and my reason for a tribute to the Doolittle Tokyo Raid."

"I doubt if you want to talk about celebrating the Doolittle Raid in Japan. That would not sit well with the Japanese. Listen, I do have a friend in Singapore who may help you. His name is Ram Acuchi. Ram is a wheeler and dealer of all kinds of stuff, mostly black market things. I can contact him and see if he has any ideas, okay?" Charlie kept laughing while he walked along with Chip. "Fireworks on your plane for a special Tokyo party? Yeah, right. Mr. Reed, are you on some kind of meds?"

When Chip and Charlie returned after a three-hour flight, they were met by Jack Anderson, who told Chip he had to contact Bud West right away. It was very important. Chip thanked Anderson and told Charlie he would meet him again in the morning to go over the inventory items they would need already on board the Duck. He also told Charlie that he needed to advise the Chinese government and file a flight plan, telling them where they were going tomorrow, traveling to their first destination, Hengyang or Quzhou.

The phone call with Bud West was not pleasant, and it put Chip on the defensive. Bud told him they were really concerned about his health as they had a call from his doctor friend in Ft. Lauderdale and also Dr. Webber in Orlando. They concluded you could have a serious problem operating your plane and not continue on but to make plans to fly home as soon as he could. Bud went on telling Chip he talked to Wayne, who was healthy again and would fly to Hong Kong with Betty and meet with the FBO people and the shipping company they had used to make plans to ship the Duck back home.

Chip did not argue with Bud or challenge his comments. He simply told him he would go ahead and make plans for the Duck to be shipped back home soon. He told him there was no need for Wayne to come to

China. Chip said he could work everything out in Hong Kong and advise him later. Chip hung up the phone and fell across the bed with his head spinning, trying to figure out what to do. Were things more serious than he thought about his health? He thought he was feeling good, just fighting his nerves and emotions on what to do about his plans.

The phone rang again. This time it was Charlie, and he had at least some good news. "Mr. Reed, my friend Ram came through as I figured, and he can help get you the fireworks. But it won't be easy or cheap. He will need an advance and have the fireworks set up for pickup in Shanghai at a customer's warehouse. Of course, this is all being done without the government knowing anything. He himself would go to the warehouse and meet with us to talk about how to package the materials. He needs to know the size of the compartment where you will be storing them on the plane."

"How much in advance does he need?" Chip asked.

"Ram says if you want at least two tons, the total will be around fifteen thousand dollars plus whatever packaging has to be done. I have the bank information where to wire the money."

This call made the difference in Chip's thinking. He was going on with his mission.

"Charlie, call your friend and tell him I will wire more than half the amount today. I will pay him the balance when we meet. I will get you all the measurements and give them to you. Listen, Charlie. We have to move fast. I have to get back to the States earlier than planned. How fast can you and your friend get set up at this warehouse?"

"I will call him right now. He says he already can get about 1,800 pounds and can get more. Should I get more for you?"

"Ah, no, Charlie, that is plenty, I am sure, and remember we have a long trip across the China Sea to Japan. By the way, you have no problem going in and out of Japan, do you?"

"No, sir, I just need to get some paperwork done through the Chinese customs office and check with the Japanese embassy here. Not to worry. I will call Ram right now and set up a delivery place at the International Airport in Shanghai or wherever Ram suggests making the transfer."

"I will meet you at 0700 in the morning, and we will begin heading up to Shanghai with whatever stops I would like to make and pick up fuel if needed. I will leave the flight plan up to you maybe Chung King should be our first stop. So work on the flight plan and notify the Chinese officials."

Bud West's Office
Kissimmee, Florida

"Bud, there is definitely something going on with Chip, and I think you feel the same as I do," Dolly said as she handed him a cup of coffee. "It has been more than a week since we heard anything from him and his plans for the Duck and leaving Hong Kong."

"You know, you're right, Dolly. I talked to Wayne last night, and he told me he did not think Chip had any problems with his health as he never spoke about it."

"Dolly, see if you can get a number on Lee. Maybe we have a number we can reach her at and get her thoughts on Chip's condition. You might think about checking with Linda too. Do you think Linda may know about Chip and these doctor visits?" Bud got up from his chair and headed for the door.

"Sara, see if you can call that clinic that keeps bugging us about finding Chip and see if they will give you any information on what is going on with him, and you'd better let them know he is in China flying his plane. I believe his doctor's name is Webber.

"I'm going over to his trailer and see if I can find any information there—at least the phone numbers for Linda and Lee. I have a key to his trailer somewhere in the hangar, and I will get back to you when I see what I can find."

An hour later Bud had found the key to Chip's mobile home and turned on all the lights and began looking around the galley area, which was a nightmare of papers and odd pieces of clothing thrown about. When he got to his desk, he found a closed business envelope sealed and addressed "To whoever finds this."

At first, he put the envelope back down and started looking for address books. Then he laughed to himself. "What the hell was Chip thinking about leaving an envelope with no name and a strange message to anyone finding the envelope?"

Bud opened the envelope and found two pages of a handwritten letter addressed to no one. He read the letter not once or twice but three times and headed out the door to his office, running all the way.

He flew into his office, yelling for Sara who was standing right in front of him. He was sweating and shaking as he handed the letter to Sara. He could hardly speak and then started swearing at Chip and tossing books and papers on his desk to the floor.

"That crazy son of a bitch is going to kill himself," Bud screamed out.

Sara read the letter twice and handed it to Dolly, who read the letter and burst into tears.

Bud ordered Sara to get Wayne and Betty over as fast as they could. "We have a serious problem for sure. He is going to Japan to find that auto factory who built that sports car that killed his wife and son and going to crash into it. His letter clearly says this was his intention for years to settle the debt with the company that he says ruined his life, and added that a Jap killed Roy as well."

"Oh my God, that might explain why he has been ducking those doctor calls. There is something really wrong with him," Sara said as she picked up the phone and called Wayne, who then told Betty. Betty called back to tell them they were on their way.

The five of them were sitting around Bud's office trying to figure out what to do next. Bud said he would get on the phone to the FBO at Hong Kong International. He was hoping to talk to someone at the FBO that Chip was flying out of. It took nearly two hours before he made contact with a mechanic at Aero Asia. The man said he knew the plane was in good condition as he helped work on it. He also told Wayne that the bomber was fully serviced and left two days ago but had no idea where it was going. Bud hung up and tried checking with Aero Asia management but no response.

Bud called the hotel number Chip had left and learned that Chip had checked out two days ago and left no forwarding information.

"Bud, why not call that FBO again, Aero Asia, and get someone in management who would possibly know more about Chip's plans," Sara suggested.

"You are right, Sara. I should have done that when I had that mechanic on the line. I will call again right now. Damn, I forgot I had a contact there. Chip gave me his name and told me it is the guy who was picking up those spare engines." Bud ran through a stack of papers on his desk.

"I found it. His name is Jack Anderson, the manager of the FBO. I have his direct line."

Aero Asia Office
Hong Kong International Airport
China

"Mr. West, Chip was here with his copilot, Charlie Chea, and left me a check for the engines to pick them up and store them. That was two days ago, and they were in a bit of a hurry. I thought I heard Chip tell Charlie they were cutting the trip short and would be heading for I believe to Chung King or Shanghai, not sure which."

"Mr. Anderson, can you get me the phone numbers of the air controller at Hong Kong International? When Chip and Charlie departed, they must have filed a flight plan or at least told the tower where they were heading?"

Bud was able to talk to an air traffic controller, a man named Wang Wie. He explained the US Army B-25 did take off at 0900 two days ago and filed a flight plan for Shanghai with a stop in Fuzho or Wenzhou, depending on weather. The weather had not been good along the coast for the past week, and nothing had been heard about the plane since. He said that the plane was going to be escorted by the Chinese Air Force fighters while it was in China airspace. He said he had no idea why it was so unless the plane was heading for some military air base and required escorts.

"Thank you." Bud hung up the phone and suggested to Wayne that they call the State Department and see what they could do to help find Chip. He suggested they should also contact the two embassies in DC where they went to get clearances for China and Japan. Wayne said that was a great idea and went to Bud's motor home to search for the information on the two embassies.

Wayne was lucky. He found the business cards of two of the Chinese officials they had met in DC. He called one of them and created a story, which he explained the best he could. He had learned that Chip Reed's plane may have an electrical problem that one of the mechanics hadn't previously reported.

Lt. Colonel Chen Pei told Wayne they received a report two days ago that the US Army B-25 was somewhere in China airspace, and according to air traffic control, it was heading for Shanghai.

He told Wayne he would track down the plane through their defense command and air traffic control at Shanghai International. He questioned Wayne over and over about what was wrong with the plane. Wayne told him it was nothing serious but that the owner, Mr. Charles Reed, needed to contact his home base.

"Shit Wayne, that may not have been a smart move. Maybe we should just be truthful and tell the Chinese that Chip may be very sick and needs to not be flying at all and see that he is grounded when he is located."

Aboard the Ruptured Duck

Charlie had checked with Hong Kong weather service and was told they would be running into rain and thunderstorms moving westward from the East China Sea. Shanghai was reporting partly cloudy, no storms. Charlie was very familiar with southeast China, and he recommended that they land at Nanchang about seven hundred miles due north. They would refuel and rest up, and weather permitting they would leave the next morning for Shanghai, six hundred miles northeast. He had good friends at Nanchang and would like to show off the Duck. Chip recalled that Nanchang was a city the Raiders may have gone through en route to Chungking.

After landing at Nanchang, they spent the night at a local hotel and continued on to Shanghai nearly six hundred miles northeast. When they refueled, they noted the bladder tank was leaking around the filler and managed to get help to drain off some of the fuel. Chip recalled Bud warning him about this filler leak and told Charlie to make a note to be sure they did not exceed 250 gallons refueling at Shanghai.

Chip and Charlie took off at daybreak and ducked a number of serious storms in their path to Shanghai. At times Chip took the Duck down to minimum altitudes to keep visuals on the many small towns in their path. Chip kept thinking these towns probably looked the same as they were when the Doolittle Raiders were in China.

Charlie kept busy on the radios getting weather information from Shanghai Central when he could get through. Chip did all the flying and at no time reached for the autopilot, but now he felt exhaustion setting in after nearly three hours. He would shake and hold his arms and massage his shoulders. Charlie asked a few times to take the controls, but Chip said no.

After many long hours and one stop, they found clear skies, and Shanghai came into view. Charlie called Shanghai Control Center for landing instructions, and in no time they were on final approach to land. As soon as they landed, they received instructions from ground to taxi to the north end of the field to an FBO called Hangar 1.

A reception was waiting to greet them when they reached Hanger 1. A large group of people, including many government officials, the press, and many older Chinese military veterans wanted to celebrate the arrival of the Mitchell B-25.

Chip's original plan was to land at Chuchow Field, where the Raiders were supposed to land on April 18, 1942 but weather prevented the plan. After refueling, the Doolittle planes were to continue on to Chung King and turn their planes over to General Chennault. None of the planes made it to Chuchow.

At Chuchow, city officials and a large group of citizens heard a B-25 was landing at the airport and became excited about the opportunity to see it. Most local elderly Chinese had only seen the wreckage of Doolittle bombers. Chip learned later that the city of ChuChow were told there would be a Doolittle plane visiting the airport, so they prepared a large reception. Chip had to change his plans. ChuChow was surrounded with storms.

Chip and Charlie taxied up to Hangar 1, where a gathering of people stood, including many military uniformed men who were standing at attention. There were also a few well-dressed civilian officials and many members of the press. A man with wands approached the Duck to give Chip directions on where to park.

"Mr. Reed, I just spotted Ram over to your right near that black panel truck. I think he is staying clear of any of the officials waiting to greet you. When we get off the plane, I will run over to see him and make sure he has your package ready."

"Charlie, wait a minute," Chip got out of his seat and unzipped his flight suit. He removed a long flat belt from around his waist and opened it up. He pulled many hundred-dollar bills out of it, then opened his brief case and gave Charlie ten thousand dollars.

"Charlie, you give this money to Ram, which should more than cover the expense of the packaging. If there is any more to be paid, I will send it to his bank later when I get to the hotel."

Charlie nodded his head and put the roll of bills into his pockets.

"We smell like a couple of homeless guys from Hoboken. I hope they understand we have been in this plane for nearly seven hours."

After shutting down the engines and going through the post flight checklist, they talked about any maintenance they would need before leaving for Japan. Chip followed Charlie down the crew ladder, and Charlie immediately ran toward the black van.

Chip was greeted by two Chinese military officers who welcomed him and said they were happy they had made it to Shanghai through all the weather in the south.

"My name is General Zhi Liyou. I am the assistant to the chief of staff of the Chinese Air Force, and this is my aide, Colonel Zhen Lu. We have messages for you from your base in Florida and from a Mr. Anderson at Hong Kong Airport. If you would please follow us to the hangar office, you will be able to meet the visiting city officials and guests who are waiting to see you and visit your plane as soon we finish our business."

Chip did not say a word, just shook hands with the two officers, picked up his flight bag, and followed them past a very excited crowd of people who were yelling and waving their hands in the air. He looked back at the Duck and was pleased to see hangar personnel putting chocks around the main gear and placing uniformed security men around the plane.

The manager of Hangar 1 appeared as they walked toward the hangar office. He reached out to shake Chip's hand. "Hello, Mr. Reed. Welcome to Shanghai and Hangar 1. My name is Tim Tao, and I am the manager here. We will take good care of your plane, and if you need any maintenance completed, we have a number of experienced mechanics who can do whatever is needed. I believe you carry your own tow bar, tools, and spare parts?"

"Yes on both counts, Mr. Tao, and my copilot, Charlie, will help take what is needed from the plane. I would like to change all the spark plugs on both engines and change oil filters, all of which are on board. That is about all that needs to be done right now."

The Chinese General took Chip into a private room in the lounge and began to question him from a long sheet of forms and papers he had in his hand. "We were requested to have your plane grounded, Mr. Reed, because of a possible mechanical problem. This came from your co-owner of the plane in Florida. He also mentioned you may have a serious health problem, and they are concerned."

"That is true, General. I had a little health problem with my blood. It seems like I am not getting enough red blood cells and lack of iron running around my veins, but that was taken care at a clinic in Hong Kong. All I needed was a shot, and it was provided at the clinic just before I left Hong Kong. I'd be happy to show you the invoice as proof if needed. It was quite expensive.

"I am not surprised, sir, that my friends at home are somewhat concerned for me. This is my first trip to China. That's all. I will call them in the United States and get this cleared up for you today. As for the mechanical problem, it is an old backup VHF radio and I had a fuel pump acting up but it was changed in Hong Kong. I have the maintenance log in the plane and can show you the plane is airworthy."

"Okay, Mr. Reed, that explains the concerns and it was not a serious mechanical problem and taken care of. As to your health problem, you say it is under control, and that is enough for me. I already checked with Hong Kong customs, immigration, and Beijing. It appears all your papers for you and your plane are in order, and you say you are healthy to fly. This is all we need to know. Here is my card, and if you need anything, please feel free to call. By the way, what you think of my English?"

"Perfect, sir, I just wish I could understand my copilot as well." Chip laughed, and the two Chinese officers tried hard to smile and agree. They had no idea Chip was kidding them.

FBO Hangar One
Hangar 14

The Duck was carefully towed into hangar 14 where the mechanics began to set up makeshift work stands around the engines. The crew provided for the work on the Duck was very professional. Chip stood guard over the removal of the cowling and did a thorough inspection of all cylinders, pushrod housing seals, any oil leaks, and all connections, including electrical and exhaust.

Charlie showed up with a worker in the black van, and he quickly acquired a forklift to help move the wood and cardboard box from the van and place it on a pallet. He found Chip and took him over to inspect the crate.

Ram introduced himself and pointed out that his crew had done a professional job on packaging the fireworks. "As you can see, we also labeled the box 'aircraft parts' in English and Chinese. We estimate the weight to be around 1,700 pounds with the crate. You can see it will easily fit up into the bomb bay with plenty of room to spare. We decided we can suspend the crate on ropes like a hammock and attach the ropes to the bomb release brackets so it can float without damaging the frames. Charlie gave me a book on the Mitchell bomber a while ago and I studied the prints on the bomb loading devices and figured out how to secure the crate."

"Ram, do you have an invoice?" Ram shook his head and handed Chip a piece of paper written in English. It said good luck and requested another thousand dollars in cash for Charlie.

Chip smiled at Charlie, took his belt off, and gave him ten hundred-dollar bills. He thanked Charlie and told him he was a piece of work. He also asked Charlie to get some help to rig the crate in the bomb bay and install the crate suspended with ropes as suggested by Ram.

Chip was able to find Tim Tao and explain he had a crate of parts that was shipped to him and needed help to have it installed in the plane. He also told Tim Tao how to suspend the crate for safety reasons.

Chip had the plane's fuel tanks topped off and explained how to get to the extra fuel tank in the bomb bay and told them it would take three hundred gallons but to only put 250 gallons in it. He then went to the office and paid the woman with plenty of cash for fuel and all the maintenance performed. He and Charlie waited until the Duck was secured in the huge hangar and then left at around ten in the evening.

Charlie had a lady friend who picked them up and dropped Chip off at a nearby Holiday Inn. Then Charlie he took off with his friend for the evening. Chip told Charlie to sleep in. He would see him around ten o'clock, knowing he would not see Charlie again.

Chip checked in and asked the front desk clerk to give him a call at six in the morning.

After a shower and shave, Chip slid into the king-size bed and put his head on the pillow. He began planning for the next morning. He opened his flight bag and took out the area maps of China, the China Sea, and Japan's west coast cities and landmarks.

For the next two hours, Chip laid out a route he thought to be the best way to get away from China and the safest ways to get to Tokyo. He took a straight edge and pencil and started making lines for his route. He located an island called Cheju-Do about halfway across the China Sea, four hundred miles from Shanghai. From there he chose to fly to Nagasaki, which was two hundred miles east, putting him on the Japanese mainland. From Nagasaki he drew a line straight to Kobe and Osaka. He looked again at the maps and thought it may be best to head east to Miyazaka and fly along the eastern seaboard, staying clear of major cities like Kobe or Osaka, which were about 250 miles from Tokyo. Taking the ruler, he went from Shanghai direct to Tokyo. It was only 680 miles to northeast. He also knew he had to do some fancy flying once over the mainland as he did not file a flight plan at Shanghai and knew he would be challenged.

At six o'clock he heard the alarm, got dressed, brushed his teeth, and went to the breakfast area for eggs and coffee. He checked out, went outside, found a cab, and went to the FBO 1 Hangar 14. When he arrived, he was able to find a young man working on a portable generator and asked him to help get his plane out of the hangar so he could run the engines. The young man went and got a small tug, hooked Chip's tow bar to the Duck's nose wheel, and slowly moved it out to the tarmac. Chip went up to the cockpit and handled the brakes. He came down and gave the mechanic a hundred-dollar bill, stowed the tow bar, and began his preflight. He reached for Charlie's notebook and got the ground and tower frequencies. He also noticed there were no workers around, and so he started both engines and let them warm up. He dialed in the ground frequency, and a voice responded. Chip asked the man for taxi clearance, weather report, local sea level pressure, and the radar frequency. The young voice gave

Chip the information he requested and told him to taxi to runway 9 and hold and call the tower.

Chip held short of runway 9 and did his run-ups, including props and magnetos drops. All was perfect, so he called the tower. The tower told Chip he was first to take off and proceed to runway 9. Winds were at sixteen miles per hour from the east. After seeing all the systems were in the green, he taxied into position on runway 9, advanced the throttles, and rolled to reach his takeoff speed and in seconds he was lifting off and climbing into cloudless sky with unlimited visibility. He was heading right into the breaking sunrise when his headset came alive.

"Army B-25, what are your intentions?" Chip hesitated and then told the tower he was just taking a local test flight, checking out his engines just serviced. The tower advised him to stay below five thousand feet and head southeast away from the airport traffic area and do testing in large open fields five miles out that were easy to find. Then he would call when he was returning to the field for landing instructions.

"Roger, Tower. Army B-25 will call when returning to airport."

Chip thought it best to confirm the message as he continued to head straight into the sun, climbing to six thousand feet, and then he turned and flew northeast until he reached the coast and the East China Sea. He looked to make sure he was taking fuel from the auxiliary tank first. This would give him at least two hours of flying before switching to the mains. He put the nose of the Duck right on the ninety-degree compass mark. The tower called and asked again about his intentions, and he told them he was still doing a test flight. This time Shanghai Control gave him headings and altitude, but he ignored the controller and kept flying east toward the China Sea.

Chip realized from there on, he would most probably be challenged many times for his flight behavior, so he decided to just go silent and not respond to any calls.

Chip saw the shoreline coming up. He put the nose of the Duck down and headed for the China Sea. He took out his notes to confirm what his first visual was on his route. It was an island called Cheju-Do more than two hundred miles ahead. After reaching the island, he would set a course southeast, heading straight to Nagasaki, two hundred miles on the Japanese mainland.

He was now flying a hundred feet above the choppy brown waters. To his south he could see a number of commercial ships heading east and west, so it had to be a major sea-lane. He needed to identify the ships to tell which ones were the military defense radar vessels. He knew China and Japan had stationary navy ships all over the China Sea, watching for any signs of aggressive flights entering their no-fly zones.

It did not take long for Chip to start getting calls from the China Air Defense Department. They were coming fast, trying to reach him and demanding to know what his plans were as he was in dangerous restricted areas. He maintained his altitude at a hundred feet but was getting nervous, so he climbed to two hundred feet. He checked his instruments to make sure his engines were running smoothly. Both cylinder heat temps were in the green, and he had twenty-five inches of manifold pressure and props steady at 1,800 rpms with his airspeed at 185 miles per hour.

"American Army B-25, I am Captain Ti Liu with the Chinese Defense Forces. I'm warning you. You are entering our no-fly zones. You need to return to the airport traffic control at Shanghai immediately where you will be cleared to land."

Unknown to Chip, the Chinese Defense Headquarters had already sent a message out to four regional bases to stand by and be prepared to send up interceptors to guide the suspicious plane out of the no-fly zone and back to the airport.

The Chinese Defense Headquarters were alerted by the Chinese Civil Aviation Authority with more information now coming from the States and also from Hangar 1, where the B-25 bomber's copilot, Charlie, was deeply confused and concerned about being left behind. He was asked many questions, and Charlie reported he was very concerned as his pilot, Charles Reed, had purchased nearly a ton of fireworks and never really explained why. He told the officials the pilot should have never taken off alone, that he was illegally flying the plane without a second pilot. He also mentioned that the pilot never notified anyone at Hangar 1 that he was actually going to take off and that there was no record of him filing a flight plan.

Colonel Zhang Jinim, a colonel with China Air Defense Headquarters, was advised by phone personally by Bud West about Chip Reed's health problem. Bud did not want to alert the Chinese or anyone about the fact that the pilot could really be on a suicide mission. However, the Chinese were now aware of the ton of fireworks on the plane and advised Bud West. This shocked Bud as now he knew Chip had the means to become a flying bomb. He had no choice. He had to advise the Colonel that the pilot and his good friend, Chip Reed, could possibly be on a suicide mission to bomb a factory in Tokyo.

Colonel Jinim wasted no time and sent word out to all commands that the American bomber's pilot was not only ill, but could be a flying bomb on a mission and heading for Japan. Although the bomber was heading out of Chinese airspace into Japan's airspace, the colonel felt obligated to pass on the information to the Japanese authorities. He was unaware the Japanese self-defense officials had already been notified of an American bomber heading their way, but they were not aware of the bomber's mission. The Japanese Defense Command took standard operating procedures dealing with any plane entering their airspace. They had a network of tracking ships stationed all over the China Sea, and a number of navy ships had already alerted Japan's Self-Defense Forces that a bogey was heading their way. The news from the China Defense Force earlier explained who the bogey was and informed them that it was on a mission heading for the Japanese homeland.

Chip had a tough time keeping the Duck level at less than two hundred feet at times while trying to read the map of Japan he had on his lap. He knew the he had to fly at least 1,200 miles to reach Tokyo and that he would be stretching the fuel even though he had extra fuel with the bladder tank. He leaned out his engines, keeping his manifold pressures at twenty-four inches at 1,700 rpms. He knew flying low at the cruising speeds of 195 miles per hour was burning up his reserve fast. He needed to find the island called Cheju-Do, which was about 180 miles northeast. From there he would head east to find Japan's mainland and Nagasaki, where he would make a decision. Nagasaki had a major airport, and he guessed plenty of air traffic. He looked again at the chart of Japan and the area and noticed a large island west of Nagasaki and a city called Goto. He decided to play it safe and stay well south of Nagasaki and head for Miyazaki, which was more than two hundred miles south of Tokyo.

He had many hours to go, but weather appeared to be building up to his northeast. He realized he might have a tough time picking up weather reports when he got inland. He looked again at his notes and thought there was a chance he could possibly make it to Osaka or Kobe before the storms, but he was about to hear some troubling news from the Japanese Defense Forces. They told him that he would never be allowed to land anywhere except a military air base.

Suddenly, two Mig-21s appeared close by and alongside of him on his wingtips. Their pilots were giving him hand signals to turn around. They kept moving in and out close to him making him nervous. He pulled back both throttles, forcing the Migs to fly ahead of him. He saw they were trying everything to slow down by lowering flaps and their landing gears. Chip opened his throttles and put the Duck in a shallow dive. He saw the two Migs use afterburners and bank west, heading back to China. He won his first battle of the day.

All the major centers from Hong Kong to Shanghai had been alerted about the Army B-25 flying into their no-fly zones and keeping low to avoid radar tracking. There were reports from the Navy Defense Forces that they had tracked him over the China Sea near Shanghai but had lost him. The Japanese Aviation Authority was also trying to contact him, asking him to switch to their military frequency. Should he enter their airspace, he was to obey all their commands. If he did reach Japan's mainland, he was not to fly near or over cities and nearby suburbs.

The Duck was performing like a Swiss watch with everything running in the green. It had good oil pressure and no overheating engines or misfires, and the autopilot was working perfectly. Plus the weather was clear for now. What more could he ask for? He located a bottle of water, opened it, and poured it over his face and washed his hands. He tried to relax after rechecking his settings, and he moved his seat back so he could stretch his arms and legs.

For the first time since he had left Shanghai, he began to think about what he was planning to do. He thought about Linda, his good friends Bud and Dolly West, and his friends Wayne and Betty. He realized that he was not only being a coward facing his own life but that he would end up a murderer in the eyes of those he loved and every American at home. For the first time, he thought about how many innocent men and women he might kill with his act of vengeance. This did not change his mind. He was going to make the owners and builders of the Zoto automobiles pay for building their killing machines.

He felt a chill run through his body and felt beads of sweat running down his spine and broke out in a sweat around his forehead and the back of his neck. He thought it was only nerves, recalling he had the same sensation at the Titusville air show after he flew over the runway where the detonations occurred under his plane.

Chip reached again for the bottle of water and washed his face and poured the rest over his head and rubbed his eyes. He once again began feeling his arms and shoulders begin to ache and tingling in his fingers. While looking ahead, he saw his first landfall. It was the island called Cheju-Do on the horizon. It wouldn't be much longer before he would see the mainland and one of Japan's busiest ports, Nagasaki.

CHAPTER 39

Bud West's Office
Warbird Museum
Kissimmee, Florida
1000 hours

Bud, Dolly, and Wayne were on the phones, working with the Chinese and Japanese embassies in DC, FAA, Homeland Security, and the State Department. Everyone was trying to figure out a way to get to Chip and talk to him directly. They had been given the frequencies from Shanghai Central and the Chinese Aviation Authority, but they were not able to get the military frequencies they wanted to use.

Wayne was working with a number of Japanese officials at the embassy who were calling their contacts in Japan at the Self-Defense Forces Headquarters. They also contacted the commanding officer of the Fifth Air Force at Yokaota Air Force Base. The messages arriving from the Japanese Self-Defense Forces were not complimentary. They were not happy about having a Mitchell B-25 flying over their cities for any reason and were very vocal about the situation, including complaining directly to the US State Department in DC.

The China Sea

Meanwhile over the China Sea, Chip began to think about the Doolittle crewmembers who had to fly from a carrier for four hours before they reached Japan and then six to seven hours flying into thunderstorms before they reached China. However, Chip reminded himself that there were two pilots in each plane he was only one, and he knew he had at least eight hours ahead of him.

With all the communications going on, he suddenly wondered if the Japanese knew he had a plane loaded with explosives. Did his copilot advise the authorities and government agencies about his load of fireworks and his plans for Tokyo? Were they told from communications with Bud West about my intentions? Would Bud tell them where he was heading and that he wanted to destroy a factory? He also started to wonder if the Japanese would shoot him down as soon as he was in their airspace? He cleared his head, again telling himself that it wouldn't happen. They didn't know about his intention, so why would they shoot him down?

Then he got the call again from Shanghai Control Center. "Army B-25, we are going to have the military take action. If you do not turn around now, we will have no choice but to take defensive action. Please change your frequency to our military channel now, and obey our orders." Chip dialed in their information and once again ignored the voice calling him in halting English from what he felt was one of the commanders in control of the Migs.

Chip decided to take the Duck down to the wave tops again. He went to full throttle and dived toward the sea. The two Migs returned out of nowhere but did not follow him down and disappeared. He became nervous, thinking they were going to send an air-to-air missile up his tail. He waited for the bang or explosion, but nothing happened. He also looked at his watch and reminded himself the auxiliary fuel should be getting near empty and that it was time to change to the mains. He turned on the fuel pumps and transfer was made, and there was no sign of a drop in fuel pressure after turning them off.

A new voice came on from the Chinese Defense Command. "Army B-25, you have left our airspace and are now in Japanese airspace. Please change your frequency to the Japanese Air Control Center at Kyusho. If you do not have their frequency, let us know, and we will be happy to give it to you."

Chip said to himself. "That's a pleasant surprise coming from the Chinese." Then he realized the Chinese were very smart. They were not going to have him shot down in their airspace when he was entering Japan's airspace and Japan were our allies, so they would let Japan take the credit for destroying him and his plane.

Once again, he just ignored the call. He had the frequency he needed, thanks to Charlie and his notes. He switched to the Japanese Self-Defense Network frequency to monitor any news about being in their airspace. He was hoping that if he was intercepted, it would be by a US Air Force fighter and not a Japanese interceptor. If that was the case, he would communicate with an American pilot.

The sun was beating hard on him through the cockpit windshield. He saw a layer of cumulus clouds scattered around three thousand feet and climbed to use the clouds to block the sun. He knew he was below any commercial airline routing, but he also knew he would be a clear radar target for all defense forces. He was in his third hour of flying from altitudes of a hundred to 3,500 feet. He had found the island he was looking for and now pointed the nose of the Duck for Nagasaki, which was less than two hours away. He tried to look once more at the map in his lap and see if he might consider changing his course and head for Hiroshima and then on to Kobe. That way he would not have to deal with the mountains to the north, and once he was over more populated areas, chances were it would be more difficult to shoot him down. But first, he had to deal with the Japanese radar and their defenses in the China Sea, so he flew down to the wave tops and leveled out at a hundred feet.

Bud West's Warbird Office
Warbird Museum
Kissimmee, Florida

Bud West, Wayne, and Dolly remained in Bud's office, going over all the maps they had on Japan and the list of air defense base locations they had learned about from the Japanese embassy. They shared these with the US Air Force too.

They tried to figure out what route Chip would be taking to reach Tokyo. Bud had worked on the fuel consumption at ninety-five to a hundred gallons per hour at speeds from 180 to 200 knots and came up with what he felt was a reasonable fuel usage for Chip and the Duck to stay airborne.

Studying the charts, Bud commented, "The way I figure Chip would know he is going to be close on fuel and will take the shortest route to Tokyo he can. We can only hope that word did not get out about his load of fireworks and his intention. We did not tell anyone from this end; however, that pilot he used in Hong Kong has already alerted the Chinese of the fireworks, and that could still be an issue if they report to Japan's Air Defense.

"I really think Chip will most likely panic and decide he may not make Tokyo and pick out some other factory or government building and settle his debt. Remember how he blew it in Titusville by not following the rules. He is a bit of a hothead, and his respect for the Japanese is nil, so he may go against his own plans if he thinks his fuel is getting too low," Wayne said.

"No, Wayne. Chip won't do that. Just look at his distance from Shanghai to Tokyo on the commercial flight routes. It shows more than 1,200 miles, and he would have enough fuel if he filled the auxiliary tank. I figure he would reach Tokyo with an hour or two of fuel left. Where are we with the Japanese folks in DC? Have they contacted their control centers and defense people?"

"Last I heard they were alerted and in the process of locating him. They will be sending up a number of F-15s to spot him. They also have all the commercial airlines watching the skies in southern Japan. He will or should be well under their flight paths, staying low as he had planned, but you and I know it will be difficult to spot him from above because of his olive drab color. He can easily blend into the countryside."

"Wayne, we have to keep working with the Japanese and US Air Force to find a way to communicate with him. I think if I can get him on the radio, I can talk him down safely. He thinks he is dying according to his final letter, but his friend and doctor in Ft. Lauderdale, who is now a little more open about what may be wrong with him, told me he wants Chip to know he is not dying. He was in an early stage of leukemia, but it's one that is easily controlled by treatments. He has to know about this if we are to save him and hundreds of innocent people at the Zoto factory."

"Do you think we should advise the Japanese officials and the US Air Force of his health problem and why he needs to land and seek treatment as soon as possible?" Wayne said as he paced back and forth past Bud's desk.

Bud picked up a phone and began the process of getting through to the Japanese Self-Defense Headquarters again to see if they were able to reach Chip on their frequencies. At the same time, he told Wayne to try to reach the US Air Force's Fifth Air Force Headquarters and find someone they could talk to about Chip and why they need to find him at all costs.

China Sea
Thirty Miles West of Japan's Mainland

Chip could see the outline of the large island with the mountains he had to pass over before he would see Nagasaki. He could see the increase of ships moving about off the south end of the island, and he figured he was on radar and being reported constantly about his presence. He thought it might be easier to fly toward Kobe once he was over Nagasaki. Then he remembered its major airport and air traffic. He must fly south and clear the city or change course and go northward to a city called Kumomoto.

He remained flying at a hundred feet as he neared the coast. He crossed over the shoreline of the large island and over the mountains and noticed straight ahead was a large city called Goto. He flew over a large bay with many ships moving and on anchor west of Nagasaki. He pulled back on the controls and leveled off high enough to clear the mountains that surrounded a large bay. Just ahead were the city of Nagasaki and its huge port. There was plenty of smoke in the north end, so he elected to bank south and fly well around Nagasaki's southern area, which was crowded with suburbs, and he began to climb and head eastward.

"Army B 25, good afternoon, sir." Chip's headset came alive with a deep, commanding American voice.

"Army, I can only guess you are on our frequency. I am Lt. Colonel William Allan, and if you look above to your right, you will see an F-15. That would be me, sir. You were spotted by a number of Japanese ships and reported to defense command. I was scrambled to find you and guide you to a safe base. I am doing all I can to help you, but you have to understand. You have created serious problems with the Japanese government. Presently, you are on radar at all defense forces operations, and I am getting orders from Japanese officials as well as my commanding officer at Yakota Air Force Base. You need to climb immediately to 3,500 feet and join up with my flight. I cannot get down to your altitude. You are much too low, sir. If you hear me, please respond."

Chip looked up, and there he was cruising at the same speed just above him.

"Colonel, I hear you loud and clear. I am on the defense force frequency. Where did you come from?"

"Sir, Yakota Air Base, and I will give you a new course change to make. We need for you to land right away, and I will guide you to the base. Do you understand me, sir?"

"I appreciate the offer, Colonel, but I have a date in Tokyo and would like to keep it today. I figured it was just a few hours away, and I don't need fuel. But thank you, Colonel."

"Army, again understand that I have orders to escort you to Yakota Air Base from Japan's Self-Defense Command. They do not want you and your B-25 flying over their cities. My commanding officer told me you will not be welcome at any civilian airport, especially Tokyo International. Understand you are a foreign plane that entered their airspace. I also need to advise you that you have two more F-15s above and just behind you and we are flying at very low speeds which is not easy for us.

"We were told who you are, Mr. Reed. One of our Japanese colonels flying with the Japanese Air Force is with my formation and says he knows you. He is flying down to join up with you on your right wing. He is flying a Japanese Air Force F-15 and would like to guide you to Yakota."

Chip could not believe his ears. "A Japanese colonel who thinks he knows me?"

There it was off his wing, a shining F-15 all painted out in Japanese "red ball" markings on the fuselage and wings. He could easily see the pilot in a bright red helmet inside the big bubble canopy waving at him.

"Well Mr. Reed, looks like we meet again. I see you have the same B-25 you flew at Titusville air show. I also see you had it totally rebuilt, and here we are again, flying together. But this time I promise I will not blow up in your flight path. I want you to know how terrible I felt after hearing you had to crash land because of the damage caused by my plane. I did come by to pay you my respects at the hospital, but you refused to see me. I came because I wanted to say how sorry I was you had to lose your friend in the crash."

Chip was totally speechless. He had his finger on the mic control button but could not talk. He just kept staring over at the colonel.

"Mr. Reed, in case you forgot, I am Colonel Ram Kaisha from the Titusville air show. My Zero's engine blew up, and parts of my plane damaged your bomber. You must remember how you punched me and cracked my jaw at the hotel. I did not bring charges because I understood your feelings at the time. I know it must have been tough being grounded by the air boss for your lack of flying abilities at the show."

Chip found his voice and responded, "Well, Colonel, I never thought we would cross paths again, and I hope you realize what damage you did that day showing off. I will not forgive you for causing the death of my friend, so just get out of my sight. If I get the chance, I will do more than just crack your jaw. It wouldn't take much right now to bank hard and take you and your plane out."

"Mr. Reed, once again, I deeply regret and apologize for the loss of your friend. I had no control over my engine when it blew up, and I had no idea you were so close behind me. I am sorry for the problems I have caused, but now you are illegally over my homeland and possibly causing a threat to my people. We need to know your plans now. If you don't obey Colonel Allan's commands to land as soon as you can, you do know you could be shot down?"

Chip gave Kaisha a snappy salute while smiling and then told him and all listening, "Colonel, go fuck off."

Colonel Kaisha did not respond. He used his afterburners and headed straight up into the blue sky, catching up with the other two F-15s.

"Army B-25, this is Colonel Allan. I'm sorry to hear that conversation, but it does not change my orders. I need you to climb now and get set up for a landing at Yakota ahead. Please contact Yakota Tower on 125.5 and get your landing instructions."

Once again, Chip ignored the colonel's commands. He flew down low over the rooftops outside of a large residential area. He changed his mind again and decided to head northeast toward cities called Hamamatsu and Hiroshima. He figured either one would be a direct path to Kobe and Osaka. He figured the Japanese or US Air Force had no intention on shooting him down over populated areas. He was also sure they had no idea about his plan to bomb a factory in Tokyo.

CHAPTER 40

US Navy Task Force 24
En Route to Yokosuka Naval Base, Japan
South Pacific Ocean

Sixty miles off the coast of southeast Japan, the carrier USS *Midway* CVA-41 turned into the wind and began launching her squadrons of Hornets, A-6s, and Tom Cats to land at Atsugi Naval Air Base. This was a standard operating procedure for carriers before they made port.

The US Midway was commissioned in 1945 and took part in many battles in the Persian and Gulf wars. She was the first aircraft carrier constructed a new type of deck that was too wide to pass through the Panama Canal. She was now under the command of Admiral Hendry "Hank" Sweeny, who had trained as a carrier pilot and had flown missions in Korea and Vietnam before being sent to the Midway as assistant air ops officer. He then became captain of the Midway after the Gulf War.

Admiral George J. Sweeny, Hank's father, began as an instructor pilot and was then sent to the Pentagon, where he worked under Captain Woe Duncan, one of the planers for the Doolittle Raid. He was later assigned to the USS Hornet as assistant air ops officer. He had the privilege of meeting Lt. Colonel James H. Doolittle at Alameda Air Station when Doolittle arrived with more than one hundred Army Air Corps airmen and sixteen B-25 bombers. The Hornet's crew was upset all their planes were stored below deck, making room for the B-25s. They did not take a shine to Doolittle's army men either as they felt they were going to the Pacific to go to war, not play taxi cab for the Army Air Corps.

Sixteen days after departing San Francisco, Captain Sweeney watched Doolittle and the sixteen planes take off for Japan on the morning of April 18, 1942. They were spotted by and reported by a Japanese fishing boat and Doolittle had to launch early more than two hundred miles further than planned. His concern now was that they would all run out of gas before reaching China. None of the Hornet's crew that morning felt the Doolittle, his airmen, and their bombers would ever make it to China.

It was not until the Hornet and her sister ship, USS *Enterprise* made it back to Pearl Harbor did they first learn the raid was a success. They were told that all planes were lost, but nobody had information on the fate of the crews.

USS Midway
Task Force 24
USS Midway

Rear Admiral Hank Sweeney made orders to his helmsman to change course for the naval base at Yokosuka. He had launched his four VF squadrons to Atsugi Naval Air Station west of Yokosuka, where they were landing that hour. The plan was to have ten days of R & R before returning to the Philippines for exercises.

"Sir, releasing the squadrons was perfect timing. Sir, take a look at this forecast that just came in. We thought that we were going to see some typical squalls coming in, but it is a full-blown depression with winds of fifty-plus and due here in an hour or so."

The young marine officer Lieutenant Donald Styles was breathing hard as he had to run up from communications center two decks down. He handed the report to the admiral and asked if he could do anything else.

Admiral Sweeney went to his desk and contacted his officer on deck. He gave orders to send out the message to the task force escorting the Midway to follow standard procedures for serious weather conditions and rough seas. All escorting ships according to standard fleet rules in heavy weather had to move out to a larger perimeter surrounding the carriers.

Ruptured Duck
North of Nagasaki

"Army B-25, sir, this is Colonel Allan staying with you at a thousand feet above you. I have only one question to ask and also to advise you if you can see ahead about ten miles to the east is not smog or smoke. Sir, you're may be heading into a storm and not a good one. I have no idea why you are flying so low. It's certainly not necessary and dangerous. It will be just a matter of time before you will no longer be in VFR conditions, and I have to believe you are well versed on instrument flying because you will need it shortly.

"Army B-25, please climb to three thousand feet and increase your speed to at least 200 miles per hour so you can join me and I will set up an ILS approach to Yokota. If you are hearing me and don't want to talk, just wave your wings so I know you are getting the message and warning of the storm heading your way."

Chip broke radio silence with the colonel. "Sir, I appreciate your information, and I do see the weather coming and planned to climb. I know there are many factories coming up with tall stacks and plenty of antennas around, so I will climb but will need new headings for Hiroshima, not your base. I don't want to land anywhere but Tokyo International, and yes, I am fully qualified for an IFR approach."

"Army, as mentioned earlier, the Japanese Air Defense has issued orders to the US Air Forces to get you down at the nearest air base, preferable one that we share with them. I am sure you will be able to get clearance from JAD Headquarters to continue on to Tokyo after the storm passes. Yokota is your only chance. Why take the risk flying blind over heavy populations?"

Chip was convinced he was not compromised and felt that they had no idea he had explosives on board or that he was planning to take out a factory in Tokyo, which made him breathe easier. He also realized he had not eaten and searched his flight suit for two candy bars he had bought at a vending machine at Hangar 1. He uncovered a candy bar and began looking for one of the cokes he had stowed. He found the bottle he relieved himself in earlier instead and now felt the urge again. He leveled off and put the Duck on autopilot. He managed to get his seat belt off and unzipped his flight suit. He was trying to relieve himself when the Duck hit a pocket and he had to take control. Now he was really miserable sitting in a wet flight suit.

"Colonel Allan, I am climbing to three thousand as requested and appreciate you staying off close by, but I will not land at Yokota, so please just give me a heading to Hiroshima or even Kobe. I think I may be close to Kobe, correct?"

"Negative, Army. You are southwest of Kobe and need to climb to level off at three thousand feet. Kobe and Osaka are overcast with storms. You need to change course now to 010 degrees to get to Yakota.

"Army, you have to understand how serious your condition is right now. As a fellow American and pilot, why are you not trying to possibly save your life and plane? For whatever reason you need to go to Tokyo, it can't be that important to possibly lose your life for."

"Colonel, I can't thank you enough for your advice and helping me right now as I cannot reach my maps and have no idea where I am. I take it I may possibly be shot down if I don't land at your base, correct?"

"Army, right now the Japanese Self-Defense and our headquarters at Yokota are trying to work out a plan for your very dangerous situation. I say dangerous as I just learned from my CO you are really on a suicide mission and have explosives on board. I was also told you plan to crash into a factory in Tokyo. Is that true? For heaven's sake, what are you thinking? Do you realize what can happen? You'll not only to kill yourself but thousands of civilians at and around the factory."

Chip could not believe what he was just told.

"Mr. Reed, you are causing serious problems for the Japanese government as well as the United Sates. The Japanese government's Self-Defense Command has heard from our State Department and the US Air Force chief of staff claiming you do not represent the United States in any degree. You are a rogue private pilot in your own bomber."

Once again, Chip was totally shocked and wanted to respond, but he was interrupted by Colonel Allan.

"Army, please stand by, do not change altitude or airspeed as I am receiving new orders from my CO. I have new orders coming in for you."

CHAPTER 41

Bud West's Office
Warbird Museum
Kissimmee, Florida

Ed Metz, one of Bud's mechanics, came into the museum and saw Bud and Dolly standing at Sara's desk. "Hey Bud, take a look at what just taxied in. It's a classic Convair 404."

Bud and Dolly both went out the door and could see a cabin door opening and a portable staircase unfold to the ground. An attractive woman dressed in a flight suit stood in the door, waving to them.

"Oh, my God, it's Linda," Dolly cried out and began to run to the plane as Linda was coming down the stairs. They met and hugged for a few moments and then began to walk toward the office.

Bud put his arms around Linda and commented how beautiful she looked. Dolly took her hand as Linda swept her hair back from her forehead.

"See, no more scars. What do you all think? Linda said, smiling and striking a pose as if for a photo op.

"You look just marvelous, Linda, and we are so happy to see you again." Dolly reached out and took her left hand, and Linda knew exactly what she was doing and looking for.

"I am still a single little lady if that is what is on your mind?" Linda said, laughing.

Bud smiled and suggested they go inside the office, where Sara was waiting to greet Linda as well.

"So what is with that dinosaur you just flew in with?" Bud inquired.

"Oh, that is one of our old executive planes that we just sold. I am on my way with the other pilot to deliver the plane to some Costa Rican fruit company in Miami. When the delivery plan came up, I volunteered to come down and to get a chance to see both of you and of course, hear what Mr. Chips is up to."

Bud suggested that Linda ask the pilot to come to the office and relax since it would take a while.

Bud and Dolly began to explain what Chip was up to and where he was, and then Bud handed Linda Chip's letter. She read it and began to cry immediately. Dolly handed her some wipes and told her she was sorry to find out this way, but at least she learned in the letter that Chip was still very much in love with her and only sorry for all the mistrust he had shown her.

"Bud, he can't do this. How do you stop him?" she said through her tears.

"Linda, we have the Chinese, the Japanese, the State Department, and the US Air Force in Japan trying to hunt him down and make him land somewhere."

"Can you talk to him, or has anyone talked to him? Surely, he can be reached on his radio, right?" Linda asked.

"We know he is listening and have had reports he was even talking to a US Air Force colonel flying an F-15 alongside him, but the colonel says he was unable to get him to land at his base. He says Chip insists on flying to Tokyo. Linda, he managed to purchase thousands of pounds of fireworks."

"My God, where did he get fireworks, and why have they let him in their airspace knowing he is on a suicide mission?"

"Linda, we don't think the Japanese authorities know about the explosives, which are fireworks he was able to get in Shanghai through the black market. They have no idea of his intentions either simply because we have not told them. We have only reported to the Chinese and Japanese embassies and the State Department that the pilot has a serious health problem and should not be flying."

"Linda, Chip befriended a young Chinese pilot to help him get the Duck in commission after she arrived by ship. They flew many hours around Hong Kong while training Charlie, and they had plans to fly to cities in China and then to Japan. This guy Charlie has connections that got Chip the fireworks. They were supposed to pick them up when they arrived at Shanghai. That is where Chip dumped the Chinese guy and headed out to Japan solo. His only hope to stay airborne right now is to use the extra fuel tank we installed. I have worked out the Duck's range, and if he is doing everything right, he had a ten- to twelve-hour flight to Tokyo from Shanghai. So far, he has made it into Japan somewhere in the south and that is all we have right now. We did learn he has an American Air Force colonel flying alongside of him and giving him instructions. We have also learned he is going into a large front of heavy storms between him and Tokyo."

"How can I reach this Colonel Allan, the Air Force guy who talks to Chip?"

Bud replied, "We could try to go through the Air Force in DC to start and then find out what air station he is flying out of. That way maybe we can communicate with him. I also have a number for the Japanese Civil Aviation Authority and see if they can help us too."

"Bud, would it be wise to tell the Air Force and the Japanese what Chip is really up to? Surely, they would not take evasive action while he was flying over populated areas, would they? If they let us hook up, we can talk to him directly. I can tell him the truth about how I feel and how he is not as terminally sick as he may think. I could give him a reason to want to save his life, and you need to tell him what you learned from the doctors, that he is not terminal and can be treated and live a long life."

Bud, Wayne, and Dolly got back on the phones and called all the agencies again to see if they could get through to Chip with their help. They decided it was best for all the authorities in DC and the Japanese Self-Defense Headquarters to know the truth not just about Chip's health but about the fireworks and his plan to destroy the Zoto auto company for killing his wife and son.

They would soon learn after talking to the Air Force at the Pentagon, all the authorities in Japan were fully aware of the fireworks aboard Chip's plane and his intentions.

Yokota Air Force Base Japan
Air Operations Officer
Colonel Jack Simms's Office

"Yes, sir, I understand. We still have two F-15s shadowing the B-25 but about to hit some heavy weather. I will call Colonel Allan and Colonel Kashia." Colonel Jack Simms, CO of the 105th Fighter Wing put the phone down and turned to Captain Chambers, his air operations officer. "Captain Chambers? That was General Wei at Self-Defense Headquarters. He was just advised this American pilot, a Chip Reed from Florida, is flying that B-25 we are tracking. They are fully aware is not only very ill, but he has a load of explosives on board and plans to crash into some car factory in Tokyo. They want him down out of the sky as soon as possible."

"Colonel Simms, that explains why Colonel Allan has not been able to get him to land. It sounds like this guy is on a mission. What are your plans now? Do we have our two F-15s just take him out before he gets into Kobe or Tokyo?"

Colonel Simms went over to the communications center and relieved Airmen 1C Schultz from his post. He took a seat and put on a headset and began to broadcast.

"Colonel Allan and Colonel Kashia, Colonel Simms here. Mr. Reed, I hope you are listening. I am Colonel Jack Simms, commanding office of the 105th fighter group and just received orders from the Japanese Self Defense Headquarters with orders you have to land immediately at our Yokota base. We also have orders if you don't to destroy you. You are running out of time, do you understand?"

"Colonel Simms, Colonel Allan here. We are getting close to entering that northeaster storm at three thousand. We were advised there is a clearing layer at nine thousand where we can maintain VFR. This storm is moving fast and will be clear in an hour or so; however, we are over populated areas presently and would be too dangerous to take any action to down the plane, sir."

"Colonel Allan, that's a roger and thank you for your information. However, that bomber has a load of fireworks on board and as briefed, we also know the pilot does has a serious health problem. We have reports we received from his Florida base, the Pentagon, and the State Department that he is on a suicide mission. He plans to crash into the Zoto automobile factory in the Tokyo area."

Chip could not believe what he was hearing from Colonel Allan and now his commanding officer. He was devastated that maybe even his friend Bud West had told the Japanese government and our State Department about his plan.

"Army 25, Allan here and I hope you heard our CO just now. We need to get you up into clear air to escort you to Yokota. The Japanese Self-Defense Headquarters is recommending there are open areas ahead and away from populated areas. If you don't obey their instructions to land at Yakota, I believe their next order will be to shoot you down. I am asking you to please reconsider your plans now. If they do send out the order and you survive and bail out, I will try to follow you down and give ordinance to your location. Do you understand what I am saying, Mr. Reed? Do you want to really end your life this way?"

"Colonel, I will climb to nine thousand," Chip responded.

Chip thought maybe he could just stall them for more time to get closer to Tokyo. They would never shoot me down over any major city or the areas around the cities. He advanced throttles and pulled back hard on the controls flying into heavy rain when he suddenly heard a large jolting bang behind him. He thought for sure they had shot him with an air-to-air a missile."

"You sons of bitches," he cried out. "For God sake, give me a break. I was trying to do what you asked. Why did you fire on me?"

"Sir, we lost visual on you in the rain but have you clearly on radar and staying with you. We did not fire anything at you unless it came from the ground. However, we were not informed of any missiles being launched and that would not happen with two friendly escorts so close to you," Colonel Allan replied.

Chip went through the motions working the controls and could see everything was normal. He was climbing at a high rate and down to 165 miles per hour. Then it hit him. "My God, it had to be the fireworks breaking loose and hitting the aft bulkhead of the bomb bay when I pulled up."

Colonel Simms received another call from JSD Headquarters. A request had been made from the base in Florida. They wanted to be patched through to Chip Reed so a special person could talk to him, someone they claimed might be able to change his mind and save his life and others. The request was granted by JSD Headquarters.

"Army 25, this is Colonel Simms. We are patching in someone from your base in Florida who needs to talk to you."

Naturally, Chip was certain he would be hearing Bud West's voice and was ready to blast off at him for calling both governments about his mission. Instead it was a sweet, soft voice that came through his headset, a voice he had not heard in a long time.

"Chip, this is Linda, and I am with Bud and Dolly and Wayne. I hope you can hear me.

"First, I want to say that I love you, Chip, with all my heart and always have. We can make a new start. I know we can. If you think you're dying, you're not. You do have a problem which can be treated, and you can live a normal life with me. Don't take your life and maybe the lives of hundreds of innocent people over a grudge to get even with a car company. Please, I beg you Chip, to find a way to get down safely for me."

Chip was unable to speak. His eyes watered, and his throat became dry, so he couldn't speak at first. "Linda, I don't know how you found out, but it does not matter now. I am so sorry for everything and realize my plans are wrong, very wrong. I promise ..."

He did not finish the rest of his questions to Linda, he was cut off by an incoming call on the frequency.

"Mr. Reed, this is Colonel Kashia. I am once again well off your port wing, and I heard your lady friend pleading with you. Now it's my turn. Nothing would please me more than to send a missile up your stubborn butt. You are over my country now and flying over thousands of my people who don't deserve or understand why they are to be destroyed by you and your plane. I might add you will not get to destroy that auto plant either. You must know you can't escape air-to-air or ground missiles, so let's work out a place to get you down safe."

"Army B-25, this is Colonel Simms. I am the only one who can give the order to shoot you down, and it will not be Colonel Kashia's decision. But we need to start planning to get you down safely now. I will keep those two F-15s with you. You are close to Kobe now, and I need to know from you exactly what you have on board. We are told you have a large load of fireworks. But can you land safely without a detonation?"

"Colonel Simms, I am not sure if I can. Yes, I am carrying nearly two thousand pounds of fireworks in a container wrapped in cardboard and wood with metal straps. The crate was installed using ropes suspended like a hammock tied to the bomb racks. When I pulled up a while ago, I heard a large bang, and I thought I was shot at. I think it was the fireworks crate breaking loose, hitting a bulk head, and possibly just lying on my bomb bay doors, I think. I also need to tell you I am running low on fuel."

"Roger that, Army 25, let me get back to you after I talk to the Japanese self-defense officials. For your information, Mr. Reed, we have put the lid on any kind of publicity on this matter at the Self-Defense Headquarters and the CO's office at the Fifth Air Force Headquarters. We hope your friends at your base will respect that order as well. We don't want to panic the people of Japan regarding a US bomber flying over their cities with explosives."

Colonel Simms continued, "Colonels Allan and Kashia, you both need to be getting close to running out of fuel. I advise you return to base as soon as I get two replacements up to stay with the B-25."

"Sir, Kashia here, I have plenty of fuel, and I want to stay with the bomber. I think the Japanese Self-Defense Force would be very understanding once they knew it was personal why I want to escort this bomber down."

"Colonel Kashia, I realize you are an honorable man among your fellow officers and the JSD officials. I will have to check with headquarters. Meanwhile, we will alert air controllers in Kobe and Tokyo of the presence of the army bomber and the two F-15s coming into their airspace soon.

"Army, Colonel Simms here. I just received a new order from the Self-Defense Command. You are to change your course right now and head due east toward Japan's eastern seaboard and the Pacific Ocean. You need to understand it has been agreed by all officials. We cannot land you at any airport considering your present situation. We have no idea what those explosives may do when you touch down. Now we know there are metal straps to consider. A hard landing with a ton of weight on them could force open the doors to open releasing the crate hitting the runway and metal straps possibly causing sparks, and who knows what could happen.

Regardless, they are not taking that chance. We came to a solution that may save your life. I want you to fly due east to the Pacific Ocean, and when you are safe out to sea, bail out, and let your plane crash into the sea. We believe you may stand a better chance for survival."

Bud West joined the conversation. "Chip, I am still on the channel, and what the colonel just suggested really makes sense. Two thousand pounds possibly sitting on the bomb bay doors could be a problem landing with enough impact to open the doors. When the time comes to ditch, I will help you down, walking through the procedure like we did in Kissimmee."

Chip hit his mic button, making up his mind to cooperate with all the authorities. "Colonel Simms and everyone on this frequency making decisions to help me, I want you to know I do understand and you are all right. I will take the colonel's advice and head for the Pacific Ocean. Colonel Simms, I don't carry a chute, so jumping out is out of the question. I have to ride her down, sir. Bud, if you're there, please put Linda on the line."

Linda was handed the phone. Chip could hear she was crying while trying to talk.

"Linda, I don't care who is listening to this conversation right now. Please understand I will do all I can to survive. I know I have to do what is only right now and realize how selfish and controlled by hate I have been all these years. Please believe I do love you and want to live to see you again."

Once again, Chip was interrupted and cut off.

"Army 25, Colonel Simms here, and I'm sorry to interfere. However, you made the right choice, but time is not on your side. I understand you are getting low on fuel, and we have more weather heading your way. We have worked out the shortest and safest route to take to the ocean. Stay on this frequency while our communications officer directs you."

"Army 25, Captain Phillip Neal here, squadron communication officer. We have a route from Osaka just north of you now. You need to change course and take ninety degrees east for 155 miles till you see a city called Hamamatsu, do you copy?"

"Roger Captain.

"Once over Hamamatsu, head 110 degrees for seventy-five miles. If your navigation is good, you will see a small volcanic island called Oshima. You need to set down as close as you can on its east windward side. We have notified the Coast Guard at Yokosuka, and they will monitor your position and sending out a cutter. You will also be in the direct path of an American task force heading to the navy base at Yokosuka, and they could possibly give you aid. Presently, they are approximately thirty-three miles southeast of Oshima Island.

"Colonel Simms, I will do as asked and will report back as soon as I have this island in sight. I have been going through some cumulus scattered clouds around 3,500 feet, and it appears be clear beneath. Can you say who will be giving me flight information from here on?"

"Mr. Reed, you will be under Tokyo Control Center and Captain Neal. They are on your frequency right now, so do as instructed by them. They know exactly where you are and the location of carrier task force as well. I wish you luck, and I'm sorry that you have to sacrifice your plane and that you have to ride it down. I know you may well get through this, and I hope to catch up to you someday. I might add   not to discourage you but to advise you—the navy is reporting some rough seas running three to four feet because of the winds ahead of a storm heading your way."

"Roger that and Colonel, thank you for staying with me."

Chip now realized he had his throttles still open from the recent climb and was burning up precious fuel. He pulled the throttles off to 1,700 rpms, reducing airspeed and manifold pressures and began to descend through the clouds.

"Army 25, this is Tokyo Center. You are at three thousand feet and thiry-eight miles from Hamamatsu heading east. Your next target will be sixty-nine miles on a heading of 105 degrees. It is the island called Oshima. It is south of the navy base at Yokosuka. Please keep this frequency open at all times for communications with all services involved."

"Army, switch to frequency 136.9 on second radio for navy communications. Colonel Simms commanded.

"Mr. Reed, Colonel Kashia here to assist you. I am coming up on your starboard wing flying a T-28 I borrowed from the local National Guard unit at Atsugi Air Station."

Chip could not believe his eyes. A beautiful gleaming white T-28 was flying alongside the Duck. "What is this all about, and are you really Colonel Kashia?" Chip asked, trying to stay on course.

"Yes, Chip Reed, it is me. I traded my F-15 for this old bird that was used in the popular movie *Tora! Tora! Tora*. It was used as a photo ship and now belongs to the Japanese National Guard's at Yokota but being used for air sea rescue by the Navy at Atsugi. I have permission to escort you while letting down and assist you to reach Oshima Island and will continue to stay with you until you ditch so I can report on your condition and location.

"Right now, Chip Reed, I need for you to continue on course so I can match your speed and altitude. You are presently descending from thirty five thousand feet and I recommend you level off now as you are approaching Hamamatsu, which you should be able to see in the distance."

"Colonel, I have no doubt that this is to make sure I leave the country, I am sure. I know what I am doing, so you can take your old American-made T-bird and go home." Chip said in anger.

"I can't do that Mr. Reed, I am under orders, and believe it or not it was my idea to help save your life, not to chase you out of my homeland. Look down to your right, we are just about to pass over Hamamatsu and closing on Oshima Island, so start slowly descending. I will stay with you until you decide when to ditch so I can report your position to air sea rescue. I sincerely hope you survive, and if you do I hope to see you again in a few days in Tokyo."

"Colonel, I know this may be too late, but I am sorry for what I did to you in Titusville at the hotel. I hope someday you can forgive me, but more important I want to sincerely thank you for your concern and keeping me company as I prepare for another crash landing, but this time I am fully responsible for destroying my plane."

"Mr. Reed, just a reminder that as you get closer over the open sea, it is very difficult to judge your height to the waves. I will try and give you information as to your position over the water before touchdown. When you think it's time, you want to try to flare out almost into a stall so you can hit as flat as you can instead of nosing in."

Before Chip could respond, his headset came alive, and a new voice cut in.

USS Long Beach
Task Force
Twenty Miles South of Oshima Island

"Army B-25, this is Lieutenant Wiser aboard the cruiser USS *Long Beach*. I have been ordered to intercept you from US Navy task force commander Admiral Sweeney on the carrier USS Midway. We have you on radar heading 125 degrees. You should have a visual on us when you reach Oshima Island. We are coming at flank speed from the southeast. When you have us in your sights stay your course and maintain at a thousand feet. We will have a destroyer close to you and ready to assist you after you ditch."

"Lieutenant, I have a load of explosives I have to try to get rid of first, and I don't want to be too close to any ship. Please let me know when you have a sighting on me. I will turn on my landing lights to help."

"Chip, Bud here. I am still with you, buddy. Listen, when you are ready to put her down, I want you to pull up and climb to six thousand feet, level off, keep throttles open, and open bomb bay doors. Put the Duck into a steep dive, and when you get near a thousand feet pull up sharp and climb again. Let's hope gravity takes over and helps you lose your package."

Chip followed Bud's orders and pulled the Duck up with full power to six thousand feet. He leveled off, and with full power he went into a dive toward the sea. He was close to five hundred feet when he recovered and was able to pull the Duck up and level off. He heard nothing release. He did hear Colonel Kashia confirm nothing hit the water.

He suddenly remembered he forgot to open the bomb bay doors. He reported to Bud and climbed back up to six thousand feet, leveled off, hit the bomb bay door's switch, and immediately began his power dive toward the sea. He pulled up with all his strength. This time he felt a bump and a small jerk on the controls. He rolled to his left to look back at the rough seas, and there it was, floating and bobbing on the white caps.

"Mr. Reed, it fell out and disintegrated when it hit," Kashia reported.

"It's gone," Chip yelled. "It's gone." There was a sigh of relief from everyone who was listening as he switched from radio to radio.

"Thanks, Bud. Now let's go over this water landing together," Chip demanded.

"Easy, buddy. First, do you think you have enough fuel to get back to the closest airport? Bud asked.

"Bud, I have been running on what appears to be on fumes. I have little time or fuel, so turning around now would be out of the question. What do you think my chances of surviving are if I ditch now?" Chip asked.

"Chip, it all comes down to how you enter into the sea. That is the key. How is the ocean surface right now?"

"I would guess to be three to four with winds from east 095 at twenty-five, says the navy."

"Okay, here is what you do—" Suddenly, Bud was interrupted.

"Army B-25, this is Admiral Sweeney aboard the USS Midway. We have you on radar along with Long Beach and a closing destroyer heading your way about five miles off my bow. Forget about ditching right now. Here is what I want you to do. Have you ever experienced a really short landing?"

Chip could not understand the admiral's question.

"I have made standard short landings, sir, and one controlled crash landing, but not a water landing."

"Army B-25, here is what you do. You continue until you see the Midway. Then enter a standard right-hand flight pattern. Go through your normal landing procedures and think of my flight deck as a short runway. We are going to coach you down like an A-6, but it is up to you to stay focused and pay attention to our instructions. Do you understand? I will have the deck prepared with our emergency net and will be blocking the end of the deck with tugs and lifting equipment just in case you don't stop in time."

Chip could not believe his ears. He was just told to land on a super carrier? "Sir, admiral sir, I don't think I can do that. Is there anyone there who can help me if I decide to try? I have a serious problem. I know I am running on fumes, sir, and I think I will be better off in the drink."

"Start your pattern, Army, I have a twin-engine prop pilot here who flies our sub hunters daily and can help you down. You have flaps and landing gear in that war bird, correct?"

"Yes sir, and I am sort of an expert on crash landings. This plane has already been in a crash landing, so I know what not to do now."

"Army B-25, this is Captain Ron Miller, and I fly the twin S-2E with two props. I just have a hook to catch me, but I have landed short without the hook too."

"Captain, is the admiral not breaking the rules letting a nonmilitary carrier plane land on is deck?" Chip inquired

"Army, Admiral here, you let me worry about that with navy headquarters. You just do what Captain Miller tells you to do. Understand?" Admiral Sweeney said in a harsh tone.

"Yes, sir," Chip replied and began to start preparing for a landing that he had never done alone before. He got out the landing procedures and began his landing checklist. He was afraid to look at the fuel gauges as he knew they were bouncing on the empty mark when he crossed over the island six minutes ago.

Chip could see the cruiser Long Beach and a destroyer heading for him, crashing through the waves, and about two miles behind, he could see the silhouette of the large carrier on the same course also plowing through the angry waves.

"Mr. Reed, Colonel Kashia here. You are in excellent hands now, and you were right. You would not be able to reach a landfall airport close enough. Good luck to you and a successful landing."

Chip watched as the T-28 flew up close to his port wing, rolled out, and climbed ahead, waving its wings.

CHAPTER 42

Bud West's Office
Warbird Museum
Kissimmee, Florida

Dolly had made coffee, and Sara had made a run to a local fast-food store and brought back an assortment of cakes and cookies. Wayne and Bud were leaning over his desk, looking the map of Japan, and trying to locate the city on the coast where Chip was told to head for. It took some time, but they finally located the navy base and the island of Oshima.

"Wayne, I just went over Chip's fuel problem again, and he was right. He may be close to running on fumes. According to my calculations, he should have run out of fuel a half hour ago." Bud then told Wayne to try to get that colonel to let him talk to Chip again.

Wayne tried calling Chip, but there we nothing coming back. "Chip seems to have left the frequency we were on earlier. We can only hope he is not in the Pacific."

"Good God, Wayne. Tone it down. Linda is in the next office, and she can hear you."

"Bud, I have Colonel Simms back on the line. He just told me Chip is okay and being helped by a T-28 and heading down to set up a ditching."

Bud got on the phone with Simms and asked if he could remain on the line to help Chip Reed with instructions on how to land a B-25 in a splashdown. Colonel Simms tried to explain the best he could that Reed was now being instructed by the US Navy for a landing on an aircraft carrier called the USS Midway.

Bud and Wayne could not believe what they just learned. They both began yelling and screaming about the good news that Chip and the Duck may be saved by an aircraft carrier! They immediately went into the next room only to find Linda lying across a sofa. She appeared to be fast asleep. Bud wanted to wake her but decided to wait. He wanted to make sure the next news he gave was that Chip and the Duck were safe aboard ship.

Chip Reed's B-25
Ruptured Duck
Over the Pacific Ocean

Chip flew past the destroyer and by the port side of the cruiser Long Beach at 1,500 feet. He could see many of the crew in slickers waving at him. He dipped his wings and continued on toward the Midway.

"Army B-25, Captain Miller, here. I want you to climb to two thousand feet I am setting you up for a left hand pattern, not right. Just maintain a left-hand pattern as you reach the Midway. We will have you on the scope, but we also are going to have a flag man on the stern with two yellow flags. He will be the man you need to watch. He will tell you if you're too high or low and your wing positions. You will have to be perfectly level on final. Right now, the carrier is turning into the wind and is expected to give you up to fifty-five miles per hour across the deck with her hull speed and the current headwinds. The Midway is going to be doing twenty-four knots. Keep that in mind on your approach. Do you copy, sir?"

"Yes, I think so. Who will tell me when to start my base and final turn?"

"That would be me when you are ready to make your base leg turn."

Chip realized he would not have a normal approach and also realized he was too close to the Midway, so he banked right to move out to what he felt was a good distance then turned into his downwind leg. He began to reduce his speed to 165 miles per hour, manifold pressures to twenty-one pounds, and lowered his flaps to one quarter.

"Army, you are coming up on your base leg pretty soon, so adjust your flaps and airspeed to your standard landing speeds. Be ready to drop your gear after you turn on final. You will need full flaps, and reduce you airspeed to at least to 120 knots or less."

"Roger that, Captain," Chip responded and scanned his instruments. In his head, he was going through landing procedures.

Chip started to realize the seriousness of his situation. *My God, that ship looks huge, but the runway is short and narrow*, he thought. He could see the net being raised and a lot of yellow machines at the end of the deck. He continued thinking about the situation and praying the net worked and the nose gear held up. If it didn't, he might go out of control.

"I just wish Bud was next to me right now as I know I am going to do something dumb and lose my plane and possibly end my life if I crash-land or put down in those seas."

Chip's headset came alive with a strong, demanding voice. "One thing at a time, Army. When you turn and see the deck and stern coming at you, make sure you're level, and get ready to flare out when you go over the stern. As soon as you hit the deck, cut off all shutoffs or firewall valves, and when you feel your main gears touchdown, close throttles and mixtures. Once your gears hit the deck, start riding your brakes until your tires blow out. We will be with you all the way and ready for any emergency, so concentrate on staying level and keep watching that guy with the flags and do as he says. If you have to make an emergency approach, bank hard left to clear the ship and head for the sea as level as you can. I doubt if you can power up for a go-around with your gear down. You know you are going to go on your back, so just land the best way you can into the sea, and we will pick you up."

Chip turned on final about two miles out and saw the carrier coming at him fast. He could clearly see the sailor with two big yellow flags on the edge of the deck giving him signs that his right wing was down. Chip reacted, and at the same time, he reached for the gear switches to drop the gear. He heard the gear drop and the three green lights come on. He glanced at his airspeed. It was dropping as he throttled back, and it read 125 miles per hour. He lifted the Duck's nose and pulled off more throttle. The flag man was again showing the right wing dipping.

His headset rang out, "You are on the glide path, Army. Don't wander or wobble. Keep steady."

The deck was coming up fast. He thought he was going to make it when the number-two engine suddenly began to sputter and the prop slowed down and stopped. He reached for the number-one throttle and increased his airspeed. He put pressure on left rudder to straighten out the Duck to get back on course as the nose began to drop. Now he had to fight with his ailerons to get the wings level, get the nose up, and maintain his airspeed.

The flagman could not believe what he was seeing as the prop on the number-two engine stopped turning. It was too late for any signals as he could see the bomber was coming fast and low and expected the B-25 to stall, hit the edge of the deck, and drop in the ship's wake.

The Duck's main gears hit the deck hard five feet from the end of the deck and took one bounce. Chip had no idea how close he came to crashing into edge of the deck and falling into the wake of the carrier. He felt the gear hit hard, bounce, and hit hard again, and he began rolling fast. He saw the net coming at him and fought to keep heading straight, putting all the pressure he could equally on the brakes. He felt the Duck hit the net and the nose wheel slam down hard on its strut. He felt the plane vibrating and shaking as it continued to roll while the brakes began to smoke and burn up. Chip looked out the windscreen, and all he could see ahead were two big yellow cranes and tugs rushing at him fast outlined by a dark, angry blue sea just beyond them.

"Shit, I must have gone through the net," Chip said to himself and braced himself for a hard crash into the big cranes and equipment.

Suddenly, the Duck came to a stop. Chip realized it became very quiet except for the sound of the number-one engine still turning and popping. He moved the mixtures to cut off and closed the throttles. The number-one engine was in its final throes when he finally switched off the two magnetos, fuel pumps, and batteries. He suddenly remembered he was supposed to do this procedure as soon as he hit the deck. He just sat taking deep breaths as he watched a crowd of sailors wearing fire gear coming at him with fire extinguishers.

Behind him he heard the crew hatch release and the crew ladder drop. Before he could undo his shoulder harness and seat belt to rise out of his seat, the young Captain Miller, who had been giving him all his instructions, was standing halfway up the crew ladder and yelling at him, "Great landing, Army. You just qualified to be a carrier pilot!"

Chip looked into Captain Miller's smiling face and thanked him for getting him on board. What he wanted to do next was to get down on the deck and give a big hug to the captain and inspect any damage, especially to the nose gear to see if it was still attached.

Once Chip was outside the Duck, he was surrounded by personnel congratulating him. He was ordered by a young lieutenant to follow him to the admiral's quarters. Chip wanted to inspect his plane first, especially the nose gear, but it was surrounded by sailors working on getting the heavy tangled net off the nose wheel and strut. He climbed back up into the Duck to get his B-4 bag, came back down, and followed the officer across the crowded deck toward the towering island structure. Then he walked through a door.

After a few walk-ups, he entered the admiral's quarters where Admiral Sweeney stood waiting to greet him. The admiral was a tall man with an athletic build, broad shoulders, and a large chest. He was half bald and wore very thick horn-rimmed glasses. He reached out with his big hand to greet Chip.

"Welcome aboard the USS Midway, Mr. Reed. This is Commander Rice, our ship's doctor, who wants to look you over and then take you down to his dungeon and give you a thorough exam." Commander Rice shook Chip's hand and asked him to take a seat close by where he immediately took his blood pressure and listened to his chest.

Chip kept apologizing for his wet jumpsuit and body odor, and he did not want to sit on a padded seat cushion and possibly soil it. He elected to stand.

"Doc Rice says you seem to be in the green for now, Mr. Reed. We had a number of talks with your base people in Florida, including a Dr. Webber? We learned that you needed special meds. Unfortunately, we do not carry the types of medications you need, but we will have it at the base when we arrive at the dock. We can take care of you there.

"I am not here to judge you for what you were planning to do, and we have been told by the authorities from fleet and the Japanese Self-Defense Headquarters, we are not to talk about it. We have orders to take no pictures, and of course, that means all navy ships personnel, including you. Nobody wants any publicity leaked out on the fact you were planning a suicide mission and going to take out some auto factory. Now is that the truth?"

Chip admitted he did plan to crash into an auto factory. He then began to explain why, but he was interrupted by the admiral.

"Mr. Reed, I am not really interested; however, whatever Japanese laws you broke or what the US or the Japanese government will want to do with you is something you will have to face later."

"What is your pleasure, Chip Reed? Scotch, Rye, a cold Bud?"

"All of them, sir," Reed said, laughing.

Chip pointed to a large painting of an aircraft carrier on the wall. "That, Mr. Reed, is a painting of the original USS Hornet, and I understand you named your plane after one that flew off her deck."

"Sir, that is correct. That carrier and my plane were a big part of my childhood dreams, and the story of that famous mission was a part of my adult life. I was fortunate. I was able to meet many of those airmen who flew that mission called the Doolittle Tokyo Raiders."

"For your information, Mr. Reed, my father was a lieutenant JG aboard the CV-6 USS Hornet and the assistant flight operations officer. Took her through her sea trials and was at Alameda when Jimmy Doolittle, his sixteen Mitchells, and more than a hundred army airmen arrived on board. The navy crew was not thrilled. They did not show any respect or act friendly until they were out to sea and learned the planes and crews were headed to bomb Tokyo. Navy spent many days helping the crews getting ready up until they were compromised by the Japanese and had to take off earlier than planned."

Admiral Sweeney went back to the small bar, poured another scotch in his glass, turned, and addressed Chip. "When your Irish friend in Florida told me the story of you and the plane, I just had to do what I could do save you both. My dad would have been thrilled to meet you and see the Ruptured Duck return to a carrier and land no less. He was on the Hornet and survived after they got hit and sunk in the battle of Santa Cruz. The Hornet did not have one birthday before the Jap torpedo planes found her. They were determined to sink her because of the Doolittle Raid. Well, we will have time to chat about the raid and hear your tale about your mission at dinner in an hour. Meanwhile, you may want to get into a shower and out of that rank jumpsuit."

"Sir, I apologize. I had a small accident and missed the bowl you might say."

The admiral and the doctor broke into hearty laughs, and Chip joined them.

"Sir, I have on question. Is it possible I can call home? I mean my base. And I really need to talk to a special lady."

"In case you forgot, Mr. Reed, her name is Linda, and of course you can call her. I will have you patched in, and you can use my desk phone." The admiral gave the order to the operator and left the cabin with the doctor, Captain Miller, and his aide.

"Linda? It's me, Chip. I am fine and calling you from the aircraft carrier USS Midway. You are not going to believe this. I landed the Duck an hour ago on her deck. Tell Bud I think the Duck is okay and in one piece. We will get her back in the air as soon as we get her home. Linda, I love you and can't wait to see you again and talk about our future."

Linda could hear that Chip was really excited and hesitated to inform him they were already fully aware of his successful landing.

"Chip, that nice admiral called us, and we all talked about how you saved yourself and the plane. We are all so proud of you. Bud says you did the almost impossible landing. Did the admiral mention we are in the process of heading for Tokyo? Bud, Dolly, Wayne, and Betty are hopefully coming in a few days and will meet with you then. Bud and Wayne are already making plans to have the Duck shipped back home. If they have to, they may have to fly it to a place called Nagasaki or maybe to Shanghai to get back on one of those Chinese freighters you used before."

"Wow, that's fantastic, Linda, and I can't wait to see you and the gang."

"Chip, you are flying back to Orlando with Betty and me, and you are going right into the hospital for treatment. There is no fooling around now, and if we have to get married in the hospital chapel, so be it. We just have to wait for Bud and Wayne to get back from getting the Duck loaded up and on its way. Bud wants to be the best man, and Dolly my maid of honor. When the time comes, you and I will pick up the Duck in San Francisco or Los Angeles or wherever she arrives. That will be our honeymoon. Roger that?"

"I love you with all my heart, and I hope Bud, Dolly, Wayne, Betty, and Sara can hear me. Thanks to all of you, including Admiral Sweeney, the US Navy, and Japanese Air Forces, the crew of USS Midway, and even Colonel Kashia. You all helped save my life and my plane. In a way that you may not understand, they made it possible for me to find and understand President Roosevelt's comments about his mysterious and famous Shangri-La. I just landed on it."

Chip said good-bye and fell back into the admiral's big chair, and without thought about his wet uncomfortable flight suit or its contents. He just wanted to take the moment to think about the past few hours of his life and what he had accomplished to save his own life and the lives of thousands of innocent Japanese civilians. Most importantly, he finally realized his lifelong hate for all Japanese people nearly ended his life that day.

As he began to feel a peace coming over him, he started to think that he now had a chance to get healthy enough to live a long life with Linda. He began to have flashes of the past, mostly about his father and his many moments of rage about the Japanese. He thought about the day he landed at LAX and learned his wife and child were killed that morning. He recalled the authorities would not let him see his wife or her car because of the degrees of damage and condition of them both. He recalled the wonderful life he had with his family, especially fishing with his son and the day he arrived at Lakeland Airport and found Roy Bergy and his B-25. He remembered his plane's test flight to Kissimmee, which Bud West had flown to his warbird hangar. He thought about the Titusville air show as well as the Jap Zero who had caused his crash landing and taken the life of his friend Roy. He remembered Lee, the motel room, and punching out the Japanese colonel. Then he recalled the times and happiness he had with Linda and the possibility of a marriage. He thought marrying Linda could lead to a wonderful life. Hopefully, they'd fly the Duck together and maybe at air shows.

Bud West's Office

Meanwhile back in Kissimmee, Florida, Bud West's office was jubilant with excitement as Bud, Dolly, Wayne, Betty, and Linda were exchanging hugs and smiles. The air was filled with laughter and even tears after the conversation with Admiral Sweeney. A bottle of red wine and a quart of Dewar's scotch suddenly appeared on Bud's desk with a stack of plastic glasses.

"My God, does anyone realize it is nearly seven in the morning?" Dolly cried out.

"Hey, instead of getting bombed before daybreak, it's time for breakfast, and we have not eaten since lunch yesterday. Let's pile into Wayne's car and head over to the Stick and Rudder for greasy eggs and bacon."

They all agreed and began to gather jackets and purses. Bud reached over and grabbed the bottle of Scotch. Dolly reacted and took it away from him.

"That's a no-no, sweetheart," she said, laughing.

Suddenly, the office door swung open, and standing like the winner of a beauty contest was Lee Walters. She was dressed to kill in an off-the-shoulder red halter and skin-tight white jeans and baseball hat displaying her long blonde hair in a ponytail flowing from the rear of the hat.

"Well, it looks like I hit the jackpot this morning. The entire family is here except for the superstar pilot, Sky King Chip Reed. Is he still in China where I left him recently? Or did he get lost in Tokyo showing off his plane?"

Dolly moved forward and separated Lee and Linda. She motioned with her arms spread out wide to stop anyone getting near her and Lee. "Lee, I don't know why you are here, or for whatever the reason, I am damn sure not interested. No one else here is interested either. You are not welcome, and I suggest you turn your skinny ass around and go back to where you came from."

"My, aren't we the big, bad pussycat? I had no idea, Dolly, you were so … shall I say bullish? I really came to hopefully see Chip, but I will settle for talking to his flying schoolteacher, Miss Amelia Air Brain, and tell her she had better have a bigger hook."

Nobody saw it coming, especially Lee Walters. Dolly came out of right field and took one open-handed swing that ended on Lee's right cheek. Lee's head twisted halfway around on her shoulders. She fell hard to her right against a stuffed chair that saved her from a hitting the wall. For a moment there was absolute silence. Bud rushed to Lee's aid as she began screaming, holding her face with both hands. She began to cuss and yell at Dolly.

Dolly gave out orders, "Bud, you and Wayne get the witch out of here. Throw her into her little red chariot." She then turned and faced Linda, who appeared to be in shock.

"I've been waiting to do that for a long time," Dolly said with a huge smile.

"Holy moly. Are you the same woman I married? Where did all that come from?" Bud laughed as he reached out and hugged her.

Aboard the USS Midway
Task Force 24

Meanwhile in the admiral's office, Chip opened his eyes. He had not realized he had drifted off. He felt a sudden tug on his sleeve and woke up looking into the youthful and smiling face of Captain Miller.

"Mr. Reed, sorry to wake you, but the admiral was concerned he had not heard from the doctor on your condition and sent me looking for you."

Chip pushed himself up and out of the chair. He stood in front of the young captain and began to apologize while looking back into the chair to see if he had done any damage from his wet and stained flight suit. He was pleased to see there were no stains or damage.

"Wow, I must have dropped off. I apologize," Chip said, holding out his hand.

"No problem, sir, and if I may say, you may have made it into the history books today with your landing a B-25 on the deck of a carrier and surviving. It's a damn shame that what you did today is never going to be disclosed by the navy to the press or anyone else for that matter."

Chip laughed as he started to walk beside the Captain toward the door. "You know, I only did what Jimmy Doolittle knew could be done with his sixteen B-25s back in 1942. If only he had had a carrier with a deck 250 feet longer than the one he took off from."

"Sir, I don't understand what you mean. Did he really expect to land bombers on a carrier?"

"Evidently, you don't know about the famous 1942 Doolittle Tokyo Raid and the USS Hornet. But not to worry, I will send you a book, or better yet, ask Admiral Sweeney about the Doolittle raid. Just don't admit you never heard about this famous raid or the history of two young navy captains who actually designed and executed the mission," Chip said as he walked behind Captain Miller. Miller stopped and turned and faced Chip with a confused look.

"Sir, if I recall, you and the admiral were talking about the painting of some old aircraft carrier hanging on the wall of the admiral's office. Could that be the Hornet you mentioned? I know it had a brass plate on its frame with the name of the ship on it. It was named after some kind of bug."

Chip laughed. "Yes, that bug is the USS Hornet, and it carried a big sting, which the Japanese Empire felt on April 18, 1942. She launched sixteen B-25s with eighty Army Air Corps volunteers to bomb Tokyo and four other major cities. Luckily, she got back to her base before she was discovered by the Japanese Navy. Later, she was at the battle of Midway and fought in the Solomon's only to be sunk by the Japanese in the battle of Santa Cruz on October 26, 1942. She officially served the US Navy only for a few months."

"Where did the Hornet originally sail from? Was it Pearl Harbor?" Miller asked.

"No, Captain, according to President Roosevelt, she sailed from Shangri-la." Chip smiled and took hold of the captain's arm and continued to walk. "Captain, I imagine you may be a bit confused by now. So you may want to ask Admiral Sweeney to join you at the OC when you dock and ask him to tell you the story about the USS Hornet. It may take a few scotches on the rocks, but it is a story you will be proud to hear and proud to pass on to your grandchildren someday. Trust me."

The loudspeaker suddenly rang out through the entire ship, "Attention, all ship personnel. Report to your stations for docking procedures, and be in proper dress on deck. We are being treated to a formal welcome from the base's commanding officer and Japanese officials."

"Mr. Reed, I may be young and not a big history fan, but I never heard of one of our bases called Shangri-la. You are putting me on, right?"

AUTHOR'S NOTE

President Franklin Roosevelt would be proud to know that the mysterious Shangri-la he created from the Oval Office on April 19, 1942, was found by a pilot in his personal B-25B seventy years later.

ABOUT THE AUTHOR

Thomas G. Casey was born in Brooklyn, New York and raised in Westfield, New Jersey.

After serving in the USAF as a flight engineer for the Military Air Command during the Korean War he moved to Florida and today lives in Sarasota with his best friend and wife Catherine and two Shih-Tzu pups, Lady and Missy.

A private pilot and experienced sailor he worked for SAIL Magazine for thirty years. His work took him to almost every island in the Caribbean calling on Governments and international chartering companies, which led him to write an adventure novel called Island Drummer. He also wrote a personal story about his job working at a New Jersey Beach hotel, Beaches Blondes and Bellhops. Most recently he wrote an illustrated children's educational book called "Angus, A Boy & His Sailboat" with his own artwork.

As a devoted fan since childhood of Jimmy Doolittle and the eighty pilots and crews who flew the famous raid on Tokyo in 1942, Tom volunteered to manage the Doolittle Tokyo Raiders Association. He and Catherine became their business managers arranging all their annual reunions and public appearances. Recently Tom was elected President of the Association to continue the legacy of their mission and their personal dedication to family and country.

Printed in the United States
By Bookmasters